LAST BREATH

THE TEMPLAR - BOOK 2

DEBRA DUNBAR

Last Breath
By
Debra Dunbar

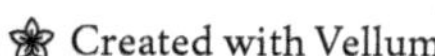 Created with Vellum

CHAPTER 1

The sky was that ominous yellow that heralds a downpour. Thunder rolled in the distance, but I knew this storm was right overhead. A burst of wind whipped the bush I was crouched behind into a frenzy, stinging me with the slap of branches. I should have headed for shelter, but there was no way I was leaving until I'd found the bastard that had killed two of my friends. He was out here somewhere, and I wouldn't rest until he was dead.

There. My muscles tensed, sword at the ready as I saw a flash of blue behind a tree. I'd lose the element of surprise by running across a twenty foot stretch of open ground, but I didn't need surprise to take this guy down. Eighteen years of lessons gave me a distinct advantage when it came to hand-to-hand sword combat.

The light dimmed with the fast-moving storm. Lightning streaked to the ground, followed almost immediately by a crash of thunder. I darted from behind the bush, hunching low. Something hit my arm, and I swung from reflex.

"Ow. Damn it. Too hard. You're hitting too hard."

Oops. Barely two hours into our LARP and I already had

a reputation for knocking grown men on their ass with my PVC and duct-taped foam sword. "Sorry. Are you okay?"

A woman got to her feet, her cape brown with dust and her beaded headdress askew. "I think my teeth flew into the next county. What's with the head-shot?"

I was used to taller opponents and had aimed blind. "Sorry," I repeated.

Now came the weird part—the part where I didn't finish her off, even though if I'd been using a real sword a mercy killing would have been in order. "On the authority of the King of Glenelg, I, Solaria Angelique Ainsworth of Middleburg, take you captive."

She glared at me, righting the beaded cap and picking a stray twig out of her long, dark-blond hair. "Think again, girlfriend. I hit you with a freeze spell. I, Melisandre the Magnificent, am the one taking *you* prisoner."

One thing I'd learned about LARPing in two short hours was that I hated mages, especially ones that added the title "magnificent" to their name. The normal rules that applied to magic didn't seem to exist in this fantasy war-game and egos trumped any hint of talent. "Freeze spell, my ass. I didn't hear any incantation, didn't trip a magical barrier. How the heck did you put a freeze spell on me?"

She pointed downward and I looked at what had smacked me in the shoulder. No way. Just…no way. "That's a beanbag. I know the rules here are kind of wacky, but in what universe does throwing a beanbag at someone constitute a magical spell?"

"I say freeze then throw the bean bag. If I hit you, you're bespelled. If I don't then you get to knock me into the ground with your sword. I hit you."

This was ridiculous. If I could run around Baltimore throwing beanbags at people and causing them to be deprived of motion, I'd be set for life. "Do you know how involved a spell like that is? Eight different types of herbs, six of them not even found in this country, a lead weight, and unbleached silk string. The astrological alignment means you can only cast it once every three months, and the chances of holding the spell static in an amulet or object until you want to release it are less than fifteen percent. For a generalized freeze spell you've got a five percent chance of success as long as you meet all the other criteria. Specialized you'd need a poppet and a drop of blood—even then your success rate only rises to ten percent."

Her mouth made a tight, thin line. "I'm the mage. You're the paladin. You're also frozen and *my* prisoner."

Paladin. I winced. I was a Templar, not some do-gooder, holier-than-thou, kamikaze-with-a-sword. Although in this game, it seemed I'd been assigned that detested role. I was wanting to whack her again with my foam sword, just on principal, but I held back. These were the rules, and I didn't want to alienate my new friends by refusing to submit to the enemy. "Fine. Lead the way, oh mighty wizardess."

Lightning flared. We both jumped and I felt a sizzle of static electricity across my skin and smelled the sharp bite of ozone. Thunder shook the ground, nearly deafening us. I dropped, pulling the other woman down with me and holding her until I was sure there wasn't another strike, or a burning tree about to come down on our heads.

"Screw the prisoner thing," the woman said, her voice shaky. "Run for that pavilion over there."

That pavilion "over there" was right where the lightning strike had come down, but it was the only shelter nearby and big, fat, cold drops of rain were beginning to splat against my plastic armor. I ran, slowing my stride to let the mage, hindered by twenty yards of fake velvet fabric, keep up. We crested a knoll and I saw smoke rising in the air.

"Fire," Melisandre the Magnificent gasped.

But in this case, where there was smoke, there wasn't necessarily fire, at least not the normal incendiary kind. My skin crawled as I saw the smoke twisting like blue tentacles, as it rose then looped back down to curl along the ground. I grabbed my companion's voluminous cloak.

"Stop. Stay here." I had a bad feeling about this. A really bad feeling.

The skies opened up, and the woman wrenched her garment from my grasp, shrieking as she ran for the pavilion. About twenty feet out, she stopped, her shrieks turning into one long scream.

I tried to keep the panicked look from my face as I jogged toward her. Storms were the perfect time for casting, when personal energy could be supplemented with environmental for extra oomph. I'd never seen blue smoke like this before, but had no doubt it was accompanied by chicken entrails or something equally gruesome.

It wasn't chicken guts. It was a dead body, and the blue smoke was coming from a crater where his chest should have been. My breath stopped somewhere in my own chest and I fought to keep from screaming myself. It was one thing to see dead bodies on my favorite crime show, another to come across one in a park—one that smelled of burned flesh and coppery blood.

Just because I was a Templar raised in the art of war didn't mean I'd ever actually experienced it. A dead body... this was a first for me. *Don't puke. Don't puke.* I forced my breakfast to stay put, but couldn't tear my eyes away from the corpse.

"Oh, my God. Oh, my God." Melisandre fumbled to dial her cell phone, nearly dropping it in the process.

She was going to call 911. It was too late for this guy, although I guess someone had to remove the body.

Snap out of it. Templar training included an anatomy

intensive on cadavers, and we'd all studied drawings and photos of various supernatural methods of death. Still, this was my first up-close and personal view. Time to stop freaking out and start doing my job.

My job as the only Templar in Baltimore, that is. Not a paladin. Not a Knight. But still a Templar with the responsibilities that my birthright entailed.

I took a steadying breath and bent down to examine the man, careful not to touch anything. He had on the same dark-green cloak as my companion, his eyes fixed wide in surprise, a beanbag clutched in his left hand.

"My name is Melissa Davies and his is…was Ronald Stull. We were in a role playing game, and there was a lightning strike. No, there's no way he's still alive."

She knew him. I felt a pang of sorrow. It was bad enough for me to find a stranger dead in a park, but to find a friend? Melissa was wrong, though. Ronald wasn't killed by a lightning strike. The blue smoke began to dissipate, and I saw what I'd suspected—a sigil burned into the grass beneath the body. I'd need to wait until the police, or whoever, moved him to get a look at the entire symbol, but its presence meant this wasn't a random magic act gone wrong. It was a hit.

"Did Ronald have any enemies?" I asked once Melissa had hung up.

Her hands shook as she stashed the phone. "What, like Zeus? No, he didn't have any enemies, aside from the imaginary ones in our game. He was killed by lightning."

No, he was killed by a being with an affinity for lightning, not by the electrical event itself, a being who liked to remove the lungs and heart, a being who surrounded himself with blue smoke.

A sharp pain shot through my side, and I rubbed the spot where my scar was, thinking it was a really bad time to get a muscle spasm. "Lightning doesn't usually leave a demon sigil on the ground, or produce blue smoke."

Melissa gave me a wary look, taking a step backward. "Copper chloride. It burns blue. And random burn patterns in the grass are not demon sigils."

So says the woman freezing opponents with beanbags. Although I couldn't really blame her. She didn't grow up looking at demons-gone-wild photos or autopsies of werewolf victims. This was all fantasy to her and I was a nutjob conspiracy theorist. "Sorry, I get a little carried away with the game sometimes. How well did you know him?"

She relaxed at my explanation. I'm sure I wasn't the only one running around this LARP in the Park who "confused" what everyday people considered to be reality and fantasy. Melissa could believe whatever she wanted, but Ronald hadn't been carrying around copper chloride—which causes blue flame and *green* smoke. And that *was* a sigil. I'd swear it on the Templar tattoo inked into my right wrist.

The woman turned her back on the body, hugging herself tight. The brief downpour had become a light shower, but her cloak was soaked, her hair plastered to her head in thick strands. "He joined us a few months back. Some of the guys had played online with him and asked him into the group. He was really good. Ronald could sneak up on anyone, and he was really accurate with his spells—I mean his beanbags."

None of that explained why he was dead on the ground. Unless he'd hit the wrong sorcerer with a beanbag. "Are you two the only magic users in the group?"

She nodded. "It was nice to have a backup, you know?"

I'd learned that wizards got captured a lot in this game. They ran out of beanbags, and with no armor fell quickly to a PVC and foam sword.

"What did he do? For a living, I mean."

I worked in a coffee shop, and tried not to touch the bank

account my parents kept dumping money into. This guy's cloak and jeans looked a lot more expensive than my thrift-shop purchases, so I was guessing he worked for more than minimum wage.

"I don't know. I think he was a programmer or something."

Or something. That cloak looked nice. Nicer than the one Melissa was wearing. Nicer than I'd seen in the costume shops. There was a chance Ronald took his mage persona seriously. Really, really seriously.

The wail of a siren sounded in the distance, growing louder. I looked around and picked up a stick the wind had knocked loose, then stretched it out to lift the folds of Ronald's cloak.

Melissa wiped the rain off her face and gestured toward the body. "Should you be doing that? I mean, aren't you contaminating evidence or something?"

"Evidence that Zeus struck this man down? You said yourself that he got hit by lightning. It's an accident. There *is* no evidence."

She frowned. "Well, then it's disrespectful."

It *was* disrespectful to be examining a dead man's garment while his body was still warm, but once the EMS people got here, I wouldn't have the chance.

Green cloak. Real velvet by my reckoning. Satin lined. It wasn't new from the wear around the hem and the faint stains on the lining, but it had been well taken care of. On the inside of the cloak I could see tiny slits—the openings of pockets. And I was willing to bet they weren't filled with beanbags either.

"I hear the ambulance. Can you go meet them and show them where to go?"

She hesitated, eyeing me with suspicion.

"I just moved here six months ago and have never been in

this park before today. I'm not even sure where my car is at this point."

Melissa nodded. "I'll be right back." She eyed my stick. "Stop poking him, for heaven's sake."

The moment she was out of sight, I did more than poke him. In spite of the dangers of touching a demon-slayed corpse, I dove right in, digging through the cloak pockets and mentally cataloguing spell components. Rue, wormwood, gold filings, salt. A whole lot of salt. I didn't have much time, so any papers I found I pocketed, feeling a twinge of guilt. Melissa knew him. I was hoping she knew him well enough to help the paramedics notify next of kin.

By the time the medical personnel rounded the knoll, carrying a stretcher and led by Melissa, I was standing beside the body, stick tossed aside and an innocent look carefully composed on my face.

"Holy crap."

I didn't think trained emergency staff were supposed to be quite so shaken by the sight of a dead body. After all, they'd probably been first on the scene to far more gruesome murders than this. Or not. With the blue smoke cleared, Ronald's chest cavity looked like he'd been part of some horrible sacrifice. Ribs were cracked and spread upward like bony towers. Lungs and heart were completely missing, leaving a bloody, muscle lined hole where the organs had been.

They set the stretcher down and eyed the body. "I'm thinking the lightning hit the ground, then rebounded and took him in the back."

Melissa gagged and turned her head. I leaned closer, wanting to see both the sigil and the back of the body. If the paramedic's hypothesis was correct, then the guy's backside would be a blackened, burned mess. Maybe they were right. Maybe my paranoia over the recent vampire and necromancer events was making me see magic around every corner. Ronald had a bunch of spell components in his pockets. He could have had copper sulfide and other stuff in the ones his body had blocked me from searching. He could have been killed by lightning that left an odd pattern on the ground.

Or not. The two men rolled the body over. His backside was untouched beyond the blood that had seeped under him and stained his cloak. And the burn mark on the ground was clearly a sigil.

"What the hell? Rob, take a look at this." The two men shook their head over the burn mark, commenting that it was the weirdest lightning strike they'd ever seen.

Me, too. Usually there was a blackened smoking tree, or a charred piece of earth with a circular section of burned and melted foliage radiating out from the impact area. Not this weird, squiggly burn. I tried to commit it to memory, wondering how crass I'd look if I took out my cell phone and snapped a picture. Probably pretty crass. Sigils were tricky though. One mark reversed, or slightly higher, called a completely different demon. That's why this particular form of magic required a detailed practitioner, and why it had a high rate of casualties. Had Ronald practiced magic outside of his LARP activities? If so, this might have not been a hit, but simply a case of a sloppy summoning coming back to bite him.

Like *my* sloppy summoning. I hugged myself, remembering the violent demon who had appeared instead of Vine. I'd barely managed to shove him back to hell. And I was well aware that if someone else summoned him and he got loose, he could very well come after me.

Was that what happened with Ronald?

Melissa and I followed the stretcher to the ambulance, all of us walking in silence. The rain had tapered off to a light mist. Once the sun came out, the humidity would be unbearable. I couldn't wait to shed this plastic armor, and I'm sure Melissa felt the same about her sodden cloak. She was worse off, drenched-clothing wise. The plastic armor had at least shielded some of my body from the rain, but she was soaked through. Her hair was stuck to her face and neck, the headdress absurd on top of it all. I touched a hand to my own hair, thankful for the braid that I always wore when fighting. It might not be the most flattering hairstyle for me, but at least I didn't have wet hair clinging to my skin.

The police were at the ambulance, as were the press. I recognized one of the reporters, and she nodded to me. Janice. Was it just last week we'd met to discuss the Robertson murders? She was going to think this was an odd coincidence, me being here. *I* thought it was an odd coincidence my being here.

The officers took down our names and information. It all seemed straight forward. No crime scene photos. No yellow tape. Just a guy killed by a lightning strike, and our information to ensure all the boxes were filled out on the form.

"It hit the ground right where we found him," Melissa told them. "We were in a role playing game. The others are at the other end of the park, but we were out doing reconnaissance. The lightning hit, and there was static everywhere. The thunder nearly deafened me. When the rain came down, we ran for shelter, and that's when we found him."

Straight forward. The police turned to me and I nodded. What else was I going to say? That I suspected the victim of black magic? That I believed a demon had killed him rather than a random act of nature?

"They say your odds of getting struck by lightning are about the same as winning the lottery," Janice murmured. She'd moved close behind me and was staring at my foam sword with curiosity. "Too bad he didn't buy a Powerball ticket."

I doubted one would have negated the other. And I was now wondering the odds of being killed by a demon. Probably a lot higher if the victim was involved in the dark arts.

The ambulance left. The police left. Melissa left after texting her group to tell them the news of Ronald's passing. In short time I was standing on the curb in the light rain, alone aside from a reporter who didn't seem inclined to get back into her warm, dry car.

"Can you show me where you found him?"

I hesitated, not sure whether Janice just had a morbid fascination with scenes of death, or whether she suspected something. I wanted to go back anyway to get a picture of the sigil before it was disturbed. Not that I wanted Janice or anyone else seeing me taking a photo of a spot where a man had supposedly been electrocuted to death.

"Sure. There's blood though."

The idea of blood didn't seem to bother the reporter. She fell in beside me, shortening her stride to keep pace with my shorter legs. "What were his injuries?"

Yep. Morbid. Creepy. There are things you expect a reporter to ask about, and things you don't. This was in the things you don't category. "Nothing on his back besides bloodstains. It looked like he took the lightning strike to the chest."

There. That should do it.

Nope.

"So burned, blackened skin and fabric? Or melted? Most lightning deaths are from heart failure caused from the electrical charge, but a direct strike would have left burns."

This woman missed her calling. Why was she a Baltimore City reporter and not off in a CSI crime lab, or working for the FBI?

"His rib cage was blown outward. Heart and lungs were missing. Judging from the small amount of blood and the damage to his cloak, I'd say the wounds cauterized with heat that also burned his clothing." There. That ought to shut her up.

And I just realized that I sounded as if I should be in a CSI crime lab or working for the FBI, not whipping up lattes part-time in the Inner Harbor.

Janice stopped. From the shock on her face I wondered if I hadn't gone a bit too far in my description. "You said his ribs were exposed, like something inside had exploded them outward? And heart and lungs were missing?"

"Yeah." I backpedaled, realizing that I was sounding way to knowledgeable, and pretty callous. "I've never seen lightning hit anything beyond a tree, though. And I'm no medical professional. I'm sure I was mistaken."

The reporter shook her head and began walking at a more rapid pace. I jogged to keep up. "Over there."

I pointed and we swerved left to arrive at the patch of ground with the sigil. Ronald's body had smudged the outline a bit. Hopefully enough of it was undisturbed for me to get an idea of what demon it referenced. Now if only the reporter would go away so I could snap a picture.

"Holy crap! David said one of their players had been killed—like really killed, killed. Is this where it happened?"

I looked up to see Brandi approaching, somewhat out of breath. The rest of my team was jogging up. So much for a private moment to snap a picture.

Luckily Brandi didn't have the same scruples as I did. Nor did anyone else in the group. Everyone chatted excitedly and took photos of the sigil, exclaiming that they'd never known someone who'd died by lightning.

"Umm. It's kind of tragic that this happened to one of the players." I tried to interject some humanity into the moment that was quickly becoming a paparazzi frenzy. "He was just here LARPing, and then he was dead. It could have been any of us."

"Could it?" Janice asked, leaning down to swipe a finger across the burned grass. She'd already taken her own picture of the sigil. "Why wasn't there a fire? And why is the burned section greasy?"

I knew why, but nobody would believe me if I told them. At least nobody present would believe me. Well, Janice might. She'd taken the reality of vampires and necromancers with very little convincing less than a week ago. Demons probably wouldn't be that much of a stretch for her.

"Yeah. Sucks that someone got killed like this, but honestly it couldn't have happened to a better guy," Zac chimed in. "It's like fate. It's like divine retribution or something."

So Ronald was not a favorite. No wonder everyone was busy snapping pics and tweeting.

"Melissa, their other mage, said he was new to the group?" I asked.

Brandi snorted. "New to them maybe, but not new to us. He's made the rounds and been thrown out of just about every gaming group in town. Arrogant asshole. And he cheats."

How did one cheat at throwing beanbags at an opponent? "Cheats how?"

Brad shrugged. "I don't know. In Other Worlds, he showed up with this insane character roll-up. We made him roll the stats again, just because he was plus twenty on everything. He got the same numbers. He always made his saves, always rolled max on his hit points. We made him use a set of our dice because we were beginning to think his were fixed. Still, the guy always came out on top."

"And if you argued with him, or took the last diet Mountain Dew, then your character began having the worst luck ever," Zac added. "Ones every roll. I went through three characters in one night. It was no fun, so we told him not to come back."

Sounded like a real sore loser, as well as a sore winner. "Did he get back at you guys in any way after you threw him out?"

"Food poisoning the next game night, but we couldn't really blame that on him. He wasn't even there, and the crab dip did taste a little off."

"Ronald was a total ass," Charles added. "I don't know what he was putting in his bean bags, but those suckers left a mark."

I looked down at the burned sigil in the grass. Either Ronald's luck had run out, or some gamer with a grudge had rolled a natural twenty.

CHAPTER 2

There was a box waiting for me right outside my apartment door. Lately my great grandmother had taken to sending me an odd assortment of stuff in what I assume was meant to be a care package, but this wasn't from her. I stared at it with the caution of a bomb squad technician while fingering the hilt of my sword because whoever had sent me the package was a mage.

No one had ever stolen Gran's packages, but whoever sent this wanted to make sure the neighbors didn't walk off with it. There was a nasty hex attached to it that would deliver the equivalent of an electric shock to whoever picked it up. It was a clever spell, designed to go live only when the package reached its destination. Clever, because the folks at the post office wouldn't take kindly to being zapped every time they touched the thing. The big black rune in the lower corner clearly told anyone knowledgeable in the magical arts what the hex was. It was easily dispelled with a single word.

But still I hesitated. I wasn't on particularly good terms with any mages since Haul Du had tossed me out. Maybe there *was* a bomb inside—a magical bomb that the wizard wanted to make sure detonated only in *my* face and not some random person's. But why would any of them want me dead? I hadn't done anything wrong besides hide the fact that I was a Templar from them during my initiation period.

"*Delens.*" I held my breath. The rune faded and my shoulders slumped with relief when a thick black checkmark appeared in its place. I recognized that checkmark. It was the stick-figure equivalent of a bird, and the symbol Raven used to sign all her stuff.

Normally I would have been irked that she hadn't put the mark in clear sight and saved me the near heart attack, but she had good reason to be cautious about identifying this package as from her. All the mages in Haul Du had been forbidden to have any contact with me once I was ousted. Raven had been my best friend, but she'd walked away from that friendship to stay with the magical group that had been her passion for the last decade.

It still hurt, even though I understood why she'd made the choice she had. A friendship of six months, no matter how tight, wasn't worth giving up the shared knowledge that came with being a member of Haul Du.

But this? I'd called her last week to warn her about my disastrous attempt to summon the Goetic demon Vine. Hopeful that this might be some tentative first-step toward a renewal of our friendship, I picked up the package and took it inside.

A note fell out as soon as I tore the paper off, and I opened it before the box itself.

Thought you might need this since you're clearly continuing your education on a solo basis. Please be careful. I'll be really pissed if I see your obituary in the paper. R

I smiled at the little check mark bird accompanying

Raven's initial. Whatever was inside, this note had made my day. Heck, it had made my year. When she'd turned her back on me and refused to return my messages, I'd thought I'd never hear from her again. Yes, she'd finally answered my call last week, but I figured that would be the end of it.

Evidently not. And hope was a beautiful thing. I opened the box and gasped to see the contents. It was a book, an old book nestled in clean white silk. I cradled it with the packing material as I gently pulled it from the box, careful not to get any of the oils from my hands on the fragile cover.

It was a first edition copy of the Lemegeton, translated from the original Latin, Hebrew, and French texts by Fra D.C.D.D. and Petra Marcus. Draping the silk over my fingers, I opened the cover and again caught my breath. Librarians, including Templar ones, might frown upon those who underlined in books and made notes in the margins, but magicians loved these insights by those who had come before them. Especially if the one making the notes had been Aleister Crowley himself. I traced the dark, scrawling script with a silk-covered finger and marveled that Raven had parted with such a treasure.

She'd given it to me. Monetary value aside, this book was priceless and she'd given it to me. I wrapped my gift carefully in the silk and stored it back in the box before putting it on the shelf with my other treasured manuscripts. Then I picked up my phone.

It went to voice mail. I hadn't really expected her to pick up. Yes, this was hopefully the narrowing of the breach between us, but I was still a Templar and I'm sure she didn't want to suffer the same fate as I had when it came to Haul Du.

When the beep came to leave a message, I said everything I could in two words before I hung up. "Thank you."

Less than two seconds later my phone beeped with a text.

Miss you.

I missed her, too. Hopefully this was a sign that in spite of her choice to stay with Haul Du, Raven and I would always find a way to be friends.

CHAPTER 3

As much as I wanted to immerse myself in my new book, I had work to do. I needed to catalog the contents of Ronald's pockets before I forgot what they were, go through all the scraps of paper I'd taken off his body, and see if I could figure out which demon the sigil burned into the ground under his body belonged to.

I also had a date—a real date with a human male. Zac, the guy from my LARP group, to be exact. I should have been excited. I knew *Zac* was excited. He'd barely contained himself when I'd said yes to his invitation. He'd reminded me twice at the LARP about what time he'd be at my apartment to pick me up. He'd already texted me to confirm yet again.

I wanted to cancel. A guy died in the park, and there was a lot of research I needed to do. Maybe I could ask him to reschedule—like, reschedule for some time next month.

But growing up meant doing things you didn't always feel like doing, like eating your broccoli or memorizing those Latin verb conjugations. I might have run out on taking my Oath of Knighthood, but I wasn't the kind of woman who would cancel at the last minute on a guy with the lame excuse of having to wash my hair or research demon sigils.

And I knew in my heart that I needed this date. It had been far too long, and I was two steps away from becoming a nun. If my landlord hadn't been so vehement about the no-pets clause in my lease, I probably would already have at least two cats roaming my apartment. I was considering taking up knitting. Well, no, not the last one, but I did miss having a pet. And the dating situation was becoming dire. If I was fantasizing about hot vampire guys and seriously thinking of cancelling a date to spend the evening reading the *Clavicula Salomonis Regis*, then I needed an intervention.

Zac was cute. He was fun. And he was crazy about me in a very flattering, if somewhat stalkerish, fashion. I'd do what I could for the next few hours, go on my date with Zac. Enjoy myself. Then finish up when I got back. Baby steps.

That decided, I sat down, pulled out a notebook and started writing. Fifteen minutes later I had what looked like a shopping list of magical supplies. Now to make sense of it all.

If the herbs and items in Ronald's pockets had a magical purpose, then they were separated for a reason. I grouped the items together, and began to research what spells they would most likely be used for. It was a long and carpel tunnel causing project, so I took a break midway to read the papers I'd found in the dead man's largest pocket.

A receipt for fast food. A grocery list. An address. I was just about to reverse look-up the address when there was a knock at my door. It was at least an hour before I expected Zac, and I'd had few other visitors since I'd moved to Balti-more. Well, except for one. I waited, hoping, but the locked door didn't swing open. I knew that he'd hardly be able to come by when the sun was up, but I hadn't been able to help my irrational anticipation. Tamping down my disappoint-ment at who *wasn't* at my door, I went to answer it.

It was Sarge, his nervous smile oddly contrasting with his buff, bouncer physique.

"You got a moment to chat?"

Not really, but I could hardly turn him away. Sarge was cool, one of the people I felt the stirrings of a fledgling friendship for. Normally I don't think I'd have much in common with him beyond weight training routines, but Sarge was a blood slave. His connection with the local vampire *Balaj* meant he was one of the few people in the city I could discuss the supernatural with without being accused of being a looney. And he was one of the few sources of information on vampires who didn't want to drink my blood.

"Sure! Come on in."

Sarge eyed my sword on the table and made a beeline for the sofa, launching right into his reason for the visit before his butt had even hit the cushion.

"Geraldo is going to dump me. We've been together for six months, and I know that I tempt him to indulge more than he probably should. I can't help it. I want him. I want him all the time, and...we had a fight."

Okay. Time to have a girlfriend support session with a man in love with a vampire. I moved my notes from the couch onto one of the few places on my coffee table not covered with books, then got him a pint of ice cream.

"Here." I jabbed the spoon into the open container. "It's cookie dough. Makes everything better."

I was just glad I had it to offer. A few days ago there was nothing in my apartment but some Ramen noodle packets and instant coffee but last night, when I got home, my monthly biological event led to my finding twenty-five hundred dollars in my tampon box. The vampires had paid up and Dario must have snuck in and placed it in my usual hiding spot for cash. It bothered me that I hadn't seen him since the last confrontation with the necromancer. He could have waited to give me the money in person, or left a note of some sort. Nothing. Just a wad of hundreds in a tampon box.

I'd buried my disappointment deep, hid most of the money back in the box, and went to an all-night grocery, grateful that at least I was a regular sort of girl when it came to my fertility cycles.

So I had ice cream, milk, real coffee, a quart of potato salad, and a roasted chicken. And I'd replaced my Emergency Beer—just in case.

Sarge's relationship problem might have warranted ice cream, but it didn't rise to the level of Emergency Beer. No, that ten dollar bottle of Belgian was only to be broken out in case of a demon summoning gone bad, or if *I* was the one crying over a vampire.

"So…what happened?"

They probably didn't have a lot of time left as a couple before Geraldo either broke it off, or lost control and killed Sarge. He wouldn't mean to, but vampires couldn't resist taking too much, or drinking too frequently from their blood slaves for long. At six months, their relationship had lasted longer than any I'd read about in my textbooks.

"The last two nights have been the usual. He takes care of his needs once he awakens, then I meet him around midnight. We spend the night together and he leaves my place before dawn." Sarge stabbed the ice cream with the spoon a few times. "We have sex. He marks me as his own. Sometimes we watch a movie or play 'Call of Duty.'"

Sounded like most relationships, outside of the biting. "So, why the argument? I don't mean to be ignorant, but Geraldo seems pretty attentive."

Sarge appeared determined to kill my pint of cookie dough ice cream with that spoon. "It's not the same. You'll see. Sex is good, but sex when they really drink from you is amazing. That's what I want, and I don't want to wait eight weeks for it."

I winced. Clearly there wasn't enough hit from whatever narcotic was in the vampire venom to sustain Sarge in between deep feedings. This was the nature of a relationship with a vampire, the life of a blood slave. Their venom was a drug that created a dependence and cravings that couldn't be ignored. At first it was manageable, but over time, the need was all a blood slave felt. Textbook cases had a blood slave living for four months before the vampire took their life. Geraldo seemed to have amazing control, but with Sarge pushing him, he'd eventually step up the feeding frequency until his partner was an anemic husk. Eventually Sarge would die.

I didn't know what to say. You couldn't tell an addict to lay off the smack, to walk away. You couldn't convince him that his seductive drug of choice was going to kill him. All I could do was hope the tub of ice cream that Sarge was massacring was going to help him make the right choice.

"Tonight is our night. You know, for us to really be together. I've been waiting eight weeks for this night, and I get the feeling it's going to be our last."

Sarge stopped stabbing the ice cream and set it on the coffee table next to Swift and Beachum's *Cabalistic Rites*. I looked at the sad container of melting cookie-dough, then up at Sarge. "I think that's even more reason for you to just enjoy tonight."

Because tomorrow he'd be dead? Or ditched and facing the mother of all detox? Or turned, although I'm pretty sure that discussion would have been on the table prior to tonight.

The man shook his head. "I want more. He wants more. But we both know where that will end. This whole relationship was doomed from the start."

It was. I wish I had some magical spell to lessen the addictive nature of the venom, or to allow a human to regenerate blood loss overnight. I barely knew Sarge, but I felt for him and his romantic tragedy. I wanted to be the good friend and just listen and sympathize, but it was hard to see anyone standing on the edge of a cliff and watch while they jumped.

"What do you want to happen? I mean, within the realm of reality, there are only three choices, and you're going to have to pick one. You keep going like this and you'll have a few weeks of non-stop ecstasy before you die. And I'm trying to stress the 'die' here."

He eyed the ice cream. "Part of me wants that. I'd die happy. I wouldn't suffer, Geraldo would make sure of that. Beats getting hit by a bus."

Yeah, we all died eventually. I thought of Essie and her comment when I'd brought Dario to Middleburg last week. It would totally be worth it if Sarge were over a hundred years old or terminally ill. He was a healthy young man, though. He had his whole life ahead of him, and it could be a happy life. He'd never know if he went down this path.

"Have you spoken to him about possibly turning you?" That was one of the other options. I don't know if he'd get the weeks of ecstasy—possibly only the one night before Geraldo did the deed. I wasn't sure exactly how it worked except that it involved exsanguination on both sides and an overnight blood bath.

Sarge looked shocked at my question. "That's not common. It would be a great honor, and I've put it out there that I wouldn't refuse, but that's not the sort of thing you ask. From what I've been told, it's rarely offered. Siring takes a huge toll on the vampire, and there's a lot of responsibility involved. Even the oldest of them have only turned a few dozen in their lifetime."

I blinked in surprise. Dario had twice offered it to me and

he'd never even shared my blood. It shed light onto those conversations and revealed some nuances I wasn't sure I was willing to think about right now. Not that it mattered. I'm sure that and all other offers were off the table now.

"Besides," Sarge continued. "It would completely change our relationship. In a way, we'd have a deeper connection, and we'd probably still love each other, but it wouldn't be the same."

No, there would be no sharing of blood, no drug-fueled orgasms. They'd both feed from humans, finding emotional and physical satisfaction in blood slaves. It sounded weird that Sarge would miss the obsessive need of a blood slave for his vampire, but it was true. Unfortunately, the man couldn't have his cake and eat the whole darned thing without it killing him.

"Then you need to walk away." Here came my tough love speech, the one I wasn't sure I would heed if I were in Sarge's shoes. "You walk away, get clean and find a boyfriend who isn't a vampire."

Sarge's eyes met mine. "Could you? Walk away, that is?"

Probably not. Still, I needed to be the voice of reason. "Three choices, my friend. Three. Indulge and die an early death. Break with polite convention and have the make-me-a-vampire talk. Or walk and live. There are good guys out there, Sarge. Once you come down off the venom addiction, you'll see that there are great guys out there to love who won't wind up killing you."

He smiled sadly. "You wait and see. I tried to break things off once, and went right back after a month. Sex isn't as good. No one else is as good. All you do is think about them and how incredible you feel when you're with them. I'd walk away and be living like a hollow shell, constantly missing what I'd left behind. I think I'd rather be dead."

And with that, I realized that Sarge had made his choice.

It was a choice that scared me, that brought a sting of tears to my eyes. The man stood picking up the container of soupy ice cream and taking it to my kitchen.

"Normally we meet at my house, but tonight I'm going to meet Geraldo at his place."

I waited a second, wondering the significance of this.

"I've been there before. You know how vampires are about anyone knowing where they rest. Well, blood slaves are different. I've been to his house, I've met the other vampires in the *Balaj*. I'm part of their family. It's what being a blood slave is all about."

"So you're going to ask him to turn you?" I hoped this was where Sarge was going with all of this.

He shrugged. "I'm leaving that up to him. I won't ask. I'll just be there when he wakes, so the first blood he tastes is mine. And there I'll remain, in his house."

I felt a chill as I understood. Sarge was all in. He was going to enjoy tonight, encourage Geraldo to take more than the customary pint. And he was going to remain there for his vampire every night until he had no more left to give.

"And what if he makes you leave? What if he breaks things off with you?"

I had no idea how this worked. Last month I would have assumed any vampire would jump at the chance to drain a beloved blood slave dry over the course of a few weeks. They were willing, and the vampires I'd read about wouldn't say no to an eager buffet.

But now I wasn't sure. There were things that Dario had shared which made me rethink my opinions. Geraldo's hunger might win out. If so I'd never see Sarge again. Or Geraldo might have some shred of humanity left in him. He might have strength and control over his instincts. Maybe he'd love Sarge enough to set him free.

The man shook his head. "Geraldo has said he would

leave me before he'd hurt me, but I've seen the look in his eyes. He can't help himself any more than I can help going to him tonight."

I remembered the predatory look that flashed across Dario's dark eyes on more than one occasion and agreed. The hunger would win. I got the feeling it won most every time.

My heart ached for him. "Enjoy tonight, Sarge."

He nodded, his mouth wobbling up into a smile. "I will. Oh, trust me I will completely enjoy tonight. And I better get going if I'm going to be there when Geraldo awakens. A guy's gotta get all primped up for a big date like this, you know?"

Totally. Not that I was busy primping for my own date, who would be here any minute. The difference struck me and I thought about Sarge's words. Vampire venom aside, I got the feeling he truly loved Geraldo. And I doubted their relationship had started with a date he hadn't even bothered to wash his hair for. If he *had* hair, that is. I really *should* have cancelled this thing with Zac.

I stood and gave Sarge a hug, then walked him to the door. A scrap of paper on the table caught my eye. "Hey, do you know where this is?"

I'd only been in Baltimore for six months, and was still figuring out my way around the sprawling city with its neighborhoods and suburbs.

He laughed. "Gay Street, five hundred block. Old Town Mall. It's just off Orleans. It used to be one of those pedestrian open-air markets with hip little shops but that all fell apart in the '70s. Supposedly a developer bought it and plans to turn it into housing, but right now everything is shut down and boarded up. The Mall is kind of a cool spot to take photos on urban decay and graffiti, but nothing beyond that. And I wouldn't go there at night, unless you had the boss with you, that is."

The boss. Dario. I still hadn't quite figured out why he was "the boss" and Leonora was Mistress.

"Dario and I aren't together," I hastily assured Sarge. "I'll be okay. I've got a really big sword."

The man eyed my neck. "It's clear to everyone that Dario has a thing for you. All the other vampires know you're off limits. How long are you going to hold out?"

Forever. I ignored Sarge's question and opened the door for him, again wishing him a good evening. As he edged past me, I saw Zac climbing the last flight of stairs to my apartment. The guys passed each other on the landing, doing that sizing-up thing men do. It was kinda funny, huge weight-lifter, bald-headed Sarge with his tattoos, brushing shoulders with Zac—a guy who was only a few inches taller than me and had a geeky vibe to match his slim build.

Zac smiled at me as I waited for him in my doorway. I could see the doubt in his eyes, and gave him props for not asking about the guy just leaving my apartment—the one who looked like he could bench press a Volvo.

"Sarge," I told him. "He's got boyfriend problems so we ate ice cream and chatted."

No one actually ate the ice cream, but Zac got the idea and visibly relaxed when he realized Sarge was not competing with him for my affections.

"Cool. You guys hang out often?"

I watched Sarge's bald head drop out of view as he rounded the last set of stairs. "Not really. I'll probably never see him again."

And as I ushered Zac into my apartment and closed my door, I thought how true those words were. It *was* unlikely I'd ever see Sarge again.

CHAPTER 4

Of all the places for Zac to take me on our date, he chose Sesarios. I didn't have the heart to tell him a sexy vampire, about whom I still had some rather lurid fantasies, had taken me there last. Instead I nodded and agreed that their gnocchi was amazing and that they had the best cannoli in town. I should know, I'd eaten six of them in twelve hours once. The one saving grace was that it was August, which meant the sun didn't go down until nine at night. Which meant there were no vampires dining when we were there.

Running into Dario would have been awkward, as unlikely as that prospect was, but I was more worried about being able to focus on my date-night conversation with the prickly feel of vampire energy filling the restaurant. I couldn't help but sense them, and once I knew they were there, it was hard to ignore their presence.

Instinctively my hand went to cover my Templar tattoo as the hostess seated us. I'd left off wearing the wide leather bracelet that covered it when I'd moved to Baltimore, thinking it was time for me to embrace who I was and for everyone else to accept it. Hiding it from Haul Du hadn't helped, they'd found out anyway. Might as well let everyone see the thing right up front, judge me as they may.

It hadn't been a big deal. It wasn't a big deal for most Templars although we tended to hang out with our own kind. The only real repercussion of my open display of the tattoo was that Dario had recognized me, and that had led to my project with the vampires last week.

There was an uneasy truce between Templars and vampires. I'd felt confident enough in that truce to tease Dario by sending him Bloody Marys and other nonsense for months. I didn't feel so confident walking into a vampire friendly establishment, even before dusk, with my tattoo clearly revealed.

The hostess's eyes snagged on my wrist, although to give the woman credit, her warm welcome never faltered. The waiter also kept sneaking peeks at the tattoo as he recited the specials. I hoped this wasn't going to be a problem. It seemed Templars were okay if they were accompanied by a vampire with status in the local *Balaj*, but not when they were with a human date.

Zac was either oblivious or polite enough not to comment. He took charge, asking me about my preferences and ordering dinner as well as our wine. It was more old-fashioned than I'd expected from him, but he'd done it with a friendly smile that didn't raise any of my feminist hackles.

"I half expected you to cancel after what happened in the park," he admitted sheepishly.

I'd considered it, but not for the reasons he thought. "It takes more than a dead body to make me cancel a date."

He smiled. "Well, that wasn't your run-of-the-mill dead body. Not that I've ever seen a dead body outside of a funeral viewing."

Which made me realize I had no idea what Zac actually

did besides gaming. At least I now knew that it didn't involve dead bodies. "So I take it your job isn't at the local coroner's office or in mortuary services?"

"I sell medical equipment. Mostly to hospitals, although my territory includes some private practices and urgent care facilities."

That was…well, whatever it was it didn't sound very interesting. I guess someone had to sell those things. I'm sure there would come a day when I was glad the hospital had chosen the something-something machine that caught my tumor early.

"So, are you in college? I know you work at the coffee shop part-time with Brandi."

I winced, realizing that probably sounded just as boring to him. In fact, I probably came across like a lazy bum who had no ambition whatsoever. He wasn't far from the truth.

"I have a degree in history. Which doesn't make me very employable, I guess." I laughed awkwardly. The history degree had been perfectly suitable for someone who would take their Oath and spend their life in service to the Temple. A degree, and four years of specialized training. And here I was making lattes.

"You'll find your calling." Far from bored, Zac seemed intrigued by the idea of a woman with a history degree pouring coffee part-time. "The perfect job will come along. You just have to be ready to take that chance when opportunity knocks."

I envisioned my opening the door to find a pack of harpies on the other side, tied up with a bow and ready to kill. I'm sure that's not what Zac meant. Still, I wondered whether selling medical equipment was *his* calling. Maybe he loved dealing with the doctors and technicians, telling them about the latest products and recommending things that would make their jobs easier, that might save lives. Who was I to judge another's passion?

Conversation faded, and we both began to flounder for anything discussion-worthy. I knew nothing of local politics or sports. Zac barely knew the Mona Lisa from a Degas. We both breathed a sigh of relief when dinner arrived and we turned to the one thing we knew we had in common.

"You're gonna need to dial back your swing a bit in the LARPs before you put half the other team in the hospital."

I took a bite of gnocchi and hid a smile at Zac's exaggeration. Yeah, I was hitting harder than I should, but I doubted anyone was going to wind up concussed. "All right, who complained?"

He laughed. "Well none of the guys, because no man is going to whine that a woman is hitting too hard. They did all comment admirably on the strength of your arm and your amazing reflexes, though."

I squirmed, pleased that I'd made an impression. "So who *did* whine? Let me guess—that Melisandre mage woman?"

Zac nodded. "She said you nailed her with a head shot, too."

"She's all of five feet tall," I complained. "That should have been a shoulder blow on anyone of reasonable height. Next time make her wear stilts or something."

"She said you hit her after she froze you with a spell."

Oh, that snitch. "Reflexes. And *how* is a beanbag with no verbal incantation whatsoever a spell? Bogus. Her complaints are totally bogus."

The rest of our *meal* was not bogus. We bantered about the LARP, discussed strategy for our next melee, and pondered whether the city would ever allow us to do mounted combat. Maryland's state sport *was* jousting. There totally needed to be jousting in Baltimore City parks.

The waiter cleared the plates away, and right before

coffee arrived Zac reached across the table, taking my hands in his and looking into my eyes with a serious expression.

"Aria Ainsworth, will you do me the great honor of...of joining my Anderon game Wednesday nights at my house?"

It was the oddest proposal I'd ever received. Actually it was the only proposal I'd ever received and it wasn't even a marriage one. Thankfully. I was more excited about the prospect of the Anderon game, and I demonstrated this by squealing and yanking my hands from Zac's so I could clap enthusiastically.

"Yes! Oh, yes!"

He smiled, face flushed and eyes sparkling as he reached into the messenger bag by his side and pulled out a sheet of paper. Next came a little leather bag that rattled as he sat it on the table. "Excellent. Let's roll up your character over coffee."

I'd done some research ever since I'd mistaken RPGs for rocket propelled grenades, so I looked down at the ability categories eagerly. "I want to be a chaotic good, half-dragon fighter."

Half dragon. The very thought made me want to giggle. Dragons were reptiles, and although sentient and scary-smart, they weren't physically compatible with humans. Half-dragon. Ha ha ha.

"Let's see what you roll up first."

I took the four six-sided dice and tossed them on the table. Then I added the highest three numbers. "Four."

Zac recoiled as if I'd just punched him. "Four?"

"Yeah. Is that bad?"

He swallowed a few times. "Well, ten to twelve is a normal, average score."

So four was bad. I looked down the list. Strength. Constitution. Dexterity. Intelligence. Wisdom. Charisma. A four strength would really suck, but none of the others was a great choice either. Too weak to pick up more than a sock. Keels over dead when someone sneezes at me. Stumbles over dust. Has the IQ of a toddler. Decides jumping face first into lava is a good idea. So ugly I make ugly people run and cry.

"Put it in Charisma." I was vain, but not so vain that I'd take any of those other faults over ugly.

I kept rolling. "Thirteen. Thirteen. Ten. Fifteen. Fourteen."

Okay, none of that was particularly stellar. I could take the ten in constitution, and at least be above average in the other attributes.

Zac stared at the paper then threw down his pen. "How about we do another method? Otherwise you're going to be dead by the end of next Wednesday's game."

I put myself in his capable hands, and by the time we were done, I had the makings of a reasonably proficient half-dragon fighter. We'd finished several cups of coffee. The waiter was making not-so-subtle hints that he wanted new customers at our table, and I was eyeing the setting sun thinking we should get going before the vampires started arriving.

It was dark by the time Zac walked me up to my apartment, clearly lingering in wait for an invitation to come in. I thought about it. We'd had a good time tonight, even with the awkward, rocky start. I didn't want to push this too fast, though. And I had that list of magical components to research, plus the address I'd found in Ronald's pocket. I put my key in the lock and turned to face Zac and thank him for a lovely evening. He must have seen the handwriting on the wall, because before a word came out, his mouth was on mine.

It was a nice kiss. Okay, it was a better-than-nice kiss. The guy knew what he was doing, and I'd had a ridiculously long dry spell. Before I knew it, my arms were around his neck and I was plastered to Zac, kissing him back with abandon. Maybe I *should* invite him in instead of spending the night researching the dead guy. It's not like I was friends with this Ronald. For all I knew he'd summoned a demon and improperly banished it. For all I knew he'd gotten what he deserved. I liked Zac, and he clearly liked me. A lot. I could invite him in, drag him off to bed, and not come up for air until the sun rose. It sounded like a great way to cap off the evening. Besides, no one had appointed me the supernatural investigator for Baltimore. It's not like I was a paladin or anything.

Although I kinda was. And as much as the idea of sex appealed to me, I was better off buying a vibrator than leading Zac down a path I wasn't sure I wanted to travel.

So I pulled away, running my hands across his shoulders to rest on his chest. He wasn't much taller than me, his beautiful hazel eyes nearly level with mine. "Wednesday?"

He swallowed hard. "Wednesday." His voice was husky, his hands shifting lower to cup my rear and press my pelvis against his. "Wednesday. The half-dragon will make her debut."

I smiled, pulling away once more and turning to unlock my door. "She'll be there, wings and all."

I was still smiling as I closed the door and leaned against it, listening to Zac's footsteps on the stairs. This wasn't crazy love-at-first-sight, or even lust-at-first-sight, but there was a spark of something between us. Maybe it would go somewhere, maybe it wouldn't. Either way, I was glad I hadn't cancelled on Zac tonight.

CHAPTER 5

I chewed on my lip as I looked at my phone and re-read the crime stats for the area around Old Town Mall. Sarge hadn't been exaggerating when he had warned me against going there alone at night. But night it was, and unless I wanted to wait until morning I was going to have to brave gang and drug violence. Hopefully not alone, though. I'd never have considered dragging Zac to such a place, but a vampire was different. *They* were the big scary in the night, and they also had dealings with the local gangs and drug lords that might make them recognizably off limits, and thus me off limits by association. Sarge had suggested I bring Dario, but there was one problem with that idea—I didn't know where the vampire was. I'd been searching for the last hour with no luck and was about to give up.

One more pub. If Dario wasn't here, I'd need to go out on my own and see what the address on this slip of paper revealed. Hopefully I wouldn't get shot. I was fairly certain I could hold my own when it came to hand-to-hand combat, and I was pretty good at dealing with assailants carrying knives. Guns were a whole different thing, though. I needed to ask Mom to send up my vest from back home. I hated wearing that thing. It wasn't exactly standard issue for us Templars, but I'd picked one up while training to fight manticores. Seems Kevlar was just as good at protecting against poisoned darts as it was bullets.

Vampires weren't impervious to bullets but the projectiles didn't kill them. Shooting a vampire just pissed them off, and a pissed off vampire was a deadly one. Besides, I was thinking with Dario around there wouldn't be any shooting going on at all.

Not that I was completely sure he'd accompany me even if I did manage to track him down. I hadn't heard from him since our last encounter with the necromancer, and leaving a bunch of money in my tampon box didn't exactly constitute forgiveness.

I'd betrayed his trust. I'd withheld information and vampires had died. No matter what I did, I wasn't sure anything would make up for that. He might still have a "thing" for me, but that didn't mean he'd ever forgive me for what I'd done. I should let it go, let this...whatever we had die a slow death. I should just head out to Old Town Mall on my own. I had a sword. I had skills. There was no reason for me to be trying to hunt down Dario to ask him to accompany me. One more place, then I'd assume this was a sign to leave well enough alone.

Reilly's was a typical Baltimore pub with over twenty microbrew specialties on tap and sports events on every television. I weaved my way through the front tables and the bar area to the back where the dart games drew quite a crowd, even on a Saturday evening. I looked about, then sighed as I headed around the side room to the exit. And that's where I saw him. His back was to me, but I could sense the static-feel of vampire anywhere, and I'd come to know Dario's particular energy, even if I hadn't recognized his broad shoulders.

I was a Templar. I probably felt different to him than the humans around me. He must have sensed me, but he didn't budge an inch. I realized why when I saw that he had company. It had never bothered me before. Dario was always with a different woman, picking up his meal of choice for the evening. I'd still sent him drinks and notes on napkins, not caring whether or not he had a "date."

But this time it bothered me. I wasn't sure why. A vampire had to eat. She was a meal. And if she was more… well, that was none of my business. Still, I hesitated. The woman across from him was leaning forward, spilling her breasts practically out of her top. She tilted her head and laughed, flicking a strand of glossy, ebony hair behind one ear.

Awkward. It was like walking up on an ex-boyfriend while he was romancing a new girlfriend. Dario was busy. He didn't have time to escort me around a bad section of town. I should have left. But I was here, and I seemed to have a masochistic streak this evening, so I moved myself in their direction, smiling apologetically at the golden-skinned brunette as I stopped by their table.

"Hey. Can I talk to you for a quick second?" I asked Dario.

He hesitated just enough to make me feel like a vinyl siding salesman calling at dinnertime. "I'm kind of busy right this moment. Is it important?"

I felt my cheeks heat to a level that could incinerate paper. After what had happened I didn't blame him if he was giving me the cold shoulder.

What should I say? I could hardly tell him that a man died at the hands of a demon in a park this afternoon, and I was checking out an address I'd found in his pocket. That wasn't vampire business. He probably wouldn't care one bit. The only reason I was here was because Sarge suggested I shouldn't go alone and said I should have Dario accompany me.

I wanted a vampire to have my back. I wanted *this* vampire to have my back, but he was busy, and I wasn't sure the limits of our friendship at this point.

"No. I'm just heading to Old Town Mall to check something out and thought you might want to go. No problem. Talk to you later. Maybe."

I walked away, feeling like a total idiot.

"Who was that?" I heard the brunette ask Dario.

"A work associate. We did a project together last week, but it's wrapped up."

Out of the corner of my eye I saw the woman turn to look at me. "She's kind of weird. I think she has a thing for you."

I walked out the door before I could hear Dario's response. I didn't *want* to hear it. This woman was his dinner, his one-time meal for the evening, but something inside me worried that maybe she'd be more. Did he care enough about her to make her a blood slave? She might not live long, but there would still be a level of intimacy between the two of them, the idea of which made me want to pull out my sword and start slicing and dicing.

"Aria! Wait!"

I froze in place as Dario jogged up to me.

"You *do* know that Old Town Mall isn't a mall anymore, right?" He asked, standing close enough to me that I could smell the cinnamon and myrrh scent of vampire.

"I know. A demon killed some guy in the park today and he had this address in his pocket. The guy, I mean, not the demon." Crap, I could barely think straight with him standing this close. "I wanted to check it out."

He tilted his head and gave me a lopsided smile. "It's probably a drug pick-up spot. If any of the local businessmen give you grief, mention my name. Okay?"

I loved that he didn't coddle me, or forbid me to go and fuss as if I couldn't take care of myself. He'd seen me in action. He *knew* I could take care of myself, but he still gave me a trump card to play if I needed.

"Thanks. It'll probably just be a quick in and out. No big deal. And I've got my sword." I hesitated, not sure how to ask him about the other thing on my mind—well, the other thing that didn't have to do with dark-haired beauty back at his table. "Sarge…he came to see me tonight and I'm worried."

The vampire sighed, as if he had been dreading this conversation. "I don't know what to say, Aria. That's between him and Geraldo. Sarge is a grown man, a consenting adult. He gets to choose how he lives his life."

"Even if that's death?" I shot back, mad at the situation. "He's addicted. He can't walk away. And he's going to die because of it."

Dario blew out an exasperated puff of air. "People die all the time. They're mortals. They die rock climbing, drunk driving, from eating too much red meat. They die smoking, base jumping, walking down the stairs. Are you suggesting Geraldo should cut Sarge off? What if Sarge spends the next year miserable only to get hit by a meteor? Doesn't Sarge have the right to decide how he lives and how he dies?"

"Not when that decision is tainted by an addiction that is reinforced every time you feed." I caught my breath and looked back at the pub door, where Dario's date waited. "Why can't you all just do the one-night stand thing only? There are no lasting effects. You all get fed and no one dies."

Sorrow flashed in the vampire's eyes. "Because we get lonely, too. We still long for human companionship. It's more than blood. There's something life-giving about being close to a human, something that holds back the darkness and the hunger."

I felt for them, I really did, but humans eventually *died* in this exchange. Every single time. "So you hold back the darkness for six months, more if you have good control, then one night the human dies and you run out to do it all over again? How is that beneficial to either vampires or humans?"

Dario winced. "We don't 'run out to do it all over again.' We grieve. You have no idea how much we grieve over the loss of a blood slave. And knowing we're the ones who killed them makes it harder. Even the worst among us has feelings when it comes to their blood slaves. For some of us those feelings are what you would call love."

I could barely breathe as I listened to his words. He'd offered this to me. Did that mean his feelings for me ran in that direction? The whole thing was a tragedy. *We* were a tragedy. And I didn't like tragedy, not one bit.

Dario reached out a hand and tugged at the end of my braid, a sad smile on his face. "I haven't taken a blood slave in over a hundred years. That's how painful it is to lose one. That's how much we grieve."

There was a moment, charged with emotions that ricocheted between us. I swallowed hard and stepped back a pace, feeling my rear press against the brick wall of the pub. "I don't want Sarge to die. I don't want to never see him again and know he's met his end. It… It taints the sympathy I have for vampires as a species."

His smile faded as he turned away. "We are who we are. There are times when we will seem to be heroes, and times when we will seem to be monsters. We are both."

I watched him walk to the pub door, the streetlight highlighting his broad shoulders and his smooth, dark skin. Without another look my way, he vanished through the doorway—away from me and toward the beauty who waited for him inside.

CHAPTER 6

Far from the typical branched out building with anchor stores, Old Town Mall was on a brick street that had been blocked off from vehicular traffic. Lining the broad walkway was a series of boarded up shops. Graffiti covered the brick and the plywood. Papers blew about the streets and down the narrow alleyways. I'd been in some rough sections of Baltimore, but this seemed worse. There was an abandoned, ghost-town feel to the area that the 'hoods on the west side lacked.

It was dark. Seriously dark with no working street lights, the moonlight blocked by the abandoned storefronts. I wanted to use magical light, not only to figure out which store was the one on my slip of paper, but so I didn't trip over a loose brick and faceplant into the ground. I didn't, though. I didn't even pull the non-magical flashlight out of my bag. There was something about this place that demanded it remain in the dark.

My footsteps were soft but they echoed against the pathway. Where were the dealers? The junkies? Where was *anybody*? I'd expected shadows darting between buildings, or surely a hooded figure watching me from the curb. Instead I got the feeling that nothing alive remained here.

Well, nothing *human* anyway. Something was watching me. I could feel eyes on me as I made my way down the empty streets. I didn't get the static feel of vampires, but instead a coldness that ran deep through me to the bone, aching sharpest at the scar on my side. That ache was more nerve-wracking than the prospect of drug dealers and junkies with guns and knives.

I finally pulled the flashlight from my purse and held it more as a weapon than for the light it gave off. Just in case, I had my sword in the other hand, at the ready as I walked. Sarge had said there was a revitalization project in the works, and the presence of a few bulldozers backed that up, but heavy equipment was as far as it went. Most of the buildings remained standing, and those that didn't looked as though nature had done the demolition and not construction equipment.

I repeated the building number under my breath, shining my light upward along doorways. Half the buildings didn't *have* numbers, and given the chipped, peeling nature of the ones that did I wasn't sure which one five-twenty-four was. Taking a guess, I approached one. The door had two-by-fours nailed in random angles across the frame. I tested the door itself with the butt of my flashlight and nearly had a heart attack when it swung inward.

The light revealed nothing beyond dust and broken shelves as far as I could see, but I wanted to check further. Wedging myself between the two-by-fours, I squeezed through the tight space and into the old store. It looked to have been some sort of gallery. The front room was spacious with bent metal easels past the broken shelving. Electrical wires sprang from chipped plaster, above where paintings must have once hung.

It took me a few seconds to realize that the energy inside the building was…normal. I still felt as if I were watched, but the chill was gone. Walking backward, I squeezed through the door and stood directly in front of the building. Then I edged the way I'd come down the sidewalk until I hit the point where my side ached and the cold ran through me once more. It was as if someone had drawn a line in the pavement that the cold energy could not cross. I took a few steps forward and again it vanished. I still felt watched, but I got the impression whoever it was couldn't cross this invisible line, that they were waiting for the fence to come down so they could spring.

I scraped my foot along the brick but saw no symbols. A magical circle worked both ways—as a method to keep energy and spirits contained within and to keep them out. There were many magical workings that were safer conducted inside a circle where stray energy couldn't muck up the results. And, of course, there were times when a putting yourself into the cage of a circle kept the big and bad from ripping you to shreds. Temporarily, that is. Eventually you had to come out and most supernatural creatures were very good at waiting.

But there were no sigils, no symbols, no runes. What kind of circle could hold energy back while remaining so…open?

I returned to the building, figuring the answer would be at this address on the slip of paper from Ronald's pocket. Inside, I searched the far recesses of the old gallery, finding nothing but a pile of broken furniture, dust, and old shelving.

As I made my way around the front room of the building, something moved in the corner. I jumped, poising my sword to strike as I swung my flashlight around. It was a rat. The creature stared at me with eyes reflecting crimson in the light. Then it turned and left, deciding I wasn't a threat.

I turned to leave too, but a faint, familiar scent held me in place. Sage.

Those who followed the various ceremonial magic paths didn't rely as heavily upon the herb as the Native Americans, or even Wiccans, did but that didn't mean we didn't occasionally find it useful. Sage was for protection. Smudging rid the magical space of bad spirits. Yes, it had other uses, but in my experience, sage only came into play when you were about to practice in an area with a sketchy supernatural history—or when you needed to clean up after a ritual gone wrong.

Of course, if you practiced black magic a ritual gone wrong was often a ritual gone right.

I sniffed, noting the lack of footprints in the dust as I made my way toward the back gallery. Whoever had been here, they either had a hide-your-tracks spell, or they were using another entrance. I was betting on the former, otherwise why leave the front door unlocked and free of wards. In fact, the lack of wards was something bothering me almost as much as the lack of symbols on the circle perimeter. The aroma of burning sage and the invisible line that blocked a cold energy was all I had here. Maybe I had the wrong building. Maybe some kids had been hanging out on a back step, smoking some weird herbal blend and blowing it in through the broken windows. Maybe I was thinking of any excuse I could not to go farther.

I wasn't always such a coward, but that dead body today had shaken me more than I wanted to admit. The image of an empty rib cage sprang from my memory and I shut my eyes, shaking my head. Now wasn't the time to freak out. Sage. It was just sage, and despite what I knew its uses could be, there were other, far more innocuous explanations for the smell. I'd seen no blood, no salt, no wards or runes or magical symbols of any kind.

And the icy energy? I was going to ignore that, stiffen my spine and just keep going.

The middle room of the gallery was as filthy as the front one, and free of any hint of magical undertakings. The rear room was the same. I noted the back entrance was a locked steel door, and that the windows were tightly sealed with plywood boards. Nothing. I nearly collapsed in relief, shaky from the adrenaline that had fled my body. I was so relieved that I almost missed the little saucepan just inside the back door. It was the cheap kind that you find at thrift stores, aluminum with yellow sides splattered with stains and burn marks. Inside was a pile of ashes. Burned sage leaves curled gray on a charred bundle of twigs. Someone had smudged the building, but it looked like they hadn't done anything *but* smudge. I doubt they would have gone to all the bother to remove all trace of their magical workings only to leave an old pot of ashes by the doorway. But why go to the trouble to smudge and not use the building?

I frowned down at the ashes, remembering ceremonies and spells from my own grimoire and other research. Sage to clear the space either before or after the ritual—or both. But sometimes sage was used *during* a ritual, on the outside of a magical space.

It was to keep the bad shit away that might be drawn to a dark working. Or even keep the bad shit contained in case the protections inside the circle failed. I caught my breath, adrenaline surging again as I peered into the pot and took out my keychain.

In spite of regular church attendance, Sunday school, and education in a variety of spiritual belief systems, my family wasn't what I'd call particularly religious. But we *were* Templars, and when you were born with a mission from God, you tended to follow the general path. My keychain was a seven inch, 14k gold crucifix. It was perfect for fending off vampires, but also could serve as a faith-based focus to bless a space or guard against malevolent spirits.

It was also very useful for digging into a pot of ashes when I wasn't sure if what was in there would take my finger off. I wasn't about to risk my sword, or the butter knife that I'd swiped from my kitchen and spent long nights spelling. The keychain was expensive but replaceable, and beyond its spiritual significance, it wasn't imbued with any magical powers whose presence might set off a particularly stealthy ward.

I stirred the ashes, waiting for them to settle before shining the light downward into the pot and peering over the edge. There, among the burned leaves was a shining white bone. I grimaced, wishing I'd brought tweezers. I really needed some kind of Templar readiness kit if I was going to start doing these things regularly. A multi-tool. Some rope and bungee cords. Chalk and a mirror. A Glock.

I dumped the pot over, spilling the ashes and bone onto the dusty ground. If only I'd been packing a tissue, or paper towel. Something else to add to my Templar kit. But I didn't have any handy and this old gallery was empty of anything except broken shelving.

The moment the mixture hit the ground I felt it. Icy winds that stirred nothing. Something tickled along my spine and I jumped, spinning with my sword outstretched. It encountered only air. And the beam from my flashlight revealed nothing.

But it was cold—way too cold for an August night. My breath fogged the air in front of me and from out of the silence I heard a scream.

Some noises practically stop your heart, some send a surge of adrenaline through it, some cause you to cower and cringe. This one locked me in place. I could do nothing but stand and wait for the wail to end. It tapered off with another rush of cold, and abruptly everything returned to normal. I began sweating from the sudden change in temperature, and noted the faint noise of crickets that had been silent before.

My body desperately wanted to flee, but my mind prevailed. I still had that feeling of being watched, still felt the lingering remains of cold energy, but whatever that Big Bad had been, I got the impression it was gone. For now. Which meant I needed to hurry if I was going to figure out what the heck was going on here in Old Town Mall, and what Ronald Stull had to do with any of it. Starting with the contents of this pot.

Turning back around, I picked up the bone and hurriedly stuck it in my jacket pocket, exhaling when I didn't burst into flames or fall through the floor. I knew a lot of stuff, but bone identification wasn't on the list. I wasn't sure I even had the correct texts to figure out what animal the bone was from, and the answer would be important. Every little detail was important when it came to magic. Whether the bone was a crow or a cat or a rat would mean all the difference in exactly what the practitioner was smudging to protect against, as well as give me some indication of what the icy presence had been.

But in the meantime, I had some adjoining buildings to search, and the thought gave me the creeps. Smudging an empty building either meant the area of ritual was large or whatever they didn't want to find them was pretty scary. Either one made me think twice about proceeding. I could go home, check out what this bone was, then come back in the daylight when less scary stuff was up and about.

But that left time for someone to clean up after themselves. Besides, daytime posed its own risks and I doubted whoever was in charge of revitalizing this area would like a woman prowling around the condemned buildings. It was now, or quite possibly never.

The next store was locked up tight. I squeezed down the narrow side alleyway to the rear and found the back door equally secure. Looking in through the gaps in the window boards, I didn't see anything out of the ordinary. Which left either the building on the other side of the gallery, or one across the street.

I was feeling a bit like a coward so I tried the one across the street. The door was nailed shut, but with some wiggling and considerable muttered curses I was able to wedge myself through two boards that blocked a rear window.

It wasn't the smell of sage that came to me the moment I got inside but something else. The thick, sweet, coppery scent of blood hit my nose. It was summer, and in spite of the thunderstorm, today had been hot. Either the blood had been used in a ritual within the last day, or something had been added to it to help keep it fresh. Steeling myself for the worst, I readied my sword and my flashlight, and walked forward.

This building had been sectioned off into a maze with shelves and partitions. No wonder they'd gone out of business because the layout was a shoplifter's dream. No employee could hope to be able to see what customers were doing with all little nooks, crannies, and aisles to hide in. There weren't enough security cameras in the world to monitor this kind of layout. And it wasn't even ideal for magic. As I'd learned trying to do a summoning in my apartment, carpet, walls, and fixtures meant the biggest space for a circle was teeny tiny. Summoning a demon was dicey enough without pissing one off by summoning them into a space too small to even turn around in.

Of course, not all magic was geared toward summoning. I'd always been fascinated by the greater spirits and that had been the avenue that the majority of my clandestine studies had taken. I was well aware that there were many rituals that benefited from a small, enclosed space. So I wasn't overly surprised when I rounded a corner and laid eyes on a literal blood bath.

Bath. As in bathtub. Not one of those beautiful, clawed-foot ones that you see in posh home-improvement magazines either. This bathtub looked like something out of a third-world hillbilly digest. It was little more than a white plastic hundred gallon stock feeder, and it was more red than white.

I choked back the bile that rose in my throat. Flies swarmed all over the tub. Blood stained the sides and the linoleum floor beneath, nearly obscuring the white chalk circles and symbols. I needed to take pictures of the magical space to research later, but I only had two hands and was reluctant to put down either my flashlight or my sword.

The sword won. I propped the flashlight up on a nearby shelf and pulled out my cell phone, snapping pictures as I held the weapon with a white-knuckled grip. That done, I pocketed the phone, picked up the flashlight and moved forward to look inside the tub.

I had no fear of triggering wards or encountering residual magic from the ritual. Death magic was horrific, but it was efficient. Every last bit of energy derived from the killing went to its intended purpose. As messy as the site was from a crime-scene perspective, it wasn't at all messy from a magical one.

Not that those facts made me feel any better. Something had died in that tub and I didn't want to know what. But Ronald had died too, and clearly he'd been connected to whatever went down here. From what my LARP friends said, Ronald's death had been no great tragedy, but he was still a human being. He was still somebody's son or husband or brother. And beyond that, a mage doing sacrificial magic in my city was unacceptable. Spells powered by the murder of another human weren't all unicorn sparkles and fairy dust, and besides the spell, death magic drew bad stuff. Beings of the underworld were attracted to it. No doubt that was why they'd smudged a large area around the ritual with sage.

I looked over the edge of the tub and choked. This wasn't a run-of-the-mill death spell, if there was such a thing. This was the stuff of nightmares, and no amount of sage and bones was going to help us if what happened here was what I thought it was.

CHAPTER 7

I'd at least had the forethought to stash my sword and butter knife back in my car before the police arrived. Yes, I called the police. As much as I didn't want to deal with all the questions and red-tape bureaucracy, I couldn't leave a dead woman to rot in the ruins of an abandoned store.

I also called Janice, leaving her a message to meet me for breakfast in the morning. She'd been a huge help to me before, and I'd sorta agreed to give her first scoop on this sort of thing. What the reporter was going to actually do with a demon slaying and a death-magic ritual murder, I had no idea.

My next call was to Raven. I was shocked out of my mind when she picked up on the first ring.

"Aria, you need to get out of town. Go visit your family for a few weeks or something, but get out of town."

Huh? Did she know? How could she have known? It had been a long time since I'd seen Raven, but the woman I knew never would have participated in the ritual I'd seen in that building.

"There's a mage here in Baltimore doing human sacrifice. I was calling to warn *you*."

"They do that there. And shit is going down. It's been going down for a while, but now it's really going down. Stay out of it and get out of town."

They do that there? I was in Baltimore, not some island in the South Pacific full of natives with strange customs that included human sacrifice.

"You *know*? This is commonplace? Mages in Baltimore regularly power their magic through murder?"

Raven made a soft noise. "Not all groups are Haul Du. This is not your fight, Aria. Get out of there."

How could this *not* be my fight? "Raven, there is a woman dead in a bathtub. A mage died this afternoon by a demon's hand. I might not have been in Haul Du for long, but this sort of thing shouldn't be a regular occurrence."

"Who was the mage?"

I replied before I even wondered at her question. "Ronald Stull."

I heard her snort. "He was an ass. No loss there."

Probably not, but that didn't mean I could just walk away from a demon loose and out of hell, or a woman who'd been murdered to power another's magic. "I need to know who the mages are that did this. Which wizards in Baltimore are performing human sacrifice?"

"Hell if I know. Look, Aria, we don't associate with those guys. The only reason I know Ronald Stull is because he screwed Reynard over on a luck charm once. Other than that, we don't hang with them. They do death magic. It's an acceptable magical practice. If there are a few bad apples who take it too far and use human sacrifice, then I don't know about it. I've heard rumors, but that's it. All I can tell you is some magical violence is brewing and you need to be out of the way. Got it?"

No, I didn't, but before I could respond, she'd hung up. I knew better than to try and call her again, so instead I sat by my car and waited for the police. I didn't have to wait for long.

Within minutes the place was overrun with red and blue lights. They'd moved a few of the barriers aside and driven right down the brick pedestrian path to park in front of the crime scene. I followed on foot, catching up with them as they were swarming the building like a group of armed ants.

I hugged myself, knowing that whatever story I told them was going to make me look suspicious. And I'd need to think up something fast. I couldn't exactly tell the law I was a Templar, and that even though I'd refused to take my Oath I still had a self-imposed duty to sleuth supernatural occurrences in my adoptive city. And confiscate powerful magical items so they could be secured in The Temple. And protect Pilgrims on the Path—whatever that meant anymore...

The looney bin might have better meals than I'd eaten this past month, but they didn't run around parks in plastic armor with foam swords or spend hours crafting cappuccinos and butter nut lattes for a caffeine-deprived public. I liked my life, and I really liked the direction it was heading. Well, except for tonight. Tonight sucked.

A man in uniform approached me. "Are you the one who found the body?"

I had an urge to laugh. I was the only one here beyond the rats and flies. Yeah, I'd found the body. It wasn't like the police presence had drawn a curious crowd of onlookers. The area had remained a ghost town even with lights flashing everywhere.

And I got the feeling that was an odd thing. Old Town Mall wasn't in the middle of nowhere, it was smack dab in the city. There were neighborhoods nearby. I'm sure people cut through this area on their way home or to activities elsewhere in Baltimore. I was the only one here besides the police, and I'd been the only one here since I'd arrived.

Death magic wasn't something that reacted well to disturbances, and someone wandering into the middle of your sacrificial ritual would be pretty bad. Whoever had done this wasn't just morally bankrupt, they were powerful enough to protect the area from intruders—both living and those of the spirit world. But why wasn't I affected? The coldness of whatever had been held outside the ritual area, as well as the humans that normally frequent this area had all been kept away, but I'd passed right through the barrier. I'd driven down here, walked up the street and poked through the stores like nothing had happened.

"Yes. I found the body."

He nodded and motioned me over to a squad car where a man with crumpled khakis, a crumpled shirt, and crumpled hair stood. The uniformed guy left, and Man-Who-Doesn't-Own-An-Iron and I stared at each other.

"You found the body?"

"Yeah. You always sleep in your clothes?" It was too late for this, and I'd been through enough today. Two dead bodies, and my former best friend admitting that death magic was a normal occurrence in Baltimore? Yeah, not a good day. That's the only explanation I had for my snappish reply.

"No, but I couldn't exactly show up to a crime scene naked."

He dug around in the squad car for a pen and notebook while I gaped. Is this the way cops talked to people? It seemed terribly unprofessional, but then again so did his appearance. And I couldn't help but run my eyes over him, rather intrigued by the idea of him naked at a crime scene. It was hard to tell what was under the wrinkled clothing, but I'll admit I was mildly interested in finding out.

"Name?"

"Solaria Angelique Ainsworth."

He blinked, his pen pausing on the pad of paper. I produced my license and handed it to him, figuring it was easier than spelling out the God-awful name my parents had "gifted" me with.

"Virginia," he commented, holding the laminated card up to the light.

"I moved here six months ago. I know, I know. I need to get a Maryland license at this point. I promise it's on my agenda."

It wasn't. I was hoarding my stash of cash from the vampire job, and changing my license plus the registration on my car would take pretty much every last dime I had.

"College?"

He was a man of few words as well as less-than-ideal grooming habits, and I still didn't know his name. I'd finished college four years ago, but at least he hadn't mistaken me for thirty like the vampires had.

"Graduated. I work part-time at Holy Grounds off Pratt." He raised an eyebrow and I felt the need to elaborate. "History degrees don't carry much weight in the job world. I can tell you all about the fourth crusade while I whip up a cinnamon dolce latte though."

He smiled. And he was kind of cute when he did so. Although I wasn't exactly the best judge of men right now. It had been a really long dry spell for me. Maybe I *should* have taken the night off and invited Zac into my apartment and my bed. There was no trusting my judgement at this point. One smile, and I was ready to start throwing panties.

"Huh?" I realized he'd asked me a question and was waiting patiently for the answer.

"Can you tell me exactly what happened, starting with

what brought you here to when you discovered the deceased?"

Oh yeah. Story time. I took my license back and stashed it in my pocket, feeling the outline of the bone I'd taken from the sage pot as I did.

"There was a guy, a customer on my shift today, who ask me to meet him and gave me this address. I came here, went in, and looked for him. That's when I found the body."

Did I mention how I was the worst storyteller ever? I think my Latin is slightly worse, but making crap up is a close second. It's why I was always in trouble as a child. I could never concoct anything plausible enough to cast a hint of doubt on what naughtiness I'd actually been up to.

"So a man asked you to meet him after dark in an abandoned store in a bad part of town—a store you needed to climb through a window to enter."

I produced the slip of paper with the address on it and gave it to the cop. Or detective. Whatever he was.

He looked at it and slid it between the pages of his notebook. "And how hot was this guy? I mean, he had to have been a total Adonis for you to show up here. You do know who Adonis is, do you?"

Jerk. "My history degree did include basic Greek and Roman mythology, but I may be a bit rusty."

"Well, you don't seem to be high, but I've got to say I doubt your 'cute guy' story. I really don't care if you were meeting a dealer here. I'm not in Vice, I'm in Homicide, and I'm trying to investigate a murder. And I really need to check out this dealer of yours if he's selling drugs in a building where a gruesome murder has taken place.

Gruesome. He hadn't even been in there yet, hadn't seen the tub of blood and the symbols around the floor. Just wait 'til he got an eyeful of that one. Unless there was a magician moonlighting by dealing smack, he wouldn't find the killer by roughing up the local drug lords.

"I don't do drugs, although I do enjoy an occasional alcoholic beverage. Look, I'm still fairly new in town. The guy said it was a mall, so I figured we were going to hook-up in the parking lot outside a Sears or something. I'll admit this wasn't what I expected, but I figured after driving down here I'd see if he was inside."

His eyes shot to mine. "And you weren't afraid? A young, beautiful woman in a bad part of town casually leaves her car, walks down a dark pathway flanked on either side by abandoned buildings, and climbs through the window of a boarded up store. Seems rather reckless."

Beautiful? I'd been sometimes called pretty, but no one outside of my parents had ever claimed I was beautiful. I held the detective's gaze and smiled. "I assure you that I am completely capable of defending myself against any attacker."

Well, almost any. And the detective didn't realize that at the time I'd been clutching the sword, now in my car, with a panicked grasp. Yeah I was afraid, but I'd been taught that fear was a good thing. It kept you from doing stupid stuff. Sometimes it kept you alive.

"Okay, ninja girl from Middleburg, Virginia. I'll buy that. Now why were you in the building across the street from the address on this slip of paper?"

Oops. Yeah, that. I shrugged, giving him another vacuous look. "I couldn't read the numbers very well in the dark."

I was blowing this whole thing. I couldn't act like a ditz one moment, antagonize the cop another, then go on to give him "I'm a badass" vibes. If I didn't get my act together, I was going to wind up in jail, or at the very least down at the station for a very long night of questioning.

"What's in the building across the street? The address on the paper?"

Wrinkled clothing or not, this guy was sharp. "Nothing. The door was unlocked and I went in but there was nothing there except a pot by the back doorway with some ashes in it. I figured I had the wrong building, so I checked this one out."

He shook his head. "A pot? With ashes?"

I sucked at lying, and I was really wanting to go back to my apartment and do a little research before going go to bed so I figured it was time to try the truth.

"Burnt sage. In a saucepan." No way I was telling him about the bone. At least, not until I'd figured out what it was.

"Sage."

Okay. The one word responses were getting on my nerves, especially now that he'd started repeating me.

"Sage. Sage sticks are sold in bundles in new age or magical supply stores, and sometimes at craft fairs. They're often burned with lemon verbena or prairie grass to sanctify a holy space or to protect against malevolent spirits."

He blinked. "Malev…malevolent?"

"Malevolent. You do know that word? I don't have a dictionary on hand, but I'm sure you can Google it on your phone."

Oh, I was being very bad. It would serve me right if I spent the night in jail.

Detective Crumpled Pants didn't seem offended by my slight. "So you believe that someone was practicing a spiritual something or another across the street? And I guess it's an amazing coincidence that there was a murder in this building, here?"

Might as well get this over with and get to bed, whether that be in my apartment or in a jail cell.

"It's not just your run-of-the-mill murder in there," I told him. "It was a ritualistic sacrifice. I won't know exactly to what purpose until I do some research, but there was some bad juju going on in there, and the sage across the street was to make sure dark fae, gremlins, hellhounds, or demon avatars didn't interfere."

He stared at me open mouthed. "I'm rethinking my drug dealer theory. What exactly did you take and why did it have such a delayed reaction?"

I pulled out my phone and scrolled through the pictures. "These aren't the best quality. I'm sure your CSI dudes in there will have much better shots."

"You took pictures?" He voice rose in volume. "You encounter a dead body with blood everywhere, and you snap selfies?"

"I did *not* take selfies! And I didn't see what had been sacrificed until after I'd taken the pictures. For all I knew it could have been a dog or a hundred rats."

The man drew himself up. It was then that I realized he was quite a bit taller than me, and that in spite of his slim build, he was fairly buff. I might have given him the bravado speech earlier, but I wasn't sure that this guy couldn't pummel me to a bloody smear. Especially if I didn't have my sword. Although if I tried to skewer him, he'd probably just shoot me. My eyes went to the gun in the holster at his shoulder.

"History major. History of what? The idea of a slaughtered dog or a hundred rat corpses doesn't faze you? You sneak into an abandoned building for a romantic tryst, find a tub of blood with some kind of satanic symbols around it, and you take pictures first and call the cops later?"

There was a lot to refute in his statement, but I seized on the most egregious. "Black magic has nothing to do with Satan. Well, it might depending on if they were summoning demons or not. But beyond that, those who follow Satanism as it exists today don't truly worship Satan as defined by the Christian church."

I saw several police exit the building out of the corner of

my eye, and saw a team enter with a collapsible stretcher. The man in front of me tilted his head, as if he wasn't sure whether to charge me with murder or not.

"I didn't kill her," I argued. "I came to the address on that paper, and I'll admit that I got nosy. And I know a lot about this stuff. I've spent my whole life studying this. My father has a library full of old manuscripts, and I've had access to some of the oldest texts in Europe. I'm going to find out what's going on here because that's what I do. That's my calling. It's what I was born to do. I'm happy to share information with you as long as you keep an open mind, and as long as you don't lock me in a cell. Or shoot me. I'd really like it if you didn't shoot me."

He looked over my shoulder, then dug a business card out of his pocket and handed it to me. "Stay here until I speak with the techs. But just in case the dark fae spirit you away in the next five minutes, I'd like it if you call me in the morning, once you complete your research."

Now it was my turn to stare at him in astonishment. The man walked past me, brushing my shoulder lightly with his arm on the way. I held the card between my thumb and forefinger, watching as he spoke with the white suited, booted people. Then I tore my gaze away and looked at the card.

Detective Justin Tremelay. My mind screeched a one-eighty. Tremelay. Bernard of Tremelay had been the Grand Master of The Temple in 1153. It was a weird coincidence that the very detective investigating this case had a last name that harkened back to our Order's roots.

So many of the Templar families had been exterminated after that black Friday when the King of France demanded the Pope denounce us as heretics. Our family had survived, as had many of the English and German families. Areas where the King of France had scant hold hadn't suffered as badly as those within his reach. A few of the Italian families had also survived, sheltered by the decentralized power structure of the duchy system in that country. But the Tremelays had been wiped out—at least we'd thought. Not that it mattered. The guy thought I was high, or a crazy academic who saw the occult in everything.

Or not. I watched as he jerked his head to look over at me, his mouth a tight line. Just as quickly he turned to face the tech and continued speaking with him. *Told you so.*

A few seconds later he was jogging back over to me. "I'm sure I don't need to tell you that we don't want details of this murder to be made public at this time."

Or at any time, I thought. I'd promised Janice that I'd clue her in on any goings-on, but I wasn't sure how she'd run a story like this. Breaking the news of an occult murder that police were keeping under wraps would be a huge scoop and it would also send the public into a tailspin of terror. Gang violence was a daily occurrence in this town. Ritualistic human sacrifice was not. That would be up to Janice to spin how she needed, though. A promise was a promise, and I couldn't hold this sort of thing back from her. Especially when I might need her help. These two murders were somehow linked—Ronald Stull's demon-related death, and this ritual. It could be a coincidence that one of the mages involved in this ritual got sloppy with a demon summoning, or it could be something more.

And that got my brain working. Maybe Ronald hadn't screwed up a summoning and got himself killed. Maybe the demon had been a supernatural hit man. Mages who worked death magic, especially death magic using human sacrifice, had to have secrets. If Ronald had been widely reviled as an asshole, perhaps one of his buddies had killed him.

There might not be a direct cause and effect from one murder to the other. Not that anything I had right now was more than just theory. I needed to figure out what the bone was, what the symbols and magical parameters told me the death ritual was for, and what the sigil under a very dead Ronald indicated. Lots of unknowns.

"What do you think about all this?"

I jerked my attention back to the detective. He was asking my opinion? Well, that was quite the change from stupid-girl-looking-to-buy-drugs label I'd had previously.

"I'll let you know what I think once I do some research. I've got an early shift at the coffee shop, but hopefully I can get a few hours in before I head off to sleep." There was no need to tell him I'd probably pull an all-nighter on this one. I'd been pulling a lot of those in the last few weeks. It's not like I'd be able to sleep with all this running around in my brain. I was one of those people that couldn't rest until I got the answers I was looking for.

"The coffee shop on Pratt." The detective consulted his notes. "What is your current home address?"

I told him, then gave an exaggerated yawn. "Well, better get back home if I'm going to be digging through books before bed."

I headed toward my car, with the detective keeping pace beside me. "Books? Wouldn't the internet be easier?"

"Yeah, if I wanted to sort through millions of wacky, fake-magic sites and video game references. Most of the real stuff isn't on the internet."

"Isn't everything on the internet nowadays?" He'd stuffed the little notebook in his back pocket.

"No magic user is going to put his carefully crafted spells up on the internet for a bored Goth teen in Cleveland to perform. Would you want some novice trying to summon a lesser demon, or in this case performing death magic? It's irresponsible to throw stuff like that out there for the uninitiated to mangle with potentially deadly conse-quences."

He paused by my car as I fumbled in my pocket for my keys.

"So you really *do* know how to do this stuff? You're a wizard who just happened to stumble upon this because she was meeting a hot guy?"

I unlocked the car. "I'm not a wizard, I'm a Templar with minor skills in certain areas of magical practice."

I knew enough to be dangerous. And based upon my last attempt at summoning, dangerous was exactly what magic was in the hands of anyone below an adept level. Which included me. Simple wards and illusion, that's what I was going to stick to from now on. No more demonology for me, and definitely not anything remotely close to death magic.

"You've got a sword in your car."

Crap. I did. Trusty was on the front seat, close enough for me to grab if I needed it. And I thought it very interesting that Detective Tremelay noticed the sword even with the look-away spell. *Very* interesting.

"I…I do reenactments." I did. Sort of.

He leaned in and squinted at the foam sword and plastic armor still in the back seat of my car. "You wouldn't have happened to have been at the park this afternoon where that reenactor guy got hit by lightning, were you?"

Double crap. My name was on the police report, so there was no sense lying about that one. "Yes. I was with another person during the storm and we were the ones who found him."

"What an amazing coincidence." His eyes met mine, and I felt like a bug pinned to a board. "I look forward to your call tomorrow morning to update me about the results of your research, Miss Ainsworth."

I started my car. "Aria. I'll call you. And in the meantime you might want to see if there are any photos from the crime scene of the lightning strike death this afternoon. You might be very interested in the burn pattern under the body."

I pulled away before he could respond, a smirk curling up one corner of my mouth. This was fun, taunting the somewhat slovenly Detective Justin Tremelay. He might still think I was a bit off my rocker, but at least he was willing to consider information from all sources when faced with a ritual murder. And he hadn't hauled me off to jail.

And he was interesting, in a rumpled, middle-aged sort of way.

CHAPTER 8

*I*n spite of my pooh-poohing the internet, that's exactly where I went to try to identify the bone. I might have a library's worth of books on mythology, various supernatural beings, and magical spells, but when it came to naturalistic pursuits, it was a big fat zero. Edible plants, mushrooms, butterflies, birds, and animal bones all were subjects I'd never explored beyond the bare basics. Templars weren't expected to forage for food, survive the zombie apocalypse, or track wild animals, thus I couldn't tell an oriole from a robin. For all I knew, this bone was from someone's chicken lunch.

Three hours later I knew what the bone wasn't. It wasn't human. It wasn't a skull or vertebrae. And it wasn't from a bird.

That was about it. All the long bones looked the same, in spite of expert instruction to look for ball ends, notches and curves. If this was a long bone, then it was from a fairly small animal—a squirrel or maybe a rabbit or cat. Heck if I knew. Luckily one university site offered an identification service, so I took the best pictures I could with my phone and sent them off with the fifty dollar fee, wincing at the expenditure. There were no vampires bankrolling this investigation, and I doubted Detective Sleeps-in-his-Clothes would chip in to cover my expenses. I'd need to start watching my funds, or I'd be right back where I started two weeks ago—behind on rent and living on a Ramen noodle diet.

Then I turned my attention to the symbols at the death magic ritual. Most of them I quickly crossed off as the usual runes a mage would use when delineating a protective space for spell-work. Slowly I made my way through the remaining symbols until I'd identified all but one. They'd performed a type of protection spell, one used to keep the casters safe as well as to contain...something. That something was the remaining symbol.

I wasn't all that worried in spite of the fact the mages had poured an obscene amount of power into this spell. The symbol wasn't the sigil of a Goetic demon, and I was fairly certain it wasn't any of the major demons either. It didn't follow the same lines of the sigils indicating higher spirits. This one seemed home-grown.

A lot of magic was. This symbol could represent a rival mage. To keep them safe from a magical hit, such as what I suspected happened to Ronald. It could be to contain an actual person—to keep another wizard in his hometown, or to hold his magical working back.

If the latter, that would require a huge amount of magical energy. Restricting someone's movements was more difficult than a charm to win a scratch-off. If the spell also acted as a magical shield...well, no wonder the human sacrifice. It would take me forever to puzzle out who or what the target of this spell was, and I didn't have forever. The specifics of whatever the mages were containing would have to wait because I had only a few hours left before I needed to get ready for work.

I eyed the clock and started in on the research I should be able to finish before my shift began—the sigil under Ronald's body. Enlarging the pictures from my phone, I copied the sigil onto paper, drawing the blurred sections in red. There were several possibilities that I noted as I pored over my reference books, but as the sun was beginning to lighten the eastern sky, I hit pay dirt. Even with the blurred sections from rain and the shifting of the body on the grass, the sigil burned into the ground under Ronald's body could be none other than Araziel.

The angel of Taurus, which was the astrological sign associated with the Hierophant in Tarot. The Magician. The Light of God. Often confused with Azrael, who was cast out of heaven as one of the leaders of the tenth choir who engaged in carnal relations with human women. Araziel was little known outside of Cabalistic circles or those who specialized in higher spirits.

Goetic demons were one thing. They were lesser demons, inclined to help rather than attack. Summoning a Goetic demon took skill and confidence. Summoning a higher demon took adept status and enough power to compel and bind. But summoning an *angel*? My blood ran cold at the thought.

Of all the stupid, reckless things to do. Demons were sort of like us. Well, sort of like super-powered serial killer psychopaths, but still there was a frame of reference there. A practitioner could study them and anticipate their actions. They were somewhat predictable, their motivations and actions tended along well-worn pathways. Angels were inscrutable, impersonal, and unpredictable. In spite of all the cute cherub statues and the prevalence of personal, spiritual attachments, the actual beings were nothing like what people thought they were. Of all the ghouls, demons, demigods I could encounter in the course of my life, angels scared me the most.

And Araziel wasn't an angel I'd even think of calling upon. He was the angel who separated the soul from the body upon death, kind of a godly grim reaper. Which was all fine and good if the person in question was actually dead before the angel's action. In theory, angels were on a tight leash connected to the firm hand of God, but we were beings of free will and so were the higher spirits.

If one of us were foolish enough to summon an angel, to unhook the leash from the collar, well, who knows how long they'd roam among us before they were called back home. And who knows how their morality would twist and change if an angel found himself in the physical realm among humans.

I rubbed my eyes, wondering if this was an occasion for Emergency Beer. Probably not. The way the last few weeks had gone I had a feeling there was a bigger Oh Shit occurrence in my future that would be more worthy of Emergency Beer than this revelation. Still, Araziel was bad news. I had no idea how to track a loose angel, or send it back under heavenly controls.

I eyed the orange streaks of dawn through my window. With any luck I could grab a quick nap before I needed to get ready for work. Of course, that meant I'd have nothing to tell Detective Wrinkle Pants when I called him later. It would probably be a day or so before I heard back from the bone people, and telling him an angel was involved in Ronald's death wouldn't do much for my credibility in this investigation. I needed to press on and see if I could determine anything concrete about the murder at Old Town Mall, otherwise I was likely to lose Detective Tremelay's confidence. And I found myself oddly reluctant to lose the one person in the city police department likely to take me seriously when I discussed summoning and magical societies. Well, somewhat seriously.

An hour later I threw in the towel. I was too tired to do more than stare at the pages, and I needed to get a minimal amount of sleep before my shift. At least I had a list of possibilities, and I'd hit the research again after I got off work.

CHAPTER 9

Janice met me a few blocks down from the coffee shop at a smoothie shop. The protein and energy-enriched drink wasn't exactly my idea of a liquid breakfast, but since the reporter was paying, I wasn't complaining.

"So the dead guy in the park is involved with a group of occultists who are killing people as part of their magical rituals?"

I'd told her everything, from the angel-on-the-loose right down to the unidentified bone in the sage pot. In typical reporter style, Janice had seized on the one thing she could run a headline with.

"In a nutshell, yes. The police haven't released anything. It was pretty gruesome."

Janice nodded. "Normally I'd run with it, but I'm thinking of waiting a few days. I've been tracking down some missing persons' reports and I think it might be connected to this."

And this is why I risked angering Detective Tremelay and Baltimore's finest to spill the beans to Janice. Raven had said the Baltimore group were regular practitioners of death magic. There was a good chance that this dead woman at Old Town Mall hadn't been their only human victim, and if Janice had a lead on others, I wanted to know.

"People go missing all the time—homeless, junkies, runaway teens." The reporter tapped a pen to her paper. "These aren't those kind of people. Four of the missing had loose ties to the occult—a psychic, a woman who wrote about local ghosts and seemed to believe what she wrote, and two Pagans. The religious Pagans, not the motorcycle gang Pagans. All of them went missing within the last two months."

That did seem like an odd pattern.

"Two accountants. A waiter. Three home improvement contractors," Janice continued. I shook my head, not understanding the connection.

"Let's just say the word about town is that there's a gang you don't want to piss off. No threats. No extortion. No violence-as-a-warning. You just disappear."

A gang of mages. It seemed kind of risky behavior, though. They had to have some big egos to go nabbing accountants and the like without the fear of getting caught. Could that be part of the magic they were spinning? Something that shielded them from detection? Ten people in two months was a lot to go missing.

And it was a lot of murder to power their magic. Could a protection and containment spell need *that* much energy, or were they doing something else, too? I also wondered if the quality of the victim mattered, or would the death of any human do? Would it matter in other, non-human sacrifice? Was a purebred attack-trained Doberman a better victim than a trusting mutt from the pound? If they needed upstanding citizens to get the biggest bang for their magic, then it made sense to take out those who had angered or hindered them in the process, killing two birds with one stone.

I thanked Janice for the smoothie and headed to work, mulling the whole thing over in my head. The lunch rush was just tapering off when I saw Detective Tremelay come through the door. The man appeared to have the same pants on as last night, although his shirt was clean and looked as though it had been neatly pressed at one time in the last century or so.

I'd been running late this morning and hadn't been able to call him as promised. I'd planned to grab a few moments on my break to connect, but it seemed he was too eager to wait. Either that or he wanted a coffee this lovely Sunday afternoon.

Actually I was surprised he'd bothered. I'd thought that in the cold light of day he'd write me off as a crazy girl whose talk of magic seemed even more improbable than it had in the dark of Old Town Mall. I really didn't expect him to walk into my coffee shop. And I certainly didn't expect him to order an iced, caramel mocha, soy latte.

"We've got coconut milk." It was good to have a second non-dairy option for the scores of lactose intolerant.

"Nah. Soy. I hate coconut."

I wrote the order on a cup and Brandi sidled up to me, posture-perfect as she smiled at the detective.

"Hi," she purred. I got the hint.

"Brandi, this is Detective Justin Tremelay." I handed her the cup.

She eyed the order. "Extra shot of caramel? My way of thanking the city P.D."

My eyes nearly rolled out of my head. I loved Brandi, but this guy was twice her age and couldn't manage to iron his pants. Although, now that I thought about it, he *was* her type.

And that bothered me. It shouldn't. Sheesh, was I now

collecting guys? They're mine. They're all mine. Yeah, the detective was cute in a slovenly public servant kind of way, but he'd not shown a lick of interest in me. Vampire, geeky LARP guy, and now a middle-aged detective. What was next, the garbage man and the landlord?

I smiled. "Have a seat. Brandi can bring your coffee out to you."

He shot a quick glance at the blond, looking surprisingly like a cornered rabbit. "Actually I need to speak with you. Can you spare a few moments?"

I cast Brandi an apologetic look. She shrugged. "Okay," I told the detective. "Only a few, though. I've got another hour on my shift."

That would be my excuse if questions got too uncomfortable. Although with the lack of customers right now, I'd need to claim an urgent task in the stock room to get away.

Tremelay sat on one of the sofas, throwing one arm across the back and scanning the various mugs and accessories on the sale shelves. I tried not to stare at him as Brandi mixed up his iced latte. I'm sure he wanted to discuss the case but I didn't have much to tell him. In a fit of paranoia I checked my phone, wishing that the bone dudes would hurry it up and get back to me. It's not like this was a griffon, and I doubted they were flooded with bone identification requests.

Brandi still gave him an extra shot of caramel. I'll give the girl props for her optimism. Tremelay took the cup, raising his eyebrows as he sipped.

"Please tell that girl that I have a daughter her age."

I snorted. Not that Brandi would care. Girl had her type.

"Got a daughter my age, too?" Seriously? *That* came out of my mouth? Oh for crying out loud, I needed to get a boyfriend—one that wasn't a vampire or a middle-aged man. Zac. I should have asked Zac to spend the night last night. Maybe then I wouldn't be hitting on every guy I saw.

"I wasn't *quite* that precocious. Any kids claiming to be mine would need to be under thirty."

Did I need to rethink my moisturizer routine, or what? This was the second person in two weeks who had assumed I was older than my actual age. I *was* twenty-six.

Let it go. I took a deep breath. "There is some information that I'm still waiting on. What I do know is that the death at the Mall and the park are related. The death magic ritual was used to power a protective and containment spell. Protect and contain what or whom, I don't know." I thought about my conversation with Janice and decided to throw in the extra info. "I doubt that woman last night was their only victim. Protection and containment spells wear off, and if they needed the energy of a sacrifice to protect them, then it's something dangerous enough to warrant repeated spells."

Which also got me to thinking that I needed to figure out what exactly they were trying to protect themselves from. If it was the angel that had killed Ronald, then why not just use the sigil? There had to be a reason they were using that odd symbol.

"I'm sure if there were more of what happened last night, we would have heard about it. There aren't many places in Baltimore you can leave a dead woman in a bathtub with occult symbols everywhere and not eventually have it discovered."

True. But if they needed to kill off ten or so people in the last two months, they would have been more careful about it. "Maybe we found the one last night before they had a chance to clean up and dispose of the body. Maybe they had an emergency or were interrupted before they could cover it all up. I'm thinking you need to look at other missing persons' reports and consider other victims."

He pursed his lips and nodded before taking another sip

of the coffee. "Point taken. I'll dig around the reports and see what I can find."

Good. And there was one more thing I needed to tell him. "The sigil under the park death is for Araziel."

Tremelay waved a hand. "Can you elaborate? Who is this Araziel, and can I bring him, or her, in for questioning?"

Now that would be something I'd like to see. "Araziel is an angel—the one who separates the soul from the physical body at the time of death. Which leaves me wondering if the angel was the one who actually caused the death or not. He, although angels aren't gendered, isn't supposed to be a reaper or an angel of justice. Araziel is a collector, a sorter. I'm still trying to figure out what the angel has to do with any of this."

The detective sucked down a large gulp of his beverage and trained his steely, hazel gaze on me. "And what does the guy who you claim was killed by an angel in the park have to do with the ritual murder in the Mall. What's the connection beyond the freak factor?"

Here is where I admitted to lying to the authorities of the land. "I was one of the women who discovered the dead man in the park. He had a paper in his cape pockets with the address in Old Town Mall. That's why I went there."

"Rifling a dead guy's pockets. Taking photos of a murder site. I worry about you, Ainsworth. This isn't sane behavior, you know." Tremelay rubbed his forehead. "Besides that, I checked into that park case. We're still waiting for the coroner to tell us what exploded the guy's chest outward and where his lungs and heart went to. You think the same freaks who sacrificed that woman in Old Town Mall sent a killer angel after the guy in the park?"

"They're related, I just don't know how. Yet." And now for my big favor. "I need to go back to the Mall, to look for something. Can you accompany me?"

I needed him to bring legitimacy to my investigation, and

to bring the murderers to civil justice if they were of the human and not supernatural type. And he needed me. Otherwise he'd be chasing his tail, looking for Goth Satanists who most likely had nothing to do with any of this.

"I'll take you, but that building is still considered a crime scene. I can't have you contaminating anything."

"It's the side buildings I want to look at."

He raised an eyebrow. "The building across the street from the murder, the one written on the piece of paper you found on the dead guy in the park? Does this have something to do with the saucepan with burned twigs?"

I nodded. "A smudge stick. The buildings on either side of the murder site should have the same, as should the building behind it. Four quarters. Compass points. The murderers wanted to keep something outside of their ritual. If I can find out what, that will help me figure out exactly what they were doing when they killed that woman."

"Bethany Scarborough."

I blinked, thinking his interjection of some woman's name to be downright random.

"The victim." Tremelay consulted his notebook. "Fifty-five. Unmarried. Lives alone aside from a cat. She's an insurance adjuster working at an office in Columbia. Lives in Westminster."

And she was a death-magic sacrifice in Baltimore. None of that made sense. "Did she do drugs? Did she make it a habit of dating men she met on the internet?" Or perhaps Janice was right and she'd pissed off the wrong mage.

The detective shrugged. "I've got interviews this afternoon and tomorrow with her co-workers. Family is from out of town and they were shocked to find out she was dead. According to them, she was a stereotypical, unmarried, cat-lady, spinster homebody. Of course, family are always the last to know, especially when they don't live nearby."

I shook my head wondering how the woman he'd just described had wound up the subject of a magical ritual. An insurance adjuster from Westminster?

"I need to bring her killer to justice." There was something in Detective Tremelay's eyes that I completely identified with. There was a reason he was a cop, and I wanted to believe it was the Templar blood in his veins.

"Me, too. And I want to make sure what happened to Bethany and Ronald doesn't happen to anyone else."

"Do you think there's something at these other buildings that will lead us to the killer? I know you said the guy in the park was killed by an angel, but this woman at the Mall definitely died by human hands."

Maybe. Eventually. "I don't know, but I'll do my best to find out. Magical societies are a tight bunch. There are areas of specialty and practitioners tend to know who does what. Once I figure out a few things, then it's just a matter of time until I find the mage responsible."

I thought once more about my conversation with Raven. She'd known about the death magic. She'd wanted me to get out of town. There was a chance she knew the killers. Although getting her to cough up names would be pretty close to impossible. Mages were tight-lipped, even with rivalries and feuds. She was Haul Du. I was cast out. We might be making baby steps to repairing our friendship, but that didn't mean she was going to start ratting out fellow practitioners.

"What if we find out it's some druggie on bath salts? Or a Satanist?"

Oh for crying out loud, not the Satanist thing again. "I doubt someone on salts would have a steady enough hand to draw those symbols, let alone conduct a ritual murder. And followers of the Church of Satan don't conduct ritual murders." They didn't conduct murders at all, but I doubted I would be able to convince Detective Tremelay of that fact.

He stood, taking his latte with him. "I'll pick you up at your place at five. And the only reason I'm entertaining any of this is because I want this sicko behind bars as soon as possible. Anybody with such a careless disregard for human life isn't someone I want loose on the streets of my city."

And on that, we were in complete agreement.

CHAPTER 10

The note on my door was short and to the point: *Fort McHenry. 3:00.*

I ripped it from the door and ran for my car, knowing I'd have to hustle to make this meeting. And hustle to get back in time for my five o'clock with Tremelay. I know it sounds weird that I'd go haring off like this to meet up with some weirdo that stuck a note on my door, but it wasn't the words that had me squealing down the road, it was the symbol under the place and time—the same home-grown symbol used in the sacrificial ritual I'd discovered last night.

If this guy, or gal, was involved with the death magic group or had information about them, I was throwing everything aside to meet up. Magical groups were hard to infiltrate. I'd take anything I could that wouldn't mean me spending weeks working through networks and nosing around.

I realized I had a bit of a problem once I pulled into Fort McHenry. The park wasn't exactly the size that would make it meeting-friendly, and my note hadn't specified exactly where I should be at three o'clock. I'd never been there before, and only vaguely knew the site's importance in the War of 1812, so I figured I'd start at the beginning—in the Visitor Center.

I was a few minutes early, so I perused the gift shop, giving my donation and receiving a brochure for a self-guided tour that claimed to provide a riveting historical experience of about an hour. Huh. I liked history, although my degree had leaned more toward the European Middle Ages and Renaissance. If there wasn't a LARP next weekend, I would definitely come back.

"The orientation film is beginning."

I spun around to see a portly man in a park-service uniform attempting to herd me toward another room with his round arms.

"Oh, that's okay. I'm meeting someone." I had no idea if I was meeting them here or not, but it was three o'clock and I was keeping my eyes open for…whoever. Would he or she be in a cloak? Have a banner with the symbol on it to help me recognize them? I had no idea.

"Another one won't start until three thirty, so you best make this one." The man shooed me again. I moved toward the room just to avoid getting whacked by those thick arms. They were like giant hams, I swear.

"I'll tell your friend you're in there." An arm shot out with surprising speed as I tried to side-step the doorway. "Go on in."

Far be it for me to get into a brawl with the staff. I edged into the room, taking a seat as close to the door as possible so I could still look out. Thankfully, they left it open as they began the film.

It was hard not to get sucked in. I'd admired the Fort's layout upon arrival. It was a fascinating defensive structure, positioned perfectly to safeguard the harbor and the city. Just as I was becoming engrossed in the complexities of defending against twenty-five hours of bombardment by British guns and rockets, a man slid through the doorway and sat beside me.

"Shade," the man muttered.

"Ainsworth," I muttered back. Was Shade his magical name or his last name? I hoped this was my Deep Throat contact and not just some weirdo commenting on the window treatments.

"The Templar. Most of us wish you'd go back to Virginia, me included, but I want you to know that none of us have any intentions of doing you violence."

"It's a free country. I get to live wherever I want to." That sounded rather churlish, but his statement that a group of mages in Baltimore was aware of my existence as well as his reassurance about my safety threw me. *Someone* must have violent intentions toward me if he felt the need to bring it up.

"I knew it would eventually come to this. You blew the perimeter last night at the Mall," he continued, his tone somewhat accusatory. "Triggered a domino ward. Be warned that I'm not the only one who knows."

Knew what? That I was there? "So? The worst I could be accused of is trespassing. You all are facing first-degree murder."

Shade shifted, sucking in a sharp breath. "We *all* perform death magic, but believe me when I say that the majority of us do not condone human sacrifice or soul magic."

Soul magic. My blood ran cold at the thought. I'd suspected it when I saw the odd knife mark on the victim's breast bone, but hadn't been sure.

"How many do? And is your group willing to turn them in?"

The mage laughed bitterly. "Used to be only one or two would even *think* about using humans to power a spell, but now most of the group is involved. You don't understand. None of us *want* this. We have to. There's something... We have to. A few must die for many to live."

Not that excuse again. How many unwilling victims lost their lives to protect the masses, only to have the masses fall anyway? These things were always temporary and not worth it.

"I don't care if you all are single-handedly holding back the apocalypse, a woman died. A *real* woman, not some animated character in a video game. Her name was Bethany Scarborough, and she was an insurance adjuster, living happily with her cat in Westminster. She's dead. And I get the feeling she wasn't the first. The police are already checking through missing persons' reports. It's just a matter of time before they close in on you. Turn in those responsible and there might be an easier sentence for the rest."

That's how it worked on television anyway. I was assuming it was the same in real life.

He snorted in the face of my threat. "We're not sacrificing humans because we get our jollies off on that sort of thing. We *had* to. And when it was clear that wasn't working, we had to turn to soul magic. And now... I'm not sure anything is going to work."

There was nothing that could be worth the cost of a human life, or a human soul, and now Shade had just confirmed Janice's theory that Bethany Scarborough hadn't been the first. "It's murder. The cops are involved, and I am, too. You're going to have to face justice for what you've done."

"I won't be here. I'm leaving tonight and starting fresh, as far from Baltimore as possible. And I'm not the only one. Do you think we don't know it's going to come crashing down now that the police know? And you... A Templar in Baltimore is a serious thorn in our side. It's all falling apart and once we stop the spells…well, you should probably leave Baltimore, too."

Golly gee, the drama.

"It's not just that," Shade waved a hand. "I was there Friday night. Normally I refuse, but Creek had to take his Mom to the hospital and they needed a thirteenth person."

"You were there?" It was all I could do to keep my voice hushed. This man sitting next to me had watched a woman being murdered and done nothing to help her. Who *does* that? What kind of monster does that? I ground my teeth, wishing I had the flexibility to yank my sword out and show him exactly how that woman must have felt.

"Yes, I was there," he shot back. "And something went wrong. The ritual was successful, but something was drawn in and the smudge perimeter barely managed to keep it out. We could feel it, cold and angry as it bashed against the walls. It's that fucking soul magic, I just know it. We'd only used it once before Friday. I heard the previous week's ritual went okay, but Friday night's definitely didn't."

I saw red, barely able to process what Shade was saying. Previous week? They were killing a person every week? And they'd *twice* done soul magic—the darkest of all the magical arts.

"That's why we left everything there," Shade continued. "Why we didn't even dismiss the outer circle. Everyone just wanted to get away as fast as they could, and we were all worried that if we opened the circle enough to clean up the body, whatever was out there would get us."

Cowards. Murderous cowards. "Who's in charge? Who killed her?"

Shade swallowed audibly. "Breaker. Gryla is our leader, but this was Breaker's thing. He picks the subjects and orga-nizes the rituals. He's the one who lets the blood and collects the energy."

In other words, he's the one who chooses and kills the sacrifice. I ground my teeth. "Who is Breaker? Tell me and you'll have a head start out of the city. Keep quiet and I'll drag you in myself."

The mage seemed unaffected by my threats. "Doesn't matter. He's dead. Breaker's name is Ronald Stull. The morning after the ritual—the ritual where something tried to get in and tear us apart—he died by a lightning strike in a park. I doubt that's a coincidence. And that's one more reason for me to get out of town."

Oh snap. Seems karma had rebounded hard on Ronald Stull, but not in the form of a weather event. "It wasn't the lightning that killed him, it was an angel." I leaned closer to Shade. "Araziel. I've got no idea who summoned an angel, or what Ronald did to piss him off, but from what you're saying Araziel took exception to your ritual Friday night. Run all you want, there's no escaping an angel if he wants you dead."

The mage clasped trembling hands together in a futile attempt to still them. "We warded against psychopomps— well, against the avatars anyway. Nothing we could do would completely guard against an angel. Araziel. Shit. Poor Breaker."

I wasn't feeling so sorry for the guy. "I need a list of names, Shade."

He got to his feet in a rush. "No. It's bad enough that I might have the cops and an angel on my back, I'm not putting myself in a position to be cursed by twenty-four mages. No way."

I reached out to grab his arm and my hand passed right through him. Illusion. Clever bastard. He turned to me, face pale. It was a good illusion. If I hadn't just tried to touch him I would swear he stood right in front of me.

"It wasn't just Breaker," he said as he edged toward the door. "There's an outsider, a stranger. He's at the rituals and is always masked. I got the feeling he and Breaker were close, that this last subject was the stranger's selection and not Breaker's. *He's* the one you want. Everyone else…well, we were just trying to keep the city safe."

I opened my mouth to argue, but the illusion vanished. It was an exercise in futility, but I still ran out into the visitor center, and then to the parking lot to see if I could catch a glimpse of Shade's physical form. He had to be nearby. Illusions from a great distance were tricky.

Nothing. He was gone and I got the impression that I'd never see him again. That left twenty-four other mages who were guilty of murder by association, regardless of their reasons. Twenty-four mages and one stranger.

CHAPTER 11

Thank heaven for miracles. The bone guy must have been particularly intrigued by my case because I had an email from him just as I was running into my apartment.

It was a one word email. *Dog.*

I winced, not liking what that meant. If I found dog bones in all the other makeshift crucibles, then my worst fears would have been realized. If not, if the other quarters held the bones of different animals, then this ritual murder was headed in a completely different direction.

Dog in the north. If there was bird in the east, fish in the west, and a dead scorpion in the south, then the murderer was spelling for control. Usually those rituals were a sort of course correction in the mage's life, but with death magic involved the spellcaster would be going for a more dramatic effect—control over another, over a group of people, or even over a higher spirit. It would take more than one human sacrifice to gain dominion over a demon, and a heck of a lot more to control an angel. Harnessing the quarters wasn't the best scenario, but it was hardly the worst. If a mage was casting for control, then they'd be lining up more kills.

But with dog in all four quarters, they'd be doing far worse. Which was why I was praying that the other saucepans held a variety of animal bones.

I found myself with a half-hour before my fieldtrip to Old Town Mall, so I decided to do some digging. Internet searches for Bethany Scarborough were sadly bland. She was on a few professional network social media sites, listing her resume and work experience. Other than that, nada. I frowned, curious as to why she'd not been on Facebook or other sites. On a whim I looked through Instagram cat pictures, but found nothing beyond the fact that millions of people love posting pictures of their cats on the internet.

Ronald Stull had the internet presence that Bethany lacked. In keeping with his asshole persona, Ronald had been a member of several chat rooms, both advocating *and* railing against gun control. He seemed particularly upset about immigrants and felt the government was spying on him. After reading his posts, I figured he was probably right. Homeland Security watch list or not, there was nothing online to indicate he was a practitioner of death magic. Not surprising. Wiccans and pagans tended to proclaim their religious leanings often and loudly, trying to convince a skeptical public that they only worked magic for good. Ceremonial magicians…not so much. Many of them did keep away from hexes and curses or anything in the gray area that separated black magic from white. Most dipped more than their toes in those waters. Thus most were very careful about who knew what they did on Saturday nights.

Which was why I'd been kicked out of the magical group Haul Du the moment they'd discovered I was a Templar. It had been hard enough to gain entry. I'd been studying magic since I was six, and had needed to walk a fine line between appearing like a thrill-seeker idiot and far too experienced for a layman. After my initiation, I'd been welcomed to the group's DC location and spent some of the happiest months of my life studying and practicing with those who shared my passion.

Then some jealous asshole got suspicious and figured out who I really was. Racist jerks kicked me out without anything resembling a fair trial. It seems Templars weren't welcome at Haul Du.

No surprise there. That's the reason I'd worn wide leather cuffs on both wrists, the right one covering my Templar tattoo. Ever since I'd been kicked out I put away the cuffs. I was a Templar, and if someone had a problem with that, well, too bad.

All that bad blood meant I couldn't call my former buddies in DC to ask them to weigh in on Araziel or if they knew who beyond Ronald Stull was involved in sacrificial magic.

I'd told the Detective that magical groups were tight. They were. My Haul Du contacts in DC might not have encountered Ronald in person, but they would know who Breaker was if he'd so much as borrowed an occult text from the public library. Luckily there was one other place for me to check. Sage and lemongrass were available at any grocery store, but other magical materials were more difficult to obtain. The internet was usually the go-to source, but only if you were planning ahead for a ritual. There were always those moments when you metaphorically needed to borrow a cup of sugar in the middle of the night, and for that there were magic shops.

They sometimes hid in plain sight as new age retail stores or palm reading services, but everyone in the magical community knew what really went on in those back rooms. There was one in DC, and another in Ellicott City just outside of Baltimore. One in the morning, Christmas at midnight, Halloween at dusk, you could call a number or show up with a password and you'd gain entrance to what was pretty much the Walmart of the magical world.

I didn't have time to drive down to Ellicott City, but I was putting it on my agenda. I also put one other thing onto my agenda. As soon as Detective Tremelay and I were done with our trip to Old Town Mall, I needed to track down Dario and clue him in about what was going on in Baltimore.

It wasn't just because I wanted to see him or indulge in additional masochism. I'd withheld information from him before and betrayed his trust. I wasn't about to do that again. Death magic with human sacrifice, and an angel on the loose? Even if it didn't threaten the *Balaj*, I was going to make sure Dario knew what was happening. I'd go see him now, but it was still daylight, and in August it would remain so until probably after nine at night. I didn't see my trip to Old Town Mall taking longer than a few hours. Plenty of time to race through a dozen pubs afterward to search for a vampire.

A visit to an abandoned slum that was the go-to spot for drug dealers and murderous thugs as well as those practicing death magic might not warrant extra care in my personal beauty routine, but if I was going to hit a bunch of bars afterward I might as well look good. Because…well, I didn't really want to think too much about why at this point my beauty routine was suddenly so important.

Shoving those thoughts aside, I straightened my crazy dark-brown hair, slapped on some mascara and a flattering shade of plum lipstick, and on a whim threw on the push-up bra.

Push-up bra clearly needed a shirt to show off the gravity defying effects of said enhancement device, so I dug out a tank-top that looked like it had been painted onto my skin. And then I got out the skinny jeans. I drew the line at heels, though. After trying to outrun an angry john in heeled sandals last week, I was wary of non-serviceable footwear.

I winced as I saw my appearance in the mirror. I could see Brandi wearing something like this, but not a Templar who was trying to convince a much older detective that she was a credible source of information, and then later meet with a vampire who was clearly no longer interested. Unfortunately I didn't have time to change because there was a knock at the door.

Crap. I ran from the bedroom. Easily ran, because I was wearing my sneakers and not the four inch platform shoes that would have completed my sleazy outfit. Whipping open the door, I took a deep breath, no doubt exaggerating the cleavage enhancement of my attire.

"Hi."

The detective stared wordlessly at my chest, his eyes widening. "Are you...? I thought we were going to check out the crime scene at the Mall. Do you have a date or something? Should I come back?"

Date or something? I was such an idiot when it came to men. He knew I'd been at work earlier today. There was *really* no excuse for my skintight clothing right now. I took another breath, noticing that his eyes were remaining fixed on my chest no matter how he tried to raise them. Yeah, I had boobs. Yeah, he was a guy. But he wasn't into me in any way beyond the fact that I was two steps from naked in front of him.

"Ready to go? Let me get my sword." I hesitated, my hand on the scabbard. "Is it okay if I take my sword? I'm a Templar. I kind of go everywhere with it."

He smirked, his eyes finally rising to look at my face. "You weren't wearing it at the coffee shop today. You didn't have it on when we responded to the crime scene last night. Clearly you *don't* take it everywhere."

"Would you go to Old Town Mall without your gun?" Of course he had the legal right to carry his gun. Gigantic swords were a bit different. Knives where the blade folded down and weren't the spring-operated switchblade type were allowed regardless of blade length. So if I could fold Trusty's thirty inch blade into a gigantic hilt, I could carry it around legally. Bastard swords didn't fold.

"Point taken. And since my gun and I are both accompanying you, there is no need for you to take your sword."

I knew I was going to have this argument one day, but had been hoping it wouldn't be today. "It's sheathed. Legally I'm allowed to carry and transport it."

"Yes, but there's that whole intent thing. The sword is considered a dangerous weapon whose sole purpose is to injure. It's not a fishing knife or a hunting knife. You're not going to a reenactment or a Renaissance Fair."

I wasn't a lawyer and didn't play one on TV, but I was still going to try and argue my way out of this. "It's *not* a dangerous weapon, it's a tool. Gutting fish, skinning deer, lopping the heads off vampires, creating a holy space to protect the both of us against undead. Same stuff. It's a tool."

The detective tilted his head, one eyebrow raised. "Sorry. Not buying that one. Crazy women who think that they're Templar Knights and are on a mission to protect the world from vampires and Satanists don't get a pass on concealed carry law."

"It's not concealed," I argued. "Plain sight in the car and strapped to my back. There's no intent to harm humans."

"It's a *sword*." Tremelay's voice was getting louder. I wondered what my neighbors were thinking about this discussion. "You're not bringing an illegal weapon to a crime scene."

"A sword is totally legal. There's nothing in Maryland law that indicates a restriction on blade length. It's not a switchblade or a throwing star. I've got no intent to harm someone. Case law shows the definition of dangerous weapon outside named illegal weapons hinges on the utility purposes of the knife and intent."

"It's not a knife, it's a sword."

And now the detective was shouting. Stupid Maryland. I wished I was still in Virginia where these things were so much easier.

"It's a religious object." This was my last ditch effort, and it was a long shot.

He rolled his eyes. "Get a rosary. You're not carrying around a sword the size of a first-grader just so you can pray."

I hesitated. There was my keychain crucifix as well as my spelled butter knife. *That* couldn't be considered a weapon by any stretch of the imagination. Still, it bothered me to be heading out without my sword strapped to my back. Funny how I'd lived here six months with it hidden under my mattress and now I wanted it everywhere I went. My sudden attachment to the weapon, and yes it was a weapon, hadn't anything to do with being a Templar. None of my family went grocery shopping wearing their swords. I couldn't think of any other Templar who had their sword constantly with them.

Maybe I was going crazy, but I felt like I needed it. I felt naked without it. Even locking it in the car while I worked bothered me.

"Then I'm going to drive separately from you. There's nothing you can do about my bringing the sword in my own car. It will be in plain sight and it's in the sheath."

The detective sighed then glared at the weapon. "Fine.

You can bring it with us in my car, but it *stays* in the car. I don't want to see you wearing it around. Got it?"

I hid a smirk and gathered up the sword. Whatever. We'd continue this argument when we got there, and if I lost, then at least my sword would be nearby in the car. And if things went wrong…well, from what I'd read the most he could charge me with was a misdemeanor.

CHAPTER 12

I did lose that argument, and Trusty remained in the car as the detective and I walked the dark pathway of the Mall. There wasn't that heavy, menacing feel that I'd gotten from the area the night before. Some of that could have been that the sun was still up and there were a few people milling about the streets. Some of it could have been that I was with someone instead completely alone, and that someone had a gun. Not that his forty cal would do him any good against a demon, or really even a skilled magic user. Some of it could have been that I broke the smudge barrier, and whatever had been pacing the edges had left. Either way, the area felt cleaner, lighter. Well, as clean and light as a row of abandoned stores could feel.

We went to the house where I'd found the smudge stick and dog bone and I watched while Tremelay surveyed the outside of the building. For what, I had no idea. The whole time he walked around, taking note of every tag of graffiti and visually checking with me to make sure it wasn't part of a magical symbol. I wondered whether I should tell him about my meeting with Shade. He'd been pretty accepting of the whole Templar and magic thing so far, but I think it was more about gaining information into the killer's mind-set than any belief in what I did.

Shade. How could I tell Tremelay that an angel had killed his prime suspect, and that I'd met with an illusion who'd not given me any other names or valuable information before disappearing into thin air? Yeah. Better keep my mouth shut on that one.

Done with his graffiti surveillance, the detective made his way around the building, inspecting the entrances and windows. The old store wasn't public property, and Tremelay informed me he couldn't officially break into the building. He could, however, go inside to investigate when there was a clear sign that someone else had been doing the breaking and entering. So we walked around to the rear of the building and I pointed out the broken boards and windows. Evidently that was enough for the detective to wiggle himself through the window.

Yeah. I'm bad. I didn't tell him the front door was unlocked and open. It was much more fun watching him crawl through a window.

"Here." I showed him the saucepan and the burned remains of the sage by the back door of the building.

"Doesn't smell like it's been burned recently," he said leaning down to sniff at the sage bits.

"It would have been burned Friday night during the ritual," I explained. And here's where I confessed to more illegal activity. "I found a bone in this pot which turned out to be from a dog."

His eyebrows shot up. "Dog? Is the rest of the dog somewhere else?"

Oh God, I hoped not. "It's not a sacrifice like what happened to Bethany Scarborough. Practitioners can get dog bones either from roadkill, pet crematoriums, or if they're the squeamish sort, from magical supply shops."

I pulled the dog bone out of my pocket and showed it to Tremelay. He turned it over in his hand a few times then stared up at me. "They sell these on the internet, too?"

"Yeah, if you know where to go. There are lots of magical rituals that involve the use of animal bones, feathers, snake skins, etc. It's not powering the ritual, so there's no need to have a sacrifice of the animal. The bones are used to channel the energy or to create a barrier. Their use is symbolic."

He slipped the dog bone into his pocket. "So you're expecting to see this at four locations equidistant from the crime scene?"

I nodded. "I haven't been to the other buildings. You may need to take a little walk around while I discover clear signs of illegal entry, if you know what I mean."

The detective gave me a stern look. "Ainsworth, you are a whole lot of trouble. And I'm still thinking that you might just be a crazy woman."

I *was* trouble, and I probably was crazy too, but I was the only one he knew that had any idea of what was going on here.

There was a vacant lot next to the building where Bethany had been sacrificed. Knowing the need for the spell perimeter to be a circle rather than an oval or a polygon, we walked the weed-infested lot, Tremelay taking one side and me the other. These types of magical circles didn't *have* to be perfectly round, but the further they got from an ideal shape, the less effective they were at holding out, or in, energy.

It was slow going. The weeds hid huge chunks of concrete and rock from whatever structure had once stood here. The mages wouldn't have wanted to set the place on fire, but it only took a small clearing of weeds, or a space between two pieces of rock to set up the smudge pot. After the fifth time nearly twisting my ankle in the debris, I heard Tremelay give a shout.

Getting to him was an exercise in agility. Once again I was glad at my choice of sensible footwear over sexy heels. The saucepot was on top of a flat piece of concrete, wedged between two pieces of rusted, jutting rebar. Inside were burnt pieces of sage, and a bone.

Tremelay handed me a pair of latex gloves and I slipped them on. Then I held my breath as I picked up the bone to examine it. We were in the east quarter, and the bone I held wasn't the hollow bone of a bird. "I think it's another dog bone." My heart sank, but I wanted to check the other two quarters just to make sure.

The detective held out a plastic bag and I slipped the bone inside, noting that he closed it and wrote the details of where we found it on the outside of the bag before pocketing it. "Okay. Onward."

We prowled the dilapidated building at the south corner and again I pulled a bone out of the smudge pot. "Well, this isn't a scorpion, so I think I know what we're dealing with," I told Tremelay.

"I'll admit I'm a little weirded out that you just shoved your hand in there with the possibility that a scorpion was under those ashes. Honestly this whole thing is beginning to weird me out. What *are* we dealing with? You can tell me later what your theory would have been if you'd yanked a scorpion out of that pot."

"Dog bone in four quarters is meant to keep something out of the ritual. When you're conducting magic, it's a waste to have energy flying around all over the place, so a circle is primarily meant to concentrate the energy inside for the greatest effect. Likewise, you don't want to broadcast what you're doing all over the natural and supernatural world— that's the second purpose of a circle. All the magic for the ritual would have been going on inside the line of symbols surrounding the tub with the body. That was the circle holding the energy in. This one." I waved my hand at the smudge pot. "Was meant to keep something out."

"Keep what out? I notice you didn't say keep 'someone' out."

I fingered the smooth edges of the bone then plopped it into the outstretched bag. Shade had said they'd warded against this, and I'd suspected he was telling the truth, but it was good to have it all confirmed by physical evidence. "Dogs are psychopomps. They separate the soul from the body and allow it to move on to the afterlife. Birds and other animals can be psychopomps too, but dogs are the traditionally symbolic animal."

Shade had particularly mentioned psychopomps and the need to keep them out. I was guessing that was a common practice when doing sacrificial magic. No one needed a reaper showing up to screw up your ritual, and especially no one needed a psychopomp snatching the soul you were about to use to power your spell. It was all so horrid, so dark. It made sense from a logic point of view, but made my skin crawl as a member of the human race.

"Psychopomps? Wait, you said they separate the soul from the body at death, like that angel Azrael you mentioned today."

I winced. "Araziel. It's really important not to mix those two up. And yes, Araziel is considered a psychopomp. He's an angel, so he'd be the ultimate psychopomp."

This detective wasn't slow on the uptake. I was honestly thrilled to be partnering with someone who didn't discount my knowledge and who was catching on so quickly. Normally I wouldn't have thought about teaming up with a non-Templar, let alone a cop who wouldn't let me carry my sword around, but there was a human behind these murders.

I could do my best to take care of a demon or angel, and I certainly would come down heavy on any magician abusing his power, but it would be beyond my Templar responsibilities to bring a human to justice. We'd done plenty of that during the Crusades with horrible consequences and centuries of what I could only call bad karma. Nowadays we left that sort of judgement to the civil legal system.

Tremelay frowned. "So the angel that killed the gamer in the park might have been drawn to this ritual? If the people who killed Bethany Scarborough took steps to keep the angel out, that means it was around *before* it killed the man in the park."

I was thinking so. The presence Slade had mentioned that had scared them into leaving before cleaning up post-ritual? The unlikely coincidence that the mage who'd done the soul magic, who'd wielded the knife, was the one killed the next morning by Araziel? I had no idea how the angel had arrived here and why, but clearly he took exception to soul magic as an usurpation of his psychopomp duties.

But that was my theory, and I had nothing concrete right now to back it up.

"I'm thinking yes, but I'm not positive. Araziel might have been around back then or not. Death magic can be just about the energy of taking a life, or it can be about the soul. Either way the mages wouldn't want a psychopomp of any kind to release Bethany's soul."

The detective looked horrified at my words. "So her soul is still stuck in her body? What does that mean?"

It was time for Death 101. "No, if her soul had still been in her body it would have been released when the runes were smudged by me and your crime scene guys. Animal psychopomps are mainly symbolic. Sometimes an actual animal arrives, an avatar that releases the soul. Sometimes they remain in the spirit world, invisible to our eye. I doubt the mages went to all this trouble to keep a psychopomp out just to leave Bethany's soul in her body. They would have used it in their ritual."

The detective stared at me a moment, his hand brushing the top of his gun. "You're scaring me, Ainsworth. You should be doing those séances and ghost tours down in Fells Point."

It scared me, too, but I wasn't about to admit it to this guy. "I need to research death magic that involves the soul. This all seems excessive for a protection and containment ritual. It makes me a little worried about what they're holding back."

What Shade had said made me more than uneasy. He seemed genuinely fearful about whatever they were protecting the city from. Maybe they were holding back a high level demon, although banishment would have been a more appropriate response. An angel? A crazy mage with an artifact? A vampire *Balaj* with an artifact? I'd taken the scepter but who's to say Leonora or another group didn't have something else in their treasure chests.

"I need to figure out what they were doing," I mused.

Tremelay shook his head. "I know what they were doing, they were killing a woman. I don't care about their mumbo jumbo, I just want to find out who they are and gather enough evidence to put them away. Especially if you're right and this wasn't their only murder."

This was the nature of our partnership. Tremelay gets the mages. I take care of whatever magical fallout their death magic ritual produced. And the angel. I shivered, thinking I'd rather swap with the detective.

"I'm not well connected enough with the magical community for them to give me any information on this, and they're certainly not going to communicate with the police."

I went on to tell the detective about the magical shop in

Ellicott City, and my hope that between the pair of us we could pressure/convince them into telling us who bought dog bones, a blood sacrifice crucible, and whatever the heck someone needed to trap a soul.

"I take it this store isn't open past six at night?"

"Actually it's a twenty-four-seven kind of place. Are you proposing a road trip?" I smiled, thinking if we hurried, I could still catch up with Dario before midnight, before he was likely to have picked his dinner for the evening and headed off to enjoy a meal.

Tremelay nodded. "I'll drive, but the sword stays in the trunk. No bringing it into the store."

I snorted. "No problem." I could hardly trot into a magical supply shop with a Templar sword strapped to my back. In fact, I was going to need the leather cuff I'd thrown in my bag to cover my tattoo. Hopefully word hadn't spread about me and my dismissal from Haul Du. I was banking that the magical group hadn't wanted to admit they'd allowed one of my Order admittance. Otherwise I was going to find that door shut firmly in my face.

Tremelay looked down at the dog bone in the bag, pulling it out to examine it carefully in his gloved hand. With a smooth flick of his wrist, he rolled the bone up and over each finger. "So one more quarter to check then we head to this magical shop?"

I was eager to get going. Magic shop, meet up with Dario, then the research that was going to take most of the rest of my evening. Plus I was determined to actually get some sleep tonight. "There's really no need. Dog bone in three quarters pretty much guarantees there will be a dog bone in the fourth."

The bone made one more rotation around his fingers. The guy was pretty good at this. I'll bet with some practice he could do sleight of hand magic. Or be mighty lethal with a knife. I wondered how he'd do with a sword.

"Let's check anyway, just to be thorough." He grinned. "If there winds up being a scorpion when you stick your hand in that pot, I want to see it."

"Fine. Let's hurry though. I've got stuff to do and if I don't get some sleep I'm going to start hallucinating." We climbed through the broken window and replaced the splintered wooden slat. "That's a thing, you know. Sleep deprivation and all that."

"How could you tell they were hallucinations? I mean, you see wizards and demons on a regular basis."

"Yes but they're not dancing in tutus across the rooftops."

We crossed the street to where the west quarter of the circle would be. "Do you need to take a walk while I magically unlock this door? I mean while I discover where the vagrants have broken into the building?"

"No need." Tremelay nudged the door with his toe and it swung inward.

The downstairs of the small dilapidated brownstone had probably been some sort of retail establishment with separate entrances to the apartments upstairs. The door opened to a large room with several stained mattresses on the floor. Garbage bags lined the walls. Sprawled across the filthy floor at the end of the mattresses were two dead bodies.

I knew they were dead because they lay on their backs, white ribs pointing toward the sky.

"I'm guessing we're not going to find those two guy's lungs or hearts?" Tremelay asked.

"Or livers, or kidneys, or anything else." I tilted my head to see the mess of splattered blood that coated the mattress underneath the corpses. Araziel. I doubted there was more than one being running around Baltimore ripping the insides out of people.

But why? Had the angel been drawn here to collect Bethany's soul only to find his path blocked? And if so, why kill these two…junkies?

"Hey," I asked Tremelay who was on his phone. "Did you get anything from the coroner on exactly when Bethany Scarborough died?"

He pulled the phone from his ear. "Friday night around midnight."

If these two had just been in the wrong place at the wrong time, shooting up while Bethany died, then that put their deaths at the same time—nearly two nights ago. But this was late August. I might be a layman when it came to the intricacies of decomposition, but I doubted these two had been dead that long.

One more thing to research. I just didn't know enough about psychopomps, let alone an angelic one. If Araziel had been unable to perform his duties, had that caused the shift from assisting a soul to actually killing people? Was this a normal side effect of death magic that practitioners had to account for? If so, these mages neglected to take care of this little detail.

CHAPTER 13

For the second time in two nights Old Town Mall was lit up with blue and red lights, as well as the sound of police radios and running engines that dispelled the eerie quiet which had previously blanketed the area. My presence was being explained alternately as an unpaid consultant and a witness. Unpaid. Story of my life.

There had been no storms or lightning in the area to blame these deaths on, yet this clearly linked Ronald Stull's death to the area of Bethany Scarborough's murder. Everyone stared at the two dead junkies, gagging and conjecturing about the "sick fuck" who could do such a thing. And everyone was bandying around the terms Satanist and occult. This brought the death toll to four. Araziel three, death mages one.

"I've asked for a list of missing persons' reports in the last two months, concentrating on any reports in the last forty-eight hours. I agree with you that there have to be bodies we haven't found that are connected to this."

I blinked at Tremelay's words. Forty-eight hours meant they were doing a sacrifice each night, but I'd figured no more than once a week. Unless he didn't mean the sacrificial victims but the angel. Did he think Araziel had become some sort of angelic spree murderer? "Which crime? Do you mean these death-by-angel murders, or the sacrifice?"

His mouth set in a grim line. "Both, but let's look at these first. Let's say I do believe you and there's an angel running, or flying, around killing people. Why the guy in the park? Dude was minding his own business and wham, his chest gets ripped out. I can see these two may have stumbled upon some bad shit and got taken out, either by killers who didn't want witnesses or a killer angel, but why the guy in the park?"

I winced, wondering how to tell him this. "I have a rather secretive source that led me to believe that Ronald Stull, the guy in the park, was involved in Bethany's murder. That's why he was killed. Although I don't see why Araziel would kill these junkies."

Tremelay glared. "Who is this source?"

Shit. "It's all very Watergate. I don't know him. I never actually met him. He claims to have been in the group and actually witnessed Bethany's murder. He says Ronald Stull did it, and that he organized other murders that my source did not have direct knowledge of or exposure to. He also claims that there is an unknown person outside the magical group that facilitated and participated in the murders."

There was a moment when I thought Tremelay's eyeballs were going to burn holes through me. "And of course this guy has vanished to Mexico or somewhere with a new identity, never to be seen again?" I nodded. "Well if a miracle occurs and you hear from him, please let me know next time."

I swallowed and nodded again.

Tremelay sighed. "Okay back to the angel. Why is one here? You're my expert, so tell me your theories."

That, I could do. "When I was thinking it was a demon, I'd assumed it was either a botched summoning where the mage didn't banish or bind properly, or that it was a hit. It's dangerous and could cost you your soul, but a skilled mage can summon a higher level demon as a sort of hit man."

He shook his head. "But an angel doesn't fit in those categories?"

"No. First off, no one summons an angel. You can't bind or banish them, and they don't perform services like demons. They're way too dangerous. And they don't do assassination jobs either."

"So why did an angel kill your mage in the park? And why did an angel kill these two?"

"Well, Ronald Stull could have been in the wrong place at the wrong time. Araziel senses a death, comes to collect a soul, and can't get in because of the smudge circle. The angel goes bonkers, and maybe kills these two by accident? Then tracks down Ronald the next morning and takes revenge?" I shook my head. "I don't know. Maybe the angel is on a cleansing mission, killing those who practice dark arts…and addicts."

It sounded lame. Even I didn't believe it. But I really had no idea why Araziel was here, and why the angel had killed those he had.

"Let's say someone is directing this angel, using it as a weapon. I know you said they weren't assassins, but if a well-meaning mage—a vigilante of sorts—summoned Araziel, then perhaps he, or she, convinced the angel these murders would serve a greater good."

"Maybe." I shrugged.

"So, concentrating on the angel killings, if we think about these three victims, what ties them together beyond proximity to a place where soul magic and an occult murder occurred? What can help us predict this angel, or the angel's puppetmaster's, next move? And how does an angel tie in with mages sacrificing people to power their magic?"

I winced at the term puppetmaster. Angels weren't puppets by any stretch of the imagination. Demons either. "The connection could *be* the mages who did the death ritual, or Ronald Stull, or even the sacrificial victim. At this point the only common thread is the death magic."

The detective made a note in his book. "Hopefully we can winnow that down after we visit the magic shop. I need to get an in, a few names of people in this magical community that I can question. And tomorrow I'm going to see if I can get a warrant to go through Ronald Stull's house."

I wished I could help him with the second one. My former group, Haul Du, was DC based and I hadn't been with them long enough to meet mages from other regions. The only practitioner I knew in Baltimore was a necromancer, and he was a solitary—unaffiliated with any organized group.

"Let's talk about the victim," Tremelay continued. "Bethany Scarborough. She's not the sort of woman that a bunch of killers would grab off the street. She's risky in terms of a potential victim. She's a professional woman who wouldn't easily be lured into a bad area of town by strangers."

If Janice was right, then there might be some connection between Bethany and the mages. It could be as simple as she cut one of them off in traffic. If so, we'd never track them down through her.

"What if they grabbed her in a grocery store parking lot or car jacked her or something? I mean, she did live alone. There was plenty of opportunity."

"But why her? There are easier victims. Was there something about her that made her ideal? Virgin sacrifice or something?"

I shivered at the notion. Not all single, middle-aged cat ladies were virgins. Heck most men and women nowadays *weren't* virgins. If the killers needed a virgin sacrifice, they were better off snatching a child. "I didn't think of that. There *are* some magics that require a virgin. Most of them are sex magic, but a few involve death magic."

I didn't have the stomach to tell them most of those rituals involved sacrifice to summon a demigod. Really, really scary stuff. I didn't know anyone who would be stupid enough to mess with that sort of thing. But then again, someone was responsible for Araziel's presence here. An angel wasn't that much different than a demigod.

Tremelay scratched his chin. "How would they have known whether or not she was a virgin, though? She was fifty-five. Even if she hadn't had sex in ages, she still might have had that one hook-up in high school."

"That's what I was thinking. It's not the sort of thing you discuss in casual conversation with people. Can you see walking up to a stranger, or your insurance adjuster and asking if she's a virgin? Plus what if she lied?"

"They had to have known her, either in person or over the internet. And there's something about her, some reason that they chose her instead of an easier victim."

I agreed. But in addition to finding out who these mages were, I needed to track down and put an angel back on his leash. There were some books in my personal library I could refer to, but when it came to all things holy, I'd need to go to the source—the Librarian Knights of the Temple. My Dad was one, and as much as two trips home to Middleburg in one month might pain me, it was just what I was going to have to do.

The Knights Templar didn't take requests for information via phone or the internet. These things needed to be done in person. My choice was my Dad, or crazy Uncle Beo up in the

Hamptons. Beo was a whole lot of fun at a party, but when it came to knowledge of the supernatural and spiritual world, I was going to go to Dad. I'd just have to figure out when I could squeeze in a visit between my job and other activities. I would need to work fast given that people seemed to be dying left and right around here.

Fingering the crucifix keychain in my pocket, I looked up at Tremelay. "So what do we do now?"

His shoulders straightened, a look of anger on his face as he once again glanced toward the dead. "I'll be up all night working this and going through missing persons' reports. Do you think the magic shop can wait until morning?"

Actually that was perfect. It was now after dark, and I really wanted to see if I could find Dario before I dove into my own research. "Sure. I don't work tomorrow, so we can go as early as you like."

We. I tried to hide the excitement that didn't seem suitable given the gruesome scene around us. We. That meant I was still in the game. And that's where I intended to stay.

CHAPTER 14

It took me a couple of hours to find Dario. He wasn't at any of his usual pick-up spots, and when I finally tracked him down at a little gastropub off Calvert Street I saw why. His companion tonight was the same dark-haired beauty he'd been with last night.

The realization hit me like a fist in my stomach. I adjusted the skintight tanktop over my push-up bra, feeling ridiculously sleazy. I wanted to leave. I wanted to turn right around and leave. But Dario needed to know what was going on. I owed it to him to tell him. And the significance of him being with the same woman two nights in a row shouldn't stop me.

I'd turned him down. Repeatedly. He'd moved on, and clearly found someone else to fill the role of blood slave. I don't know how I could have thought he would keep on picking up random women each night, denying himself of a meaningful relationship with someone when he'd gone without a blood slave for over a century. *I'd* gone out on a date with Zac, had seriously contemplated sleeping with him. I was moving on, and so had Dario.

I walked up to the table. The vampire didn't seem particularly surprised to see me. He smiled warmly. His companion scowled.

"Sorry to interrupt. There are a few things going on that I wanted to make you aware of. Can I have a minute? And then I'll be out of your hair." The last part was addressed to the woman with what I hoped was an apologetic smile. Her glare never faltered, so I turned my gaze back to Dario.

Our eyes connected. He didn't seem angry or bitter. The look on his face was one of…concern.

"Of course. Giselle, do you mind?"

Giselle looked very much like she minded. Her hand clenched in her lap, just out of Dario's line of vision, and I was pretty sure she was wishing she could shank me right now. "Can I stay? Please?"

Oh gag. Saccharine smile, purring voice. Blech. The woman flipped her hair over her shoulder and I saw the faint fang marks. He'd marked her. Of course he'd marked her. Two nights in a row. Blood slave. She was bound to have those marks. And she was pretty darned obvious about making sure I saw them.

Dario's eyes flickered to her face. "Yes. You can stay if you wish."

Well, that pretty much removed any doubt I might have. I wasn't about to stand at the end of their table like a waiter and deliver my news, so I pulled a chair over, flipped it around, and straddled it.

"There are a group of mages who performed a sacrificial death magic ritual in Old Town Mall which involved using the victim's soul. A source informs me that this isn't the only time they've done this sort of ritual. To complicate things further, the magic was used in a spell to contain and protect against something or someone which the magical community seems to feel is horrific enough to warrant killing people to protect against. It's got to be pretty darned scary if they're needing that much energy."

The vampire didn't even blink. "Go on."

Go on? I guess the *Balaj* didn't give a rat's ass about mages killing humans, or whatever big-bad they were trying to guard the city against.

"The mage who organized and performed these death magic rituals was killed yesterday afternoon by an angel. Two others have also been killed by the same angel."

That got a reaction, minimal though it was. "Should we be concerned?"

Oh no. Just go on about your business. No worries here. Sheesh. Vampires. Any doubt I'd had a few minutes ago over my choices was gone now.

"Death magic? Well, if you're concerned that they're poaching on your food source, yes. If you think whatever they're guarding against might be a threat to you, yes. If you're worried that they're powerful enough to decide to rid the city of vampires, yes."

"That's not our concern," he interrupted. "We have dealings with the local magical community. They do not take our marked humans. They limit their activities. We stay out of their way and leave them alone. I'm more interested in whether the angel is a concern or not."

It took me a few moments to wrap my head around this. The vampires knew mages were performing human sacrifice and had given it the thumbs-up. *Dario* had given it the thumbs-up. All of this was making me revisit my view of them.

"The angel is Araziel. He's a psychopomp." At Dario's blank look I continued. "He separates the soul from the body at the time of death. Vampires are technically dead. We saw what happened last week when a necromancer yanked the souls out of vampires. Araziel can do the same, only with a more dramatic flair. And he's not as easy to stop as a bunch of specters."

"But that's humans," Dario mused. "He's an angel, so he'd be concerned with humans. Heaven's messengers are not interested in harvesting our souls."

No, I guessed not. "In the normal course of things, you'd probably be right, but Araziel is an angel off of his heavenly leash. He isn't just harvesting the souls of the dead, he's killing them, and there are two dead junkies to back that theory up. I've got no idea what his criteria are in who he graces with his services, but I thought you might want to know."

Dario nodded. "I appreciate the head's up. Is there anything we can do to remain out of his sights? And how long do you expect this angel to be prowling the city?"

"I don't know the answers to either of those questions. I've got some research to do tonight, and more tomorrow. I'll let you know what I find out."

I stood, and Dario did also.

"I think we should meet regularly to exchange this sort of information," he said. "On both sides. I want to ensure you know what's going on with the *Balaj* and any issues at our end, too."

Huh? I just stared at him.

"You're a Templar, and you've clearly taken it upon your-self to police supernatural activities in the city. We're the largest paranormal community here. If we're to coexist, then we need to have regular meetings."

"Liaisons." What a weird idea. Actually, what a good idea, despite the fact that my stomach churned over the thought of seeing Dario regularly. Would Giselle be at these meetings, like a living accessory? How involved were blood slaves in their vampire's night-to-night business dealings?

"Yes." He picked up a napkin and wrote a number on it,

handing it to me. "This is my cell number. Call me tomorrow night and brief me. We should probably think about setting up a weekly schedule. Or maybe meet each evening, say at Sesarios."

I pocketed the number, feeling like a deer in headlights. Sesarios. Would we have dinner there every night? Cannoli? It was kind of our place and the idea of having what would become an emotionless business meeting there bothered me.

Would Giselle be there, too? Awkward.

"I'll give you my number." I scrambled in my purse for a pen, but Dario waved me away.

"No need. I have your number. Call me tomorrow."

He remained standing until after I'd left the building, Giselle stiff-faced across the table from him. It wasn't until after I'd gotten home that I realized he'd never introduced me, that he'd never included her in our conversation. And that the woman's trembling hand had reached up to touch the fang marks as we spoke.

It was petty of me, but *that* made me feel pretty damned good.

CHAPTER 15

*D*etective Tremelay was waiting outside my apartment as soon as I got home.

"Thank God you're here. I tried your number twice. Why didn't you pick up?"

I glanced down at my phone, seeing the missed messages. "I was in a meeting and forgot to turn the ringer back on. What's up?"

Another death magic ritual? More angel deaths? Whatever I expected, it wasn't what came out of the detective's mouth.

"Two dead in DC. I've got a friend there in homicide, and we chat about cases. He called me right away with something he called a satanic ritual gone wrong. I'm on my way, but I really wanted to take my expert along."

Oh, hell yeah. Not that I was thrilled to hear of two people dead in DC, but I was excited that I was now the detective's go-to on these sort of things. It gave me an odd thrill to be his expert. Almost as much of a thrill as I got from being the newly appointed liaison to the vampires. Although appointed probably wasn't the right term.

The drive to DC was a quick one. Tremelay had insisted I stash my sword in the trunk, saying we were out of his jurisdiction and we were there by invitation. Evidently it would be bad form for me to show up with a bastard sword across my lap in the front seat, even though I noticed the detective didn't stash his service weapon in the trunk with my sword.

The crime scene tape was all around the brick rancher, but there was only the one cruiser in the driveway with one cop standing at wary attention beside it. Tremelay and the other officer nodded and exchanged a few words.

The man looked me over. "Who in the hell is this?"

Tremelay had already performed the short introduction to Detective Anthony Zrubek, so I doubted it was my name he was demanding. He was Mutt to Tremelay's Jeff, short with dark skin, a round belly and a bald head. What hair he lacked on his head, he made up for in the elaborate mustache that drooped over his upper lip and twisted downward at the edges. It was like a cross between a Fu Manchu and a Tom Selleck. I was fascinated and couldn't keep my eyes off it.

"She's a consultant on matters of the occult. She's been working with me on the ritual sacrifice case I told you about."

Detective Zrubek shuddered. Evidently Tremelay had spared none of the details when telling his friend about the murder.

"Shouldn't she be wearing flowing robes with pentagrams or something?" He looked me over, his mustache twitching.

"I'm a Templar," I explained. "We study a variety of supernatural matters as part of our education, but I've specialized in magical practices dealing with Goetic demons and other spirit beings. I also spent a few months as a member of one of the largest ceremonial magic groups in the northeast."

"Templar? As in Templar Knight? Like the Crusades and

all that? Where's your sword?" He clearly had seized on the first part of my speech to the exclusion of the rest.

"I made her leave it in the trunk," Tremelay chimed in. "You should see it. Thing is huge. She claims it's some kind of religious tool, but one swing and someone's gonna lose a head."

"I'm not a Knight."

Neither paid any attention to me.

"A real sword? No shit! I didn't think you guys allowed that sort of thing in Baltimore."

Tremelay shot me a narrowed look. "We don't. At least not on public property. She can carry it in her car to reenactments and stuff, but no sword fighting on public property."

Oh good Lord. "Can we see the crime scene now or do you guys want to play show and tell with my sword?"

Zrubek looked for a second like he was considering the show and tell option. "Two adult males age forty to fifty. They looked to be slashed apart with a weapon that had multiple curved blades."

"Like Freddy Kruger?" I asked.

"Like bear claws?" Tremelay added.

The other detective tilted his head, for a brief moment. "The M.E. will have to weigh in on that one. Since we don't have any reports of escaped bears from the National Zoo, I'm going to assume a human with a multi-bladed weapon."

Huh. Still, could have been a werewolf. Last I'd heard there was one running around the Blue Ridge Mountains. They weren't fond of urban areas, but I didn't want to rule it out.

Detective Zrubek showed us the pictures on his cell phone. It looked like the two men had run bleeding throughout the house, flinging red droplets on the walls and ceilings as they passed. Two bodies were facedown on the floor in a sea of red, their clothing shredded in long deep slashes.

I crossed werewolf and escaped bear off my list of suspects. I also crossed off angel, at least if Araziel was keeping to his former method of killing. Angels were pretty anal when it came to patterns.

"Why did you think this case was related to the ones in Baltimore?" Tremelay asked. "The three in Baltimore had their rib cages spread upward. These two are face down, but I'm assuming they're not missing all of their internal organs. None of the Baltimore victims had these slashes on their backs."

"You'll see when you get inside. These guys were into some serious satanic magic crap. Even if there was a guy with a fist full of box cutters who killed them, I figured the magic shit was enough of a tie-in to warrant a phone call. Can't be a coincidence. I don't recall the last time I've seen wizard types dead and I've been working homicide for the last twenty years."

I'll admit I was interested. "What's that in the one guy's hand?" I asked, pointing at the picture on the cell phone.

Zrubek swiped and held the phone out to me. I caught my breath as I looked at the picture, zooming in just to make sure.

"Dude tried to defend himself," the detective commented. "We're hoping the blood on the knife has a DNA hit to something in the database."

It wouldn't.

"A Bowie," Tremelay chimed in. "Looks about twenty inch with a thirteen inch blade. Sharp, too."

I stared at him, openmouthed.

"What?" He grinned sheepishly. "I know my knives."

Color me impressed. "It's not just any Bowie. See that little mark down there? That's a magical symbol. The blade can be either iron, which is a bitch to keep from rusting, bone, obsidian, or silver. They're purpose built, and unlike ceremonial daggers, these suckers are made for defense."

Now it was the two cops turn to stare at me. "What? I know my magical weapons."

"From what I saw the blade was metal. I thought steel, but maybe iron. I'm no expert."

"If it's steel or iron, then no wonder the pair of them are dead." I scrolled back a few pictures and enlarged the picture to show a sigil burned into the floor off to the side of the victims. "That's a demon sigil. Innyhal to be precise."

Innyhal wasn't one of the lesser demons. Haul Du only summoned Goetic demons for information and divination, but Innyhal was a major demon affiliated with Mars and all that the god of war symbolized. To summon him was to summon an assassin.

I didn't know what the heck happened. A lot can go wrong when summoning demons, as I'd recently learned. Either way, I still didn't see where these cases were related besides the activities surrounding the deceased.

"So you're saying a demon killed these two guys?" The impressed expression was gone from Zrubek's face and Tremelay looked embarrassed. Guess I was back to being a weirdo again. So much for expert occult witness.

"Yeah. The good news is these things just don't pop over here uninvited. Someone summoned him, and that someone is your murderer."

Bad news was there was a demon running around, and if the summoner didn't banish it, then it would be my job to send it back to hell. I rubbed my side where the burn scar was acting up. Templars banished demons. It was part of our job description, although we didn't have cause to do it much in the last few centuries. Most modern mages were too smart to mess with the higher level spirits, and the ones who did were careful to keep their practice hidden and to send the demon back as quickly as possible. A slip up would get you a slap on the wrist from the Templars. I wasn't sure what we would do to a repeat offender.

Great. An angel I needed to track down, and now a demon. It made me wonder about Araziel's summoning. What if the magician had been trying for Azrael? Although bringing one of the princes of hell into this plane was certifiably insane, so was bringing an angel. Of course, so was bringing Innyhal.

Was this the same mage? If so, he or she had a lot to answer for. Although judging from the crime scene in the photos, the mage responsible for Innyhal's appearance might have already paid for summoning the otherworldly being. That might mean case closed for Tremelay and Zrubek, but not for me. Dead mages meant I had a demon *and* an angel potentially running around the area without any sort of direction or control. I was in for a fun week.

"All righty then. Benton Leigh and David Alban, killed by a demon with super-sharp claws. Can we prosecute this Innyhal? Do Miranda rights mean anything to a demon? Can he afford a lawyer or will one need to be appointed to him?" Zrubek flipped through a notepad that looked eerily like the one Tremelay carried. Did they order those things in bulk? Standard police issue?

Wait. I narrowed my eyes in thought. Benton Leigh? David Alban? "Hey, I know those guys."

Now I had the attention of both detectives.

"Remember I said I used to be in a magical group? Well, we don't use our real names and people are understandably cagy about their identities, but things occasionally slip out."

Slip out. As in magical tracers, and other ways of identifying people. Once I tracked them, it was easy to do some internet research on their homes, places of business, and even license plate numbers. Did I mention I'd held an unhealthy grudge after getting kicked out of Haul Du? I didn't hex or curse them or anything, but I figured if they were going to out me, I was going to at least know the legal names and current addresses of everyone in the group that I could manage to dig up.

"David Alban went by Tempest. Benton Leigh was known as Oak. They weren't Masters, but they certainly knew enough to safely summon a greater demon. If they were the ones that brought this demon over, then this massacre shouldn't have happened."

Zrubek pocketed his phone. "Well, it did. Shall we go in? Gloves and booties folks. We've processed the scene, but I still want to keep it clean just in case."

We slipped the elastic-edged booties on at the doorstep along with the latex gloves. Once inside I wandered, trying to recreate the events of the night without disturbing anything. The living room was a wreck. A rapier had been yanked from a wall hanger and had been stuck clear through the drywall, the scabbard crumpled on the floor. End tables were knocked over, figurines smashed. I winced. Everything in the room had been of magical use. They may have looked like decorations, but even the nesting dolls had spells imbedded in them. Tempest took his magic seriously.

Bloodstains and patterns in the dining room showed where the two had died even to my neophyte eyes. I followed the trail of broken furniture and headed carefully down the steps to the basement.

In a normal house it would have been carpeted with a sectional sofa and a big screen television along with a wet bar in the corner. This was a mage's house—clearly an unwed mage with no children. The floor was cement with the double circle acid-etched into the surface. Just the basics. Sigils, as well as different geometric shapes depending on what the mage was working on could be added as needed. A workbench stood off to the side with typical supplies neatly stacked. Candles, various herbs and stones, jars with bones, feathers, and fur alternated with carefully organized books on the shelves that lines the walls. I was struck with a pang of jealousy. My little apartment could never support such an amazing magical space as this.

My family home in Middleburg could. It was one more thing I'd left behind when I'd refused to take my Oath of Knighthood and walked away from that life. I jammed my hands in the pockets of my jeans just to keep away from the temptation to steal the amazing array of supplies Tempest had in this room.

I took one look at the circle and knew we were dealing with a summoning gone wrong, and not a hit. There had been an intended victim of assassination, but it hadn't been Tempest or Oak. They'd summoned Innyhal, and no one brought that demon over for peaceful purposes. Something had gone wrong here, and in addition to tracking down a loose demon, I wanted to find out exactly what *had* gone wrong. Any opportunity to learn from another's mistakes, especially if that mistake had cost two mages their lives.

But for now I needed to focus on the immediate threat of a loose demon. The circle had been set up for summoning, and from what I could see Tempest had taken every precaution. The runes looked neatly drawn. He'd foregone the usual containment triangle in favor of a stronger pentagram one. Sigils for Innyhal were at each point to hold the demon in place. I walked widdershins around the summoning area, careful not to smudge anything, but could see no weaknesses where the demon would have been able to break free.

But he *had* broken free. And Oak, in a last attempt to send him back, had hastily drawn the sigil upstairs right where he'd taken his last breath. Just a few moments more and he would have had the banishing sign ready for his bloody hand to activate. He'd never gotten the chance.

"Anything?" Tremelay asked. The two detectives were at the bottom of the staircase, watching me with curiosity.

"They're the ones who brought the demon over, but I can't see any screw-ups here. Maybe the incantation was faulty."

I completed the circle, making the sign of the cross just in case my lap of the magical area had triggered anything, then walked over to the workbench. The grimoire lay open, a crow's feather marking the page. When summoning a Goetic demon, there was never any need to let them out of the circle. The magician brought them here, made offerings and threats, then returned them to hell once the demon coughed up the information. Even though I'd never intentionally summoned one, I did know that protocols were different for higher demons. Rarely were they brought here for information. No, mages summoned higher demons because they wanted them to *do* something—and doing something required letting them out of the protective area of the circle.

That's what scared the stuffing out of me. Demons were scary enough without letting them out of the circle. The request, the parameters of their release, had to be very specifically worded, otherwise somebody died. Otherwise lots of somebodies died. If this demon hadn't escaped the summoning area due to a mistake there, then he found a loophole in the rules and restrictions of his release and took advantage of it.

And once the summoner was dead, all bets were off. Demon. Here. No rules. It was scarier in some ways than the idea of an angel off their heavenly leash. Angels lived by rules and order in their own weird, otherworldly way. Demons were chaos incarnate. They did whatever the heck they wanted. And they wouldn't go back unless forced to.

I read the beautifully written script, outlining the ritual with a gloved finger. The summoning was textbook. I cringed when I read what the demon's task was.

"Guys? I think I have our link here. Leigh and Alban were summoning a demon for a hit. They wanted Innyhal to kill a group of people up in Baltimore."

"Who? Does it list the names? We'll need to warn them." Tremelay walked over toward me, giving the summoning circle a wary glance as he passed it.

Of course he'd want to warn them, as well as bring them in for questioning. If their names were in this book, they were most likely knowledgeable of, if not involved in, the Baltimore murders.

"Their full names are here." Demons needed exact names to perform their tasks. Because there were so many people in the world nowadays, they often required current address and date of birth. It sounded silly, but if you didn't want every Kimberly Ann Cannon in the state of Maryland to be killed, you needed to be specific.

But there was no need to warn these people. Once the summoner was killed, the deal was off and a demon was free to slaughter whomever they wanted. Oddly, they tended to stay clear of their original targets, kind of a final fuck-you toward their summoner. Of the twenty-five names on this list, twenty-four would be safe. Technically so would one other, since he was already dead.

"Ronald Stephen Stull," Tremelay read. "Yep. There's our connection."

Tempest hadn't known that Ronald was dead when he summoned this demon. How very ironic. Of course, the question now was why had Tempest and Oak wanted Ronald dead, and why had an angel beaten them to it?

Because *someone* had summoned that angel.

Zrubek made his way over to us. "So a demon kills these

two. An angel kills three in Baltimore. And a group of psychos sacrifice a woman in Old Town Mall. Sounds like a bunch of Satanists to me."

Oh for Pete's sake. Would they ever stop pinning this on the poor Satanists?

"I think we may have two warring magical groups, but I'm not ruling out the possibility that this was a personal grudge."

Twenty-five names. That sounded about right for a magical organization, and Shade had mentioned twenty-four mages, excluding himself, were in the Baltimore group.

Unlike witches, ceremonial magicians liked to keep their groups between twenty and fifty in number. More than fifty and sub-factions broke off. Less than twenty and there wasn't enough energy for serious magical work. I thought about Shade and his insistence that they were protecting Baltimore from something big and bad. They'd needed thirteen in ceremony, but if there was a necessity for regular sacrifice, it would have been important to swap mages to ensure fresh sources of energy to protect the boundaries of the ritual.

Twenty-five. Why would Tempest and Oak want them all dead? Raven had spoken as if there was no love lost between the groups, but murder?

Zrubek stared at me. "Warring magical groups? Is that like gang warfare?"

"Yeah, only instead of bullets they shoot demons and curses at each other." I shooed the pair. "You guys go outside. I need to try and send this demon back where he came from and I really don't want you both to wind up dead in the cross fire."

The two detectives didn't budge.

"There's no way I'm leaving you alone at a crime scene," Zrubek commented.

"There's no way I'm leaving you alone to summon a demon," Tremelay added.

I felt all warm and fuzzy at the last statement. He believed me, and he thought *he* could help defend me against a demon. If he'd been trained as a Templar like his ancestors had been, he might have been of assistance—very welcome assistance. But since he wasn't, I was going to have to do this one solo.

Which scared the crap out of me. That demon who'd come when I'd summoned Vine last week had been a high level demon, and I'd barely been able to banish him. This was going to be tough.

"Fine, but I'm going to need to set up wards for the pair of you, and I'll need my sword."

No one appeared to be rushing to comply. "Wards?" Zrubek asked. "As in drawing those squiggly things? You can't do that in here. It's a crime scene."

"And you can't draw your sword in public," Tremelay said. "Can't this wait until you're back home with all your magical supplies? It's not like you can use candles and herbs and stuff from a crime scene."

He had a point. There was one thing I *could* do, though. I took some detailed pictures of the circle and sigils as well as the pages in the grimoire. Then as soon as the detectives were looking elsewhere, I pocketed a few items. A sigil should be enough to call the demon back to me, but a few items from the room would seal the deal. I didn't need Innyhal refusing to come to me. This demon was bad news and as the sooner he was back in hell the better.

"Ready." I smiled at the two men and headed up the stairs. It was pushing on toward dawn. An hour back to my apartment in Fells Point, a few hours prepping for my confrontation with the demon. If Tremelay came over at noon to go to the magic shop, I might be able to sneak in a few hours of sleep. That is, if the demon hadn't killed me first.

I heard the heavy footsteps of the men coming up the stairs…then felt a presence. Hair prickled up at the back of my neck right before I heard a loud noise. I spun around. The door to the basement had slammed shut, the refrigerator tilted sideways to block it shut. Black smoke swirled upward from the floor, coalescing into a shape.

I didn't wait to see what form Innyhal took, I ran. The lights flickered and went out, plunging the house into darkness. I could hear the two detectives shouting and bashing against the basement door. I made it through the kitchen and into the dining room, banging my shin on a fallen table and tripping over a lamp. Stumbling forward, I hit the wall instead of the living room doorway, and fell face-first onto the bloody rug.

It was still damp and sticky, smelling of copper and urine. I dug my nails into the fibers of the plush carpet and pulled my feet under me in an effort to launch myself through the doorway. It took seconds for a demon to form. It would take me longer than that to get out of here and to my sword.

"Haxa Luz." A globe of light flew from my hand. It was enough for me to see the doorway and the obstacles in the living room. I felt the demon behind me and dove forward. Razor sharp claws slashed through the back of my shirt, stinging as they striped my skin.

There was a cracking sound. Tremelay and Zrubek must be smashing the basement door open with whatever they found downstairs. I ran through the front door, slamming it shut behind me.

"Pechar."

The quick spell locked the front door and threw the dead bolt. It wouldn't be enough to stop the demon, but I hoped it would slow him. My back felt as if it were on fire as I ran for

Tremelay's car, the scar on my side a dull throb. As soon as my hand hit the trunk I realized my dilemma. Like a typical cop, the detective had locked the car, and thus the trunk. My sword was safely inside, out of reach.

That was the last time I got pressured into leaving my primary weapon in the trunk. I dug through my pockets for my keychain, well aware that it was a paltry substitute for my sword. The gold crucifix might be a deterrent to vampires, but it wouldn't do much against a demon.

It was better than nothing.

I spun around, my cross held high, and got my first look at my pursuer. He had the body of a human, as so many demons did. Beyond that, Innyhal was a mish-mash of creatures. His legs were bird-like, his head that of a lion with four eyes. His hands ended with knives instead of fingers— five seven inch, double edged blades. He bared his teeth as he slowly approached, clicking the knife-claws against one another.

"T'voghnel anmijapes." I shouted. It was the Templar blessing to banish. I'd used it successfully last week with the demon I'd somehow summoned in Vine's place.

Innyhal hesitated, shaking his head as though I'd just hit him with a low-level stun gun. Then he made a noise that sounded like a cross between a laugh and a roar and kept on walking.

Why hadn't it worked? I was a Templar. This was my birthright. Why hadn't it worked? All I knew was that I was shaking like a leaf in a hurricane, standing in front of a sedan with a keychain held in the air. And my side was killing me. It felt like needles were digging into my ribs. And if I didn't get out of here, a whole lot more was going to be digging into my ribs.

The front door slammed open and I heard gunshots. Holes sprouted all over Innyhal's body, purple blood blooming from the wounds. Tremelay and Zrubek kept shooting until their clips were empty, even though their bullets did less to stop the demon than my Templar blessing had.

I ran. Innyhal didn't want them, he wanted me. He wanted the one being who was determined to send him back to hell. Some say demons aren't smart, well, they're wrong. They *are* smart, and self-preservation is their number one priority. Right now, I was the threat. Two cops with guns weren't. He'd come after me, and if he killed me, Tremelay and Zrubek would be next. Not because they were threats, but just because they were handy.

I'm fast, but I'm human. I barely got to the end of the driveway before I felt claws slashing through the remains of my shirt. The cuts weren't deep, but one of the demon's knives hooked on my belt, and as sharp as they were, it caught long enough to knock me to the ground before the edge sliced through the leather. I rolled, trying to avoid the ten slashing blades, but one dug into my side. My breath left me as the pain of Innyhal's claws cut through the skin and muscle right where my scar was.

In that moment when you're facing death, weird things go through your head. My weird thought was that at least the knife cuts would accent the round burn mark that had inexplicably appeared on my waist this summer.

The demon snarled, saliva dripping from fangs in what my pain-filled delirium was taking to be triumph. Then his face changed. Four eyes widened, rolling backward into his head until all I saw were the whites. His body convulsed and white foam flew from his mouth. The claws left my body, and Innyhal clutched himself, pawing as if he were trying to remove parasites from his skin. Slowly he dissolved into a writhing mass of smoke, flying upward with a scream that nearly deafened me.

I panted and rested my head back on the grassy lawn, weak from the adrenaline rush and the pain in my side. Out of the corner of my eye I saw the two men running toward me. Tremelay was loading another clip into his pistol as if another round of bullets might do what the first dozen or so hadn't.

"Holy shit, what was that?" Zrubek asked, his pistol at the ready as he spun around looking for the demon.

"It was a demon. Innyhal, the one who killed Benton Leigh and David Alban," I told him, dreading getting up to check my injuries. Maybe if I just lay here a few hours, they would all go away.

"Is it gone?" Zrubek was still spinning around, peering with narrowed eyes into the bushes.

"As far as I know." *Still laying here. Still hoping I don't have big gaping holes through my torso.*

"You okay?" Tremelay appeared just as ready as the other detective, but his eyes were roaming over my body instead of the surrounding area. Too late I thought of my skimpy, tight attire. Wow, I must be practically naked after having the tank top nearly sliced off me. Although I doubted bloody claw marks were a sexy addition to my skin.

"Yeah." I took his outstretched hand and stood, gingerly feeling my waist. The skin was totally smooth where Innyhal had dug into my side. Well, smooth except for the round lumpy scar. I took a deep breath in relief and winced. My back hadn't fared such a miraculous recovery. I turned around to show Tremelay. "Stitches? Or will I be okay with a shower of hydrogen peroxide?"

At my words Tremelay flipped the safety on his pistol and stuck it in his back waistband. Before I knew what was going on he was yanking the shredded bits of my tank top aside and running his hands over my skin. It felt good—really good. It took me a second to realize that his hands on my waist and back were all I felt at that moment.

"I think you'll be okay with some tape and a tube or two of antibiotic cream. I saw him stab you in the waist, but all you've got are these cuts on your back. How the heck did you manage that? What, are Templars Kevlar-coated when it comes to demon claws or something?"

Not hardly. My hands joined his, but I felt nothing on my skin beyond a few old scars which included the circular shaped burn on the side of my waist. Reaching around to my back, I encountered the jagged edge of broken skin, my hand wet as it came away. Ugh. I should be happy I wasn't bleeding out on the grass from a stab wound to the side, but my lack of serious injury troubled me.

I'd been pointedly ignoring that burn mark, but now I needed to face the cold, hard, sucky reality of what had really happened. That demon who'd appeared last week instead of Vine had gotten out of the circle and pinned me on the ground. Before I managed to banish the thing it must have marked me. That was the only explanation I had for the scar that had appeared out of nowhere. It looked old, but I'm positive it hadn't been there before my summoning attempt.

Some demon had marked me. The thought made me sick, even though I knew in my heart that was probably what had saved me from Innyhal's attack. It's probably the reason I hadn't suffered any lasting damage from the claws.

And it was probably the reason my blessing hadn't worked. How the heck was I going to get out of this? All my blessings worked just fine last week. Could it be they no longer worked on demons because one had slapped his claim on me? No, I refused to believe that. Demons could only take a person if they willingly traded their soul and I'd done no such thing. Yes, I'd summoned one, but only for information. There had been no bargain. And even if there had, the wrong demon had arrived. I had to be mistaken. The mark was just a scar from my near miss last week. My Kevlar-coating had to be some Templar thing that I'd been unaware of. The reason the blessing hadn't worked tonight was that in my fear I'd mispronounced a word.

I sucked at lying, even when I was trying to lie to myself.

CHAPTER 16

I'd planned on calling Janice to give her a quick update, then banishing Innyhal when I returned home, but instead I was doing some early morning home improvement. Thank heaven for those twenty-four hour Walmart stores who happened to have floor leveler in their fix-er-up section. I bought every box they had and spent the hours before dawn with the carpet and padding rolled against the wall, ensuring I had a smooth even surface for magical rituals. It hurt like hell, every outstretched arm and scoot on my knees across the floor pulling at the taped-up wounds under my T-shirt. Tremelay had been a good nurse, even if he hadn't been carrying the narcotics I now desperately longed for.

I should have been sleeping. I should have been sprawled on my stomach on the bed, drooling with prescription pain-killers, but I had a job to do and I was determined to do it right—especially when the price I'd pay was my own life.

I'll admit there was some jealousy of Tempest's work-room driving my handyman efforts, but it was mixed with fear. Oak and Tempest had been skilled mages with decades of experience. If they screwed up enough to wind up dead, then I didn't stand a chance. I wasn't sure if the demon mark on my side was a result of an error on my part or not, but I was determined to not half-ass this sort of thing again.

Yes, the wisest course would be to swear off ceremonial magic, but that wasn't going to happen. I just needed to be better at it and more careful. I knew there would come a time when I'd have to conjure or spell or summon and I wanted to be prepared. And there most definitely would come a time when I had to perform a ritual to get this demon mark off me. What ritual, I didn't know, but that research was pretty close to the top of my list.

And I couldn't ignore the fact that there was a higher demon running around the tri-state area—one I had failed to banish. As humiliating as it was, I needed to call in a Knight. Dad was a Librarian Knight, but Mom and my two siblings were Guardians. Roman was in Leesburg, Mom even farther away in Middleburg, but I knew Athena was at a symposium up in Philly this week.

My sister and I were the closest in age, but she was still seven years my senior. I'd been my parents' midlife baby, the pesky kid following my teenage brother and sister around. We were tight, but with gaps of seven and ten years, we weren't *that* tight. Still, Athena seemed thrilled when I called, telling me about her seminar on cursed objects and asking about the weekend's LARP. When the small talk had run on for a respectable length of time, I reluctantly turned to conversation to my problem. Reluctant because I hated to admit my failure, and in all honesty the seminar on cursed objects *did* sound pretty cool.

"Innyhal? Are you sure it was him? A high level demon loose in DC? Holy gauntlets, Aria, you get *all* the luck."

I was momentarily stunned into silence that Athena would consider being nearly killed by a demon luck. How bored were Guardians these days when human sacrifices, reaper angels, and rogue demons were experiences to be envied?

"Yeah, it was Innyhal. The sigil was unmistakable even if the four-eyed, lion-headed form wasn't. I really need your help, though. I tried to banish him and for some reason it didn't work."

Some reason. I wasn't about to admit to my sister that I'd probably gotten myself demon-marked. It was bad enough that I had to swallow my pride and tell her I failed to banish a demon. Me. A Templar. Even though I wasn't a Knight, I was still empowered as part of our holy mission to send Satan's minions back to hell. Gah, it was so humiliating.

There was a moment of silence from Athena—a poignant moment. I felt like I'd just admitted to peeing my bed at night or something.

"I'll be right down. Let me wrap up a breakfast meeting with Elder Eustache and I'll meet you at your apartment."

Typical. She hadn't asked if I had to work at my job, because for all the other Templars this *was* their job—their only job. Although, to be fair, a demon loose in the city did trump my responsibilities to corporate America. "What time? I'm helping a civilian detective on the death-magic sacrifice and we had plans this morning. I can switch them if I need to."

Civilian. It made me want to laugh that as a Templar the police were considered civilians.

"Make it noon? You know how Elder Eustache talks and I haven't even packed yet. It's not an emergency, is it? Innyhal is all about death, warfare, and slaughter but I've read that he likes to plan a bit more than the usual Mars demons."

True. "Outside of the two mages who summoned him, I haven't heard of any other deaths." Plus most demons preferred to kill at night, when the lack of light added to the terror of their murders.

"Noon, then. Oh, and I've got a package from Gran for you. I was going to swing by on my way home and drop if off anyway."

I read between the lines, or in this case, words. The package was Athena's excuse for a visit. I smiled at the thought that she'd wanted to visit me—the only one of my family to do so since I left six months ago. Not that it was completely their fault. I hadn't left on the best of terms, and I'm sure they all wanted to give me my space so I could get through my little tantrum then come home and take my Oath of Knighthood.

Athena *wanted* to visit. She'd asked about the LARP, seemed genuinely interested in my life here—excited even. Could this be a sign that my family might eventually accept my choices? Lord, I hoped so.

I was exhausted, but I had a few more calls to make. I made quick work of briefing Janice, telling her the link between the DC mages with their hit list, and the Baltimore killings.

"I want to run this tomorrow morning," she warned.

I winced. Would the story scare off the mages we were trying to catch? Plus I wasn't sure leaking the story about the sacrifice would do much beyond panicking the public. "The victims might not even have known the mages responsible for this. I know you think there's a motive, a method for selection, but I'm not completely convinced."

"I'm running it, Aria," she announced. From the tone of her voice I knew she wouldn't be swayed. "People need to know. Maybe someone has seen something. Maybe one of their co-mages feels guilty and will come forward."

I thought of Shade. He hadn't necessarily felt guilty. As distasteful as he found the sacrifices, he'd believed them to be a necessary evil. Running this story was only going to make them close ranks.

Shit. Tremelay was going to kill me. "Don't implicate Ronald Stull or mention him yet," I warned. "I've got no proof beyond a slip of paper in his pocket with an address, his name on a hit list, and the word of a mage who wouldn't even face me in person that he's involved. Leave this all vague and anonymous so we have time to bring these people in."

The line was silent for a few moments. "Okay. I'll leave out Ronald Stull as well as the DC demon killings, and just run this as a death-magic, human sacrifice. I can add in the others once we figure out how they fit together."

It was the best I could hope for. I promised to keep Janice in the loop, and received the same assurances from her. Then I hung up and dialed another number.

It was yet another attempt on my part to reach Raven. I'd called her from Tremelay's car on the way back from DC. I'd called her while standing in the checkout line at the Walmart. I'd called her while on my knees smearing gray stuff all over my floor. I couldn't stop caring about someone —or worrying about them—just because they'd had to make a choice between me and their magical organization. She'd chosen Haul Du, but I knew deep down inside that decision bothered her just as much as it bothered me. Two Haul Du mages had died last night. Maybe she was the one who needed to get out of town and hide in Virginia for a week or two.

This time she picked up the phone. "Aria, stop calling me. I've got hundreds of problems I'm dealing with right now. Are you in Virginia with your family?"

"No, I'm in Baltimore." Before she could scold me, I rushed right into the topic at hand. "Tempest and Oak are dead. They were summoning a high demon named Innyhal in order to kill a list of twenty-five Baltimore area mages. Innyhal got out, killed them, and is on the loose."

I heard her sharp intake of breath. "Oak and Tempest are dead?"

"Yeah. And now there's a demon running around DC. What the heck is going on, Raven?"

"A feud between Haul Du and the Baltimore group. I can't tell you the details, but it's gotten ugly and people have died."

"And what started this feud? Because it needs to stop before any more innocent people get killed."

Raven made an impatient sound. "That's what some of us are trying to do. Your interference won't help, Aria. And you're liable to get yourself killed in the crossfire. Just go visit your parents and let us handle it."

That stung. I might not be an adept in the magical community, but I did have my skills. And honestly, these mages hadn't been doing a great job at handling the situation so far. "Oh, so more get killed like Tempest and Oak? More Baltimore mages and junkies get their souls ripped out by an angel? More people are sacrificed in a death magic ritual used to contain some really scary thing that, frankly, I'm a little afraid to conjecture on? Raven, you guys are in over your heads."

I felt her frustration through the phone. "Maybe we are, but this is an internal matter. I'm sorry it—wait. Did you say an *angel* was ripping the souls out of people?"

Yeah, I'd had a hard time believing it, too. "Araziel. He killed one of the mages that was on Tempest and Oak's hit list, and two junkies on the barrier where the sacrifice took place. So now there's a demon running around loose, an angel equally loose, Baltimore mages killing people, and Haul Du members summoning higher level demons to kill others. And summoning them badly. Did I mention they got themselves killed?"

"I gotta go." Raven sounded distracted, like she hadn't heard half of my rant. "I'll call you later."

"Raven, you need to tell me—" Too late. She'd hung up and I got the feeling she wouldn't answer if I called again.

Oh well. I'd done my duty—more than my duty. I'd called to give her the heads-up. I'd told her what was going on. She could go to Dark Iron, the head of Haul Du with it all. I didn't care. He'd be in a better position to protect them from a loose demon than a marked, not-a-Knight Templar.

After my call with Raven I tip-toed around the edge of my living room so as to not step in the drying floor leveler, and crashed on my bed for a much needed nap. It seemed my head had barely touched the pillow before there was a knock on my door.

"I'll be right there!" It took me a while to negotiate my way around the floor leveler, then some gymnastics to figure out how to open the door without planting my foot in it. It probably wouldn't have mattered right at the edge, but I wanted as large a space to work with as I could manage.

"What the hell?" Tremelay stared at the floor, then at me perched against the wall like a tight-rope walker. "Is that cement? What are you doing?"

"I can't properly delineate a circle on plywood with huge gaps between the sheets, and there are times when I need to do magic. It's floor leveler."

The detective took a step inside, gingerly making his way around the edge to the kitchen. "You're never getting your security deposit back. You know that, right?"

My hopes for ever seeing my security deposit had long vanished. "Any more deaths happen while I was catching some Z's?"

"Not that we've discovered. I did find out that Bethany Scarborough knew one of last night's deceased. It seems she'd worked on a burglary claim Benton Leigh filed last winter."

It was a weird coincidence, but I still filed it away in my noggin. It was a connection, the only one we had. Could Oak and Tempest have been *involved* in the death magic ritual that killed Bethany? It didn't seem their sort of thing, but I'd been wrong about people before, and Shade had mentioned a stranger who was involved. Perhaps there had been a double cross of sorts going on. Raven did say it was an internal matter. Maybe there was more to this feud than just two rival magical groups who employed different methods in their practice.

Although if Oak had been involved with the Baltimore mages, why would he have chosen an insurance adjuster as his victim? Unless he had a reason to be pissed at her and was killing two birds with one stone.

"Any details on the claim? Did Benton Leigh receive money from the insurance policy?"

Tremelay consulted his notepad. It had been rapidly filling up in the last few days. "Yeah. Says the claim paid out. Television, some DVDs, artwork and jewelry. Not a huge amount was taken. Seems like the normal steal-what-you-can-pawn robbery."

Okay, so no grudge against the insurance adjuster, then. I yanked my hair back into a ponytail, rubbing at the sheet marks that I was sure were on my face. Then I followed the detective out, grabbing my purse and my sword before locking the door behind me—both with the deadbolt and with a magical hex. It wouldn't do to have the landlord waltz in unannounced and see my unauthorized modifications.

Tremelay sighed, staring pointedly at my sword. "Front seat out of view, and please keep it sheathed unless a lion-headed monster attacks."

I hid a grin. "Gotcha."

"One more thing," he said after we'd both climbed in and were on our way. "The two dead junkie guys? Cause of death was obviously due to the removal of organs essential for life, but both had enough heroin in their systems to kill them."

I shook my head, thinking what a tragedy it was that most addicts were on a short road to overdose.

"It's still murder," he added.

"Well, then let's arrest this angel and throw the book at him." It wasn't nice of me to rub in the fact that he would probably never be able to see the killer brought to justice, but I was more than a bit on edge after my close call with the demon last night.

"I'm trying to figure out how I can arrest the person who summoned the angel," he snapped back. "The angel is a weapon, just like a gun."

No, not exactly. "Let's concentrate on the death magic for now and decide how to handle the killing by angel and killing by demon later."

CHAPTER 17

Setting Sun was the type of shop you went to if you wanted scented candles, ornamental potpourri holders, or decorative primitive figurines. Farther back in the store you'd find essential oils, dried herbs and tea blends, and a variety of generic protection and divination materials. Through the back curtain, past the meditation/yoga space was a door. It looked like your standard emergency exit door with a push bar and shiny gray paint. The difference was what you would see when you went through. And the fact that you could push on that bar all day but the door wouldn't open without a key.

Staff had the key, and it wasn't on a keychain. Plus they wouldn't open that door for just anybody. There were reasons spells beyond the simplest of charms required difficult-to-get materials and very specific incantations. The world would be a frightening place if everyone could throw curses around or summon demons with a few days practice and a handful of grass from their backyard.

Of course, the world was a frightening place when skilled mages were bold enough to sacrifice a woman and use her body and soul for dark magic. Or when mages summoned demons and angels into this world without proper skill and know-how. And yes, I was including myself in that category, given my botched summoning last week.

The guy behind the counter smelled of patchouli and had a shock of fire-engine red hair that stood out to each side of his head from a center part. The woman he was ringing up made a joke about the weather, and he laughed. It was a squeaky, high-pitched laugh that reminded me of a Muppet.

Once the customer left, Elmo approached us smiling. "What can I help the two of you with?" Before either of us could reply, the smile left his face. "Wait. I know you. You're that Templar girl."

Seriously? I'd never been in this store or met this guy. I'd covered my tattoo with the wide leather bracelet. Was there a wanted poster out with my picture on it? *Curses shall rain down on those who speak or sell candles to this Templar?*

Thankfully Tremelay stepped up. "Yes, she is. And I'm a cop." He flashed his badge and Elmo winced.

"Fine. *You* can buy candles. *She* can't."

Racist pigs. "I'm working as a consultant with the police department about a series of murders in Baltimore."

"The murderers killed people with candles?" Elmo was being deliberately obtuse. It annoyed me almost as much as his freaky hairdo.

Tremelay took over the interrogation. "No, the murderers performed a magical ritual in which they sacrificed a woman. Now, I know you sell more than candles here, and as the nearest shop carrying ceremonial magic supplies, it makes sense that the killers might be customers of yours." The detective put away his badge. He was amazingly calm given the clerk's hostility.

Fear tightened the clerk's face. "What exactly do you need?"

The detective looked over to me and I motioned for him to continue to take the lead. He was getting more information with his cop-talk than I would as a Templar.

"We're trying to find out who bought dog bones in the last month."

Elmo gave an exaggerated shrug. "Lots of people. Dog bones are top of the list when you're doing magic that involves a psychopomp."

Spiritualists sometimes used them. Although not your run-of-the-mill ghost chaser with their pocket EMF and motion sensing cameras, or even priests. The only ones who tended to use dog bones in clearing a haunted room were those with skills in necromancy. I knew of only one necromancer in the Baltimore area, and although I'm sure Russell did have dog bones, he would have shelled out the extra for a skull rather than use these dinky toy-dog leg bones.

"These people do death magic," I said. "They buy dog bones in sets of four, along with blood chalices and knives for sacrificial work. These aren't necromancers."

Elmo looked around the store then began twisting his hands together. "That's pretty much every mage in Baltimore. You know that. You used to hang with Haul Du before they kicked you out. They go straight to the source in Baltimore."

I suddenly felt like someone was sitting on my chest—someone who weighed over four hundred pounds. "Source?"

The clerk swallowed hard. "Source. I mean, I don't do that sort of thing. I don't ask my customers what they're doing with the stuff they buy. It's not my place to judge."

He couldn't mean what I thought he meant. I glanced over at Tremelay, who was staring at the pair of us as if we were suddenly speaking an alien language. "They *ail* do soul work? All of them?"

"No! Well, not usually. You need a soul trap for that

sort of thing. They can take decades to put together, but only if you've got the specific skill-set to make your own. Existing ones aren't easy to come by. Cheap ones are a couple thousand, but if you're going to go to the effort to kill someone and take their soul, you want to maximize the energy output. A good soul trap can be fifty grand, if you can manage to find one for sale, that is."

"Sell one lately?" Tremelay asked.

Elmo's eyes bugged out. "You kidding? We deal in basic magical supplies, not high-end stuff like that. I don't even remember the last time I *saw* one for sale."

"But someone in Baltimore has one," I told him.

The clerk nodded. "I heard the rumors, although I think it's a recent acquisition."

This whole thing was making me ill. Fifty grand so you could murder someone and use their soul to power a ritual. "I know the mages in Baltimore do death magic, but usually that's just animals, not humans and *souls*. That's...sick."

"And summoning demons isn't? Where do you think demons get their power? This is just cutting out the middle-man. It's safer."

Safer except for the victim being sacrificed. Yes, demons took souls, but that was with the consent of the human. There were deals, an exchange of sorts. What we were talking about was murder.

He must have seen the horror on my face, because he quickly backpedaled. "I've never seen it. That's just what people say. It's probably just a rumor. I doubt they're using anything more than chickens and rats."

"We need a list of who bought dog bones, blood chalices, and sacrificial knives." Tremelay wasn't buying the guy's sudden ignorance any more than I was.

Elmo shook his head. "I can't. They'll kill me. It's not just one or two mages, it's a lot. I'll be ruined if word gets out that I gave up that kind of information."

"You'll be ruined if I have to subpoena that information," Tremelay told him.

The guy set his jaw. "All you get is a list of customers who bought candles. You don't seriously think those guys pay by credit card or personal check, do you? They don't even use their real names. I honestly can't help you."

I pulled out a picture I'd downloaded off the internet of Ronald Stull. "This guy one of them?"

Elmo took a step back and swallowed hard. "I can't remember."

I was about to get my sword to see if that would jog the guy's memory a bit, but Tremelay had a different idea.

"Okay, then what do you remember? Help me out here, buddy so I don't need to get your shop shut down for trafficking in human remains and illegal, endangered-species animal parts."

Elmo winced. "Look, ever since they got the soul trap, the Baltimore group does soul work. They're *all* involved with death magic, but in the last few months they started sacrificial magic. I think their group is twenty to thirty mages. They call themselves Fiore Noir."

Ugh. Never trust a magical group whose name mixes romance languages. I waved the picture at Elmo once more. "So Ronald Stull was part of Fiore Noir?"

The clerk chewed his lip. "Breaker. That guy…he's got a reputation for revenge. You gotta understand, I say anything and I'll be the next guy bleeding out in their circle."

"He's dead. Is he part of Fiore Noir and can you describe any of the other members?"

Elmo practically slumped with relief. "Yeah, he's Fiore Noir. He isn't their leader, but I got the feeling he had a lot of influence and was in charge of some of their major magical workings. He was the one who came out to buy supplies. I don't know any other mages who I can specifically say were in Fiore Noir, but Breaker had a friend. This guy made Breaker look like a saint. Big guy, mid-fifties, I'd guess. One look and you knew not to cross him. I didn't even want to meet his eyes, you know? Anyway, from what I hear, he's the one who loaned Fiore Noir the soul trap."

The stranger. Unfortunately big, mean-looking mid-fifties guys weren't a rare occurrence in Baltimore.

"Anything else you remember?" Tremelay asked. "Names, even magical ones? Dates or times for their rituals? Locations?"

Elmo thought a moment then nodded. "I overheard Breaker last week on the phone. From what he said, I think they were doing their rituals near Security Boulevard. There's a big park there with a stream running through it."

"Dead Run," Tremelay mused. I had no idea where that was, although I'd driven by signs for Security Boulevard a few times since I'd moved here. "It's a narrow winding park, but there are some spots where there's nothing nearby beyond the highway. That area's mostly businesses. Perfect place to conduct midnight activity unseen."

The clerk nodded. "Yeah, that's it. Something went wrong last time, so they moved to a spot with lots of abandoned buildings."

Old Town Mall. The detective and I exchanged knowing looks. Was it wrong to be this excited? It was a decent lead, even if we didn't have names and addresses of the mages involved. From what Elmo said, Bethany's sacrifice had been the first in the Mall, but, like Janice had suspected, it wasn't this Fiore Noir group's first death magic ritual. I got a feeling that a search of Dead Run would reveal signs of an abandoned ritual space, and possibly the remains of previous victims. Unless the group had some mass disposal site, they probably had left the bodies there. Transporting dead was risky. It would have been easier to dig a giant hole and toss them all into it.

"One last thing." I pulled another picture out of my pocket. "Do you recognize this woman?"

Elmo looked at the picture of Bethany Scarborough and shook his head. "No. I've never seen her in the shop before."

I didn't get the feeling he was lying. We had some forward momentum on the mages who'd killed her, but still no clue as to why they'd chosen Bethany. I was still in the dark as to why Benton and Alban had wanted to kill a list of people—the entirety of the Fiore Noir mages it sounded like. And then there was that angel. What role did Araziel play in any of this?

And one more thing. "How did you know who I was?"

Elmo smirked. "Haul Du made a big deal when they threw you out. Yeah, it was kind of embarrassing that you'd fooled them for eight months, but they were more interested in making sure you didn't gain entry to any other group than preserving their dignity."

Great. "So you're not allowed to sell me anything? Or are you supposed to report me to someone?"

He sniffed. "Both. There's a price on your head. Normally I'd be all about collecting that bounty, but it's not enough to risk pissing off a bunch of Templars. I don't need that kind of hurt coming down on me. Besides, it's like five hundred dollars. Chump change."

I was so shocked I could barely wrap my brain around his words. A price on my head? Me? "The DC group put a bounty on me? Dark Iron put a bounty on me? Like a dead or alive bounty?"

"Someone in that DC group would be happy see you dead, and they'd pay for it, too. The Baltimore group, Fiore Noir just wants you out of town. Forever."

CHAPTER 18

"You thinking what I'm thinking?" I asked Tremelay as we climbed into his car.

"I'm thinking I've got a busy day ahead of me," he replied. "I'm gonna try and pull a few guys to help us search Dead Run for signs of rituals and possibly other victims. Then I need to file for that warrant on Ronald Stull's place, and fast track that list of names we got from the DC house."

"Our killers are on that list," I told him. Actually from what we'd been told the entire list had been complicit in at least one murder. Probably more. If Elmo was right and all of Fiore Noir had participated, there was a lot they needed to answer to.

And then there was this lame bounty on my head. What the heck was that about? I could see Fiore Noir being nervous about having a Templar in their backyard when they were doing soul magic, but who at Haul Du would care enough to throw a few bucks at anyone who took me out? I was a member for only eight months, and when they threw me out, I left quietly. Yeah, Dark Iron seemed to have a particularly large stick up his ass when it came to me, but disliking someone intensely was a far cry from putting out a passive-aggressive plea for their murder.

I needed to call Raven. I couldn't see a mage psycho enough to kill just to please Dark Iron, but it worried me. Was Elmo being dramatic? Would I find myself plowed down by a city bus one day, or hit on the head with a chunk of falling cement just so some mage could score a few hundred dollars?

I'm sure it was nothing. Mages just didn't murder people they casually disliked. Elmo was trying to scare me. It worked, but I wasn't going to let my paranoia distract me from this case. I had things to do.

"So, wanna grab a bite before we start hiking through Dead Run? Our drive-through choices seem to be burgers or chicken."

Yum, especially if the detective was paying. But I had a tight schedule today. "I'm meeting my sister at my place at noon to banish that demon from DC, and I've got some prep work to do first."

"Call me when you're done and I'll let you know where we are in our search. You can come out and meet me."

Were we *friends*? I mean, I know I was an expert witness and all that, but Detective Tremelay seemed unusually eager for my company. Although searching for dead bodies and magical sites in a suburban wilderness hardly seemed the sort of thing buddies would do together. Well, normal buddies anyway.

My phone chimed and I looked down at the message. "I'm probably gonna be tied up most of the day. Can you call me and let me know if you find anything? Otherwise I'll check in with you later tonight."

He'd have to search Dead Run alone because I just got a message I'd been waiting all day for.

I knew Bethany Scarborough. Pissed. So fucking pissed that I'm going to tell you everything I know. Meet me at O'Grady's in Westminster at five.

Raven. And as interested as I was to figure out how Bethany was connected to all this beyond the settlement of an insurance claim, I was happier to know my ex-friend was going to fully cooperate and that she'd reached out to *me* to help.

CHAPTER 19

"This...this has got to be the craziest thing I've ever seen."

Athena was strangely enchanted by my tiny, ratty apartment. She was equally enchanted by the double circle with two sets of symbols that I'd just finished painting on my dry, gray floor. My sister handed me a box and threw her coat on the sofa before kneeling down to inspect my work. I winced, thinking about what the floor leveler was going to do to her creamy linen pants. Although her pants were the least of her worries. Athena drove a dark blue Mercedes S class that she'd left in my parking lot in between the twenty-year-old Geo Metro with mismatched body panels and an AMC Gremlin that looked like it hadn't moved from its space since 1978. She'd be lucky if there was a scrap of metal left on that car when she went to leave.

"What are you going to do in this thing? I've seen you make charms before and you've never used something this elaborate."

"It will concentrate any magical energies, so anything I do will have more oomph. Everyone should have one of these.

They're very useful." I opened up the box and unwrapped the contents. One was a Breyer horse—a four inch tall chestnut mare that reminded me of a painting back home. One was a resin fox, tail curled around his legs as he sat. The third was a prickly brush hedgehog with a smirk painted on his wooden face. I put them up on the book shelf with the others and stood back to admire them. Great grandma Essie was... eccentric. She was also well over one hundred years old. I had no idea why she was sending me all these little animals, but they'd been arriving steadily by post over the last week.

"They're cute. Are they all from Gran?" Athena shook her head. "Got any idea what they're for?"

"Decoration?" Essie was a witch, so there was a remote chance the figurines could be intended for magical purposes. Or they were just ornaments. Maybe she was spending way too much time on eBay. Shrugging, I went into the kitchen to grab my sister a drink.

"So, I've got some news." Athena shot me a mischievous grin. "We didn't want to jinx things, so Pietrus and I haven't said anything about it yet, but we have a baby."

I squealed, leaving the sodas I'd pulled from the fridge on the counter and running to hug my sister. And then wincing as she hugged me in return, my fresh scabs from my injuries pulling all along my back.

Athena and her husband had been trying unsuccessfully to get pregnant since their wedding. Adoption was unusual for Templar families, but we'd all supported their choice when the pair had made the announcement two years ago that they had filled out an application.

"Name? Son? Daughter? Does he look like his papa?" I teased.

"She's six months old and we're calling her Jet. Pietrus and I fly to Seoul next week to meet her and hopefully bring her home."

I cried. Tough girl me broke down and actually sobbed on my sister's shoulder. She did the same and by the time we pulled away from each other we were a soggy mess. "I'm so happy for you both," I told her, wiping my eyes.

She reached out a hand to cup my cheek. It was an unusual display of affection for our reserved family. "I hope one day *you* are so blessed."

I laughed. "Might need to find myself a husband first, unless you think Mom and Dad will be okay with the whole unwed mother thing."

Athena snorted. "Well, you make a darned good Auntie in the meantime."

There was that. I handed her one of the sodas and raised mine. "To baby Jet, may her parents not kill Auntie Aria for spoiling her rotten."

"Here, here." Athena took a sip, then folded her arms across her chest. "So what's the plan with this demon? I've never hunted one down before. Do we need a '67 Impala?"

Soda nearly came from my nose at her joke. This *would* be new to her, though. Templars didn't hunt down demons. We hadn't hunted down much of anything in centuries. Hundreds of years ago we banished any evil that crossed our paths, threatened our pilgrims, or tried to attack the Temple. Otherwise we pretty much ignored it. I knew what the elders' opinions of this endeavor would be. Foolish humans called the infernal forces to their side and suffered the consequences. They'd counsel we leave the demon for Haul Du to handle. That's how humans learned the lessons of hubris. If we jumped in and saved the day all the time, then there would be no need for personal responsibility. The elders wouldn't lose any sleep about innocent deaths. God would protect the innocent.

I didn't agree with that kind of thinking. And the fact that Athena was by my side meant she must feel the same. I doubted the novelty of demon banishment or the ties of our familial bond were the only reason she'd rushed out early on her symposium.

"We're going to summon the demon. We've got his name and his sigil. I've got a copy of the original summoning that ties him to this world."

Athena again made a circuit around the circle, eyeing the symbols. "Seriously? You can do that? I know you were messing around with Goetic demons last year with the group in DC, but Innyhal is a completely different class."

"Which is why we need to summon him. I don't know about you, but I don't have time to go driving all over Maryland and DC looking for Innyhal, even if we did have a sweet ride of an Impala." Summoning wasn't just for bringing demons over from hell, it was also for bringing them to heel and holding them in place while you sent them home.

Athena pursed her lips. "Banishing is easier the Templar way."

Yeah, when it actually worked. "Well, I'll summon him here, then you can banish him the Templar way. Sound good?"

My sister grinned, looking far younger than her thirty-five years. "Only if you show me how to do this summoning thing. Just for research, you know. It's always good to know how these things work in case I'm on call when the Temple comes under attack."

The Temple hadn't come under attack in over eight hundred years, but I understood the need for preparedness. There was stuff hidden away there that should never see the light of day.

"Deal."

I got out the chalk and got to work. The portions of the magical space that were universal to all spells I'd done in paint, but chalk would make up the specifics for today's work. The benefit was that it would be easy to clean off with a wet sponge when done. The drawback was that it was oh-so-easy to smudge, and chalk didn't provide quite the clean lines that paint did. Such tradeoffs in magic were commonplace.

Athena followed me, making thoughtful noises but otherwise respectful of my need to concentrate. Done, I stepped back and flexed my cramped hands. "Showtime!"

We pulled our swords, but I set mine on the kitchen table because I needed both hands free to summon. I'd copied down the relevant parts of Benton and Alban's ritual because trying to read from grainy cell-phone photos during a summoning was a good way to get killed. They'd preferred their rituals in weird, mangled Latin, which had never been my strong suit and wasn't the language I used when performing magic. It was important for me to tie as much of this as I could to the original summoning, so mangled Latin it was. Hopefully my failing marks in the ancient language wouldn't end up causing my death today.

Paper in hand, I poured a glass of cheap wine and put both the bottle and the glass just inside the inner circle. Then I dimmed the lights and pulled the shades before lighting the candles. Slowly I moved from quarter to quarter, calling for the energy, spooling it into the confines of the circle and locking in the protective space. I was extra careful, worried about a repeat performance of what happened the last time I'd summoned.

The candlelight danced against the walls. It gave the room a romantic ambiance, even for noon in August. For a brief moment I'd wished I was enjoying the cheap wine with a male companion rather than summoning a demon.

"Ready." Athena held her sword less as a weapon and more as a religious object. It was a wise move given that she didn't have the magical enhancements on her sword like I did. For Templars, their sword was a weapon of steel as well as one of faith. Maybe I was lacking a bit in the faith department because I'd added magic into the mix.

I got right down to business with the evocation. Evocation because I was commanding an appearance rather than politely requesting one. Hence the floor covered with symbols and geometric shapes. Normally I'd never consider summoning a demon at noon, but we weren't really moving one across the planes, simply calling one from wherever the heck he'd gone into my apartment.

"Innyhal. *Iam non dico vos mihi.*" I picked up my sword, putting the force of my will into each word. A breeze blew through the room, stirring the curtains and flickering the candle flames.

"*Apparebis in conspectus meo et praecepta meo quae praecepero summonds.*" The wind picked up speed, swirling like a lazy cyclone. Suddenly the ambient light from outside dimmed, plunging the room into a darkness relieved only by the candles. Athena stood opposite me, lit from below like a warrior from a horror movie.

"*Veni,* Innyhal. *Veni. Ego praecipio vobis.*"

The wind on the outside of the circle died abruptly, leaving an eerie silence and a near vacuum. Now the candles flickered outward, pushed by the energies held tightly within the summoning triangle. A column of smoke rose, blocking my view of Athena. I heard the sound of our breathing, like an oncoming train compared to the quiet around me.

The smoke coalesced into a bipedal shape—a shape with a snouted head and a flowing mane. Gigantic birdlike legs formed, like the lower half of an ostrich had been attached to a human torso. I took a breath and looked into the four eyes of Innyhal.

The scar on my side ached. Now was not the time for that

to act up, so I clenched my teeth and tightened my grip on my sword.

"Bitch. I should have killed you when I had my claws in you."

Yeah, why hadn't he? I wasn't sure I wanted Athena to hear the answer, I wasn't sure *I* wanted to hear the answer, so I kept that question silent.

"The two humans who brought you here from hell, what task did they want you to accomplish? What did you need to do before they would return you to hell?"

His snout widened into a toothy grin. "What I do best, girl. Kill."

Duh. I figured that. "And who did they want you to kill?" Who? Whom? I wasn't sure if appropriate grammar mattered in this instance or not.

He shrugged, a peculiar movement for a man with a lion head. "They had a list. We didn't get that far."

I'd taken a photo of the list. Tremelay and Zrubek were already working on those connections. I was simply relieved that if the worst happened and we didn't manage to banish this demon, he wasn't planning on continuing with the organized hit he'd been brought over to do.

Of course, that meant he would just go around killing whoever struck his fancy. Still not a good plan. "Why did they want those people dead?"

It was a long shot. Even with the bizarre head and four eyes, I could read the look of incredulity on Innyhal's face. "Because they did, that's why. I don't concern myself with petty human emotions. Silly creatures needing a reason to end another's life when the sheer joy of slicing humans into little strips is the only reason necessary."

He was lying. Don't ask me how I knew. It's not like I'm used to reading the facial expressions of lions or anything.

"I demand you, held in my circle under my command,

answer me truthfully. Why did the mages want those humans to die?"

The demon shook his head, like I'd just zapped him with static shock on his giant furry ruff. "They killed some friends of theirs. Doesn't matter though because Mansi wants them dead, too. They take souls. They take that which is ours."

I caught my breath. Who had Fiore Noir killed that were friends with Tempest and Oak? And who was Mansi? Across from me Athena raised her eyebrows and mouthed *"Souls?"*

They take that which is ours. Maybe working soul magic put a giant crosshair on your chest when it came to demons. I know I had a dangerous creature testing the power of my circle, but my intellectual curiosity had kicked in.

"So all those who practice sacrificial magic are enemies of the demons?"

He hesitated, four eyes narrowing. "Humans kill humans. It's truly a beautiful thing, but souls belong to us. Souls are not for the humans to take."

I remembered the dog bones keeping the psychopomps from Bethany. They'd used her soul, not just her death, to power their spell. Evidently that sort of thing pissed off demons, and I wasn't sure why.

"Don't you all take the soul when the deal is struck? When the human sells it to you?" Did they object to the practice in general, or were there demon-claimed souls still in bodies that were being stolen? What was going on here?

"Aria," Athena interrupted in a whisper. "Can we stop talking and start banishing?"

No. Because I wasn't done with Innyhal yet. "How do you keep track of your humans if you don't at least take part of their souls during your deal?"

I didn't get it. A human who'd sold his soul would be of no use in death magic beyond the energy his actual murder created. No amount of dog bones would have helped hold fast a soul that was already gone.

Innyhal approached the edge of the circle, runes lighting and sizzling as he ran a claw along them. "Rotted meat is far sweeter than fresh from the kill. Sometimes we want a soul to stew in the actions of its vessel before feasting. We leave an owned soul occasionally so it is at its peak when it comes time for us to dine."

Gah, I hated demons. Rotted food metaphors were probably all I was going to get out of this one. Athena was right, it was past time to send Innyhal home.

"Mali spiritus mandabo ne redirect ab orbe nostro navibus expellas rursus convocari."

Innyhal paced the confines of the circle as I spoke. Athena held her sword aloft, ready to banish this demon the Templar way if the ritual Oak and Tempest had written didn't work.

The demon paused, staring directly at Athena. My sister didn't even waver, her gaze steady as she made eye contact with Innyhal. He smiled that lion smile and I was the one who wavered. Why was he smiling?

"Vade et amplius iam. Go now."

He didn't "go now." He just continued to smile and reached one of his long, pointy dagger claws through the line of protective symbols. Suddenly I realized my mistake. I'd needed to replicate Tempest and Oak's summoning circle in order to call Innyhal here—the very summoning circle that had failed to hold the demon the last time it had been used.

"Athena!" I jumped, crashing through the chalk lines past Innyhal to leap on my sister. The flickering symbols stung my skin like an electric shock as I passed through. Athena and I hit the ground, both of our swords clattering from our hands. She gasped, the air knocked from her lungs. I gasped too, but from the scorch of fire across my already injured back. I frantically ripped off my shirt, feeling the scabs peel along with the strips of cloth.

Flinging the burned shirt aside, I reached for my fallen sword only to see it slide away from my hand.

"I don't care *who* has marked you, you'll die for this, Templar."

I crawled for the sword. *"T'voghnel anmijapes."*

It was a desperate attempt, the only card I had to play right now. The banishment didn't work this time either. Innyhal laughed at my effort and grabbed my hair, yanking me into the circle. This time the symbols didn't sting, the circle already having been broken. What *did* hurt was the demon's hand twisting my hair and his claws scratching my bare stomach.

"T'voghnel anmijapes."

The claws left my waist at Athena's words but the demon still kept his grip on my hair. I heard the clang of a sword, heard my sister's shriek. I swung out a foot in a blind attempt to kick the demon. It wouldn't do much good, but I couldn't just let this demon play crack-the-whip with my hair, or let him kill both my sister and me.

Suddenly the demon howled like Satan's hounds had their teeth in him. There's no way my foot had done that much pain, but inexplicably Innyhal's grip on my hair loosened.

I twisted free and rolled, springing to my feet as soon as I was clear of the circle.

"Aria!" Athena kicked my sword over to me. She was clutching her hand, her own sword sticking through one of my kitchen cabinets. I grabbed Trusty, whirled around…and stared. There wasn't just one demon in my house, there were two. Innyhal stood in the broken circle, his four eyes bulging as a demon of black smoke and fire squeezed inky hands around his neck. The smoke demon grinned, his sharp teeth white. And then he winked at me and threw Innyhal at my feet.

I hesitated.

"Well? Go ahead. My gift to you, little Templar." The smoke demon cocked his head, his eyes dancing coals of orange and red. "I won't request anything of you in return for this. Consider it…what do you humans call it? A freebie?"

The demon at my feet made a choking sound, snapping me out of my state of shock.

"*T'voghnel anmijapes.*" I swung my sword downward, plunging it into the demon's chest. *This* time the banishment worked. Innyhal screamed, his body hardening then shattering into a million bits of shale.

Without hesitating I raised my sword again.

The smoke demon laughed, and I swung wide missing him entirely.

"Yes, yes. Back to hell with me, too. Until next time, little Templar." The smoke swirled and the demon vanished, but not before raining little sparks all over my living room. I raced about, still clutching my sword as I stamped out the embers. Then I went to help my sister.

"Aria?" Athena panted, still clutching her hand. "What in hell was *that* thing?"

CHAPTER 20

O'Grady's was, true to its name, an Irish pub. It was also housed in an old stone building with a winding staircase to the upper restaurant floor, tapestries on the walls, and scotch eggs. Raven was late. I was halfway through my dinner and starting to worry when she finally arrived.

It was as if time had stood still since I'd last seen my friend. Her windblown light-brown hair had burgundy tips which matched her leather jacket. There was even a red stone in the hoop through the side of her nose. Smile lines crinkled at the edges of her eyes as she saw me, but there was a weary look about her face that hadn't been there before. Without a word she grabbed me in a hug like she never wanted to let go. I crushed her back, my eyes watering at the pain her hands on my back caused. Didn't matter. She could have rubbed salt in the wounds and I still would have relished this hug.

"Missed you," I told her.

"Missed you, too. I was an idiot to put Haul Du in front of a friendship. Life is too damned short to do that kind of thing. People die without warning and then there are all sorts of regrets. I don't want there to ever be regrets."

I had no idea what had spurred this maudlin speech from the usually cheerful and salty friend. We pulled away and sat, Raven looking in horror at the contents of my plate.

"What the hell are you eating, Kite?"

Kite. I'd taken a magical name just as everyone in Haul Du did, but once I was kicked out no one used it. Raven had called me Aria the few times we'd communicated since then. It was like I'd been stripped of my name as well as my identity with the group. Hearing her call me that once again stirred up memories and feelings of resentment that I really wished I could let go.

But in a way it felt good, as if I was once more her sister in the magical arts. I wasn't just that Templar outsider anymore.

I waved a fork at my plate. "It's a Scotch egg—hardboiled egg wrapped up in a bunch of ground sausage then deep fried."

"With gravy on top." She wrinkled her bejeweled nose and sniffed. "You Brits are so weird."

My family had been in America since before the Revolution, long before Raven's ancestors had stepped off the boat from Italy, but there was no use arguing. In her mind, my family had never fully left jolly old England.

I wanted to ask her how she was, whether she'd managed to get that sweetwater spell to work, if her little French bulldog had ever stopped terrorizing the neighbor's cat. Was she still dating Reynard, who was just as foxy as his namesake, or had that gone down in flames as I'd predicted? I didn't have the chance to ask. Before I could say a word she rested her chin on steepled hands and looked sorrowfully into my eyes.

"I can't believe Bliss is dead. I heard the news and I

decided I just didn't care anymore what Dark Iron said, whether he kicked me out of Haul Du or not. The guy hates me anyway. I don't know why I put up with his abusive crap for so long. He's got his favorites, and everyone else can die as far as he cares."

I squirmed thinking of Elmo's comment at the shop. Maybe it wasn't personal. Maybe Dark Iron hated everyone and secretly put five hundred dollar bounties on a whole list of people.

Raven shifted angrily in her seat. "Dark Iron is such a cold bastard. He didn't care. He didn't care when the Dupont Circle guys died, and he didn't care about Bliss either. 'Just as well,' he said. Can you believe it? Bliss was so sweet. Everyone liked her. Murdered, sacrificed by those assholes. And nobody seems to care."

Wait, *Bliss*? Bethany Scarborough was practicing? Nothing I'd read about her said "mage."

Most mages were stealthy, keeping their magical activities secret. Some were downright paranoid. I guess Bliss had been in the latter category. "She was part of the Baltimore group? Why would they have sacrificed one of their own? Did she find out something she shouldn't have known about? Get on a powerful mage's wrong side?"

Raven shook her head, eyes practically sparking with anger. "She was with *us*, part of Haul Du. At first I thought it was a robbery or something. That's what they told me when I called to check on her at her job. Why her? Why would someone have sacrificed her?"

My friend's voice was raising in volume to the point where other patrons were beginning to look at us. I tapped a finger to my lips and shook my head. "Death magic. They took her soul."

Bethany was part of Haul Du? It actually made sense if there was a feud going on between them and Fiore Noir.

Although grabbing a member of a rival group for a ritual sacrifice was truly taking this fight over the line. It was one thing to throw spells at one another, even send demons after one another, but to kill another mage, to take their soul… somehow it seemed far more nefarious than sacrificing an innocent insurance adjuster from Westminster.

And Dark Iron didn't care? What a crappy attitude for a leader to have when a rival group kills one of your members.

For a second I wondered if Tempest and Oak had been trying to avenge Bethany's death by sending Innyhal after Fiore Noir. Although knowing those two I couldn't see that they would have valued the life of a "nice" woman enough to risk their lives avenging hers. Yes, there was the slight against their organization, but I wasn't sure Bliss's death would have been enough of a slap in the face—especially if Dark Iron hadn't been bothered about her death. There must have been other friends whose sacrifice bothered them enough they were making a deal with a demon for assassination—a deal that cost them their lives.

"I'm *so fucking pissed*. You've got no idea how fucking pissed I am." Raven seemed to change before me, from quirky mage with a nose ring to an avenging Valkyrie. "Why would they do that to Bliss? Why? She only practiced the whitest of magic. She wouldn't even *attend* when we summoned Goetic demons. She'd never done anything to anger the Fiore Noir group. Ever. She was a *nice* person. She never associated with Fiore Noir. She didn't even know them. Why would anyone do this to her?"

It was the same question I had. "Is it possible she was looking into changing groups? Baltimore is closer, and if she wasn't into demonology then Haul Du doesn't seem like that good of a fit for her magic."

"No!" Raven recoiled. "Baltimore is just…they're sloppy and careless and they do death magic. I don't think every one of them sacrifices humans, but Bliss never would have belonged to a group that killed cats and rabbits. Plus, they lack appreciation for the details and nuances of magical work. I know death magic, outside of human sacrifice, doesn't violate any laws in the magical community, but they're a bunch of loose cannons, every single one of them. We've filed complaints before about their methods. I've got no idea how they stay affiliated. They're back-alley, low-class scum."

That speech didn't sound at all like Raven. I recognized Reynard's party line a mile away. Of course, most of Haul Du would have agreed with him. Their dedication to careful research and attention to detail was one of the things that had drawn me to the group.

"Well, maybe she insulted them? Kind of like you just did, although maybe to their faces?"

Raven shook her head. "Not Bliss. She was a kind person. I can't believe *anyone* would harm her."

I had hoped Raven knew what was behind Bethany's murder, but it seemed she was just as stumped as I was. "I know you're risking your membership with Haul Du just meeting with me like this, and I truly appreciate it because I need your help." I went on to tell Raven all the details I'd left out of my phone messages.

She sat for a moment, then shook her head. "I'm actually not surprised Tempest and Oak tried to kill Fiore Noir. They threatened to in a meeting last week. Most everyone figured it just was a threat, but I saw how angry they were and feared they might actually do it. Dark Iron didn't sanction their plan, but he didn't exactly forbid them either. I got the feeling that if they'd succeeded, all would have been swept under the rug." She frowned. "This isn't the group I joined. Haul Du shouldn't turn the other way while people are killed or condone the summoning of demons for murder. There are channels to lodge a complaint when there's suspicion of wrongdoing, ways of addressing those suspicions without summoning up an assassination demon."

"Innyhal told me, under a binding of truth, that he'd been summoned to kill the people on that list—Fiore Noir. The cops and I found the list along with the summoning ritual. No one summons a Mars demon unless they intend to murder. Tempest and Oak have already paid for that. Now it's up to us to make sure that those who killed Bliss as well as others with their death magic rituals, pay for their crimes. I swear by my sword, Raven, that I'm going to bring these people to justice. Baltimore is *my* town."

Raven nodded. "And I'm with you one hundred percent of the way. This weird feud between Haul Du and Fiore Noir? I'll let you know every last detail. I don't know the names of who is in Fiore Noir, but there are ways of finding that out—servitor spells, or certain demons who might be able to give me that information."

Which made me think about something Innyhal had said. Hadn't he said that the demons were angry with Fiore Noir for taking souls? That humans were taking what the demons felt belonged to them? There was something there at the edge of my brain, tickling for me to let it in. I just had to figure out the connection.

Raven took a deep breath, one fingernail tracing the woodgrain of the surface. "There were rumors that the accident at Dupont Circle last week *wasn't* an accident. It's what started this whole feud between Haul Du and Fiore Noir and what set off Tempest and Oak."

"What? What accident?" I'd been rather busy last week dealing with vampires and a necromancer, and had no idea what Raven was talking about.

"Last Thursday there was a gas leak at a gallery in Dupont Circle and before it could be capped off or the area evacuated the building exploded. It was all over the news, didn't you see it? Twelve people were killed. Three of them were Haul Du mages who were there for a pre-opening dedication."

No, I hadn't heard. Some mages did charms and protective magic for a fee, but normally that was a one-person sort of thing. This dedication must have been complex if it had required three mages to do the ritual. And obviously it hadn't been completed, or the explosion wouldn't have occurred. There was no use paying big money for protective magic if it didn't guard against such accidents.

"Why would anyone think a gas leak and an explosion was intentional? Had the mages received threats?" I made a mental note to ask Tremelay to call Zrubek and get more details on the explosion.

"The fire marshall ruled it accidental, and no, there were no threats, but Reynard had heard that it was a hit, that someone had paid Fiore Noir to take them out. When he asked, Dark Iron said Reynard was to ignore it. That he'd take care of it himself. I don't know if Reynard talked to Tempest and Oak or not, but the next day the whole group was up in arms over the rumor."

I leaned closer. "How did Reynard find out? Could it have just been someone trying to stir up trouble between the groups? I can't see Dark Iron ignoring a blatant attack on Haul Du mages."

Raven shook her head. "Remember I said Dark Iron had favorites? Well, these guys weren't part of his inner circle. They had all gone down to Argentina a few months back and ever since they returned things have been icy between the four of them. Maybe Dark Iron didn't care enough about the dead mages to stir up trouble with Fiore Noir, or maybe he was trying to handle it himself diplomatically. We didn't really have any solid proof that it was a Fiore Noir attack.

It's not like we could go in wands-ablaze on a bunch of rumors."

I thought for a second. "The guy at the supply shop in Ellicott City? The one who laughs like Elmo? He said Fiore Noir wanted me out of Baltimore, but that someone in Haul Du wanted me dead and was willing to pay five hundred dollars for the deed. Do you think...?"

I could hardly complete the sentence. It was one thing for Dark Iron to turn the other way while someone took out a mage who had lost his favor. I'm sure he'd dance at my funeral. But could he possibly be involved in murder? He was an asshole. He just didn't care if certain people died. That didn't mean he had anything to do with their demise.

Raven choked back a laugh. "Right. Dark Iron wouldn't spend five hundred dollars if it would save his mother's life. He's cheap. He hates you, but you're out of his hair. You're not causing any problems. That idiot in Ellicott City was just yanking your chain. There's no hit on you."

Good. Because I hated looking over my shoulder.

"Three mages died, and now Bliss?" Raven shook her head in disbelief. "What's the use of being affiliated with Haul Du if Dark Iron isn't going to have your back in stuff like this? Word gets out that any of us who aren't his buddies are fair game...? Shit, we cut the wrong person off in traffic, and that's it."

She was right. It made me glad for once that I was no longer with the group and that I had a different group who always had my back. Being a Templar carried weight, but it wasn't just the organization as a whole that protected me, it was my family. The Elders might, like Dark Iron, turn the other way if I got killed doing something they didn't agree with, but my family wouldn't.

I wanted Raven to have that, too. "I've got your back. I might not have the skills of Dark Iron and other mages in

Haul Du, but I've got a big sword and a whole lot of loyalty. Consider it my vow—I won't ever turn away when you're in trouble. And I would never let a wrongful death go unavenged."

Her eyes sparkled, suddenly wet and she sniffed. "I'm sorry. I'm so sorry that I chose Haul Du over our friendship. It's a mistake I won't make again."

I reached across the table and grabbed her hands, nearly knocking my plate of Scotch eggs to the floor. "It's all water under the bridge, Raven. I'm just glad to have my best friend back."

I *was* glad. I felt like I could conquer the world with Raven by my side. I had my family, I had new gamer friends, I had a detective who actually believed me when I told him about demons and magic. And now I had my best friend.

And once this was all over, we were going to have a major catch-up session. When this was over. I took a deep breath, knowing there was still a crime to solve. "Okay, so what does any of this Dupont Circle stuff have to do with Bethany being murdered? Or Ronald Stull being killed by an angel?"

Raven's eyes met mine. "That's why I wanted you to meet me here. When you said angel, I wondered. And when I found out Bliss was dead…well I started to put two and two together."

Thank goodness someone could. "I'm glad you've got answers because I have no idea what an angel has to do with any of this."

Raven pushed back her seat and stood. "Pay for your Irish eggs and come with me. There's something I want you to see."

CHAPTER 21

Raven drove us the six blocks to Bethany Scarborough's one-story house on the edge of town. The impatiens hanging in baskets from the porch roof were wilted, but it was clear Bliss had taken great care with her home. The grass was mowed in even strips. Flower beds were weeded and mulched. The only smudges on the windows were where a huge calico cat sat, pressing her nose against the glass. Raven pulled a key from her pocket and unlocked the door.

"She gave me this a few months back to check on her cat while she was away at a conference." Raven grinned sheepishly. "Yeah, it's an hour each way for me, but like I said, she is—was—so nice. She didn't want to put Grace in a boarding kennel. I don't blame her."

Grace was the gigantic cat who greeted us with a loud squawk and circled around our legs. I bent down and picked her up, estimating the creature's weight at nearly twenty pounds.

"Does no one feed you? Is poor kitty starving with her owner gone? Aww, sweetie."

Raven grinned and motioned to the automatic feeder in the corner. "Bliss wasn't one to say 'no' when it came to her fur baby. I swear that cat weighs more than I do."

I stroked Grace's soft fur, feeling the vibration of her purr against my hand. "Who's going to take care of her with Bliss gone?"

Not me. Not with the no-pet clause in my lease. It was bad enough that I was summoning demons in my apartment. A cat would get me tossed out on the curb. But...oh how I missed having a pet. Back home there had been cats and dogs and horses galore. We'd snuck them into the house every chance we got, even the ponies. I'll never forget Mom's face the day she walked in on our Shetland pony in the dining room munching the flowers in their vases.

"Bliss's sister is coming up from Florida." Raven smiled wistfully as she reached out a hand to scratch Grace under the chin. "I'd take her, but Rocket would eat her alive."

"She's twice the size of Rocket." I'd met Raven's Frenchie several times and marveled that such a sweet, energetic dog could harbor such a profound hatred toward everything feline.

I set the cat down on a nearby chair, feeling rather bummed that I wasn't bringing her home with me. Lease or not, I missed having something, or someone, for company in my apartment. But I doubted Raven had brought me here to meet Bliss's cat. As cute and obviously loved as the creature was, the calico wasn't a familiar. It took the right animal, the right bond, and a substantial amount of time to create a familiar—so much time that many mages claimed it couldn't be done, that any familiar had to be a pre-existing magic-imbued animal that came across the mage and chose them rather than the other way around.

"See?" Raven waved a hand around the room.

That's when I actually looked. And saw. "Bliss was an *angel*-worshiper?"

Raven winced. "No! She felt they were the more appropriate spirit to commune with and to ask guidance of. No one knew but me. The only reason *I* knew is because I was taking care of her cat and stumbled across one of her charms."

"So she hid all this when she went out of town?" I walked around the room, amazed. The prints that covered the walls were all of museum masterpieces—and all featured scenes that included angels. None of that would have hinted at more than a slightly obsessive interest had it not been for the sigils. Worked into the embroidered pillows, the drapes that covered the windows, the lampshades were sigils of angels. It was crazy.

"No. We've all got some protective work in our homes, and it's not like anyone in Haul Du would recognize an angel sigil. After I found the charm, I looked a few up and figured it out."

"Was she summoning them or something? Why else would she hide this from the group?" The only difference between this and what the rest of the members of Haul Du did was that there were no lesser angels. They were *all* big dogs, and they were *all* dangerous. It wasn't that summoning a demon was preferable, it was that summoning something that didn't have the power to destroy a small city in the time it took to exhale was preferable.

"What do *you* think Dark Iron would do if he found out Bliss, the mage who wouldn't even attend a Goetic summoning, was communing with angels?"

I winced. She would have gotten tossed out. I'm surprised she hadn't been tossed out the first time she refused to attend a Goetic summoning. Dark Iron didn't like it when people didn't follow his rules.

"And Bliss would never summon an angel." Raven continued. "She did communicate with them, but it was always through the veil."

That was a relief. Most demons refused to give you the time of day unless you brought them over, but angels must be different. Well, more than the usual differences when compared to demons.

"Do you think she might have summoned one out of fear? Maybe she knew the Baltimore group was after her, and brought forth an angel to protect her?"

Raven gave me a look. It was the look she gave me when I was so far off base it wasn't even funny. "Bliss wasn't an idiot, and she wasn't incapable of defending herself. If she was worried about those mages she would have stepped up her home and personal defenses. She would have charged a set of charms, or an amulet. She wouldn't have gone nuclear and summoned an *angel*."

Yeah. I guess not. "Would it be okay to look around?"

Raven nodded. "That's why I brought you here. I'm hoping between the two of us we can find something to let us know why Bliss was killed, who specifically in Fiore Noir killed her, and what Araziel has to do with any of this."

I was pretty sure the list of names we had would lead us to who did it but I knew what Raven meant. Again I thought about the Stranger. Sometimes the one holding the knife wasn't the real killer.

Raven picked up a statue from an end table and walked purposely into the bedroom. The room was Spartan compared to the frill I'd expected. White, French country style furniture lined the room. The powder-blue comforter and throw pillows were unadorned with lace or the embroidered sigils that filled the ones in the living room. Besides the reading lamps, the only object on any of the bedside tables was a book.

Leather-bound. And covered with enough magic to blow my hand clear off my arm if I touched it.

Raven raised the cat figurine and brought it down on the cover of the book. *"Aprire!"*

I ducked as bits of porcelain exploded across the room. The black leather of the book shimmered, then turned white.

"Rock beats paper," Raven commented. I laughed, thinking how much I'd missed her. She picked up the book, brushing the porcelain dust from the cover before she handed it to me. "Here. You look through this while I check her kitchen and the downstairs."

I didn't argue. Yes, I was a Templar and all that, but Raven had decades of magical knowledge. After my disastrous afternoon with not one but two demons, I was happy to let her face off against any magical protections while I read Bliss's grimoire.

I settled down on the edge of the bed, trying to ignore the pops, crackles, and occasional yelps from the rest of the house. Each mage composed their personal grimoire according to their own needs. For some, it was simply a reference book of spells with notations about changes and additions, successes and failures. For others it was more of a diary, a memoire of their magical journey. Bethany Scarborough's grimoire was the latter. Early pages were filled with charms, dates, and notes referencing other books. The more recent entries started halfway through the volume. I hesitated, realizing that she'd color-coded her sections from that point forward depending on which angel spirit she was working with.

It was fascinating. Bliss was careful, opening a line of communication with an angelic spirit that only allowed the pair of them to message back and forth. Early communications were through dreams and synchronicity, which meant Bliss had to do a considerable amount of interpretation.

Slowly she winnowed her list of spirit contacts down until she was opening her mind in meditation to only a few of them.

The last month she'd only communicated with one angel —Araziel. The last entry had me catching my breath. She'd trusted the angel enough to open the veil and allow him through. She'd invited him in, allowed him physical entry onto this plane.

Angels weren't like demons. They couldn't be bound. They couldn't be constrained within a circle. That's why no one messed with them. Bliss had. Her grimoire was full of entries of how she and the angel had conversed about the nature of divinity, the issues surrounding humanity. One evening they'd discussed the smell of leaves after an autumn rain, the beauty of a sunset, how soft Grace's fur felt under Bliss's hand.

I shut the grimoire, feeling lost, tiny, inept. I'd known Araziel was off his divine leash, had seen his victims, but what was I going to do about it?

Bliss said she'd closed the veil leaving the angel on the other side, but not without a gift. When summoning demons, there was always an offering. Evidently there was similar protocol when inviting an angel into your presence. How had the angel remained? Everything in her grimoire painted Bliss to be a cautious mage. She wouldn't have screwed up and left an opening for the angel to return. Or would she?

I rubbed the mark on my side, remembering how the smoke demon had appeared this afternoon. I hadn't summoned him, and when I'd banished him last time I'd done it the Templar way. There were no loopholes, yet he'd been able to return today without my requesting his presence. He'd marked me, and evidently that gave him an opening through the veil so he could cross at will. I wondered if Bliss had been similarly marked?

Did…did angels do that? I know they were supposed to be spirits of good, full of God's grace. But good was a rather subjective concept, and as a Templar we'd come to view angels with a wary eye.

I looked down at the white leather of the journal grimoire, smoothed my hand over the unmarked cover. Araziel. Maybe he'd marked Bliss with much kinder intentions than the demon had marked me. But even if he'd had good intentions, he'd killed. His role as a psychopomp, as a reaper of souls had taken a dark turn.

Or had it? Tremelay had said the two junkies had enough heroin in their system to have died anyway. And maybe Ronald Stull *had* been struck by lightning. That would make Araziel less of a murderer and more of a…I don't know, a Kevorkian angel. Not that I condoned that sort of thing. At least not in all cases. And there was something else. I got the feeling there was something I was missing in these three deaths.

"Kite? Aria?"

"Yeah. Still in the bedroom."

"Can you come down here? I want you to see something."

I put the grimoire back on the bedside table and made my way down to the basement of the house. Unlike Tempest, Bliss hadn't converted hers into a magical space. At least, not a traditional magical space. There was carpet on the floor, a huge sofa with chocolate brown plush upholstery and crimson accent pillows. A flat-screen television hung on the wall, a bookshelf piled high with movies under it. Across from the television sat a giant fluffy pillow. It was the sort of thing I'd expect someone to buy for a Great Dane bed. And in front of the dog pillow was an altar.

Altar was the only way I could describe it. There was an oak cabinet a foot high with a ring of candles on top. In the center was a mortar filled with fragments of burned paper and herbs. She'd meditated here, communed with her angel spirits here, sent her prayers heavenward on wings of smoke and ash here.

"Look." Raven reached down in front of the altar and picked up a shining object. It was a gold filigree chain, a series of charms dangling from the end—one a wing, one a half-moon, one a scythe.

"Angels of the night," I murmured, taking the necklace from Raven to examine closely. "She had an affinity for reapers."

"I also found this." Raven pushed a piece of paper in my hand, her voice choked. "I didn't know. I don't think anybody knew. Bliss never told."

It was a report. Along with five paragraphs of medical mumbo-jumbo was the diagnosis—cancer. Bethany had stage four bone cancer. Six months to a year even with treatment. The test results were dated two months ago; which was the exact time she'd ended communication with all angels except Araziel.

"She willingly took his mark," I said softly. "She wanted *him* to be the one who took her soul when the time came."

He was the angel she knew best, the one she'd developed a connection with. Some people made their wills, took care of final arrangements, decided what to prioritize on their bucket list. Bliss gave an angel what amounted to a proxy. When her death came, she wanted a familiar face by her side. I felt for her. I felt sad that I hadn't known her.

And I felt angry that she hadn't had the death she'd wanted. Instead of giving her soul unto an angel's care, she'd had it forced from her dying body and used to power a spell. Tremelay might want to bring these fuckers to justice, but I was suddenly filled with a desire to lop their heads off with my sword.

And Araziel. I thought about my demon mark, about the

venom in Innyhal's voice when he spoke of humans taking souls that weren't theirs for the taking. Angels and demons had differences, but at their core were surprising similarities. Fiore Noir had killed Bethany Scarborough and taken her soul—a soul that had been claimed by another. A demon would have been furious and hell-bent on revenge. Angels were supposedly beings without emotion, but even if Araziel hadn't felt the same gut-wrenching anger of a demon, he would have seen the injustice. What is promised to one should not be taken. *Thou shalt not steal.*

I thought of Ronald Stull lying dead in the park and revised my theory that he'd been hit by lightning. There had been nothing killing him beyond an angel looking to right a wrong. Maybe Araziel had reaped the two junkie's souls a bit early, but I was convinced that Ronald's death had been an angelic form of justice.

And if I was right, Tremelay wouldn't get his arrests and I wouldn't get the satisfaction of beheading these mages with my sword. Because vengeance would belong to an angel.

CHAPTER 22

We'd driven all the way back in Baltimore, so I could show Raven my apartment and brainstorm at my favorite local on ways to rein in an angel when Tremelay called. As expected, they'd found signs of magic ritual at Dead Run along with several bodies.

"Know where Dead Run is?" I asked Raven.

"Uh, no?"

I grinned. "Wanna come with me? I could use both a navigator and an experienced mage."

Raven leaned back in her seat, slugging down the rest of her beer. "Nope. No way. I heard you say bodies. I'll face down an angry demon any day rather than get within a hundred feet of a corpse. There's a reason I don't do death magic. I cry over roadkill, Aria. I avoid funerals at all cost. Dead bodies are gonna send me right over the edge."

I didn't blame her one bit. I'd seen my share of dead bodies in the last few days and wasn't looking forward to a repeat experience this evening. Still, I'd seen Bethany's body. This couldn't be any worse.

It was.

Thankfully Tremelay met me in a parking area, because I wasn't sure I would otherwise have been able to find the site. Dead Run paralleled Security Boulevard, a swath of green on either side of a meandering creek. There were other parks and even a few cemeteries nearby, turning the entire area into a small bit of solitude. Well, solitude aside from the sounds of traffic on the well-traveled road that was hidden by a thick line of trees and briars.

The ritual spots were well hidden. We sloshed through the creek and scrambled up a muddy bank, then nearly crawled under a thick cover of vines to reach them. Once through the brush, I saw a clearing with the remains of several magical circles. They'd squeezed them in, five in this tiny space.

"They moved." I muttered, waving my hand toward the numbered crime-scene signs. "Mages can't do this sort of ritual in the same place without a huge cleansing. It's easier to shift ten feet over."

I'd never performed this type of magic, but I understood why they'd done this. When creating charms or amulets, or even summoning Goetic demons, a magical space soaked up some of the energy from each use. That was normally a good thing—a mage wanted to be able to rely on an extra punch of energy if needed. But death magic was like a sort of strip mine. The murder, the soul, the energy of the site, it all went into the intended storage device. Which left the area bare and battered, and somewhat vulnerable.

Unusable. Just walking across the abandoned spaces made me feel tired. It was as if the ground itself were trying to leach the life-force from my body. It was one more thing that would have made the Baltimore group inelegant, unsophisticated, and brutish in the eyes of their DC counterparts.

"What do you think?" Tremelay asked. There were several other officers, ones in uniform, who looked at us curiously.

Here's where I pretended to be an expert. "These sites were clearly used for death magic. The symbols may have worn away or been removed, but there are still signs of the magical space. There were sacrifices here, one in each spot. No more than one, though. So five people died here, unless there's another clearing with additional sites."

The two dudes in blue looked impressed. Tremelay less so. "Is there anything here that can tie the ritual areas to a specific victim? I want your take on it before I get the CSI guys in here to rip up grass and stuff for DNA."

I shook my head. "Honestly the techs will do a better job than me at pinpointing who died where. The victim doesn't change the method of the ceremony."

Different victims had different levels of energy to give, though. It made me think of Bliss with her cancer and her angel mark. Would her energy have been less than ideal? Was her soul less potent because of its mark? Had her death, as horrible as it was, yielded a disappointing result for the mages?

The thought enraged me. As much as I wanted Tremelay to bring them to justice, part of me hoped that Araziel *did* catch them. I hope the angel took his time about it, too. Although with angels that wasn't likely. Justice was justice. An eye for an eye. Personal suffering as punishment wouldn't mean as much to an angel as it would to a human.

"The bodies are over here." Tremelay's voice was soft. He'd walked over to me, careful to avoid smudging the circles further. I felt his hand on my arm, gently urging me forward.

I didn't want to go. I'd been grossed out and intrigued when I'd seen Ronald's body. I'd been horrified when I'd discovered Bethany in the sacrificial tub. But this... Somehow in the last few days this whole thing had burrowed through my academic interest in demons and magic and landed in the freak out zone. I'd been in Bliss's house. I'd petted her cat. I'd read her journal. These weren't just bodies. These were people whose hopes and dreams had come crashing down with the stab of a knife. And with soul magic, they didn't even have the promise of an afterlife to look forward to. It was the worst of wrongs, and I couldn't look dispassionately upon their remains.

But I had to. Anything I could find out that might help Tremelay find the killers and put an end to this was worth it. And didn't these people deserve to be mourned? Didn't they deserve to have their deaths regarded with a sense of outrage, their bodies and their pain burned into my memory forever? I might be a stranger, but the connection of a stranger was better than remaining undiscovered in a park for years, or becoming a John Doe among so many at the morgue.

The bodies were laid out in an adjoining clearing, lined up on tarps and in various stages of decomposition. It was August in Maryland. I'd been upwind before, but no fortuitous breeze could lessen the stench that hit me when I approached that clearing.

Tremelay cleared his throat. "There was a ditch, kind of like a mass grave but it wasn't completely filled in. They didn't use lime or anything to speed decomposition or hide the smell. It's like they knew they'd be gone and using another site by the time these were found."

Five ritual areas. Five bodies. I looked at the nearest one, blackened and still oozing. "Probably dead for two weeks," the nearby tech mentioned. "Although it's hard to tell exactly. There's a lot we'll have to factor in before we can get a solid timeline on these guys."

I yanked my shirt up to cover my nose and mouth, not caring if I was flashing my bra to the techs and Tremelay. Then I looked upward into the leafy canopy and pushed down my nausea. It was just flesh, just decomposing flesh. I needed to get over it and help.

So I did. I compared this to the only frame of reference I had—road kill. Two weeks in the August heat, but in the bottom of a ditch and sheltered from the sun. I didn't envy these crime scene techs their job. Not in the least bit.

The tech kindly waited for me to get a grip before continuing. "These other ones were probably killed on the following days in order, the last one four days ago."

I walked by the victims, trying to find anything in their faces and naked bodies that I could use.

The tech walked with me, gesturing toward the line of corpses. "We'll need to wait for the M.E. to weigh in, but none of them appears to have been restrained by rope or tape. They may have been drugged. We'll see what the tox screens say."

They'd say no. Drugged victims wouldn't yield as much energy and wouldn't be worth all this effort. I'd done some research in my spare moments and although I didn't have a vast store of information on death magic, some of the dark arts books I'd acquired due to their demonology chapters did outline the basics of the rituals. It was a disturbing read. The victims were held by the arms and legs, but still fully aware at the time of the ritual. It was recommended the victim be in a state of panic at the moment of sacrifice. Terror lent an extra punch to the energy collected. The whole thing made me sick.

I put some much needed distance between myself and the bodies. "So no marks at all? No signs they were smacked on the head when they were taken, or bruises anywhere?"

The tech shook his head. "It's summer and it's been kinda hot the last few weeks. Decomposition is pretty bad on the older ones. There are some tattoos and scars I can make out on the recent ones. This last one has a really weird burn mark on his waist."

That was an odd coincidence when I also had a "weird" burn mark on *my* waist. Did the guy work in food service and have a run-in with a hot pan? Because it would be beyond strange for two people to have the same demon-mark on their left side.

"See? It looks like a cigar burn, only it's bigger. And it's completely round. It must have hurt like heck to leave a scar like that. That's a third-degree burn kind of scar."

My brain did a one-eighty. I held my breath and leaned down to look at the man's waist. His skin had a mottled tone and was stretched considerably in bloat, but the round mark on his side was as clear as the nose on my face. And as clear as the scar on my own side. It couldn't have been a coincidence. This man, this last victim, he had been marked. Demon marked.

But was it a demon or an angel? I closed my eyes, trying to recall what I could of Bliss's naked body sprawled in the tub. Try as I might, I couldn't remember if she had the same mark or not. She had to have *something* on her that confirmed my suspicions about her deal with Araziel.

"Hey, Tremelay," I called. The detective turned his head toward me. "Can you call down to the morgue and ask them if Bethany Scarborough had any scars on her waist? Round, like a really fat cigar burn or a hickey. Raised skin. White. It should have been obvious."

The detective tilted his head, one eyebrow arching skyward. "Okay. I'll check."

I looked again at the body before me. "Any idea who this is? Who any of them are?"

The tech shook his head again. "They were naked with nothing to ID them. I took fingerprints of the ones I could. If they're in the system, we'll know by tomorrow. If not…well, it depends on whether they match any missing persons' reports or not."

"Ainsworth!" I looked up and saw Tremelay motioning to me. With an apologetic smile at the tech, I jogged over to him.

"M.E. says there *was* a mark, but it's not what you described. It looks to be more like a birthmark of sorts and it's right over the center of her chest. He's sending a picture."

"The heart chakra," I commented.

"I don't know about chakra, but it's not over her heart. It's right in the center of her sternum. But the mark does kinda look like a heart."

"That's where the chakra is," I replied. "It's not over the heart organ, it's on a center line with the other chakras. It's called the heart chakra because it's the focal point for compassion and mercy."

His phone dinged and he swiped it, raising his eyebrows as he handed it to me.

I looked down at the picture of a brown birthmark in the rough shape of a heart right between the curve of two breasts. It was perfectly placed, and I was darned sure it hadn't been there since Bethany's birth. Still, it was best to check these things before I went off on crazy theories.

"Can you do one more thing? Check with Bethany's immediate family and see if she had this mark from when she was a child?"

Tremelay took his phone back, his eyes never leaving my face. "What are you thinking, Ainsworth? It doesn't look like a tattoo or any kind of burn. It looks like a birthmark."

I raised the side of my shirt. "The point is it *doesn't* look like this."

The detective bent over, tilting his head to look at my waist. I felt fingers lightly touching the skin next to the mark, then nothing as they drifted over the raised surface of the scar.

"Damn. That's a nasty burn scar, Ainsworth. And this connects to the birthmark on the victim how?"

"It means…" I took a deep breath, nervous about admitting this to anyone. "It means that Bethany wasn't marked by a demon. This scar on my waist? I'm marked by a demon. And that last victim over there was, too."

He stood upright, and I couldn't quite read the expression on his face. "So what's the mark over the heart chakra then?"

"I think Bethany was marked by an angel—the very same angel who killed Ronald Stull and the two junkies." I told Tremelay about what I'd found at Bliss's house, what I'd read in her journal grimoire.

"So this Araziel marked her, but not to kill her. He marked her so he could ease her transition at the time of death?"

I nodded. "I think so."

"Damn. That's just…sad. He never got to collect her soul."

I nodded again. "And I think he's upset about that. Not in a demon kind of way upset, but in a things-didn't-go-according-to-God's-plan kind of upset."

The detective pursed his lips, glancing over toward the line of bodies. "So the guy over there with the demon mark…?"

"I think, and I'm reaching a bit here, but I think whatever demon had his claws in that dead guy is mighty angry."

"Someone stole his soul," the detective commented.

I nodded. "Whatever demon marked that man didn't get the opportunity to take his soul. He'll want revenge. And the angel that marked Bliss, I mean Bethany? He's going to want justice. And justice for an angel doesn't involve a trial by their peers and fair sentencing."

Tremelay nodded, but I got the feeling he wasn't really

listening. Before I realized what he was doing, the detective reached out a hand and put it against my waist. "And you? How long do you have before a demon comes to collect on this?"

I looked down, feeling the warmth of his hand against me even through the cotton of my shirt.

"I've got no idea. But trust me, once this is over I'm doing everything I can to get this mark off of my skin and off of my soul."

CHAPTER 23

I drove home alone, the sun setting in my rear view mirror as the skyline of Baltimore rose before me. Athena had headed home right after our banishing to her husband and to dreams of a baby girl. Tremelay was heading back to check progress on our hit list as well as the search of Ronald Stull's apartment.

I had never felt so lonely or afraid.

I was demon marked. People had been murdered in a horrific manner. A woman, a dying woman who only wanted to feel a sense of connection in her last moments, had spent those very moments in terror and despair. I felt like I was spinning my wheels. We had a list of names, but unless Tremelay could find concrete proof he'd have no way to prosecute the mages. It's not like I had the skills to help him with any of that either. The only thing left for me to do was figure out how to rein in Araziel before the angel killed anyone else, although there hadn't been any further victims since the junkies at Old Town Mall. If they'd died Friday, that meant the angel hadn't killed in three days. Perhaps he'd returned through the veil, satisfied that justice was served.

As convenient as that would be, part of me wished he'd remain and take out the rest of the murderers. I had no faith that Tremelay could make any charges stick, and it made me ill to think the mages might get away with murder.

"It would be easier if Araziel just killed them all," I muttered to myself as I pulled in my parking area. Easier. An eye for an eye, with no way for them to wiggle out of punishment.

My demon-mark ached and I rubbed it, reminded that there was yet another thing I needed to do. Even if Araziel had returned to his heavenly home, my work would not be done until I was free from that smoke demon.

I locked my car and sensed the prickle of magic as soon as the alarm chirped. Without thinking, I swung my sword, still in its scabbard, and felt the blade impact someone behind me who went down with a hard "oof".

I spun around, my heart lurching as I saw a tiny elderly woman sprawled across the dirty asphalt, clutching her shoulder. Oh my God. Did I...did I just hit a little old lady with my sword? Thankfully it had been in its scabbard or I would have quite possibly taken her arm off. As it was I probably broke her shoulder.

Slinging the offending weapon over my shoulder I bent down. "Are you okay? I didn't know you were behind me. I heard...felt..."

I couldn't tell her I'd felt a magical spell about to go off and swung blindly out of instinct. After all I'd been through the last three days, I was a bit jumpy, but that wasn't an excuse for nearly skewering this woman. Although this *was* Baltimore, and creeping up on people tended to have consequences.

"I've had worse," the woman grumbled, brushing away my offer of a hand and struggling to her feet. "Serves me right for sneaking up on a Templar."

She knew I was a Templar. I thought again about the crackle of magic in the air and looked at the woman more closely. I'd judge her to be in her seventies, her silver hair in a stylish bob, deep creases around her eyes and mouth. Her pants suit was stylish, but the rabbit's foot keychain she clutched in her hand didn't look like she'd bought it at a curio shop.

I gripped my sword again, fully aware I couldn't go around bashing the elderly because they had a poorly preserved good-luck charm as a keychain. Magic again sparked in the air. She eyed my sword, her mouth in a grim line. I eyed the rabbit's foot, my expression probably just as tense.

"I won't swing if you don't," she said. Sheesh, even her voice sounded grandmotherly, like she should be baking me cookies and not preparing to drop a magical anvil on my head.

"Deal." I was outclassed anyway. Whatever spell she had in mind, it would hit me before my still-sheathed sword got near her. The rabbit's foot went into her pants pocket and I took my hand off the sword.

"I'm Gryla," she announced. I waited but no additional information came. They way she'd said the name, I'd been sure it was about to be followed by at least one descriptive adjective, like "the great," "the deadly," or at the very least "the gray."

Instead her eyebrows went up. "Gryla? Head of Fiore Noir? The Baltimore group of mages?"

Duh. Six months in Baltimore and I'd never bothered to find out her name. Heck, I'd just discovered the *group* name and that they did death magic. I really needed to get with the program here. And hadn't Shade mentioned her name? I'd been so intent on Ronald Stull that I'd completely forgotten.

"I'm Solaria Angelique Ainsworth, Templar. Nice to meet you."

Nice to meet you. No, it was not nice to meet her. She was the leader of a group of murderers. I had no actual proof that *she'd* had a hand in the sacrifices, or killed anything beyond quite possibly a rabbit, but she was their leader. At the very least she was aware and complicit in the crimes. But what to do? Could I make a citizen's arrest? I'd need to get that rabbit's foot away from her and I wasn't sure how any passerby would take my assaulting an older woman.

"I need to show you something."

That was not what I'd expected her to say. I still hadn't figured out how I was going to manage to detain her until Tremelay could get here. And now I was dreading whatever it was she wanted to show me. Death mages—it couldn't be anything good.

"I'll drive." She motioned toward a little, sporty, red Honda at the curb, careful to keep her hands away from the pocket with the keychain.

"Uh. No. I'm not getting in a car with you and driving who knows where just so you can 'show me something.'"

Irritation creased her face. "Then you drive."

Yeah. Sure. I'll drive, leaving her hands free to hex me while I navigated traffic. No way. "Just tell me what it is you want me to see."

I hoped it wasn't any more dead bodies. I really didn't want to see any more dead bodies. Gryla carefully slid her cell phone from a pocket and tapped, turning the screen toward me.

It *was* more dead bodies. These ones weren't neatly laid out in a ritual space, nor were they hollowed out with their ribs pointing to the sky. These bodies were torn to bits, like they'd been stuffed through a gigantic food processor. I so didn't need to see this.

"Okay?" It was an idiotic response, but the pictures were out of any context and my brain was still busy processing the gruesome scene.

"Demons." She pocketed the phone.

What the heck? "I banished the demon this afternoon. When did this occur?"

"Sometime between seven and eight tonight. Seven of us were meeting to discuss an upcoming bit of spell-work. I should have been there, but was detained by a very polite detective who had some questions to ask me about my name being on a list."

Of course. She was Fiore Noir. Her name *would* be on the list. The image of scattered body parts flashed again in my mind. "You walked in on that?"

Gryla nodded, her hand trembling slightly as she pocketed the phone. "The detective wanted to know if I knew two men from DC who had been killed while conducting an occult ritual. I'm not an idiot. I know the DC mages summon demons. If my name's on a list, it means I was a target for assassination."

"But I banished that demon," I exclaimed. "There's no way he could have come back. You all are safe from that hit."

Heck, they were safe before. Innyhal killed Tempest and Oak, but seemed to have no inclination to follow through on the list. Actually, he didn't seem at all interested in what was going on between the mage groups, beyond being angry about Fiore Noir taking souls. Then I remembered. Innyhal had said Mansi was pissed about the soul magic. There was a corpse in Dead Run with a demon mark on his waist. I was willing to bet that mark was Mansi's. And if so, Araziel wasn't the only being who had it out for the Fiore Noir mages.

"I knew we shouldn't have done that Dupont Circle job." Gryla's jaw clenched. "I hate that sort of thing, but that was the price for being able to use the soul trap. It's not like those things are easy to come by and we had no choice. I knew there would be repercussions. I told Breaker this would happen, but he assured me there would be no backlash."

She thought Haul Du had done this, that a mage had summoned another demon to kill their group. Maybe. Given what Tempest and Oak had tried to do, I couldn't rule it out, but there was still the matter of the demon-marked corpse and this Mansi. Either way, if this truly had been a demon slaying, my work tonight wasn't done. Araziel hadn't killed in days, but this was six dead just tonight. If I didn't act fast, there would be no one left for Tremelay to arrest.

"Are you sure it was a demon, or demons, that killed the mages?"

"Yes, I'm sure," she snapped. "The place reeked of sulfur. No bullets. No knife cuts. These people were ripped apart. If that didn't convince me, the display of heads with internal organs crammed in their mouths did."

I winced, thankful she hadn't show me *that* picture.

"I'll help you with the demon problem," I told Gryla. "But I'll need some of your mages to assist in the banishment. Think they'd be willing to do that?"

She swallowed hard and nodded. "Goetica isn't our thing. We can assist with general ritual set-up and powering the boundaries, but we don't have the experience to deal with the demon ourselves."

No, that would be me and Raven. But first I needed to figure out who or what I was dealing with, and for that I was going to have to do something that made my stomach turn.

As carefully as Gryla had done, I pulled my cell phone out and showed her the list. "Can you tell me which of these mages were in that room?"

She paled. "That's the list? Stars above, that's the entire Fiore Noir group right there." Taking my phone, she highlighted six of the names, then hesitated and highlighted two more. "Ronald Stull is already dead, but you knew that. Bill Foley is known as Shade. He left town Sunday morning. His place is cleaned out. He's off the grid. I'm Beverly Bright."

I made a quick note. That left seventeen mages, including Gryla. Still plenty to prosecute if we could get to them before the demons and angel did. "We'll do the ritual tomorrow midnight. Can you bring as many people as possible? We'll need all the energy we can muster."

The mage nodded. "Some might not come. They're scared. I'd be surprised if half those people don't run off like Shade did, especially once the word gets out what happened tonight."

Some was better than none. I slid my phone into my pocket, thinking I needed to call Raven and hope she was free, both tonight and tomorrow night.

"One more thing," Gryla added. "You're missing a name on that list."

I hadn't forgotten. "The Stranger."

"Breaker knew him well. He's the one who approached us with the soul trap and offered to let us use it. Conditions were that those three Haul Du mages died in such a way that everyone thought it was an accident, and that he got to be present at the rituals where we used the soul trap."

Sounded like someone had a big beef with Haul Du. "Do you have any way of finding out who this stranger is?"

A smile creased her face. "I'm sure Breaker wasn't the only mage in Fiore Noir who knew him. I'll ask around, and if no one talks, well I'll just kill a chicken or two and all will be revealed."

CHAPTER 24

Raven drove over and we ran out to pick up Chinese before getting to work. Summoning was dangerous enough. I didn't want to do it on an empty stomach, even if Gryla's last words kept running through my head.

Needless to say, I made sure we didn't order anything with chicken.

Scrying with fresh avian blood went right out of my head when I saw what was in my parking space. One of the other tenants had visitors who liked to co-opt my spot, so I'd spelled it. They were less likely to want to park in a space that looked like someone had vomited an all-you-can-eat buffet there. There wasn't an old Mazda taking up my spot this time. There was a dead body.

The guy was on his back, spread-eagle as if he were recreating Da Vinci's Renaissance Man. His ribs pointed to the sky and I was pretty darned sure that once I walked over and looked down, I'd see an empty chest cavity.

How could this happen? I had no idea what Araziel had been doing the last three days, but it seemed he wasn't gone after all. And now, in addition to sending a demon back to hell, I still needed to deal with a killer angel.

It scared me like nothing had so far this week. Araziel, right outside my apartment building. Had the angel killed a random passerby and dumped him here, or was this this dead guy another mage from the Fiore Noir list?

"Is this a common thing for you Templars?" Raven was trying not to look at the dead body, her complexion somewhat green.

"I'm beginning to think it's a common thing for me." I pulled my car in one of my neighbor's spots, making a mental note to move it later before it got towed.

It must have just happened, otherwise there would have been a crowd around the body and cops on the way. We both stood, me looking down at the body, Raven feigning interest in the vomit illusion. As suspected, the chest cavity was empty. There was also the typical lack of blood. Did Araziel somehow cauterize as he killed? Without blood it was hard to tell if the angel had whacked the guy here or brought him to my doorstep like a cat would a dead mouse offering.

"Another demon slaying or is this the angel guy?" Raven's voice was overloud as she struggled to keep from losing her calm.

"Angel."

She took a sharp breath. "Bliss's angel? Bliss's angel is still running around killing people?"

"I think he's killing very specific people. Well, aside from two who I think may have been collateral damage."

Specific people, which meant if my theory was correct, this dead man was on our list of Fiore Noir. I'd gone through Ronald Stull's pockets. There was no reason for me to be squeamish about going through this guy's, so I did.

Raven watched horrified. Or maybe fascinated. It was hard to tell, but I was betting on the first. My tough friend wasn't so tough when it came to corpses. Not that I blamed her. I'd been trained to be a warrior and still felt my heart flip every time. My first dead body was less than a week ago and somehow I'd seen a dozen or so since then. Jaded in a matter of days.

The dead man wore his pants a little on the snug side, so there was some jostling of the body as I searched it. Plus I'd needed to nearly flip him over to get the wallet out of his back pocket. The contents of his pockets weren't as interesting as Ronald's had been. This man had car keys, some change, and a wallet. I pulled out the ID and read the name, then stuck it back in his pants pocket.

John Ash. I wiped my hands on my own pants and pulled out my cell phone. Sure enough, the name was on the list from Alban's house.

"Okay let's go. You got the Chinese food?"

Raven blinked at me. "Yeah. Are we just going to leave him here?"

"I'm working with the police on similar murders. This guy is in my parking spot. Guess how long I'll be tied up talking to the cops?" Tremelay was probably still busy processing the Dead Run crime scene. I'd call him later. In the meantime I had work to do if I was going to be ready to summon a demon by tomorrow midnight. This was Fells Point. Someone would come across John Ash soon enough and call it in. If not, I'd do it once I got some answers.

Raven grimaced. "Good point."

If we missed our midnight window, I wouldn't get the answers I needed for tomorrow night. Yes, the smoke demon seemed able and willing to show up even at noon, but I wanted this to be on *my* terms. And I wanted to make sure Raven could help me. I'd screwed up two summonings so far. I might be a little stubborn about it, but I was beginning to realize my limitations and the price I'd pay for ignoring them. That demon had marked me. He could clearly come and go at will. I needed someone with experience to ensure he went back to hell without taking my soul with him.

Once upstairs, I pushed aside my guilt over leaving a dead guy on the pavement and began rolling up my rug while Raven pulled the food out and put it on the kitchen table. John Ash was a murderer. He deserved what he got. Besides, I couldn't really judge angelic morality. Ash might not have known Bliss was angel-marked, but that didn't excuse what he did. How many non-marked people had died at his hands, their very souls stolen away? The mood I was in tonight I was more than ready to cheer Araziel on.

Except I wasn't sure where the angel would stop. After everyone died from the list, would he continue on to cleanse the world of some other wrong? I couldn't allow an angel vigilante to run around.

Not that I knew what to do about it. I couldn't banish him. I couldn't control him. I'd need to talk to Dad and see if there were any texts dealing with this kind of situation. Or maybe I could convince Athena to put me in contact with someone at The Temple.

"Here." Raven shoved a container of noodles and a pair of chopsticks into my hands. "You eat. I'll work on the circle."

I did just that, watching my friend work. It was amazing the little differences I could see between what she was scribing and what I'd done last time. Just watching her made me feel like a silly amateur. Book knowledge was nothing compared to experience, and I was realizing that my scant months of experience in Haul Du hadn't been enough. What an arrogant jerk I'd been to think myself a peer to people who had been practicing magic on a daily basis for years. I should have stuck to charms and simple spells and held off higher works until I'd put in the legwork needed to do it safely.

Of course that would mean having someone to mentor me. Difficult, since none of the magical groups would associate with me. Heck, I couldn't even buy a candle in a magic shop anymore. There was allegedly a price on my head, for Pete's sake.

"There. See how I looped fire and Sagittarius so there's an overlap across the edge? That will strengthen your southern quarter. If a demon's going to try to break out, he'll always go for the southern quarter first."

I set the noodles on the counter and walked over to look closely at the chalk marks. "Okay. So the demon finds the circle reinforced here. Won't he just move around the perimeter until he finds a weak spot?"

Which was what Innyhal had done.

Raven grinned up at me. "That's why we put a spark-spell right here." She pointed to the tip of the arrow in the Sagittarius symbol. "The demon sees the spark and thinks he's discovered a weakness, so he keeps working the south quarter."

I shook my head in confusion. "Then you have a demon who isn't paying any attention to you because he's bashing himself against the fire rune. Why bother? Can't you just make the circle super reinforced all the way around?"

Raven chuckled, bending her head to continue her chalk-work. "Yeah, if you only want to have a conversation with the demon, then that's fine. If you want a favor, or a gift then you have to leave enough of an opening to receive it. Circles need to be porous enough for there to be an exchange of energy, otherwise why bother summoning a demon at all? Just go read a book or something."

I was beginning to understand. "Open enough to receive what you want, but strong enough to hold a demon. Like a chain link fence?"

She nodded. "Yep. And there's another reason you don't

want to lock the circle down too tight. It makes you look weak. Anyone *that* paranoid is someone who is going to eventually screw up, someone who doesn't have a whole lot of confidence in their spells so they layer them on top of each other as back up. Demons love that shit. They'll scream and rage and cause a scene, then flatter the mage with praise of his amazing spell-work. But one day there will be a tiny crack and they'll be on him like flies on shit. Well-crafted spells with an open weave show the demon that you're skilled and confident."

"The demon thinks that if he breaks through, you've got enough power to whoop his ass outside the circle."

"Exactly." Raven eyed the eternity symbol for a second, then thickened one of the lines. "You could be bluffing, but I'd suggest if you're going to summon even the most helpful of Goetic demon, you have a backup, because sooner or later one of them is going to get out."

I looked over at my sword. Maybe I wasn't as inept as I thought. Other mages might have amulets, but I had a conse-crated weapon. I also had my blessing, although that didn't seem to be consistently working lately. I rubbed the mark on my side and wondered if it would ever work again. Was I forever tainted? Had some of the advantages I had as a soldier of God been revoked? There was nothing that said Templars couldn't summon demons. King Solomon had bound them and put them to work building the Temple with God's blessing.

You're no King Solomon. My father's words rang from my memory. I wasn't. And Templars generally frowned upon dealing with higher spirits. Librarian Templars felt summoning for information was cheating and not worth the risk. Guardian Templars got twitchy at the idea of a demon on this side of the veil, with the possible threat to the Temple and all it held. Knights in general felt the only place for a demon was in hell. And although they'd never say it out loud, they weren't at ease at any sign there might be an angel among us. Messengers of God…well, they often carried a message no one wanted to hear.

"There." Raven stood and rolled her neck before handing the chalk to me. "I'm going to eat while you draw the sigils. I know you're good at that. Heck, you're probably better at that than I am."

Her praise did more for my self-confidence than if King Solomon had delivered it himself. I might have hidden from my Latin lessons, but as a child I could never get enough of sigil work. I'd buried my nose in books of demon and angel lore, spent hours in the null room drawing and charging. I could feel the energy as my chalk moved along the floor, the different mix of emotion and sensation that each sigil developed as the lines came together. Raven was scraping the last of her Kung Pao Beef out of the container by the time I was done. I stood. I stretched. And I knew even before I saw Raven's nod that I'd done a good job.

"So who are we summoning?" Raven walked around the outside of the circle, surveying my work with an appreciative eye.

"I've got no idea."

She jerked to a stop, staring at me open mouthed. "What do you mean? You can't just open the veil and do a blanket summoning. That's suicide."

I wasn't sure how to explain this to her without getting into my demon mark. I'd rather she not know about that. It was bad enough that Tremelay and Athena knew. Raven would think I was even more of an idiot, screwing up and getting myself marked. It was so embarrassing.

Tempest and Oak had screwed up and gotten killed. That made me better than them, although I doubted my survival had much to do with superior magical skills.

"Remember when I called you and told you not to summon Vine? That some other demon, a powerful, higher level one, had come in his stead?" I waited for her to nod. "I banished him, but not before he got out of the circle and marked me."

I heard her sharp intake of breath. "Let me see."

I pulled up my shirt and felt her fingers on my skin.

"Oh, Aria. Damn it all." There was a hitch in her voice as she said the last word. Then she murmured something in Greek under her breath and the mark felt like it was on fire. Not wanting to look like a wimp, I squinted, gritted my teeth and rode out the pain.

"It's a Sun demon." Her hands left my waist and she walked over to the window, her back toward me. "It's our fault. It's *my* fault. We took you in, taught you the bare basics, then we threw you out."

As bitter as I was about it, the whole thing wasn't *completely* their fault. "I'm a Templar. I hid that from you. I hate that it makes a difference to the entire magical community though."

She shook her head. "They're afraid. Even if you haven't taken your Oath, you're still obligated to snatch any magical artifact and take it to the Temple. Plus there's the whole secrecy thing. Templars *have* to share information. We have an expectation of non-disclosure, and you can't guarantee that."

No I couldn't. It still hurt, though.

When Raven finally turned back toward me, her eyes were steely. "I'll help you with this."

"I know. I really appreciate it, too."

"No. I mean after. I don't care what any of them say. I don't care if they throw me out. After we take care of the bastards who killed Bliss, I'm going to help you get rid of that demon mark."

I nearly wept with relief. I'd been so afraid, and hadn't known where to turn. Raven might not be a Master, but with her help I felt there was some chance of saving my soul.

"I don't know this demon's name or anything about him. He showed up today uninvited when my sister and I were trying to banish another demon."

She wiped a hand across her eyes and straightened. "The one Tempest and Oak summoned?"

"Yeah. Innyhal. We managed to send him back to hell, but it was touch and go for a moment there. The demon that marked me appeared. He's black smoke with red eyes. Humanoid, but kind of fluid in shape and form. He helped us subdue Innyhal, he said as a gift, then left."

Raven chewed on her bottom lip. "You didn't banish him?"

"The first time he came when I was trying to summon Vine. I banished him using the Templar blessing. He left immediately, but he'd already marked me by that point. The second time he appeared, I neither summoned nor banished him."

She nodded. "The mark. It always gives them an opening. They have a tie to the human they have claimed and that way they can keep track of you."

It made sense. That's why Innyhal hadn't originally wanted to kill me. He knew this other demon would be pissed, and whoever the smoke demon was, clearly he wasn't someone to piss off lightly.

"I'm not sure how I can get him to come back since I don't know his name or sigil. I was thinking if I tried to summon Vine again he might appear."

"It's certainly a better idea than just opening up a doorway for any Sun demons," Raven commented drily.

"Vine it is. Or rather not-Vine."

I pulled out my Grimoire and showed Raven the sigil and

ritual I'd followed last time. She read it carefully then nodded.

"That's it. Nice job, by the way. You've got all the I's dotted and T's crossed here."

"So why do you think I got Mr. Smoky and not Vine?"

She shrugged. "Demons. Could be he's assumed Vine's presence, that he's killed him."

"Killed him? A demon? I didn't think they *could* be killed."

Raven grinned. "Not by us. At least not without some crazy weapon that you Knights probably have locked away in the Temple. I do think they can kill each other, but from what I understand the original demon isn't truly dead. They can come back."

I couldn't help but laugh. "What, like in a soap opera? We saw Roberto plunge to his death on the rocks below, but it was really just a dream, or his evil twin, or there was a giant moonbounce just out of sight that saved him at the last moment."

She grinned. "No idea. When I get to hell, I'll let you know. It's almost midnight. Let's do this thing."

Raven lit the candles and incense, securing the magical space with additional care. I put out the offering of wine, then got my sword.

"You sure?" Raven nodded to the weapon. "That's a little confrontational."

"And answering the summons meant for another demon, breaking out of a circle, and marking me isn't confrontational?"

She pursed her lips. "Point taken. Go ahead Templar girl. Bring this thing over."

Templar girl. It's what the smoke demon had called me.

I was scared—bone chilling, can't-make-my-hands-stop-shaking scared. There was a time when Templars faced their fears every day. Our lives weren't like that anymore. Well, at least other Templars' lives weren't. I was different. This path I'd chosen meant I'd need to get real comfortable with racing hearts and shaking hands.

"I invoke, conjure, and command thee spirit to appear before me in this circle. Come into this circle and give answers, faithful and true, to all my questions. Come peaceably without delay into my presence." Drawing Vine's sigil on a piece of parchment I touched it to the flame of the candle in the southern quarter and tossed it into the metal bowl.

"Vine, I request your presence. Appear before me and hear my appeal."

This was more difficult than it should have been because I wasn't actually calling Vine, I was calling whoever seemed to be answering his doorbell. I sat down to meditate, but instead of focusing on a vision of the Goetic demon in my mind, I thought of another. A creature of black smoke and red eyes, who spoke with a deep, husky voice.

Centering, balancing, I let go of this world and called out, "Vine, I respectfully ask you to appear. I need your knowledge, and would like to share an offering with you"

As before, a surge of energy hit the room, rocking me backward. The candle flames went sideways, incense smoke flattened on the ground in a spiral around the outer edge of the circle. Raven uttered a soft curse, staring hard at the center of the circle where dark smoke curled lazily from the floor.

I felt a presence pressing against me. Starting in the southern quarter, the flames atop the black candles went out one by one. I heard a stirring sound, a shuffling of leaves and a crackle of fire, then the symbols around the circle glowed bright white. The curl of midnight smoke thickened, rising in a column from the floor and flowing outward to the border of symbols.

The pressure against my chest increased, and I noticed

that Raven felt it, too. She grimaced, placing one hand against her stomach, holding the other hand outward to push her energy into the protective barrier of runes. I took tiny breaths and tried not to panic. I had help. Raven knew what she was doing. I wasn't here, facing this monster alone. Someone, for once, had my back.

The black smoke coalesced into a bipedal shape. Eyes glowed like coals, blue flames around the edges. In the dim light of the apartment I could see the impressive horns rising from his head, the gnash of sharp, white teeth in a black snout.

"What is your name and why do you answer my call for Vine?"

I might as well figure out who I was dealing with, along with some idea of what happened to the demon I'd originally summoned.

The demon poked at the southern corner. Sparks flew from the runes, and I had a momentary fear of burning down my apartment.

"Lovely distraction you have here, my Templar girl. Did your helper assist you? Am I to be so transfixed by such shiny things that I don't notice this house of cards you think to hold me in?"

Crap. I held my breath and shot a quick glance over at Raven. Her face was puffed out and red from the exertion of holding the circle intact. Ideally the symbols should hold the barrier on their own. Who was this demon that it took an experienced mage's entire attention just to contain?

And I wasn't sure she was even doing that. Raven might be holding this demon in place for now, but I got the impression that with one flick of his smoky finger, he'd be free. And that every last bit of power both Raven and I possessed couldn't stop him if he wanted out of the circle.

"Who are you and what have you done with Vine?" I was

incapable of formal speech at this point. Heck, I was incapable of just about any speech at all.

The demon folded his insubstantial arms across his chest. For a non-solid creature he seemed pretty darned solid right now, as if the smoke were only a covering over an actual flesh and blood form.

"Why is there concern over a minor demon such as Vine? Stop calling for him, lest I become jealous. *Thou shalt put none before me*, Templar girl."

Exodus 20:3, although I noticed that even in the attempt to co-opt God's Word, he didn't have the balls to refer to himself as in the same league.

"I can't call on you. I don't know your name. Thrice asked in a circle of runes, what is your name?"

There. I'd managed to regain my composure enough to phrase my request in the proper fashion. Three times was the most he'd be able to wiggle out of answering my question. If the circle held, that is.

The demon seemed pleased. I had no idea how I knew this. The expressionless face had not changed, he still held the same stance. The only thing that moved was the smoke that cloaked him, shifting and rolling like an ocean tide.

"You may address me as Balsur. That is the name you may use when you ask me to appear before you, and when you beg me for mercy."

This wasn't a demon you demanded anything of, and I got the feeling he wasn't stretching the truth about the beg-for-mercy thing. He might be a higher power, heck, he might be a really, really higher power, but it never did a mage any good to grovel before hell's minions. I might doubt my abilities, but to bluff before a demon was to have a smidgeon of a chance at staying alive.

"What is your station, Balsur? How many do you command, and which Duke do you call your Master?"

He laughed. I heard the exterior walls of the building creak with the force of it. My new window groaned in the sill. Something tickled in my ear and without even touching it to look, I knew it was blood.

"There is only one I call Master. I will tell you no more than that, little Templar, even if you ask me thrice. Suffice it to know I command legions and that Vine will not be answering any summons in the future."

I fought a moment of panic as the demon again placed a finger against the edge of the circle. One of the symbols dimmed, then went black. I heard Raven whimper.

The circle was broken, but still Balsur remained inside.

"Curiosity, my sweet girl, will be your downfall. What is it you wish? I have knowledge of things you have only dreamed of. Come sit by my feet and I will fill you up with all I know."

I wasn't about to sit at that thing's feet. Dealing with demons was a terrifying prospect, one that would lose me my soul if I wasn't careful. I'd been marked. This Balsur clearly wanted me to be his for all eternity. I needed to proceed very cautiously if I wanted to make sure that didn't happen.

"In the last day I have seen another who was demon-marked. He was killed in a magical ceremony, his soul claimed by the mage. I would like to know what claims demons have on their marked, if they are able to come and go as they please and keep track of those souls they someday wish to take. I would also like to know what happens when another takes a marked soul."

The silence as Balsur considered my request was punctuated by small gasps emanating from Raven. I wondered if she'd remember any of this once the demon left, if she'd need to sleep for days to recover.

"You refer to Mansi's mark. Humans are not usually so careless as to take a soul meant for hell. The only reason we allow them to take souls at all is because there are so many to choose from. '*When you reap the harvest of your land, do not reap to the very edges of your field or gather the gleanings of your harvest.*'"

Leviticus 19:9. It actually wasn't all that disturbing to have a demon quote Leviticus at me. What *was* disturbing was that he equated "allowing" humans to harvest souls as a part of a death magic ritual to the charity of leaving scraps of wheat in the field for the poor.

Balsur ran a finger along the three runes in front of him. They darkened. Raven made a gurgling noise. "We can cross the veil through the strength of our mark. It is an added benefit that allows us to ensure the soul flourishes and ripens as we wish it to. Nurturing the souls we plan to harvest is part of the joy in having access to this plane, as is seeking out other beings worthy of our attention."

This was not just a run-of-the-mill demon. Sun, Raven had said. I'd need to research that further, once I got the horrendous image of demons "nurturing" souls out of my head.

"As for what claims we have on our marked, the answer is none. Your soul is your own, Solaria Angelique Ainsworth, and it will remain your own until you willingly hand it over into my care. The mark is simply a way to keep track of our favorite fruit in an orchard of billions, and to ensure none other tastes what is meant for our table alone."

I felt like I was going to throw up. The coal-red eyes held mine, and with a sweep he extinguished the remaining runes. There was no sound from Raven. There was nothing visible in the darkness of my apartment but those red eyes staring into my own.

"I would be very angry if someone else had the effrontery to dine on you, Templar girl. Whoever did so would suffer.

And I would ensure that others knew the price they would pay for such a trespass."

"Is Mansi the one who killed the six Fiore Noir mages this evening?"

The eyes moved closer. I tried to keep my breath even. Balsur wouldn't kill me—not while my soul still belonged to me. Although Raven… I swallowed hard and tried not to let my thoughts wander in that direction.

"Tonight was a group effort. Shall I give you their names? Yes, I think I will. I enjoy watching you in action. Something stirs in me to see you battle so fiercely against evil, knowing that one day you will lie in its embrace. Mansi. Dalgas. Gi'nar. Pinen."

Four demons. Four. I'd struggled to banish Innyhal even with my sister's help. Who was I kidding? If Balsur hadn't stepped in, Innyhal might still be here while Athena and I lay dead on the floor. How was I to banish *four* demons?

I felt an icy tendril of smoke against my hand and my thoughts snapped back to Balsur. "Please accept my offering in return for your information. Return to hell directly, not to appear unless summoned again."

It wasn't a very formal close to the summoning, and my voice squeaked like I'd been inhaling helium. Balsur, unsurprisingly, did not obey.

"A paltry offering, Solaria Angelique Ainsworth. Now that you understand the value of my services, I expect your next offering to be of substantially greater value."

He'd not get my soul. Cheap wine was all I had to offer, and if he didn't like it he could always refuse to appear. But there was no way I could speak to him with such defiance while he stroked my skin, free from the broken circle, so I just nodded.

"I ask that you return to hell directly, not to appear unless summoned again."

Ask. Not demand. Because I didn't have enough confidence to demand anything of this demon and I really didn't want to piss him off.

He chuckled, icy insubstantial fingers leaving my arm. "Very well, Templar. But only because you asked so very nicely. Until we meet again."

Again there was a vacuum in the room, as if everything were being sucked toward the center of the circle. The red eyes vanished, and even though I'd turned them off before we began, my lights flickered on.

I immediately ran to Raven who was sitting on the floor, cupping a bloody nose and wheezing like an asthmatic. "You okay?"

She nodded. "Kleenex?"

Her voice sounded thick and gurgly. I had no tissues of any brand, so I ran into the bathroom, yanked the toilet paper off the roll and handed it to her.

"Damn, that is the scariest mother fucking demon I've ever seen. That was horror movie scary. Damn."

I wasn't sure what to say. I agreed with her. And the scariest part was that I had this demon's mark on my side. Raven went through half a roll of toilet paper, finally standing with a wad of it wedged up her nose.

"Well, bring out the books, girlfriend. We've got four demons to research and banish."

I blinked at her. "But they're targeting Fiore Noir, Baltimore mages, not your Haul Du ones. These are the very mages who killed Bliss, who orchestrated the deaths at Dupont Circle."

"And these are demons who won't care about collateral damage, won't worry about the mother with three kids at the park when they start ripping limbs off people. Demons kill. Yeah, I may want Fiore Noir dead, but demons won't really care how many hundreds of others die because they happened to be in the wrong place at the wrong time."

I didn't want them roaming around anymore than Raven did. And I'd rather Fiore Noir face justice at Tremelay's hands than ones from hell. So I went over to one of my many bookshelves that lines the walls and began pulling down books. Raven took them from me, spreading them out on the table. This was going to be a long night. I wasn't sure if we'd have time to do any minor banishments before sunrise when the magical spell would prove less effective. After my difficult time with Innyhal, I wasn't eager to dive into *four* more banishments in a twenty-four hour period. And I wasn't sure Raven would have the strength for it either.

I felt a hand on my shoulder. "Hey."

When I turned Raven was staring at me intently. It would have been a poignant moment in our friendship had she not had wads of toilet paper stuffed up her nose.

"I'm helping you get that mark off of you. That Balsur... I'm helping you. If it's the last thing I do I'll make sure that mark is removed. That demon isn't getting your soul, and he's not getting a free pass here on your skin either."

Again I felt a wash of relief flow through me. Balsur had kicked her ass. He'd casually blown past her magic, overcome her charged circle with a flick of his finger. But it still felt good to know someone was on my side. Together we'd figure this out.

She'd once been the closest thing I'd ever had to a best friend. I'd been crushed when Haul Du had thrown me out and she'd turned her back on me with the rest of the mages. But now...? Just talking with her the last few days brought back to me how much we'd had in common, how much I'd enjoyed our easy banter. My bestie was back. I wondered if she liked to LARP?

"Thanks. Let's take care of all this demon/human sacrifice/angel bullshit, then we'll turn our attention to Balsur.

She picked up one of the books and plopped down on the sofa, one of the blood-soaked chunks of toilet paper falling out of her nose as she threw her feet up on the cushions. "Deal. I gotta ask though—Solaria Angelique Ainsworth? What the fuck kind of name is that?"

CHAPTER 25

e were buried in demonology reference books and sticky notes when someone started banging on my door.

"Police!" I recognized Tremelay's voice even with an unfamiliar edge of panic in it. "Ainsworth! You in there?"

Ugh. I'd forgotten about the dead guy in my parking space.

"Coming!"

I threw open the door. The detective sagged with relief, his eyes traveling over me. "I need you to come downstairs and see something."

I shot Raven a quick look and she waved me on, her nose buried in a thick leather-bound tome. Stepping into the hallway, I shut the door behind me and followed Tremelay down the stairs.

"I'm so sorry. I should have called you but I knew you were dealing with the other crime scene, and there was something I had to do right at midnight."

He halted on the steps so abruptly I nearly ran into his

backside, his face incredulous as he spun around to face me. "You knew? You just left them there for other tenants to find?"

"I know, I know. I meant to call you right after the summoning, but Raven and I jumped right into research. I figured he wasn't going anywhere, and the quicker we can banish the four demons running around the city the better."

It sounded lame. I could have spared the time for one phone call, but honestly I'd been so shaken up from my encounter with Balsur that I'd forgotten.

Tremelay shook his head, murmuring something about crazy women and continued down the stairs. I winced and followed, already seeing the flash of blue and red through the open door to the apartment building.

John Ash had company. There wasn't just one dead guy in my parking space, there were five. They were neatly stacked side by side, evenly spaced. Either this angel had an OCD streak, or the police had moved them.

Tremelay waved his hand toward the bodies. "I'm guessing here, but our angel is back? Not happy with druggies and a cosplay guy in a park, he's now killing accountants and engineers and displaying them at your doorstep like gruesome offerings?"

I sighed, running a hand through my hair. How much sleep had Tremelay gotten in the past few days? Probably not much more than I had. One of the cops walking up to us had a steaming cup of coffee in hand, and I eyed it enviously, wishing this was all over with so I could catch some shut-eye.

"John Ash. He's the one with the beard at the end. He's also one of the names on the list we found at David Alban's house in DC. I'm sure if you get the ID on the others you'll see they're on the list, too."

I quickly told Tremelay about what we'd found at Bliss's house and my theory on why Araziel was killing these guys, as well as what my chat with Balsur had revealed about the mass murder this evening. Gryla's information I attributed to Balsur, not wanting to get into my confrontation with the elderly woman in my parking lot. Besides, I had no idea where those dead mages were. Hopefully she or someone else had already alerted the police about *that* crime scene.

"Vigilante angel and demons bent on revenge." The detective shook his head, then turned his scowl on me. "And you went through the guy's pockets to get his ID, leaving your fingerprints all over him? Then you left him here in the parking lot while you ran upstairs to summon another demon?"

I knew that I wasn't keeping up my end of the collaboration bargain. And although a crime was a crime, I hoped Tremelay would agree that stopping the four demons topped stopping Araziel.

The detective paced in frustration. "Will there be any of these mages left to prosecute for Bethany Scarborough and the Dead Run murders or is the angel going to take care of this with his own, twisted, heavenly justice?"

Well, that, too. I'm sure the higher ups in the police department were having a fit over all this. Riots and gang killings were bad enough; serial-killer mages and mass-murdering supernatural beings weren't going to do much for Baltimore's already tarnished public image.

"There are plenty of other names on that list." Eleven by my quick mental tally. I just needed to make sure Tremelay got to them first. How the heck was I going to rein in a vigilante angel? Although there had to be a reason he was leaving these dead guys in my parking space. One corpse, I could write off as a coincidence. Maybe the mage had found me through the guy at the magical shop and was coming to talk to me as Gryla had, then just happened to have been killed here. But I doubted five guys individually were milling about my parking space when the angel tracked them down.

Why me? I glanced down at the illusion of vomit I'd put in my space to ensure visitors didn't park there. One of the dead guys was half in it, and the police seemed to be giving the fake puke just as much respect as they were the bodies. It was my magic, stamped with an energy signature that would identify me as the mage to anyone who knew enough of the arts to successfully do an identification spell. It was a high-level spell, and tricky, with lots of false readings. But an angel might not find such a thing difficult.

I'd marked this space as mine through my magic. The angel had to be making some sort of contact here. It was a start. It was an opening I could use to perhaps sway the angel into stopping these killings and letting us humans handle justice ourselves.

"Look, I really want to concentrate on bringing this angel in and stopping him, but I need to prioritize. And four demons on a killing spree come first."

"But they're all after the same guys. The angel and four demons are all killing our murder suspects. Can't you stop them all at once, like a mass banishing or something?"

I wish. "You can't really banish angels. Let me take care of the demons first. The angel…" I looked down at the dead bodies all lined up in my parking space. There was some-thing I was missing here, something that my sleep-deprived brain wasn't registering. "I'm gonna try something tomorrow and see if I can get the angel to come see me. A sort of parlay."

The police cars and obvious activity had drawn quite a crowd in spite of the early morning hour. It was still dark, but people clustered under the streetlights, watching. Some looked like they'd just gotten off third shift work, others heading out for an early job. There were some partygoers who were wild-haired and bleary-eyed. Were any of *them* Fiore Noir mages, come to see what had happened to their colleagues? Were any of them demons possessing a human to keep from being detected? I doubted any were Araziel. An angel would have no need for stealth, no fear of anything.

Which made me wonder, where *was* Araziel? Did he manifest in a human form, or was he whizzing around like a breeze or like the lightning strike at the park right before Ronald Stull had been killed? How the heck was I going to find him?

Probably the same way I was going to call the four demons. Summoning. Although I was hoping Dad would have some added information for me—information that he might be willing to part with over the phone since I didn't have time for the obligatory face-to-face visit. Four demons and an angel, plus the eleven members of Fiore Noir that remained among the living, and this mysterious "stranger" with his soul trap and a grudge against three Haul Du mages. I had a lot of work to do and a shift at the coffee shop in six hours.

"Do you need anything else from me?" I asked Tremelay. A few more hours of research with Raven, some sleep, work, a quick phone call, then we'd start banishing. Hopefully neither of us would get killed.

"No. I'll swing by your work later today if anything comes up." The detective waved a hand at my very full parking spot. "We'll need to rope this off. Hope you've got somewhere else to park for the next day or so."

I didn't, aside from finding a space on the street.

Crap. I hadn't just forgotten about the dead guy, I'd forgotten to move my car. And sure enough when I looked a few spots over to where I'd left it, I found a Hyundai instead of my old Toyota Camry.

Great. I was demon marked. I had four demons, an angel, and a group of black magic mages to deal with. I had to work in six hours. *And* my car had been towed.

CHAPTER 26

*R*aven snapped a book shut and slid it onto the coffee table before rubbing her eyes. "Well, the good news is that Dalgas, Gi'nar, and Pinen all report to Mansi."

I didn't get how that was good news, so I just blinked and waited for her to continue.

"Balsur said the marked guy was one of Mansi's, so I'm going to put my money on the others riding across the veil on his mark as opposed to having their own marked human gateway from hell."

I was exhausted, but not so much that I missed the impact of her statement. "They can do that? So a high level demon, like Balsur, can bring a legion or two of his demons over on the strength of the mark he's placed on me?"

"I hope not. It's a mathematical formula based on the level of the demon, the strength of the mark, and the influence of the human on the veil. And don't ask, because I have no idea what the formula is. That was lost hundreds of years ago. It's probably in a book locked up somewhere in your Temple or something."

Raven was sounding grumpy, but my heart jumped with excitement at the thought. I'd love to get my hands on that formula. If Dad had it somewhere I'd be set. If not…well, I wouldn't be allowed inside the Temple without first taking my Oath of Knighthood.

"Okay, let's hope Balsur isn't planning on an invasion or anything and think about Mansi instead. How does that work? If a demon gets a free ride across the veil on the strength of his mark, and drags three with him, does that mean we only have to banish Mansi?"

Raven shrugged. "In theory. You've got more pull with the man upstairs than I do, so maybe you should start praying, because it's going to be hard enough to banish Mansi. If we have to get rid of three more demons after that—demons who will know we're on their trail and coming for them— we're screwed. Royally screwed."

My mind felt like it was full of mashed potatoes. I desperately needed sleep, but knew it would evade me if I didn't get this off my mind. "Do we need to summon and hold all four? I'm assuming if we don't, the other three will attack us while we have Mansi in the circle."

Raven ran a hand through her hair. "Fuck. Fuck. You're right. After tonight's fiasco with that Balsur, I'm not sure I can hold that many in the circle. And if your Templar banishment is on the fritz…"

Yeah. That. "I spoke to Gryla this evening and she pledged to bring as many Fiore Noir mages as she can round up to help."

Raven glared at me. "I'll risk myself to save these assholes from death-by-demons because I don't like the idea of innocents dying, but I'm *not* standing beside them in a ritual. Not."

"We can't do it ourselves. No one at Haul Du would help us, you know that. Fiore Noir is getting slaughtered out there. They'll help, and right now we need all the help we can get."

Raven made a low growl noise and threw up her hands. "Fine. You're right. We need more than two mages to do this. They might not be experienced, but they're highly motivated. I'm warning you now that if Mansi or any of his cronies get out, I'm using the Fiore Noir mages as a human shield."

Fair enough. "They'll be here just before midnight. Can you make sure you're here early enough to help get set up?"

"Sure." Raven ran a hand through her crimson-tipped hair. "You do know that your detective friend will want the mages turned over to him. Are you planning on having him wait outside the door to grab them after the ritual? How are you going to make a deal with these mages to banish the demons, then flip them over to the cops? Isn't that a bit double-crossy?"

I winced. She was right. "He just wants them for questioning and he's already spoken to a few of them. I don't think he has anything yet he can really arrest them on."

Raven's glare pinned me in place. "And you'll tell them that? Let them know that you'll help save their lives by getting rid of these demons, and the angel, but they'll need to face human justice on their own?"

I took a deep breath. "Yeah. A prison sentence or being ripped apart by a demon? Or having your soul torn through your rib cage along with all your internal organs by an angel?"

"I'd take prison." Raven grimaced. "And I'd figure out a way to get out of town and change my name between you banishing the demons and my arrest."

That would be on Tremelay's plate, not mine. Although bringing the murderers to justice was on my plate too, if I was completely honest with myself.

Raven sighed. "There's no way I'm driving home tonight.

I get your bed. I'll work on research and the particulars of the banishment while you're serving up coffee tomorrow. I don't need to do that at night."

"Go to bed." I waved her to my room and curled up on the couch with Lawrence and Singtha's *Beyond the Veil.*

The sun was up and the traffic outside my window was roaring with the morning commute by the time I snapped the book shut, finally feeling confident that this might work without any of us dying. I glanced out the window and was contemplating curling up with Raven in my bed when my phone rang. I jumped, heart racing at the loud sound. Snatching it off the dining table, I blindly pressed the answer button to silence the thing before it woke Raven up.

"Aria?"

It was Dad. What the heck was Dad doing calling me at… okay, it *was* eight o'clock. Not exactly early, especially by my father's standards.

"Morning, Dad." It wasn't the cheerful greeting I was trying for. I was just too darned tired.

"Are you okay, honey? Athena called last night and told us about the banishing. Her hands are all blistered, and she said your back was burned. Something about claw marks, too."

Of course. Nothing in my family was ever a secret. I guessed I should be glad that Athena had waited on the story until she'd gotten home rather than calling from the road seconds after she'd left my apartment.

"Some mages summoned an assassination demon in DC and it got loose. It slashed my back. Athena and I returned it to hell, but not before he burned her hands and the back of my shirt. We're fine, Dad. I'm fine."

Actually I wasn't feeling all that fine. Raven had slapped some additional salve on my back and re-bandaged me up, but each twist and turn of my body pulled at the injured skin.

Making coffee this afternoon was going to be an exercise in pain management.

"Athena said it was Innyhal." Dad's voice was worried. "He's definitely banished?"

"Yes." I waited, holding my breath for what was to come next. Athena surely told him about Balsur. My sister was smart. She'd connected the dots, and although she hadn't insisted on every detail about my obvious familiarity with the demon, she knew. And she surely told Dad.

"So Athena says you also have an angel running around up there in Baltimore?"

I let out the held breath with a whoosh. What? No insistence that I come home so the entire family as well as the Temple elders could examine my demon mark and chastise me for my carelessness? Maybe Athena had kept that to herself after all.

"Araziel. There are some death-magic mages up here and a few were doing human sacrifice. They took a woman's soul that had been promised to Araziel, and the angel's gone on a bit of a reaper-bender as a result."

Dad made a tsk-tsk noise. "Angels are mission-oriented. No doubt Araziel believes he is simply delivering justice. Once he finishes with those he feels wronged the woman, he'll make his way back to heaven."

"He's leaving dead people in my parking space," I blurted. "And he killed two junkies who just happened to be nearby. It's not cool, Dad—both the mercy killing and dumping corpses in my parking spot. I had to park somewhere else and I got towed."

Sheesh, that sounded so petty and selfish, but I was tired. And I was beginning to wonder how I was going to get my car back.

"You can't banish an angel, Aria. You can call one and try to reason with him, but you can't banish him."

"I know." I shook my head to clear the thick feeling of sleep rapidly descending on me. "What can I say to him, Dad? And how do I respectfully summon him? He's one of God's messengers. I'm endowed with my powers by the hand of God. I assume that's why my parking spot has become a repository for his dead. I want to lean on that tie between us without insulting him."

"No circle. No candles or incense. Nothing except the sigil to burn and your sword held as a holy symbol. They hear prayers, Aria. Pray and he will come. Humble yourself and he will want to honor your request."

Humble. I wasn't all that good at humble, but I was quickly learning. "Thanks, Dad."

It was information freely given without an in-person visit. I appreciated my father bending the rules, and knew he only did so because he was worried about me.

"Get some sleep, sweetie. We'll talk later when you're more rested. I'm concerned about the problems in that city you're calling your home. I'd prefer my daughter not fight a hopeless battle in the land of Sodom and Gomorrah."

In the last two weeks I'd faced a necromancer and the resident *Balaj* of vampires, demons, an angel, and two groups of mages. I was beginning to think Dad's reference to the twin cities of sin was spot on, but how could I walk away? We were supposed to safeguard Pilgrims on the Path. I was absolutely convinced there were pilgrims here in Baltimore that needed my protection. What sort of Templar was I if I walked away and let them perish in a sea of evil?

"The Crusades, Dad? We've always fought hopeless battles. I'm just doing my job, Knight or not."

"Sleep tight, my daughter."

I hung up the phone smiling, because underneath all the worry there had been a note of pride in my father's voice.

And that was something that energized me more than a solid eight hours of sleep ever could.

CHAPTER 27

I'd ended up snoozing on the couch and waking up late, throwing clean clothes over a hastily washed body and grabbing my sword and phone as I ran out the door. It wasn't until I'd hit the bottom of the staircase that I'd remembered my car.

Crap. Double crap. I quickly copied down the number for the towing company on the parking lot sign, then decided to waste money on a cab. I didn't have time to walk, or even jog, to work. Cab fare. Towing fines. There wasn't going to be enough of my vampire-job money to last me another month if this kept up. I'd need to start being poverty-line frugal, or get a second job. Although how I was supposed to find time to work a second job with my Templar duties, I had no idea.

Digging my phone out of my purse to dial for a cab, I saw I'd missed calls last night. Had it rung? I hadn't remembered hearing any call besides my Dad's.

Frowning, I called for the cab, then checked my settings. Do Not Disturb. Ugh. It had seemed like a good idea when we were in the middle of summoning Balsur and once again I'd forgotten to take the setting off when done. Dad's had come through, as I'd designated his number as a priority call, but none of the others had. There were several calls from Tremelay, about the dead guys in my parking space, as well as their names and a few more calls from this morning. I scrolled through them, looking over at my space still festooned with crime scene tape and the magical vomit. How long would they block my parking space? I'd need to ask building management if I could have another one assigned to me until the police cleared it.

Dario. I'd missed three calls from the vampire. Each message became angrier as he demanded I call and update him about the angel situation. I had nothing to update him on. Other than Araziel bringing me a bunch of corpses and that I thought the vampires were safe as long as there were death magic mages left to kill, I didn't know what to tell him.

It wouldn't be enough. He'd be pissed. And I felt somewhat guilty for not prioritizing something that was important to the vampires. Dario had stuck his neck out for me a lot. Because of him, Russell was alive, practicing his necromancy and not drained of blood in a ditch somewhere.

Then there was one message from Janice that had come in just before midnight, urging me to call her. My cab pulled up and I hit re-dial, thankful that the spell on my sword was working and I hadn't been denied service for carrying the weapon.

"I tried to give you the heads-up," she announced in lieu of a greeting.

"Heads-up for what?" Maybe I should listen to my messages before dialing back next time.

"The article. This morning's paper? I *had* to run it, Aria. There was a slaughter of six people at an apartment in the West End, then all the dead bodies in the parking lot by your apartment last night? People *saw* that. It would have been negligent of me not to report it."

"What exactly did you say, Janice?" I gnawed on my lip, worried that she'd gone and spilled *all* the beans—demons, angel, death magic, and all.

"That there is a rash of killings that seems to be resulting from a feud between an occult gang from DC and one here in Baltimore, that there had been ritualistic killings and brutal murders that included innocent bystanders and lawful, working-class citizens."

Oh no. "Thanks, Janice. I'll call you later."

I hung up and stared at the phone, pretty darned sure what the messages that Tremelay had left this morning probably said. Just to make sure before I called him back, I listened to them.

Yep. Reaming me out for leaking the information. It *was* me, but he couldn't know that. It could have just as easily been someone from the station. Besides, it wasn't my fault that the bodies in my parking lot had been such a public spectacle.

Oh wait. Yeah, it had been my fault. If I'd called it in right away rather than summoning a demon and spending most of the night researching while an angel lined up corpses in my parking space, the police might have been able to handle it more quietly and do damage control. It was too late for that now, so I dialed Tremelay's number and got ready to eat some humble pie. It would be good practice for when I had to grovel before an angel later today.

"Ainsworth!" the detective screamed in my ear. Even the taxi driver winced at the sound. "What in all that's holy are you doing? Did you *read* that article? Occult gangs? Human sacrifice? Our phones are ringing off the hook. Nobody can get anything done with all the whack-jobs calling to tell me their neighbor is a Satanist who killed their dog. I've got every unsolved missing person case piled up on my desk because family members are frantic to know if their son or daughter was murdered by this occult gang."

"At least she didn't bring up the four demons on the loose or a reaper angel." I was trying to find some kind of silver lining in all this mess.

"I wish she had. No one would have believed her and the public would have labeled her a crazy. Now most of Baltimore is thinking this Janice somebody is the best investigative reporter since Watergate. If I don't show some progress on this case right now, the lieutenant is going have my head on a pike."

Crap. "Any progress on the list from the DC murder? Those guys should be suspects and there's only eleven left."

"Besides the three we managed to speak to last night, no. They've all conveniently taken leave from work. I don't have the manpower to stake out their homes and wait for them. They weren't there when we came by. I left a note and my card, but no one has called. There's too many on that list, Ainsworth. Eleven is too many people for me to do a concerted manhunt. I can't put out warrants. I've got no hard evidence that they're connected to the murders. It's all circumstantial and right now they're just persons of interest. Until I manage to grab a few and put the thumbscrews on them, I've got nothing."

I felt a twinge of guilt. "I'm working on that. I'll call you later and hopefully I'll have a few of them for you to interview. I know your lieutenant isn't going to care about this, but I've got to get rid of these demons first then see what I can do about the angel. Otherwise you won't have anyone left alive to question, let alone arrest."

I paid the cabbie and climbed out of the car, hearing Tremelay growl in my ear. "Tonight, Ainsworth. I need something by tonight."

"I'm on it. I'm at the coffee shop. Gotta go."

I threw my phone in my bag and shot Brandi an apologetic look as I raced into the back to stash my sword and purse in a locker. My back was starting to hurt again. I really needed to change the bandages and put more salve on the cuts. Honestly, I probably needed to go to the doctor or an urgent care place and have it looked at, possibly get some antibiotics or something. There was no time. If I didn't die of a necrotic tissue infection in the next couple of days, I'd carve out a few hours to have a doctor look at it.

"You okay?" Brandi shot me a quick look before turning her attention to the frother.

"Yeah." I winced. "Burned and scraped up my back a couple of days ago. Woke up late and didn't have time to take any aspirin before heading out. Oh, and my car got towed because my parking space was a crime scene so I parked in the neighbor's."

I didn't tell her about the demons, angel, and killer mages running around. There was only so much sob story I could pour on a co-worker.

She shook her head. "Girl, you have the worst luck of anyone I know. I can't help you with the towed car, but I've got some painkillers in my purse. Finish up this caramel mocha latte light whip and I'll get them."

"Bless you," I called, taking the container of steaming milk from her hand and straining it into the espresso.

She was back in a flash, taking the cup and handing me two pills. I threw them down dry and ran for the register to relieve Anna for her break. It wasn't five minutes later before I realized that whatever Brandi had given me, it wasn't aspirin.

I stared owl-eyed at the two women ordering croissants and espresso, trying to keep from falling facedown onto the cash register.

"Brandi," I hissed once the lunch crowd had thinned out. "Brandi, what *was* that stuff?"

"Percocet. I got them when I had my wisdom teeth out and saved the leftovers for emergencies."

Percocet. And I'd taken two. I was high as a kite off a controlled substance while at work. Lord knows how long these things would take to work their way out of my bloodstream. I had a sword in the storage room. I had to pick-up my towed car and drive it home. I had to summon and banish four demons and beg an angel to stop killing. I had to chat with the police later. And I was high.

"Brandi, I needed aspirin, not narcotics. I can barely think straight. How am I supposed to get through the rest of my shift?"

She giggled. "Bet your back doesn't hurt anymore."

It did, I just didn't care. Honestly right now I was finding it hard to care about anything. In a desperate attempt to counteract the opiates, I made a triple shot of espresso and tossed it down. Two hours left in my shift. Maybe if it was slow I could take a nap in the back room. Would this stuff work out of my system faster if I napped? Or ate a sandwich? Or drank a case of Red Bull?

I took a few deep breaths, chewed on an ice cube and struggled to stay awake. Just as I was ready to pop into the storage room for a quick snooze on the boxes of dark roast, the door chimed and I looked up to see a monster. The man shimmered before my eyes, his normal human form melting into a corpse—a corpse that had been burned in a fire.

I blinked, pretty sure I was now hallucinating. "Anna," I hissed to the redhead. "Do you see that guy over there?"

She shot me an odd look, then peered around the pastry counter at the angel. "Yeah. Why? Did he stiff you last time? Do you know him or something?"

"He's an ugly monster," I told her. I probably shouldn't

have said that, but I was relieved that she actually *saw* the man. And, you know, drugs.

Anna pursed her lips, pulling her head back as if she was concerned I might be a rabid animal. Then she leaned around the counter again, this time looking a little bit longer. "Aria, that's just *mean*. He's not my type, but it's not like he's hideous or anything. Not enough leather for me, you know? I don't really go for those emo hipster types."

Did she not see the charred skin melting off his body? I leaned across the counter, too, the realization that we were both staring at this man trickling into my foggy brain.

I blinked a few times, then rubbed my eyes. It was a guy— a college-age boy with skinny jeans and a button-down sky-blue shirt, a leather bag over one shoulder. His blond hair hung low across one eye, the other side practically shaved. Anna was right, she didn't go for this kinda guy. I didn't either.

Stupid drugs.

"Does he know we don't do table service?" I asked Anna. We were both still draped over the counter staring at the man who was scrolling through something on his phone.

"It's slow," she replied. "Won't kill you to do a little customer service and take his order."

I should have asked Brandi or her to do it, given my current state, but I was curious to get a better look at this guy who I could have sworn was pretty close to a human candle when he came through the door. Pushing myself back from the counter and nearly falling into the stack of cups behind me, I got my balance, smoothed down my shirt, and tried to walk in a straight line as I approached the customer.

He didn't look up at me, so after a few moments of standing by the table, swaying slightly, I decided to speak. "Uh, hi. Normally customers come up to the counter to order, but we're kinda slow so I don't mind… I mean, what can I get for you?"

The guy was really focused on his cell phone, his thumbs moving so fast they were a blur. Although with the way my vision was right now, I was hardly a good judge of motion.

"Coconut milk cap, light foam? You look like a light foam, non-dairy guy. I've got gluten-free macaroons, too. Or how about—"

"It's not what you can do for me, Solaria Angelique Ainsworth, it's what I can do for you."

It was like the man spoke inside my head. If Brandi ever offered me painkillers again I was going to say no. Just say no to drugs. Wasn't that some Reagan-era slogan or something?

"I didn't quite get that." Oh screw it. "Look, I'm kinda high right now because I took something I thought was aspirin but it wasn't. Can you cut me a break and just tell me what you want. Speak slowly and look at me while you talk, and maybe I'll actually get your order right."

"Did you get my gifts last night? The moment I realized there was a Templar in town, I knew this city had a chance of salvation. Admittedly, you're not quite what I expected in a Templar Knight, but…mysterious ways and all that."

I stared at the guy, my mouth hanging open. I think there was some drool involved. Then he turned to look at me, his hands still flying on the cell phone, and I saw his eyes. They were bright blue, like the sky on a clear summer day. Bright blue. Blue not found in nature, blue.

Stupid drugs. I spun around and headed toward the storeroom.

"What does he want?" Anna asked. I paused for a second and looked at her warm brown eyes, just to make sure *they* were a normal color.

"Nothing. He's probably just cooling off from the heat outside or using our Wi-Fi or something. I need to lay down in the back for a few. Just give me fifteen to get my head on straight, okay?"

Once in the storeroom, my gaze landed on my sword propped up against the lockers in the corner. Feeling like it would be a good idea to cradle a weapon in my arms while under the influence of opiates, I grabbed it and plopped down on a box, leaning my face against the cool metal of the pommel. Slumping back, I rested against the wall, closing my eyes. I had another hour and a half on my shift. How I was going to get through it, I had no idea. I was too busy for this. I'd never been one to take drugs. Booze in moderation, yes. Drugs, no. I felt like my brain was swaddled in cotton.

A light came on in the room that made my eyelids pink. "Go away." Whoever it was, they needed to turn the storeroom lights off and leave me in peace to drool on my sword.

"I cannot. Not until I avenge the human's death. She entrusted her soul to me and I failed her. I cannot leave until those who hurt her and stole her soul pay for their evil."

I opened up my eyes and squinted at hipster boy in his skinny jeans. "You're not an employee. Get out of the storeroom. Or fill out an application so we can hire you."

He smiled sadly, his blue eyes glowing. "I didn't want to scare your fellow employees, or risk their blindness and possible insanity. But you, as a Templar, should be able to see me in my true form."

Blinding light hit my eyes. Even closed it slammed into my skull with the strength of a hammer. I raised my arm to shield them and squinted. Hipster guy looked like he'd walked through a nuclear bomb and had a very over-exposed picture taken.

That was his true form? What was with the creepy corpse thing I'd seen earlier? Okay, maybe it wasn't the drugs, especially since my head seemed less foggy. Actually my head now hurt, along with my back. I gripped my sword tighter and shut my eyes again. "Got it. Turn off the glow, sunshine. Go back to the skinny jeans and the cell phone."

He complied. The storeroom seemed dark as a windowless cellar at midnight after his impressive display. I blinked, trying to clear the stars from my eyes and get my pupils back to normal.

Humility. I wasn't sure if I'd already insulted him or not, but it was time to back pedal and start laying the respect on thick. Although he'd come to me. He seemed to think I was a step above the other humans. If he was God's messenger, then I was... I don't know, God's muscle or something.

"Araziel. I'm honored. I've never been graced with the presence of an angel. I apologize if I offended you earlier. Like I said, I accidently took some drugs and didn't trust that what I was seeing or hearing was real."

He inclined his head, those eyes of his still that disturbing shade of blue. Or were they? I blinked and squinted, wondering what the flash of orange was. If only I weren't high right now.

"When I sensed your presence, I knew our purposes were aligned. After I have delivered justice for the human's soul, I'll stay to help you rid the city of evil and create a shining home for the faithful. Baltimore will be a heaven on earth, a sanctuary for all who walk the true path. Together we can create the next Garden of Eden."

Araziel was scaring me. His words sounded wonderful... actually, no they didn't. I had a sudden vision of justice at the point of the sword with no room for repentance, no area of gray between the black and white. What he called evil might be a stumbling pilgrim to me. And I wasn't sure the citizens of Baltimore would be on board with his type of clean-sweep programs.

"Like those two junkies at Old Town Mall? You can't just go killing people. Humans make mistakes. They were given free will. Our purpose isn't to murder anyone who strays from the path."

Only God should judge. It had been a Templar mantra ever since the Crusades when we'd discovered that good and evil are sometimes in the eye of the beholder. I was a bit conflicted about the whole justice thing, but I knew I couldn't take the heavy-handed approach this angel was proposing.

"Those two were dying and their souls were tarnished by theft and deceit as well as their weakness of will. I simply assisted them." He tilted his head, as if I were a child in need of instruction into the ways of the righteous.

"*You* think they were damned, but how do you know? They might have been saved. Humans have made amazing advances in medical technology. What if those two had lived, cleaned-up, repented, and went on to do wondrous things for humanity? What if they had turned toward a righteous path and spent their lives helping others? You took their souls before they were dead."

The angel squinted, shaking his head slowly. "You know much, Templar. I see that I made a good choice in seeking you out. Together we will avenge the lost souls and rid the city of evil. With you to guide me, I will not make such a mistake again."

I squirmed at the words of flattery. There seemed something almost oily about them, as if he were herding me in the direction he wanted me to go. But I was high, I'd never dealt with an angel before, and I was unused to this sort of praise. Maybe I was just being paranoid. "We can't kill humans. We Templars did that once with terrible consequences. Our goals now are to protect the Pilgrims on the Path. The human justice system is in place to deliver punishment, not us."

The angel's mouth set in a stubborn line, irritation

flashing in those sky-blue eyes. It made me wonder how much grace one of them lost once they'd crossed the veil from heaven into our worldly plane. Stubborn wasn't a trait I'd ever thought I'd use to describe an angel, but there was no mistaking that expression.

"And from what I have seen of this city, I doubt the human justice system has the ability to adequately punish any evil. Better for me to separate their souls from the bodies, so evil no longer threatens the good. Better for us to judge now than watch innocents die because of our indecision."

This wasn't heading in a good direction. "Humans make mistakes. We're born into a world of sin and spend our lives stumbling along as best as we can. Innocence and goodness untested is weak. Our souls need to be forged in the fire. We need to walk through the evil, stumbling and falling in order for our path to have meaning. Even after a lifetime of evil, a man or woman can reach the gates of heaven by turning a corner at the very end. We are forgiven a lot if our final steps are those on a righteous path."

His eyes narrowed. "There is such horror in this city. It's our duty to cleanse it. Those who killed the humans for dark magic, who took their souls for evil, do not have the ability to turn that corner."

"Don't they? How do you know that? Perhaps God has a plan for them, too. Let the humans charge them with murder and deliver their worldly punishments. If they end their lives with hearts of evil, then they will see justice in the afterlife, too." I gripped my sword tightly, holding it upright to form a cross. "You are not an angel of justice, Araziel, and neither am I. Leave justice to the human police and to God."

He backed away from me, scowling. "The mages killed many innocents, but other innocents in this city die too. I hear their screams of pain. Do *they* not deserve to live? If only we have the courage to take a stand, then they might. How can you have seen what you have the last three days and not agree with me?"

My eyes stung with tears of frustration. "Bliss shouldn't have died. Those others shouldn't have died. But killing every human who touches sin isn't the solution. Let the mages live. Let the human law enforcement deliver justice. They will have time in prison to think on their wrongdoing."

There was a moment of silence. "What if they escape?"

Escape justice? It happened. Criminals got off on technicalities or were released early for good behavior. Tremelay had said over the phone he had nothing on these people besides circumstantial evidence and hearsay. Even if he found evidence of occult activity in their homes, that was no crime. He needed something to place them at the scene of the murders, something to tie them in with the killings, otherwise they were just guys practicing magic in their basements.

I rubbed a hand over my eyes and wondered again if I *shouldn't* just let Araziel take care of them. Tremelay would be pissed, but I'd rather face his anger than risk letting these guys wiggle off the hook. It would be so easy to have the angel kill them all. It would be clean and neat. But it wouldn't be human. It wouldn't be right. It wouldn't be in keeping with what I saw as my duties as a Templar.

"What punishment can humans give mages who are so lost that they will take a soul? How can any human prison hold them?" The angel continued.

He was right about that, too. All it took was a few phone calls and someone would sneak their grimoire in with a box of mystery novels. Guards were so busy searching for weapons and drugs that they wouldn't think twice about herbs and candles, about salt and chalk. A ruthless mage in prison would soon run the joint. And probably be out on parole after a few years. Even if Tremelay made his best case, there was nothing either the detective or I could do to ensure they actually were punished for their deeds. I could break into their houses, burn their grimoires, but they'd still be able to accumulate spells and materials in short time. The human justice system just wasn't set up to deal with mages. Or demons, angels, or vampires either. Was death the only answer when it came to certain criminals?

"We have to have faith," I told him, not quite believing those words myself. Faith seemed to be an elusive concept to me lately. "If the system fails, and these people are once again a threat to others, then I'll reconsider. Then we might have no choice but to take their lives."

I felt sick, like I'd just drawn a line in the sand. Could I do it? I'd faced the thought that I might have to kill Russell, to sacrifice one man to save hundreds of vampire lives. I'd been so glad I'd not had to make that decision in the end. But what if this time I had to? It was one thing to kill someone when you were in direct combat and fearing for your life. This would be me judging another and taking their life. Could I do it?

Even the angel looked skeptical. "You have much to do in this city, but you'll take the time to monitor these mages wherever they are incarcerated, and deliver justice yourself if the humans fail to?"

I nodded. "Let me do it. I'm the Templar. I carry the sword. It's my mission to protect the Pilgrims on the Path even if that means I sully my soul by taking a life. I'm the first line of defense for the innocents of Baltimore."

Some first line. How many had died in the past few weeks?

"You risk more lives this way," he warned me. "How will it sit with your soul if other pilgrims die because you allowed the police to deliver your justice for you?"

I felt so lost. I didn't know what I was doing, how to

reconcile my beliefs with any of this. It all sat heavy on my soul, every last bit of it. Not for the first time in the past two weeks, I wished I'd stayed home, taken my Oath and spent the rest of my life jousting and reading old manuscripts.

"I'm human. And I'm only one Templar in a city of six hundred thousand. I need to have faith in and support the humans who are also working to make this city a better place."

The angel raised an eyebrow then pulled his cell phone out of his pocket. "Twenty-four hours, Solaria Angelique Ainsworth. That's how long you have to bring these mages to human justice or I will intervene."

"Deal." He turned to leave and I hurriedly stood, remembering there was one more thing I needed to address with him. "Oh, and I'm working with the vampires. I mean, I've got that situation covered, so there's no need to do anything there."

I might no longer be feeling drugged-out, but I'd completely mangled that one.

Araziel turned to look at me over his shoulder. Did he smile? Had I imagined that? "The vampires are dead. They have traded their souls in a bargain with the devil. It's my duty to release those souls to their afterlife."

My heart pounded. This was exactly what I'd feared. "Their bargain included immortality. It's not your duty to release their souls. This is my town, under my protection, and they're my pilgrims, too."

He laughed. It had an oddly cruel note for an angel. "They're vampires, not pilgrims. How can you possibly extend your protection to them?"

I scrambled to think of something that might sway the angel. "They are capable of good, capable of redemption. They may be dead, they may have made a devil's bargain, but their souls are not yet lost. Give me a chance to save them, to bring them to grace. Don't kill them and condemn them to hell. We're in the business of saving souls, not filling the halls of hell."

His mouth twitched. "We will discuss this later. In the meantime, your fanged pilgrims need not fear. I am more concerned with those who take human souls than sending vampires to their master in hell."

I nearly slumped against the wall in relief, closing my eyes for no more than a second. When I opened them he was gone, and I'd not even heard the door open and close.

CHAPTER 28

After wasting more money on getting my car out of impound, I decided I might as well splurge and get dinner. It was after seven by the time I got back to the house, and the pizza cold after spending nearly an hour arguing with building management about my parking space. It seems they didn't care that the spot I'd paid for was roped off as a crime scene. I'd have to shell out additional money for a second space this month or risk getting towed again. More money from my rapidly depleted checking account went to the landlord, along with assurances they'd drop the second spot after thirty days.

"Thank God!" Raven dove at me and ripped the pizza box from my hands, eating a piece cold as she set the oven to warm. "You've got no food in this place beyond that leftover roast chicken. No wonder you're so skinny."

"Delivery is an option," I grumbled. She'd been able to sleep in as late as she wanted. She hadn't been fighting off narcotics and trying to negotiate with an angel while supposedly working. She didn't have claw marks and the equivalent of the worst sunburn ever on her back. I opened the fridge, just to make sure Raven hadn't drunk my Emergency Beer. She was my best friend and she was helping me out, but there was a limit to my hospitality.

"So how was your day?" Raven spoke with her mouth full as she tossed the pizza slices into the oven to warm.

It was kinda nice, coming home to someone and having them ask about my day. I thought about my date with Zac and tried to imagine us living together. Nah. Maybe I needed a roommate? My lease was up in six months, maybe Raven and I could rent a bigger place together. It would be awesome to have someone around, especially someone who knew as much about magic as Raven did.

"My reporter friend couldn't hold back on the story any longer, so all of Baltimore thinks there are two warring gangs, one of which is doing occult killings of random civilians. Tremelay, that cop friend of mine, is livid. If he doesn't make headway on these murders soon, his head is going to roll. And then he might be mad enough to take my head off, too."

"Seriously?" Raven paused her pizza-warming activities to give me a concerned look.

"No. He's a good guy though. Baltimore needs people like him in homicide. Did I tell you he's from a Templar family?"

Raven shook her head and stuffed another piece in her mouth as she shut the oven door.

"Anyway," I continued, "after I got to work, a coworker gave me opiates that I thought were aspirin, so I spent my whole shift high as a kite."

Raven snorted. "Kite. Because your magical name is Kite. That's funny."

No, it wasn't. "Araziel came in and I swear I thought I was hallucinating at first. We talked, and I think I've convinced him to stop killing and let the police handle prosecuting Bliss's murderers."

"I think I'd rather the angel kill them. There's no saying they'll wind up in jail at the end of a trial, and honestly I don't think jail is adequate punishment for what they've done."

I understood how Araziel and even Raven could feel this way. Heck, I kind of felt this way too, but laws were laws. I wasn't a vigilante. I needed to uphold our human justice system. And I was trying really hard to convince myself of this when the alternative was so appealing.

"How was your day?" I asked. "Did you manage to get everything prepped for the ritual?"

Raven nodded. "Ritual is ready, tailor-made for Mansi and his goons. I also did a bunch of research on Balsur in hopes of eventually getting that mark off you, and more on Araziel, although you seem to have that one wrapped up on your own. I'm beat."

I could imagine. I doubt I could have managed that and still be standing afterward. "I'm not convinced Araziel still won't be a problem. It may have been the drugs, but he was really weird. All about justice and ridding Baltimore of evil by killing left and right."

She rubbed her eyes, holding her half-eaten pizza slice in her mouth. "Really? Maybe he's a bit nuts from being this side of the veil. Or maybe Bliss's death made him snap. Everything I read made him seem like a gentle and caring spirit, one who eases the soul's transition at death. Nothing depicts him as an angel of justice or vengeance."

I yanked a piece of pizza out of the oven even though it still wasn't more than room temperature. "I guess even angels can pick up the sword given the right stressor. Hey, I need to get a quick nap in to recharge and hopefully sleep off the remaining effects of my prescription pain relief. Can you gather supplies? And make sure I'm up at nightfall?"

Raven gave me a thumbs-up and I headed to the

bedroom, gobbling down the piece of pizza before collapsing facedown on my bed.

* * *

ONE OF THE joys of narcotics is that they did allow for restful, dream-free sleep. I awoke not long after the sun had set, feeling refreshed and ready to banish demons. Unfortunately, my back didn't feel as wonderful as it had when I'd been medicated. I stripped off my shirt and carefully peeled off the bandages, looking at the red skin and dark scabs across my shoulder blades and waist. Grabbing a tube of antibiotic cream and a washcloth, I walked out of the bedroom to ask Raven if she'd mind playing nurse.

Raven wasn't the only one in my apartment. I froze, topless with a washcloth in one hand and a tube of cream in another and stared at Dario. His gaze lowered and I flung my arms across my chest, my face feeling as red as my back.

"What…what are you doing here?" I stuttered. Duh. The vampire had left some pretty insistent messages last night. I should have realized he'd be tracking me down come sundown.

Dario's eyebrows were practically on the ceiling as he looked at me, naked from the waist up, and then over at Raven. "Are you a couple? I hadn't realized. I'm so sorry for intruding."

Oh Lord. I just wanted to sink into the floor with embarrassment.

Raven blinked in shock. "Oh, hell no. I don't do girls. Aria's a friend. And friends feel comfortable walking around half-naked in front of each other when they're camped in a one-bedroom apartment to summon demons."

"Actually I was hoping you'd put some of this on my

back." I extended the tube, keeping one arm across my breasts.

Raven hopped off the counter. "Sure. Turn around."

I would rather do this in the bathroom away from Dario's eyes, but opted to get it over with as quickly as possible so I could get a shirt on and regain what was left of my dignity.

Raven took the tube and I turned around, wincing as the cold cream hit my back.

"That looks painful."

Dario's voice was too close and I instinctively wrapped my arms once again across my breasts.

"A demon clawed me. And then burned me. And no, you can't lick it." I have no idea why I said the last part, it just came blurting out of my mouth. Maybe I still had some of the drugs in my system, or maybe Dario seeing me half naked was making me jumpy.

"I have no intention of licking you." His voice sounded weird, and I couldn't tell if he was amused or appalled by the idea. "Where is this demon that attacked you? Did you kill it?"

"You don't kill demons," Raven scoffed, "you banish them to hell. And you hope they don't hold a grudge and track you down if they wind up summoned again and on the loose during your lifetime."

I rolled my eyes, even though no one could see. "I banished it. And I'm not particularly worried that he'll come after me again, even if he winds up summoned and out of a circle."

I wanted to sound bad-ass in front of Dario, so I left out the reason I wasn't afraid of Innyhal. And I also left out the little fact that my banishment hadn't worked, that it was Balsur who had thrown the demon back into hell.

"Good." Dario's voice sounded farther away and I felt my

muscles relax. "Your friend tells me you are banishing four more demons tonight? I'm assuming these demons are the reason you didn't call me last night and update me on the angel?"

I really longed to lay on the guilt and have him think that while he was yelling at me over my cell phone I was being torn apart by a demon, but I didn't have it in me to lie any more than I'd already done.

"I'm so sorry I didn't call you. There was a massacre of mages by a group of demons in the west side of town, then Raven and I had to summon another demon to figure out what was going on, then the angel deposited a bunch of dead bodies in my parking space and I had to deal with that. I forgot I'd put my phone on mute, and was non-stop from sunset to sunup."

Raven gave my shoulder a quick pat and handed me the tube of antibiotic cream. I headed in to the bedroom and threw a T-shirt on without bothering with a bandage or bra. It stuck uncomfortably to my back, making me wish I could just walk around topless for the rest of the evening.

I came out to find Raven and Dario both munching on the leftover pizza. The vampire extended a piece to me. "So the angel is still hunting mages? Is there any indication that he might come after us?"

I winced and told him of my conversation with Araziel today, sparing no details.

Dario stared intently at my face. "Do you think you can convince him we're redeemable and under your protection? Can you banish him or send him back to heaven? I'm not really all that comfortable with him roaming around the city with ideas of moral gentrification going through his head. Maybe with this Bliss woman dead and her murderers arrested, he'll go back to heaven?"

I shrugged. "It's hard to tell with angels. He may decide

it's his mission to stay, that he needs to make sure the death mages are penitent or punished until the end of their lives."

The vampire got that speculative, narrow-eyed look on his face that I didn't really like. "Do you think he'd leave if all the death mages involved in his human's death are gone? As in, dead-gone?"

I was beginning to realize that the vampire solution to most of the world's problems involved someone's death. "Probably not. From his conversation this afternoon he wants to turn Baltimore into a sort of nirvana for good and holy people. Which doesn't bode well for the vampires."

I hated to lay it on the line like that, but I didn't want Dario and his *Balaj* taking it upon themselves to murder every mage in Baltimore, just to make sure Araziel returned to heaven. I felt guilty as soon as I saw Dario's panicked expression.

"We can't abandon this territory, not after the centuries we've spent building up liaisons and developing our business interests. We'd be drifters again, and without the scepter, taking over another territory would be a bloody affair."

Yeah, guilt. I'd taken the scepter that unified them, that in the hands of a skilled necromancer could make a rival group walk right out of their territory and surrender it up without a fight. If Araziel took over, they'd have no choice but to flee Baltimore and try their luck somewhere else.

I had such mixed feelings over the whole thing. The vampires fell on the dark side of that gray area between good and evil. Humans were their food, and their blood slaves died sooner rather than later. They held their territory through affiliation with some of the worst of human gangs and drug cartels, and they weren't shy about killing to send a message. I didn't think them irredeemably evil, but I did disagree with their methods.

"I'm working on it. I promise you, Dario, I'm working on

it. I don't want to see your *Balaj* roaming the country without territory any more than you do. Just let me deal with these demons and the mages who are killing people first, then I'll handle the angel. Well, I'll *try* to handle the angel."

His eyes bore into mine. "You understand why I'm so concerned about this situation? Why I need you to update me first thing each evening?"

He was right. I'd put a reminder in my calendar or something because it shouldn't be impossible for me to make a quick phone call sometime after sunset. Even if I was grappling with clawed demons, there was no reason I couldn't call him eventually. Well, unless I was dead or unconscious in the hospital or something. Which made me think about what must have been running through Dario's mind last night when I hadn't answered my phone or called him back. I was surprised he hadn't come by pre-dawn and busted down my door to see if I was okay.

Although...Giselle. How the heck would he have explained that one? "Oh babe, I need to run out and check on a woman I used to want as a blood slave, just to make sure she isn't dead." I didn't know much about Giselle, but judging from the two times I'd met her, that wouldn't have gone over well.

"I promise. I'll call you at sunset and brief you."

There was a moment of silence where all sorts of emotions cycled across his gorgeous face. "No, we'll meet. Every night one hour after sunset at Sesarios. If you can't make it, you're to call me."

If I was Giselle, I wouldn't be happy about that either. I wasn't sure exactly how *I* felt about that. I'd be meeting him every night at a restaurant I'd come to think of as our place. I'm assuming we'd have a cocktail, maybe dinner. Every single night. I wavered for a second but temptation was too much for me to resist. Plus as the resident

Templar, I *needed* to meet with Dario. I needed to know about what was going on in the city from the vampires' point of view.

"Deal. Now get out of here before a bunch of mages start arriving. We've got four demons to banish." And an arrest directly following if Tremelay got the text I'd sent him. It would be best if Dario were not around for any of that.

Instead of leaving he folded his arms across his chest. "Four demons. Your back looks like hash browns from *one* demon. I'm a bit worried what four are going to do to the rest of your skin."

"So *you're* going to take on four demons to protect my pretty skin?" I snorted. "I've got a group of experienced mages coming over. I've got Raven, who can banish like a mo-fo. And there's me with all my Templar skills. I'm good."

"You most certainly are *not* good. You told me what happened last week when you tried to summon that information demon. Then one attacked you in DC and clawed you up, then burned you. Two Templars, two, and you couldn't manage to banish him?"

What the... How did he know that? I shot Raven a narrow-eyed look and she grinned at me.

"Yes, well that's why I have Raven here, and why I'm going to get the assistance of other mages."

Dario look heavenward and slowly shook his head. "I might not be a mage, but I'm a vampire. I'm pretty hard to kill, and as someone who has sold their soul, I think I'm uniquely qualified to battle hell's spirits."

Seriously? He probably had a million things to do for Leonora. He'd probably had no more than a quick snack before heading over this evening. He had a girlfriend/blood slave. Hanging out with a bunch of mages while they corralled and banished dangerous demons couldn't have been high on his to-do list this evening.

"Besides, I brought you a gift. You can't kick me out when I brought a gift."

Oh he was so right. And when he motioned to the white box on the dining room table I knew he had me. I opened the box and saw half a dozen cannoli neatly lined up inside.

"Oh yum," Raven said over my shoulder. I resisted the urge to selfishly clutch the box to my chest and instead offered her one.

"You're in," I told Dario, shoving a cannoli in my mouth and shutting the box. "I'll need you to stand back and be careful not to smudge the chalk."

He nodded and I wondered for a second if I should introduce him as a vampire or not. Before I could inquire about the correct method of introduction, there was a knock on the door. Raven opened it and I saw a crowd of three men and four women outside my door. Seven. They weren't in robes, but one of the women I recognized as Gryla, so these must be seven of the remaining eleven Fiore Noir mages. There had been twenty-five names on the list. That meant that besides Shade, four mages had either declined to participate in the banishing or had already bailed and left town. With the seven at our door, we'd be nine. It was the number of eternity, of harmony. Immortality. The perfection of the trinity, squared.

Yes, nine would do very well indeed. Raven motioned them in and I felt the sting of magic as the energy from amulets and protection charms zinged around the room. Mages were nothing if not a paranoid bunch, especially around other mages.

One of the men stepped forward. "We were reluctant when the Gryla told us about this. Working with a Templar and a member of a rival group that was more than happy to see us all dead isn't something we are eager about. We're not experienced in demonology. It's not our strength."

The woman beside him waved her hand. "It doesn't matter. None of that matters anymore. We've lost too many. It's time for this to stop. We can put aside our differences to ensure our safety."

"It wasn't Haul Du," I blurted out, waving the last bit of my cannoli for emphasis. "You all sacrificed a demon-marked human. Then you sacrificed an *angel*-marked human. So don't give me this bull about not forgiving or forgetting. You brought down a demon and an angel on your own heads, as well as human law enforcement. I'll do my best to help you with the demons and the angel, as part of my Templar responsibilities, even though I'm really tempted to just let them tear the lot of you to pieces. I'll make sure you stay alive, and I'll make darned sure you face human justice for the murders you've committed in the course of your magical doings."

The mages all spoke at once until Gryla threw up her hands and yelled for silence. "Whoa, whoa. None of us are happy doing soul magic or human sacrifice. We had to. The good of many sometimes necessitates the sacrifice of a few."

Not this again. "I don't care who or what you're afraid of," I told her. "When we're done here, you need to go down to the police station and tell the truth about who was involved in the death magic rituals. There's no escaping justice—it's just your choice whether that justice comes with a prison sentence or via demons or an angel. Your pick."

I'd had it with these folks. I was tired. My back hurt. I wanted to eat cannoli and sleep the night away, not risk my life banishing demons.

Gryla's lips thinned. "We're bonded by our practice. We take care of our own problems. And you're hardly going to let a group of demons run loose to kill whomever they choose in Baltimore, are you?"

Yeah, she had me there.

"Obviously not," I scowled. "You've got a choice. Help me banish these demons and go to the police, or I'll give the angel the green light to kill the rest of you. I don't think he's very particular about figuring out who held the knife and who didn't. He's of the kill-them-all-and-let-God-sort-them-out school, if you know what I mean."

And from the pallor of her complexion, I could tell she did.

Gryla shot a quick look around at the others who gave short nods. "Okay. Banish the demons, keep a leash on the angel, and we'll go to the police and tell them everything."

"Who's that?" The man in front pointed to Dario. "I know the woman is one of the Haul Du mages, but I've not seen him around before."

They couldn't tell. I'd always been able to sense vampires nearby, to tell them apart from humans, but I often forgot that non-Templars lacked that skill. And since they didn't recognize him, Dario must not be the liaison between the Balaj and Fiore Noir. It made me feel better to know he hadn't been personally involved with them.

"He goes by Fang. He's part of Haul Du, but a novice, so he won't actually be taking part in the banishment. He'll just be observing."

No one seemed to have a problem with this. And Raven, bless her poker-face, didn't bat an eyelid at my blatant lie. None of the other mages seemed to see through my falsehood. Surely their amulets and charms dealt with the detection of untruth? Perhaps my being a Templar put them out of whack. I'd have to ask my father when I got the chance.

"Well, let's get going," Gryla said, rubbing her palms together. A shower of sparks came from them, vanishing before they managed to set my carpet on fire. "Let us know what to do."

Raven took charge, pointing at the men. "You guys roll

the carpet up against the wall. The circle on the floor is going to need some serious reinforcing if we're going to call back and hold four demons. If you Fiore Noir mages can work on getting the circle as tight as possible, Aria and I will get finish up the sigils and the banishing scripts. Fang can get the candles and incense out of the kitchen cabinets."

"Fang" raised his eyebrows as the order, but complied. It was a relief seeing Raven supervise the undertaking.

By the time midnight approached, the circle perimeter was enhanced to a ridiculous degree. Practically my entire apartment was one large series of interlocking circles, triangles, and pentacles. Raven lit the candles and we all chanted, Dario leaning against the door and watching us with a fascinated expression. The power built until the room fairly hummed with it, the circle glowing bright white with all its runes and symbols. It was so intricate that I swear it would have held the prince of darkness himself without so much as a crack or tear.

The chanting faded. My skin prickled with the feeling of anticipation. I lit a piece of parchment, tossing it into the metal bowl. "Mansi, we summon you forth to appear before us in this circle."

I did the same with three other sigils, waiting for the demons to appear. The candles flickered, the lights of the circle brightening, but no demons appeared. They were resisting. Not that I blamed them. Demons summoned from hell were eager to appear, to serve for a taste of worldly delights, information, or the possibility of snatching a soul. Innyhal had appeared, confident that he could kick my butt. Mansi wasn't as stupid.

If he was going to fight me, I needed to go for his weakness. I slid my thumb against the blade of my sword, smearing it on the parchment as I picked it up. Holding it into the flames, I watched as the blood-laced sigil burned away. "Pinen. I command you upon my blood to appear. As Solomon before me, by the gifts given to me as a Templar, I command you to kneel in this circle and do my bidding."

It hurt to summon like this. I saw Raven's eyes widen, saw the other mage's shift nervously at my invocation of my Templar rights. As before, I stuck my finger again onto the sharp edge of my sword, then massaged it until the bead of blood dropped on the fiery parchment. It hissed, sizzling like I'd dumped a cup of water into a pan of hot grease. A long, plaintive wail filled the room and something pink and lumpy appeared in the center of the circle.

One down, three to go. I set fire to a second piece of paper, not even waiting for the first to completely extinguish before I threw it into the metal bowl. "Gi'nar! Kneel before me in this circle as you once did before Solomon himself. I command you to come to me."

Gi'nar had the fortitude not to scream, but the sickening crack his long, narrow green body made as it smashed on top of Pinen couldn't have felt good, even to a demon. Dalgas came easier with two of his brethren already inside the circle. By this point I was shaking, desperately wishing we were near the end and a warm blanket was in my immediate future. The other mages were just as bad off, sweating profusely, their eyes glazed as they concentrated on keeping the symbols around the protective space solid and bright white. Across from me, Raven looked grimly determined.

One more. I needed to call the big guy. And he wouldn't refuse this time, not when I had three of his legion bound in my circle. I lit the parchment and tossed it in the bowl, jabbing any remaining fingers that hadn't already been stuck and squeezing the droplets of blood onto the burning sigil. "Mansi. I command you once, twice, and thrice to appear in my circle and bow to my wishes."

He wasn't as strong without the other three demons to

pull from. The candles flickered, the symbols dimming to near dark before slowly regaining their light. The air in the circle shimmered and Mansi appeared, round and six-armed with squat legs and the head of a lizard. He had a huge phallus that was grotesquely covered with black scabs and oozing pustules. Ugh. Give me a war demon over a plague one any day.

"You have no right to call me here, to trap us in this circle," he snarled, spittle flying from his broad mouth, sizzling as it hit the inner edge of the circle. "I am here by invitation, with permission."

"No, you are not," I told him, taking advantage of his desire to converse to catch my breath and gather my strength. "The human you marked was killed, his soul taken. You have no more ties to this world. You and your three demons are to leave and return to hell, never to return unless summoned again."

Mansi raged, spittle flying until the inner edge of the circle smoked and dimmed. There was no more time to rest. The mages were weakening, and so was the barrier under Mansi's onslaught. The other three demons joined in and the second row of symbols flickered and died.

"Mansi, Dalgas, Gi'nar, and Pinen," Raven shouted, her hands raised. "I banish you to hell, never to return unless summoned again."

One by one, the mages around the circle repeated the banishment in hoarse, strained voices, the screams of the demons nearly drowning out their words. For a second I worried what the neighbors must be thinking. That woman below me who was always banging the handle of her broom on the ceiling was probably calling the police, or the landlord, right now.

Then I turned my sword around so the tip hovered an inch above the floor. Holding it aloft, I rested my forehead against the plain hilt, envisioning the holy responsibility of my birthright and holding that in my mind as well as in my heart.

"*T'voghnel anmijapes.*" My voice rang out louder than the screams of four demons. And then there was silence. I opened my eyes, staring into the empty circle with disbelief. I'd once had faith in this banishment, but after it had failed me twice…well, I was shocked it had worked this time.

They were gone. The outer boundaries of the circle still held, so they hadn't escaped. Besides, as furious as they were, they wouldn't have just run off if they'd managed to break through the circle, they would have attacked us. They wouldn't have left until every one of us lay dead in a pool of blood and torn entrails, paying with our lives for trapping and humiliating four demons.

Raven dismissed the circle and the seven mages slumped, their cloaks stained damp with perspiration. My whole apartment reeked—of incense and sweat, of candle wax and sulfur, of burned parchment and blood. If I wasn't evicted by the end of tomorrow I'd count myself blessed.

I wanted to turn and see Dario's reaction to all this. I wanted to eat a cannoli and possibly indulge in my Emergency Beer. I wanted to take a nap. But my work here wasn't anywhere near finished.

Seven mages got to their feet. I wasn't imagining the sudden tension in the air. With the demons gone, all bets were off. Former promises were made to be broken, and I knew better than to trust that these mages would turn themselves over to the Baltimore City police.

As two of the mages moved toward the door, Dario blocked them, baring fangs in a toothy smile.

Gryla glared at him. "We've got no problem with the *Balaj*. And we're of more value to you *outside* of jail."

"Well, we've got a problem with you," Dario replied. "One

of your sacrificial rites brought an angel down on the city. If that's the sort of careless disregard you have for our interests, then you're of no value to us at all. Be grateful you're facing jail and not an unmarked grave."

I was suddenly glad of Dario's presence. Without him this might have turned into a seven-against-two magical fight.

The mages backed slowly away from the door, eyes narrowing as they realized Dario was standing in front of the only exit to the apartment. Well, the only exit unless they wanted to throw themselves out my window and down three stories onto the pavement below. Even then, vampires were fast—fast enough for Dario to grab any mages foolishly trying to jump out my window.

"I suggest you all keep your hands out of your pockets and held quietly in front of you where we can see them," I told them, holding my sword. Dario stood his ground by the door and Raven flanked the mages on the other side, a knife in one hand and an amulet in the other.

I sent a quick text from my phone, and jumped as almost immediately there was a knock on my door.

"That was fast." Dario scooted over so I could open the door for the detective. "I have seven of them, all Fiore Noir members although I'm sure they all claim to not have any part of the murders. They'll cooperate." I glanced over at Dario. The vampire was watching the mages intently. They all stared back at him with their wide gazelle eyes. It was like a nature documentary. *Vampire hunts down prey in a Fells Point apartment.* The only difference was that these mages were going to walk out of here alive. For now.

Tremelay moved aside and other police moved into my apartment past me to cuff the mages and pat them down for weapons. I wasn't surprised at the number of magical items that were going into labeled plastic baggies. I shot Dario a grateful glance that he didn't see. Without him here tonight, this would have probably gone very badly.

The mages filed out past us and I walked Tremelay out my door into the hallway. He glared into my apartment at Dario and then down at me with a scowl. "Who the heck is that guy? Is he your personal bouncer or something?"

I was too tired to go into all this with Tremelay, and I wasn't sure he'd believe me anyway. Demons, angel, killer mages, and now vampires? That conversation would have to wait for later. "I'll tell you later. I think you'll need a bottle of whisky for this one."

The detective shook his head. "I get the feeling you're not going to tell me he's an accountant who watched one too many episodes of The Wire. Voodoo? Please tell me it's not voodoo because that stuff needs to stay down south."

I patted his shoulder. "Not voodoo. Worse. I'll tell you later. I promise."

Tremelay walked down the stairs and out the door, where the flash of red and blue lights was beginning to become a regular nightly thing. I turned to go back into my apartment where Raven was giving Dario a high-five.

It was odd seeing my best friend so casual and comfortable with the vampire that was my...whatever. Friend? Near-miss boyfriend? The vampire in question turned to me without a fang in sight, grinning his fool head off.

"I'm glad I stayed. Intimidating a group of mages was immensely satisfying, but that banishing... I think I might actually be turned on."

Who was this, and what had he done with my somber vampire friend? Raven grinned back and chuffed him on the shoulder. "Well, you're not getting any from me unless I play dentist first and yank those fangs of yours. No venom addiction for me, thank you very much. I've got enough problems with my mage lover. I know my limits."

Dario didn't even look at me, knowing my answer. The levity evaporated like it hadn't been there and in its place an odd tension filled the air.

"Thanks for your help." My gratitude was real, no matter how forced my words sounded at the moment.

He nodded his eyes warm as they turned to meet mine. "Any time. It was my pleasure. Honestly." He sighed. "But now I need to go. There are some things I need to accomplish before sunup, and I'll need to hurry."

Giselle. In an instant I saw her beautiful face, adoring eyes watching him, hand reaching up to touch the marks on her neck. My stomach twisted at the thought, but I forced it down and tried to school my features into something resembling friendly interest. "Of course. I'll walk you out."

It wasn't that Dario needed an escort, but that there were a few quick things I wanted to say to him away from Raven. Best friends didn't need to know every single detail of each other's lives, especially when it concerned vampires.

I shut the door behind us and tried to be mindful of the late hour as I tip-toed down the stairs. The neighbors most likely hated me already. Dead people in my parking space. Regular demon summonings and banishings. What had amounted to a stinglike operation that wound up with seven mages doing the perp walk out of my apartment. No sense in angering them any further than they already were.

"Tomorrow night, one hour past sunset at Sesarios," Dario reminded me. I nodded.

"How…how is Sarge?" Part of me still didn't want to know, but I felt I owed it to him, to our somewhat new friendship to at least check in about his status.

Dario halted halfway past the landing and faced me. "It's none of my business, Aria. It's not my place to stick my nose into another vampire's love life."

My heart sank at his words. "So you haven't seen him

around? You used to see him at Leonora's or out with Geraldo. You haven't seen him? Have you seen Geraldo at all?"

"Yes, I've seen Geraldo. No I haven't seen Sarge. And I haven't asked. It's not my business." Dario hesitated, then sighed. "If it makes you feel any better, Geraldo does not appear to be grieving."

I did make me feel better, but it still didn't alleviate my worry for Sarge. He was a man in love, a man addicted. He was a man marching toward his death. But I couldn't save Sarge any more than I could save a friend who was deep into heroin.

"If you see him, or if you see Geraldo again, can you let me know? I'm not asking you to pump your vampire brother for information, just let me know."

A look of frustration flitted across the vampire's face, then he nodded. I continued following him to the building door, feeling the blast of humidity even in the cool night air. Dario halted so quickly that I plowed into his back, steadying myself against him with one hand while holding the door with the other.

"Aria?" His voice sounded strained. "There's a dead man in your parking space. He looks like someone reached into his chest and yanked everything out, cracking his ribcage wide open."

No. Not after the conversation we'd had in the coffee shop. Not after he'd promised me. I peered around Dario and saw that he was right. The dead man's ribs glistened white in the moonlight, his chest cavity hollow black.

If you couldn't trust an angel to keep his word, who could you trust?

CHAPTER 29

It was Tremelay that showed up. Poor guy had just left. I doubt he'd had time to set his parking brake at the station before driving back over here.

"When do you sleep?" I asked with a sympathetic smile. I'd at least gotten my nap in this evening. I doubted the detective had even had that.

"At this rate I'll be able to schedule some sleep next month. Right now I'm running on energy drinks and coffee." He saluted me with a Styrofoam cup.

"Those mages still at the station?" I was hoping this death would remain hush-hush for as long as it took to rein Araziel in. The mages weren't likely to cooperate if they thought the angel was still delivering his own sort of justice.

"Yeah." Tremelay rubbed his face and blinked tired eyes. "They're not being the most cooperative bunch. They're scared. Seems there's one particularly ruthless guy among them who they call the Stranger. Supposedly he isn't shy about choosing those with loose lips as his victims. Or those who piss him off. Everyone is worried they'll wind up dead if he even gets wind that they were at the station for questioning."

I took out my little list. There were still three mages unaccounted for—four counting the Stranger. Had Gryla found time to determine his identity? Was there any way to find out who had brought in the soul trap and bargained for the death of three Haul Du mages?

Araziel had to have some way of determining which of the mages were involved. The angel might have killed those two junkies in a twisted act of preemptive assisted suicide, but I got the feeling he was very careful about his victims. There was a plan when it came to this angel, a method to his murders. Angels didn't need to bother about such things as search warrants or probable cause or Miranda rights. What if I were to ask, or beg, Araziel for the location of the three remaining mages as well as the identity of the elusive Stranger? Then I could point Tremelay in the right direction to gather appropriate evidence. I glanced over at the corpse in my parking space. If things moved along at a faster pace as far as human justice went, perhaps Araziel would be willing to hold off on his killing spree.

The door of the apartment building opened and Raven walked out, casting a quick glance at the dead body. I'd called it in, then gone upstairs to let her know what had happened. Practical mage that she was, Raven had volunteered to stay and continue to clean up post-ritual while I dealt with the police.

"You're never getting your parking space back," she commented.

Not that it mattered. I probably would be searching for a new apartment by the end of the week anyway. "You heading home?" I asked. She nodded.

"Don't call me before noon. Actually don't call me before sunset. I'm going to make like a vampire and sleep the day away. When I wake up..." her eyes strayed to my waist. I touched the demon mark in reflex, wincing. For a few seconds I'd actually forgotten about Balsur. There seemed to be more urgent things to deal with than the potential loss of my soul, but at Raven's reminder fear spiked through me. How long did I have before Balsur started putting pressure on me? What could a demon do that might drive me to the edge of desperation, to do things I never thought I would do? To barter my soul? I thought of Athena and the adopted daughter she was about to welcome home, of my father and mother, my brother and my two nephews, of Essie. I thought of Dario. And I looked up at Raven, my best friend. What would I do if their lives were in jeopardy?

This mark needed to go, and quick.

"Get some sleep. I'm going to speak with a certain angel once we're done here. This weekend we'll get started on my mark."

She smiled and patted me reassuringly on the shoulder. No sooner had her car pulled away from the curb than another took its place. A tall woman with long legs climbed out of the sedan, trotting her way over toward us on sensible shoes. Janice. Tremelay was going to kill me, even though I wasn't the one who called her.

"Crime scene, ma'am," one of the cops told her as she waved her press credentials in his face. "Stay this side of the tape, please."

I shot Tremelay an apologetic look and walked over to the reporter. "I don't know how you're going to spin this one. Telling the public an angel is killing murderers is only going to get you a psych eval."

She grinned. "Vigilante angel. Too bad. It would make a great front page."

I waved behind me toward the corpse. "The police are questioning some persons of interest in the 'occult gang murders.' Maybe you can reassure everyone that they're making progress and that there will soon be arrests?"

She nodded, typing into her phone. "I still like the vigilante story, even if I can't say it's supernatural. Dead is dead, and the angel/vigilante is clearly targeting the occult gang members."

I pointed to Janice's phone. "Gonna make the morning paper, or are you too late for that?"

The reporter scowled. "Too late. I can get it in the online edition though."

I was suddenly struck with an idea. I'd been wanting to keep this under wraps. To not scare off the mages being interviewed at the police station or the murderers who remained alive. Perhaps I was going about this the wrong way.

"Go ahead with the vigilante thing. Hint that the only way these occult gang members are going to stay alive is if they turn themselves in to the police and plead guilty. Maybe say that you have reason to believe the vigilante won't stop killing unless he's convinced the murderers will serve time."

Janice nodded. "Flush them out. Do you think it will work? Will they be scared enough of this angel?"

I looked over once again at the dead body. "Maybe we need a few pictures and some gory details."

The reporter wrinkled her pointed nose. "Ugh. My editor hates dead body pics, but I'll see what I can do. I've got one from last night with all the dead guys lined up in your parking space. Maybe a collage with this one and the one in the park. The public loves a good vigilante story, let's see if I can run it."

"Thanks." I left Janice and the police to their work and headed back upstairs to do what I needed to do.

The unexpected appearance of a man in skinny jeans eyeing the ceramic figures on my bookshelf about gave me a heart attack. Was this how angels worked? I thought I'd need to pray, maybe get out my Bible or something.

"So I just think of you and you show up?" I asked him after giving my blood pressure a few seconds to return to normal.

"No. I figured you'd want to talk with me after seeing my gift downstairs." The angel turned to me, a smirk on his face.

"You're about to become a vigilante, a public hero. The threat of your very violent and life-ending sort of justice will hopefully bring all the other killers to the police station to plead guilty to murder." I crossed my arms and lifted an eyebrow. "Per our conversation earlier, that should satisfy you. No need for ripping the souls out of any more mages, right?"

The smirk turned even more sly. I was beginning to think angels out of heaven quickly lost their gloss, because this guy's morals didn't seem to be on-par with mine at this time.

"See what a little justice can do? Humans don't seem bothered by the threat of jail, but show them that dead murderer downstairs and they'll walk a righteous path."

"No more separating souls from bodies, right?" I repeated, wanting something to assure me Araziel was done with this "justice."

"I will remain here until the mages all die of natural causes, just to ensure they repent and that their punishment is sufficient. If not, well I'll need to step in once more."

I didn't like the idea of Araziel hanging around for another sixty years or so, but this was better than nothing. "You said you would hold off killing. What changed your mind? There's a dead guy in my parking space and per our conversation I thought you were going to stand down and let the humans handle this."

"I was, but he was meeting with another mage, the one with the soul trap, to discuss yet another murder ritual. Your humans are too slow. How many people must die before you manage to bring these people to justice?"

He met with the Stranger? Why, oh why, couldn't Araziel have killed *him* instead? "They've planned another sacrifice? When? I need to let the police know."

Araziel turned his back to me and picked up one of the figures from my bookshelf—the little resin fox. "No idea. If you kill the remaining four then there will be no need to involve the police. Everyone will be safe."

I was getting sick of this angel and his mantra of kill-kill-kill. "Honestly I'm surprised there aren't five dead in my parking spot."

"I was tempted, believe me. I remembered my promise to you and decided to deliver justice to only this one, and leave the others for you to punish."

I scrambled for a piece of paper. "You wouldn't happen to know where I can find them, would you?"

The angel raised his eyebrows. "Am I to do all the work for you? I'll give you another twenty-four hours, Knight. After that, *I* will take care of the problem."

I nodded. "And the vampires—"

His eyes narrowed. "You are a Templar Knight, and yet you have a demon mark and you have on multiple occasions exchanged information with Satan's servants. You keep the company of lawless mages and have filled your shelves with these."

He waved the resin fox at me and I blinked in surprise. Did he think they were false idols? The little figurines were decorative items—or were they? Gifts from my great grandmother often carried charms and curses.

Araziel put the fox back on the bookshelf. "I fear you are walking the path to hell already."

I thought back to the mark on my side. How far would I go to save my Pilgrims on the Path?

"Humans have free will, Araziel," I said as deferentially as possible. "It's not your place to judge their choices or take their lives. Immortality is sometimes the worst curse of all."

He tilted his head as he stared at me. "But the humans these vampires kill? These creatures prey upon your brothers and sisters."

He was right, and it did bother me. "Are they not free to make those choices, whether it be to spend a few months as a blood slave to a vampire, or to sink into the Lethe-embrace of heroin, or to end a cycle of depression through suicide?"

A faint smile flickered across the angel's face. "I may revisit this argument with you at a later time, but for now I will leave Baltimore in your hands."

That was a lot of pressure for one young Templar, especially one who had run away from the responsibility of her Oath. It seemed that some responsibilities could never be escaped. And I was oddly thrilled at that idea. Not a Knight, but the Templar of Baltimore. I'd be a Batman with boobs and a sword who worked with a detective, a vampire, a mage, and a reporter instead of the Commissioner. A paladin without the crazy suicidal death wish morality.

"Understood."

Araziel set the resin fox back on the shelf and bowed deeply, giving me a military-style salute as he rose.

And then he was gone.

I had three mages and the Stranger to find. I had some reassurances with strings attached to give to Dario. And I had a demon mark to get rid of. All after I devoured a few of the cannoli in my fridge and collapsed into a sugar-fueled sleep. Hopefully things would be slow tomorrow at the coffee shop and I could squeeze in some internet research as I worked.

CHAPTER 30

I'd had the best sleep in days, and was happily brewing up espresso at work, fueled by a breakfast of three cannoli. One more hour and I could head home to warm up leftovers and settle down to research.

Every person in the coffee shop this morning was talking about the vigilante, the "angel of justice." I heard there were rumors of a T-shirt lauding him and how he was going to save Baltimore and rid the city of all the murderers, thugs, and dealers. Oh, and corrupt politicians. Aside from the politics, it all sounded a lot like Araziel's party line. I doubted the citizens of Baltimore would want his type of justice or his hard, inflexible line concerning who was good and who was evil.

Although I couldn't imagine any of the people I served caffeinated beverages to today would consider the vampires good. Was I the only one who saw a glimmer of virtue in them?

I might not be the vigilante that Baltimore wanted, but unleashing Araziel on them would be far worse. We had less than twenty-four hours before that happened. Thankfully,

Tremelay said after the morning paper with its graphic pictures, the seven mages in custody had become amazingly cooperative. I'd left a text message for Dario, but was going to meet him at Sesarios as planned tonight. We'd need to consider our course of action on how to keep the *Balaj* off Araziel's radar.

And best of all? It was Wednesday and tonight was the Anderon game at Zac's. Tonight I'd get to pretend to be a normal human pretending to be a half-dragon warrior. I couldn't wait.

Things were looking good, and as I glanced down to see Raven calling me, I was filled with hope that she'd found something out to help me get rid of this demon mark.

"Hey, what's up?" I wasn't really supposed to be taking calls at work, but given the amount of texting Anna did with her dozens of boyfriends, I figured one quick call wouldn't get me fired.

"I think we can get the demon mark removed," Raven announced.

Did I mention how awesome my day was? How everything was finally falling into place for me. Heck, I'd even had cannoli for *breakfast*. How more right could things be?

"I owe you big time," I told her. "I've got to meet Dario an hour after sunset, and I have a game tonight with some friends. How about tomorrow? Or maybe Friday night?"

"Sure, but…" The happy joy bubbling through me froze at Raven's nervous tone. What was wrong? "I'm not sure how easily I can get the ritual. It might be next week. Maybe more. Don't worry, I'll make it happen, I just might need to drop off the radar for a day or two."

I had a bad feeling about this. Really bad. "What do you mean 'drop off the radar'? Raven, you've got to be more specific than that."

I could practically hear her squirm through the phone.

Brian motioned me over to the espresso machine, plopping a cup down next to the beans with unwarranted emphasis. I glared at him, and motioned to the phone, cradling it against my ear as I read the order on the cup.

"The word is to stay out of Baltimore, mind our own business. Basically if we have a choice between flying out of BWI or Dulles, we're advised to use Dulles."

The loud grinding of beans drowned out the rest of Raven's conversation.

"What?" I yelled, not caring that half the customers were watching me with interest. "Something about concave?"

"I was talking with someone who has a contact at the Conclave. Dark Iron has been accused of theft of a magical object."

Magical object? One valuable enough to involve the Conclave? Yikes.

"Guess what he's accused of stealing? Guess?"

"Wait. Hold on just a sec." I finished the latte and handed it to the customer, shooting her a quick smile before turning my attention back to Raven. "What?"

"A soul trap?"

"A soul trap? You're joking."

I heard her grunt in confirmation. "Yeah, from a guy in Argentina three weeks ago. Dude is seriously pissed. I'm surprised he went through the Conclave and didn't just curse Dark Iron into the ninth circle of hell. And guess who was supposed to testify against him, all hush-hush like? The three mages who were killed in Dupont Circle."

Dark Iron was the Stranger. And if he was ruthless enough to kill three witnesses from his own group, to watch while Fiore Noir murdered people and used their souls, to have them use Bliss, then he was capable of anything. Had Bliss even known? Had she innocently gone to a meeting with the leader of her magical group, only to wind up on the sacrificial table?

"Raven, get out of DC. Go to my place in Middleburg. I'll call Mom and let her know you're coming. You'll be safe there." She would be. I don't care how powerful Dark Iron was, nobody got past Mom. Nobody.

"I will tomorrow. I've got something I need to do first."

I didn't like the tight waver in her voice. "Get out. It's not important."

"You want that demon mark off or not? That was the other part of my call to my friend this morning. Seems Dark Iron got himself marked once and has a ritual to remove it."

"No," I practically yelled. By now the whole coffee shop was staring at me. "We'll get it after he's in jail, or from someone else. I'm sure he isn't the only one who's removed a demon mark before. Get out of there."

"He's got no idea that I know. We're on reasonably good terms. Heck, Reynard is one of his closest friends. I'll tell him it's preventative, for Blaze, one of the noob's I'm mentoring."

"No." I didn't know what else to say. Panic was starting to fill my chest and steal my breath.

"I'll call you late tonight, around midnight, when I'm on my way to your parents' house. I got this, Kite. I got it."

She hung up and I stared at the phone as it blurred with the tears spilling out of my eyes. I didn't know Dark Iron's name. He was one of the few Haul Du members I'd been unable to track down in the real world. Raven was smart, sneaky, a good mage. She was tough and capable. And I was terrified for her. Dark Iron was a killer. And my soul was not worth Raven's life.

CHAPTER 31

Sean sent me home early since I was such a mess. I really had the best job. I was only a part-time employee but was constantly sleep-deprived, coming in late, leaving early, or barely able to function because I was injured. I had no idea why they put up with me, but Sean and Anna seemed very concerned that I get some rest and help my "troubled" friend.

Once home the first thing I did was call Mom and explain the situation. She put me on speaker phone so Dad could hear.

"Of course we'll shelter your friend. She's welcome here as long as she needs," Mom told me, her voice warm and sympathetic. They'd take in a total stranger, defend her if necessary from evil mages. It made me feel a connection with my family that had been missing for quite a while. Maybe we were all still Templars deep down after all.

"You need to come, too," Mom added. "The police have most of the mages in custody. They'll get the rest in the next day or so. Come down here until it all blows over."

Oh sheesh. "Would *you* run home, Mom? They'll never

catch Dark Iron. Heck, I'm not even sure I can catch Dark Iron, but I can't walk away and let the man responsible for at least five deaths walk free."

I heard her sigh. "Solaria, you be careful. I know you like to be an honorable Templar and all that, but you need to swing first and ask questions later, got it?"

"Mavia!" I heard my Dad's shocked voice in the background.

I smiled. "Will do." I'd done that and nearly broke Gryla's shoulder, but Dark Iron wasn't a little old lady, and I didn't doubt he'd try to strike first if I caught up to him.

"How are things with the angel?" My Dad asked, curiosity thick in his voice. Leave it to my father. Death mages, stolen soul traps, and he wanted to know about the angel.

"He's weird, Dad. He showed up at my coffee shop yesterday trying to convince me to rid the city of evil by killing what would probably be a good chunk of the population. I got him to agree to hold off, but then he went and killed someone else last night, saying it was preemptive to save innocent lives. Are they all like this after they cross the veil? It's like he's not even an angel anymore."

"That doesn't sound right, Aria," my father said. "I was uneasy when you told me about the two addicts, but *this* seems far outside an angel's scope. Are you sure it's Araziel? Are you sure it's an angel?"

"Yes I'm sure." My tone was a bit snappish, so I took a calming breath. "I checked the sigil and—"

The sigil. It had been under Ronald Stull, but I didn't remember seeing it under the two dead junkies. And it certainly wasn't under any of the dead in my parking space. I'd just assumed they'd been moved there post-mortem, or that Araziel hadn't bothered. But an angel would bother.

And I'd never summoned him, called him, prayed for him.

He'd just shown up conveniently every time, before I could call on him with the very specific sigil for Araziel. Shit.

"Uh, Dad? Can demons impersonate angels? Would they bother to do that? How can I tell?"

"When you call them with a sigil, then you know you've got the right one, assuming your calligraphy is properly done. Yes, demons *can* impersonate angels. They have in the past to try to encourage righteous people down a path of sin. Demons can twist the worst of deeds around so that someone believes what they are doing is right. Remember the three temptations of Jesus, how Satan cloaked his offers in the guise of a greater good. Often the desire to do the right thing can lead a person to justify horrible actions."

"All this I will give to you," he said, "if you will bow down and worship me." The passage from Matthew was very much what Araziel had been advocating. I could save the world, and it would only cost me my soul.

Balsur had marked me. He wanted my soul and how better to prepare it, and me, for an eternity in hell than have me voluntarily damn myself for the "salvation" of many. I was reasonably certain whoever the demon was impersonating Araziel it wasn't Balsur, but one of his legion. If three demons could cross the veil on the strength of Mansi's mark, then surely one of Balsur's could, too.

"They won't mention God," Dad continued. "They'll only refer to Him obliquely. They'll twist your words around. They'll flatter you. The good news is if it's a demon impersonating Araziel, then the angel has returned to heaven. One would never tolerate such a thing if he were this side of the veil."

I thought of Ronald Stull. Araziel *had* delivered justice, then gone back home. And getting rid of a demon would be a whole lot easier than getting rid of an angel. Except who was to say Balsur wouldn't just send another of his minions over to harass me.

I got the feeling he wouldn't. It wasn't his style to beat away at me with bulldog determination, employing the same technique over and over again. No, Balsur was a Sun demon, not a Mars one. He'd plan something different for next time, and he'd be patient about waiting for the right moment. Hopefully that moment would never come. As scared as I was for Raven, I hoped with all my might that she would get the ritual and that it would work.

I thanked my parents profusely for offering to shelter my friend, then hung up and promptly called Tremelay.

"Progress." The detective sounded cheerful if not well rested. "One more came in. According to everyone we've interviewed there are two more Fiore Noir members at large. Of course, every last one of them claimed they never participated in the rituals and blamed it all on the dead mages, but we've got evidence enough to nail at least four of the eight on second degree murder, and the rest as accessories."

It was good news, but all I could think about right now was Dark Iron. "I know who the Stranger is, the non-member who gave Fiore Noir the soul trap. He solicited for the murder of three people who died in the Dupont Circle explosion, as well as Bethany Scarborough. He was present at Bethany's murder and the one before."

"I'm glad you know that, because no one else does," Tremelay grumbled. "I get the feeling Ronald Stull was the only one who knew the guy and he's dead."

I told him about Dark Iron, everything Raven had told me. "I'm sure if you can catch him, you'll find the soul trap to implicate him. If the Fiore Noir people can't identify him, at least they'll know the magical device by sight."

"Can't you give me anything on the guy? Anything? I

can't put out an APB on a man who goes by Dark Iron, six foot, fiftyish with graying brown hair. Do you know what he does for a living? Where he likes to grab a beer? Anything?"

"No." Mages were protective of their personal lives and Dark Iron even more so. He'd taken to using burner phones, constantly changing email addresses and running his internet usage through offshore servers.

Tremelay sighed. "I guess I understand the need for secrecy. Even if they aren't murderers I'm sure the Baptists down the street wouldn't be pleased to find out their tax guy summoned demons on the weekend."

"Exactly." I closed my eyes for a second, wondering if Tremelay could somehow pull off a miracle and manage to find Dark Iron, preferably before Raven got herself killed.

"Look, I know this is a long shot, but my friend that helped me last night? She's meeting with him about some stuff tonight and I'm scared for her. If you could go through all the stuff you collected, put thumbscrews on Fiore Noir and see if there's anything that hints at where Dark Iron lives or who he is, I'd appreciate it."

"Your friend is meeting him?" I heard Tremelay's excitement and realized he was thinking of bugging Raven, possibly jumping in to grab the mage at the meeting.

"That's not going to work. He's paranoid. He'll have detection amulets. He'll know, Raven will die, and he'll be gone before you get him."

The detective growled. "I don't want this guy to get away."

"Me either, but it may take time. I'm a bit of an outcast in the magical community, but my friend Raven has connections. We'll eventually track him down. I'm just hoping you've got something in those boxes of case files that will help."

I heard a noise in the background, as if Tremelay was

rubbing a hand over a stubbly cheek. "All right, Ainsworth. I'll see what I can do."

I hung up, feeling completely helpless. There was a source I could go to, but I wasn't about to summon Balsur when Raven was risking her life to rid me of the demon.

Wait—I did have someone else to go to. Unfortunately he wasn't *really* Araziel so summoning him with a sigil or praying wouldn't do me any good at all. If the past day were any indication, he'd come to me. I just needed to be patient, continue to play his game, and hope that Raven was as tricky as her namesake.

CHAPTER 32

Raven had called right before the game at Zac's. I nearly wept with relief when she told me she had a copy of the ritual to remove the demon mark and was on her way to my parents' house. The Anderon game was a welcome diversion now that I knew she was okay. It was almost over. Tremelay had his people to prosecute. All I had to do was reel in Dark Iron and banish the Araziel imposter. Of course to get rid of Dark Iron, I'd *need* the Araziel imposter. That was going to be a waiting game, so I battled Orcs and Goblins with my adventuring friends, leaving Zac's house just after ten for my late-night dinner with Dario. Or meeting. Whatever it was we were doing.

The staff at Sesarios had been courteous and professional when I'd been there with Zac, but I immediately realized the difference when I walked in this time. The hostess beamed at me, welcoming me by name. Dario rose as I entered the room, waiting for the lurking waiter to slide my chair in under me before sitting once more. In seconds I had a glass of wine, a plate of calamari, and a neatly pressed napkin in my lap. I felt like the Queen of England.

Dario waved the waiter off. "So, how did your Anderon game go?"

Oh sheesh, he remembered. I'd told him last week about how I was hoping to be invited to the Wednesday night game, but hadn't mentioned why I might be a few minutes late to our meeting tonight.

"I single-handedly killed eight goblins and six orcs. Seven orcs, actually. I ate one and was informed he was *not* tasty. Hopefully we'll be able to retrieve the Heaven's Shard within the month. I have my doubts though. My team is easily distracted by festivals and gambling establishments, as well as offers to participate in side quests."

His lips twitched. "Orcs taste bad. I'll remember that if I ever encounter one."

I relaxed and took a sip of my wine. I'd missed this. I'd missed him. "I've got kind of a good-news/bad-news thing. Good news is I'm close to certain that Araziel is no longer this side of the veil."

Now *Dario* relaxed, smiling warmly and snagging a calamari from my plate. "That *is* good news."

"Not necessarily. The first kill in the park? That I'm certain was Araziel. I think he left right after that, having delivered justice for the theft of Bethany Scarborough's soul."

Dario nodded thoughtfully. "But there were other angel kills, and you've seen him since then."

I drank more wine, needing some alcoholic encouragement to confess that I'd been duped. "I believe that the being I've been communicating with is a demon who is impersonating Araziel to get to me. None of the other kills have borne the angel's sigil, and each time he's appeared on his own. I consulted with my father and he feels the same."

Dario's eyes narrowed. "Are you positive? Angel or demon might not make a big difference to you, but it does to us."

That stung. "It does make a difference to me—a huge difference. I could just summon Araziel using his sigil and know for sure, but I need to pretend to be ignorant just a while longer. I need this imposter to help me catch the rest of the killers, and then I'll send him back to hell."

"How long?"

I shrugged. "Probably no more than a couple of days. He's not patient, and he wants something from me."

Dario topped off my wine. "And that would be?"

I lifted the glass in a dramatic toast. "My soul."

His eyebrows rose. "I'm assuming he won't be getting that."

"Not if I can help it." I ate a few pieces of calamari. They were breaded with cornmeal that had been liberally spiced with Old Bay seasoning. I didn't even need to dip them in the marinara. "So how are things with the *Balaj?*"

"Tense. Leonora sees every disagreement as a threat. She doesn't realize how that kind of attitude weakens her in the eyes of the family."

"And thus weakens the *Balaj.*" I got it. A family fractured by internal conflict was vulnerable to attack, and I remembered Dario telling me of those vampires who roamed outside of established territories waiting for a chance to break in.

He nodded. "We've had to take out a few rogues in the county this week. Nothing serious, just a few unstable vampires whose actions put us all at risk. Outside of that, business as usual."

I didn't want to think too hard on what business as usual meant. "How's Bella?"

He smiled, every inch of him radiating fondness for the vampire he'd risked everything to turn. "Good. She was a little rough with one of her donors the other night, but Suzette was able to restrain her before she did any serious damage. Russell visits weekly, and I think having him in her life helps. She seems happier, and definitely more vocal after his visits."

That was good to hear. We chatted about random events in Baltimore as dinner arrived. He asked about my family, and by midnight we were walking out the door. I couldn't believe I'd spent two hours over dinner with Dario. I was so thrilled he'd made this time for me. Our relationship would never be what we both hoped, but this…this would do.

Dario walked me to my car and waited as I climbed in. "I saw Sarge last night."

My heart stuttered, and I found I couldn't reply.

"He said to tell you he is well and happy with his decision." Dario's dark eyes looked into mine, his hand reached out to touch my arm. "He looked healthy. And he did look happy."

I appreciated what he'd done. This was none of his business, but he'd take the time to check on Sarge for me. "Thank you."

The vampire smiled, stepping back to shut my car door. "Anytime, Aria. Anytime."

CHAPTER 33

I was just pulling into my second parking spot, the one without the crime-scene tape all over it, when my phone beeped. Raven should have been settled in at Middleburg by now. I figured the text was either from her, checking in, or Tremelay informing me of something about the case.

It was from an unknown number, giving me an address of a law office downtown.

I smirked, wondering who wasn't going to show up tomorrow for a meeting when the phone chimed again. This text was a picture.

A body, splayed out in a ritual circle, sliced to ribbons. I barely recognized the sobbing noises as mine as I dialed Raven. No answer. Next came my Dad, who sleepily told me that my friend had not yet arrived, but that my mother was sleeping by the front door in wait.

Oh, God. She'd left seven hours ago. She'd said she was heading to Middleburg. Oh, God.

I started my car back up and drove as fast as I could. Downtown wasn't far and parking was plentiful this time of night. I launched the Camry into a free space and ran for the building.

I had no idea why an office building was unlocked at midnight, why the elevator didn't require any special pass card, why the law offices of Shuster and Shuster had doors that were wide open. I just ran, my breath coming in short gasps as I tore through the receptionist area into the gigantic conference room.

I knew before the coppery smell of blood hit my nose, before I walked into the barren conference room and saw the lines of circles and triangles intersecting with symbols on the carpet. This ritual had been a sloppy, hurried job. The carpet blurred the symbols, and from what had burned into my memory from Bliss's sacrifice, I could tell this one was more for show than any actual magical output.

This had been Dark Iron's work, without the help of a mage skilled in death magic. I dreaded getting a close look at the victim on the carpet. Maybe Raven's car had broken down. Maybe her phone battery had died. Maybe she'd stopped in Leesburg for happy hour, got drunk, and met a hot guy.

I recognized her immediately. Raven. Dead. She had been left for me, as a warning, as a punishment, as a way to put me in my place. This was meant to scare me, to remind me that I was a baby in the world of magic, and that I was playing in a world where nobody gave a shit whether I was a Templar or not.

She was spread-eagle like a Da Vinci print, her red-tipped hair a tangled mess. He'd used U clamps to anchor her wrists and ankles to the floor. I walked toward her, not caring that I smudged the symbols or was contaminating the crime scene. With a shaking hand, I smoothed the locks of hair off her face.

She'd died pissed. Somehow it helped me push down the

nearly debilitating grief. She hadn't been afraid or crying as she died. Angry eyes glared. Her lips were drawn back in a snarl. I looked and saw that even her hands were fisted. He'd sliced her wrists, the inside of her thighs, along her waist. The cuts were neat and even, meant for pain and the drawing of blood. The other wounds on her chest weren't as neat. They looked as if someone had been trying to hack a chunk of her chest off.

Blood was neatly arranged in bowls around the inside of the circle. It was all so staged. He hadn't wanted a flood of red to dilute the impact of Raven's naked, sliced body. It was almost as though he'd cleaned the cuts and her skin, to show off all he'd done.

My hands weren't shaking quite as much as I reached my fingers out to smooth the torn skin along her breastbone. I was probably going into shock, falling into an odd numbness that would dissolve into tears and pain once I got home.

The feeling of the skin under my fingers jolted me out of my detachment. The flaps of skin were colored by more than blood, and there was an odd raised quality to the mark that I recognized. A tattoo, and a fairly recent one. Judging from the scabbing and the dark lines of ink, I was estimating that Raven had gotten this two or three days ago.

Dark Iron had hacked at the tattoo with a fury he hadn't shown in the rest of his knife work. There was one good reason for him to do that to a tattoo—it wasn't just a tattoo. Raven saw how Bliss had died, knew that Fiore Noir wasn't shy about sacrificing other mages. She'd gotten a tattoo over her heart chakra, in the same place where Araziel had placed his angel mark on Bliss.

Clever, clever girl. Raven had guarded her soul. She'd locked it down tight, to keep death mages from using it in ritual. Dark Iron may have killed her, but he hadn't taken her soul. That was Raven, kicking ass even at the end.

I stepped back, the enormity of it finally hitting me. Dead. Raven was dead. And she'd died sticking her neck out to help me. Dark Iron would pay for this. I'd track him down if it took me decades. I'd make sure he paid, whether it was through jail time or with his life. I wouldn't let my friend's death go unavenged. I yanked my phone out of my pocket but instead of dialing Tremelay, I called someone else.

"Hey. Know you're busy, but I need your help." I swallowed hard, forcing down my grief and rage. "I'll be in your debt."

CHAPTER 34

"*Y*ou're not in my debt." Dario stared down at Raven's naked body, his eyes dark and angry. "You're family, and there's no debt with family."

Family. Was that really how he thought of me?

I hated for Dario to see Raven like this, tied to the floor and naked. Even with her furious eyes and balled up fists, she seemed so vulnerable. Not that Raven ever cared if anyone saw her naked. She'd confided that she had an affection for streaking, nude beaches, sex in very public places. "It's just a body," she'd say with a shrug and a naughty grin. "Everyone's got one." Still… I felt like she should be given a bit more dignity than us memorizing every cut and bruise.

Dario stepped back and turned his eyes to mine. "So, why me? You've got the city police on speed-dial. That detective friend of yours is closing in on these people. Why call me?"

I didn't know why I'd called him, I just had. In spite of the rocky patch in our friendship, Dario had my back. I had the feeling he'd always have my back. And outside of my family, far away in Virginia, I couldn't say that about a lot of people.

I shrugged. "You told me earlier that the *Balaj* had dealings with Fiore Noir."

He nodded. "It started out with us asking them for assistance on charms, hexes, magical security. They help us, and we help them. Do you think they did this? I would have thought they'd be lying low, the few that aren't already in police custody, that is."

"No. I know who did this. It wasn't Fiore Noir."

So the *Balaj* helped the death mages and they in turn provided magical items. I wasn't sure I wanted to know what the vampires had done for the group. Screw it, I did want to know. I couldn't keep turning a blind eye to these things. "Helping Fiore Noir how?"

Dario's expression froze, stiff and impersonal. "If there was someone they needed persuaded to do or not do something, we assisted. If someone needed to be gone, they were gone."

I swallowed, remembering pseudo Araziel's words. My vampire pilgrims *were* pretty darned far from the path. "So if Leonora is all buddy-buddy with Fiore Noir, why ask *me* to look over that symbol last week? Why not go to them?"

He looked heavenward, as if I'd become mentally deficient. "We weren't sure it wasn't them. They've tried stuff in the past."

Once again my eyes strayed over the chalk symbols on the carpet to my friend's corpse. "Dark Iron killed her. He's part of Haul Du, the mages in DC, but he's been working with Fiore Noir, exchanging the use of his stolen soul trap for them killing people he wanted gone."

A muscle in the vampire's jaw twitched. "But why Raven? I thought she was tight with this guy, part of the group. Why kill her?"

"Because she knew. She knew he'd contracted to kill three Haul Du mages and Bliss. She knew he was using the soul trap. She knew that it was a stolen item that could get him dusted by the Conclave. I told her to get out of town, but she was trying to help me get rid of this demon mark."

"Demon mark?"

"Happened last week. I'm working on it."

"That's the weird burn on your waist that feels like an ice-cube when I touch it?"

I nodded, finally getting to the point of my questions. "Can you use the *Balaj* connections with Fiore Noir to give me Dark Iron?"

"I wish I could. Unfortunately most of our Fiore Noir contacts are dead. We didn't work with the ones in jail. Gryla was always careful to have someone else as our liaison. If I could, I'd give him to you with a bow on top." He motioned toward Raven. "I liked your friend. If I can help, you let me know how. I'll make it happen."

I swallowed hard. "See if you can squeeze any mages you know to get me Dark Iron. I've got Tremelay looking, too. Other than that, I guess it's up to me."

Dario put his arm around my shoulder and gave me a quick hug before releasing me. "Baltimore's Templar. Or what was it those role-playing people called you? A paladin? I'll do everything I can to find this Dark Iron. I'll even get a Renfield or two on it during daylight hours."

"Thanks." My mind raced with how the heck I was going to track down the mage. I'd never managed to learn his real name or occupation after I'd left Haul Du and eventually had let it go. Now I was regretting I hadn't tried harder.

Dario's mouth tightened as he once again looked down at Raven. His expression reminded me that he was a vampire who had done horrible things in the course of his life and had no problem continuing to do those horrible things now and in the future. "I don't know this mage, but trust me if he ever crosses my path, he'll regret it. I liked Raven. And I like you—a lot. Immortality brings with it patience. I promise you that I won't rest until this Dark Iron has paid for your friend's death."

I shivered, scared at this side of Dario, but oddly gratified. He'd avenge my friend's death. He'd protect me. He'd do anything for me.

Except these were things I needed to do on my own.

"Thank you," I said again. I meant it. I really, really meant it. "But I intend to take care of Dark Iron myself."

And now it was time to call in the cops, or at least Tremelay. I pulled out my phone and dialed, putting my hand on Dario's arm. His muscles flinched under my touch.

"I better get out of here. I don't think your detective friend is all that fond of me, and I have work to do." He reached out and touched my arm before he left. I put the phone to my ear, my eyes unable to look away from Raven's body.

"Tremelay. We have another victim."

It wasn't just another victim, though. It was Raven. And that made all the difference in the world in what I had been planning.

CHAPTER 35

It didn't truly sink in until I got home. There was the cannoli that I'd regretfully shared with Raven. There was the book she'd given me, all sorts of research texts stacked up on the coffee table with pages of her handwritten notes beside them. I picked up the notes, tears blurring my vision.

Dark Iron had sent the picture to warn me, to scare me off. This was my final warning to get out of town, to stop messing in his business. Well, Dark Iron had no idea how bad things were going to get. I'd tried to walk a Knight's path, even though I'd never taken my Oath. I'd tried to protect citizens, to presume innocence until proven guilty, to let diplomacy and the justice system work their magic. I'd tried to be the paladin my LARP friends kept calling me. I'd tried. But now Raven was dead.

What would have happened if I had ditched Tremelay and gone out on my own to hunt Fiore Noir down? What if I'd let the demons and the Araziel imposter do their thing, guiding them instead of holding them back? If I'd been more of a warrior and less of a peacemaker, then maybe Dark Iron would be dead and Raven would still be alive.

I ran my fingertips along the raised scar of my demon-mark. One call to Balsur, one trade, and revenge would be mine. I'd need to word it carefully, because demons were good at finding loopholes and wiggling out of any deal.

Raven would kill me for even thinking about it. I blinked a few times and read her notes, all about breaking links with the underworld that had been made without the practitioner's consent. It was preliminary, nothing I could use, but a good start. She'd written three pages, citing different texts and even drafting a few ideas on ritual. No, I couldn't make a bargain with Balsur when Raven had worked so hard to free me of his mark.

I just needed to be patient and wait for pseudo-Araziel to show up.

I pulled the sigil of the real angel from my pocket, smoothed the bent edges of the paper and placed it on the floor. He'd always show up right before I could call on Araziel. Maybe if I set up like I was about to summon the angel, the fake one would appear. I squinted down at the paper, but before I could make a decision, a pair of pristine-white Converse sneakers appeared at the edge of my vision. I jumped to my feet, nearly falling over the sofa as I grabbed for my sword.

"You wanted to see me?"

Pseudo-Araziel. My hand clutched at my heart instead of the weapon and I forced my breathing to slow. This guy was going to be the death of me. I really wasn't thrilled about a demon having such easy access to my apartment. It was past time for me to up my supernatural defenses and locks around my residence. Dario sneaking in during the middle of the night with pastries was okay, but this wasn't.

"Yes," I gasped. How was I going to phrase this? How

could I gain his help without revealing that I knew his deception? "Raven is dead," I finally said. "The head of her magical group killed her, the same guy who contracted for them to kill Bethany—your marked human."

He rocked back on his heels, a look of surprise on his face. "Your friend? A mage killed your friend and now you want *me* to do something about it? What happened to your 'no violence toward the humans' approach?"

I narrowed my eyes. "All but two of the Fiore Noir mages are in jail right now. I need your help to catch them. I promised you and I promised Tremelay that I'd see them all in jail. I need your help to find them and then to find the mage who killed Raven."

The "angel" nodded. "Of course, they must all be brought to justice. You're sure that the police have enough evidence to deliver justice, though? Your friend died. It would be a horrible thing for her murderer to walk free."

I knew what he was getting at, what he was pushing me to do. Honestly after seeing Raven dead, he didn't need to push. "I don't know if the police will be able to prosecute Dark Iron. If not…well, I can't let him get away."

There was a gleam in the angel's eyes. "Get your sword and I will lead you to him, as well as the other two mages. They need to either submit to human justice or die, though. That was our bargain."

It would be dawn in a few hours, but I wasn't ready to toss all night in bed, thinking of Raven and how she'd died. I threw a few items I'd been working on in my purse, slid the butter knife in one pocket and my keys in the other. Then I picked up my sword, strapping it to my back cross-body so I could draw it over my shoulder if needed.

"The deal here is that you lead me to them, and let me take charge. No ripping their souls out of their chests along with all their internal organs, okay?"

Pseudo-Araziel looked surprisingly meek. "I promise I won't kill the humans. I'll let you do it instead."

That wasn't quite what I meant, but as long as he held back, I'd take it.

Araziel navigated me through the city streets, which were less-traveled than usual in this buffer time between night and dawn. Not to say there weren't the occasional cabs, smoky-window SUVs, and bleary-eyed folks either heading home or in for an early shift. We headed northwest, through downtown and Druid Heights, skirting Rosemont and into Forest Park.

I was on edge. Baltimore had more than its fair share of urban violence. While this section wasn't the worst, it definitely wasn't anywhere close to gentrified. Homes that had once been beautiful and well-cared for suffered from a distinct lack of maintenance. I watched the street signs as we headed up Garrison Boulevard, well aware of Gwynns Falls just a few blocks over to the west as I drove north.

"Turn here."

Here was Route 26, Liberty Road. We were heading toward Howard Park, near where I remembered there being a golf course. After six months of being clueless in the city, I'd finally gotten a map and one of those tour-guide booklets, determined to figure out what was where. It wasn't easy. Baltimore wasn't huge, but it was a mess of tiny neighborhoods nestled into each other like a set of Russian dolls. What further complicated things was the gentrification that like to rename neighborhoods and change traditional boundaries in an effort to sell homes at a higher price.

"Here."

Milford Avenue. Now that we were driving past homes I slowed down, waiting for Araziel to tell me which one our target was holed up in. Tremelay had already hit their registered homes, so whichever mage this was, he or she was staying with a friend.

Which made me even more uneasy about bursting into their house in the early morning hours, brandishing a sword and accompanied by a psychotic demon impersonating an angel.

These were nice houses, all with newer aluminum siding and detached garages with alley access visible behind each home. Araziel pointed at one and I pulled to the curb, the righteous fury that had driven me out on this mission faltering. It was four in the morning. The house was dark. I couldn't go bursting in on these people, demanding to know where they'd hidden a mage. It was better for me to call Tremelay.

"Who is this one?" I asked the angel as I pulled my phone from my purse.

"Eleanor Jean Jackson. Born 1980 in Silver Spring, Maryland. This is her ex sister-in-law's house."

I hesitated. "Does she have kids? The sister-in-law, I mean, not Eleanor."

He shook his head. "She makes Eleanor stay in the garage, because she doesn't trust her. Bad things happened to her brother when the two broke up, and she always thought Eleanor had something to do with it. She never would have sheltered the mage, but she's scared of Eleanor and was worried that if she refused she'd be hit by a bus, or crushed by a falling porch roof, or suffering from seeping boils over most of her body."

"Stop." My hands were sweating as I stared at the phone. Call Tremelay. Just call Tremelay.

What if the "angel" was mistaken? Or lying? I glanced sideways at him, gnawing my lip. Should I burst in there to grab some woman on a lying demon's word, or just have Tremelay check it out in the morning?

"She was there at every murder," the angel assured me, his voice cool and impersonal. "Eleanor drew the symbols, she chanted to direct the victim's energy as they died."

And she might have slipped away by morning. I opened the car door and climbed out, shutting it quietly and pulling my sword from the scabbard. "Is Eleanor alone in the garage? Any wards of protective magic that you can see?"

Araziel shrugged. "That's not my thing. I just walk right on through whatever they've got. Nothing can hold me, nothing can hurt me."

Must be nice. I dug a bag of herbs out of my pocket along with a charm bracelet. I'd only had time to charge three of the charms, but it would have to do. Three charms for three mages.

We snuck around the side of the house, through the back yard to the garage. I paused every few feet to chant and throw some herbs in the air, just to check for spells. My companion rolled his eyes each time. He'd been doing a floaty thing beside me, his hipster guy form moving out of synchronicity with the motion of his feet. I know he didn't care if anyone saw him, if a neighbor dog started to bark or he set off a magical trap, but I did.

Reaching the garage, I did a slow circuit around the building, holding one of the charms on my bracelet as I chanted softly under my breath. The only thing that lit up was by the door. Of course. If I were going to set a ward, that's where I'd put it, too.

Remembering Raven with Bliss's warded grimoire, I pulled the butter knife out of my pocket and jammed it into the lock.

"*Fue!*" The door handle exploded outward like a tiny cannon ball. I stifled a yelp as I jumped to the side, then kicked the door open realizing that Eleanor would have been woken by the spell detonation and be ready to fight.

She was. A wind held me in place while a dozen knives flew toward my chest. I grimaced, my sword shaking as I struggled to raise it against gale-force winds.

"*Confodere!*" Ten of the knives bounced away to clatter to the cement garage floor, while two skimmed my shirt and imbedded in the wall behind me.

"Eleanor Jean Jackson, surrender to me or I will kill you." It was a bit extreme for a modern Templar, but I meant it. I didn't have time to deal with this crap. I had one other Fiore Noir mage to track down before I went after Dark Iron, and I didn't have much left in terms of energy—physical or magical. If she insisted on flinging knives and doorknobs at me, I would be forced to run her through with my sword.

A woman wearing only underwear and a snug tank-top dashed around a storage box, a pistol in her hand. I dove to the side, knowing full well that bullets beat sword. Luckily the gun wasn't pointed my way, it was pointed at fake-Araziel and the moment the woman laid eyes on my companion she froze, the gun falling from shaking hands to clatter on the floor.

I winced and jumped away, relieved when the thing didn't go off.

"No! Don't kill me. Don't."

She was pleading with the "angel," not with me. I wasn't all that thrilled about being upstaged, especially by an imposter, but if it kept me from getting shot, so be it.

"He won't as long as you come with us to the police station and plead guilty to murder."

She jerked her head toward me, her eyes enormous in the faint light of the garage. "You!"

Yes, me.

"You have killed at least seven humans by death magic, using souls to power your spells. If you don't turn yourself in right now and plead guilty to multiple counts of murder, I'll run you through."

I adjusted my grip on Trusty, but her eyes never even flickered to the sword. "It wasn't my idea to kill them. We had to. We had no choice, and now with everyone locked up, all those people we sacrificed will have died in vain."

"You *murdered* people. You stood by and watched while people screamed and pleaded for their lives, and you did it over and over again."

Eleanor winced. "I told you, we had to. It was for a greater good. Sometimes you need the extra energy that soul magic provides. Sometimes the lives of a few must be sacrificed for the benefit of many."

Not this again. The benefit of many? Whether the spell had been for material gain, knowledge, power, or even protection, it was never worth the death of those people.

"Make your choice. Die here or plead guilty to murder."

Eleanor swallowed hard, shooting a quick glance at my companion who stood silent by the open doorway, scrutinizing his fingernails. "I'll turn myself in to the police. But you don't know what you're doing. You'll be sorry."

Her threats just pissed me off further, and I'll admit I was a bit rough searching her person for magical items. The woman was practically naked, but I still took the ring and the necklace she was wearing off as well as her belly ring. I'd never seen someone charm a body piercing, but there was always a first time. After I was sure she was clean I left her in Araziel's care and went through the garage.

That's where my keychain came in handy. One of the spells I'd engraved into a spare key I'd picked up at the hardware store was a finder. In no time at all I had two scrolls, an amulet, an athame, and her grimoire. I wasn't foolish enough to open or pick any of them up, so I called Eleanor over and made her put each one into a large, plastic grocery store bag that I had stuck in my pocket.

The plastic bag was one of my favorite magical items. No, it wasn't a bag of holding like in my Wednesday night Anderon game. It was a null bag. Templars learned early on to create null spaces. It was vital for survival when dealing with magical artifacts and ancient grimoires. As each item went into the bag, I heard a pop and knew that it had been rendered harmless. As long as it was in the bag, that is. In order to safely remove it, I'd need to create a null room. I'd been meaning to do that anyway. With the circle taking up most of my living room, the null room would have to be either in my bedroom or my bathroom. I was leaning toward my bathroom. Sometimes it was important to be able to cast a spell while in the bedroom.

I folded the bag over on itself so nothing spilled out and held it in one hand along with my sword. Taking the mage's arm with my other hand I nodded to the door. "Let's go."

Araziel followed us out, oddly silent. I noticed there was a faint light on in the house, and the curtain twitched aside as we walked by, a pale face briefly visible at the window. Eleanor's sister-in-law had to have heard the commotion. It said a lot that she obviously hadn't called the police.

Eleanor sat in the backseat, as far away from the angel as possible. I had Araziel keep an eye on her while I drove. Then I escorted the mage into the police station, hoping that the look-away spell on my sword worked better on the desk clerk than it did on detective Tremelay.

It did. After leaving Eleanor there to confess and sending Tremelay a quick text, I headed back out to my car where the angel sat, still in the back seat.

"Let's catch the other Fiore Noir mage, then go after this Dark Iron." The angel/demon's eyes gleamed with excitement.

This time the "angel" directed me to an all-night diner on Saratoga Street. Great. How the heck was I going to walk into a diner with a sword on my back and a demon by my side and "arrest" a mage?

"Who is this one?"

"Charles Kennedy Jones. Born November 4, 1955, in Dundalk, Maryland."

What, no other details? I thought about how I planned to arrest a sixty-year-old man in a diner as I got out of the car and strapped Trusty to my back. "Araziel" followed me inside and pointed to the man at the counter sipping a cup of coffee and working a puzzle.

Holly's Place was…well, it was a diner. Long and narrow, with vinyl covered seats and chrome-rimmed Formica tables. They'd done a nice job on the retro look. Even the sleepy-eyed waitress in the corner was appropriately attired with a lemon-yellow dress and white apron, her hair in a tight bun. She smiled wearily at me and went back to staring at the clock. I got the unspoken message—take a seat and she'd be over, otherwise I wasn't going to even get a verbal greeting.

I slid onto the seat next to the mage.

"'Bout time you got here," he grumbled, his eyes never leaving his puzzle. "I've been waiting for you. Actually I've been waiting for him, too." He nodded toward my companion.

"Charles Kennedy Jones?" He was the only guy in here that fit the description, but it was good to be sure.

"Yep. Call me Chuck."

The guy scribbled something in his puzzle book. I peered over his shoulder. Crossword, not Sudoku or word search. My mother did crossword puzzles, too. I waited a few moments and watched him erase an answer, writing some-thing else. This was it? No declarations of innocence or accusations? No dramatic cursing of Templars and trying to attack me with flying knives?

"Um. I'm here to take you to the police station where you'll plead guilty to murder." I kept my voice low, shooting a quick glance over to the waitress to make sure she couldn't hear. I wasn't sure whether to threaten the guy with my sword or with "Araziel," given that Chuck seemed pretty peaceful.

"Okay. Don't you want to talk first?"

It was a weird question for him to ask, but the whole encounter so far had been surreal. "Talk about what?"

He shrugged, smiling at me. It was a tired smile, pulling at the deep lines bracketing his mouth and crinkling the corners of his pale blue eyes. "About the mage you really want to catch? About what's going to happen once the spell fades?"

Chuck... He had a threadbare wool coat on that look like he'd bought it used in the '70s. It was shiny at the elbows and smelled of decades of tobacco. Besides the oddity of him wearing a wool coat in the middle of August, the man looked like a regular retired, blue-collar guy, like he'd spent his life moving freight at the docks or shuffling bills of lading at a warehouse. I knew the spells powered by murder and souls had been to contain something, to protect against something. Whatever it was, twenty-five people felt justified in murdering to keep it at bay.

"Dark Iron. I already know about him. And as to what you all were doing the ritual for, I'd guess that someone screwed up a spell, and you spent your energies and countless lives protecting yourselves from whatever you conjured? Which demon is it and where do you have him trapped?"

The smile broadened. I swear if the guy had been a few decades older, fifty pounds heavier, and bearded, I would have totally gotten the Santa Claus vibes from him.

"You Haul Du mages, so tied up with your demons. When you play with the devil, you assume everyone else does, too."

No. There were all kinds of things they could have summoned that they needed to contain—an elemental, a gryphon, a banshee. Heck, maybe all three. Just because a mage turned their nose up at demons didn't mean they weren't likely to haul some otherworldly creature into this plane of existence, or even wake a sleeping monster.

"Ahh, it's no matter." He waved his hand like I was a pesky fly. "I knew we couldn't keep them contained forever. It was just a matter of time."

"Keep what contained?" I really needed to know, having visions of gryphons flying down Charles Street. What *could* be so horrible that it took regular sacrifices to contain?

His eyes twinkled, evil Santa that he was. "You'll find out soon enough. It's your town now, you're the Templar. It's your problem to deal with."

Oh no. These guys screw up and summon a monster, then dump it on my shoulders when they all get arrested for murder? No way. "What is it?" I demanded.

"Something that has slept a very long time. We didn't wake it. We didn't bring this curse upon the city. But we did take it upon ourselves to keep the city safe."

"By killing other people. Is restraining this thing really worth a dozen or more deaths every year?"

"Yes." Chuck folded up his puzzle book and stuck it in a pocket of the old coat, sliding off his stool. "Now take me to the police so I may confess my crimes. It's a relief, actually. Death magic does bad things to a person's soul. I mean, an occasional chicken or rodent is one thing, but killing a human, killing many humans…it has become more than I can bear. Time for this burden to move on to younger shoulders."

I was beginning to really worry about this monster. Not

that any monster excused murder, but I really wanted a heads-up on what I might need to deal with in the coming weeks or months.

"Tell me what Fiore Noir was trying to contain, or instead of the police, I'll let him take care of your punishment." I pointed to "Araziel" who was a few seats down sipping coffee.

The mage laughed. "I am not afraid of that. Just because I don't spend my time summoning demons doesn't mean I can't protect myself from one or banish it if needed."

Araziel-wannabe froze, coffee halfway to his lips. I schooled my face into what I hoped was a convincing look of shock. "That's an angel, not a demon. You all made the mistake of not only killing a demon-marked man, but a woman who had been angel-marked. He's here for vengeance, and you can't banish an angel."

With a flick of his wrist, a gold band dropped low on the mage's wrist. Etched symbols across the surface lit up red. "He's cheesy low-level scum, that's what he is. It's an insult, really. *Eieci, ti.* Go, I banish you." The man's voice boomed, like he was suddenly using a PA system. The angel/demon flung out a hand, but his reaction was too late. With a bang and a puff of black smoke, he was gone, leaving behind a cup that fell to the counter and rolled to its side, dumping coffee across the Formica.

The waitress screamed and hit the floor the same time the smoke detectors shrieked.

"Young lady," the mage hollered at me over the wailing alarm. "If you have any intention of being this town's protector, of fulfilling your duty as a Templar, you need to be able to tell an angel from a demon."

I'd figured it out. Granted, it had taken me a few days, but I had eventually figured it out. And now I was screwed. Balsur's minion was gone, and although that did make me a bit happy, I'd still needed him. It would have been better if Chuck had banished the demon *after* I'd gotten Dark Iron's real name and whereabouts.

The coughing waitress was standing on the counter, waving a menu at the smoke alarm. Behind her stood a guy I assumed was the cook, a befuddled expression on his face as he looked around at the dissipating smoke. Chuck was standing, but wasn't making any movements toward the door, so I watched the smoke drama and waited to speak until the alarm became silent.

"I *needed* him. Yeah, he was a demon impersonating an angel, but I was hoping to keep mum on that until I got him to lead me to the Stranger—Dark Iron of Haul Du. I've got no idea his real name or where he is."

Chuck threw a ten on the counter and headed toward the door. "Mitchell Raymond Sauer?" he chuckled. "Everyone panicked when the psychopomp tried to get through the barrier at Old Town Mall. Your Dark Iron was carrying the one thing that might cost him his life, so he hid it, intending to retrieve it later. I'm not afraid of an angel, I knew who he was coming for, so I grabbed it up on the way out."

The mage reached into his pocket and took out a small wooden container. It looked like a cheap jewelry box except for the symbol on top.

"Know how to use it?" he asked, handing it to me.

I didn't want to know how to use it. I didn't want to even be holding it, but better me than in the hands of Dark Iron.

Chuck nodded at the box. "Collect the soul in ritual, then hold it until you need it. We only used it as a channel since we were powering a spell right away, but it can be quite useful in powering magic on the fly at a later date."

This guy was sick. For all his harmless old-guy vibes, he was a psycho. "But Raven... Dark Iron tried to take her soul. How could he if you had the box since last Friday?"

He shrugged. "That dead girl downtown? Amateur. It was a hack job made to look like the previous murders to implicate one of us. Any mage worth his salt could see the guy had no idea what he was doing. Your boy might be good at demons, but he doesn't know squat about death magic."

No, he probably didn't. "You used the soul trap to find out his name."

For that Goetic mages usually relied upon a demon, although many mages could trace a person through blood, hair, or saliva. Seems this guy was skilled enough to do it through an owned item.

Chuck nodded. "Simple divination really. A two chicken job though, since the first time got me some guy down in Argentina. It's yours now. Do what you want with it. And do what you want with that Haul Du scum."

His name would help, but how the heck was Tremelay going to prosecute Dark Iron? We couldn't even link him to the soul trap since the prints on it were probably smudged. I doubted a jury would accept a divination done with two chickens as adequate proof of murder.

"Does he know you have it?"

Chuck opened the diner door and headed down the steps with me close behind. "Yep. And he really wants it back. Probably has more to do with that guy in Argentina than it being used as evidence against him."

I halted at his words then ran a few steps to keep up. "Can you do a favor for me?" It seemed weird to be asking a murderer who I was taking to the police station for a favor, but there it was.

The mage paused at the passenger door of my car, making me wonder how he knew it was mine. There was no parking lot. My Toyota was one of many cars lined up along the curb. Maybe I'd underestimated this mage. Maybe he *had* known I was coming before I'd stepped foot in the diner.

"Tomorrow. Midnight." Chuck gave me an address in Butcher's Hill. Then he pulled a little notepad out of his pocket that reminded me of Tremelay's and wrote down a number. "It's your choice whether the police take him in or you do it yourself. After all I've done, I'm not about to judge your methods of justice."

I stared at the paper in amazement as Chuck magically unlocked my car door and crawled into the passenger seat. An address and a time. I had all day to prep, and Dark Iron wouldn't expect me to be there. Well, I hoped not.

"What do you want in return for this?"

He didn't hesitate. "Four times a year, a tub of Fisher's caramel popcorn. The big tub, not that little one."

I guess if you were going to spend the rest of your life in prison, you wanted to ensure a regular delivery of comfort food. I had my cannoli, this guy had his caramel popcorn.

I climbed into my car and started it, still a bit stunned at his request. It was an easy trade, and I was so close to the end of this whole nightmare. The angel impersonator was out of the picture, at least for now. All the mages would be in Tremelay's hands. I didn't have to threaten violence to this one. Well, not much threatening, anyway. And soon I'd have Dark Iron.

The mage crinkled his nose as we pulled away from the curb. "Ugh. Your car smells like demon. Hope you've got an air-freshener at home."

CHAPTER 36

I don't know how I managed to sleep. I don't know how I managed to make it through my shift at the coffee shop. Brandi asked me how my friend Raven was doing and I burst into tears, needing to take a break in the storeroom to compose myself. After that my co-workers tip-toed around me, giving me wide-eyed stares.

I ignored calls from Tremelay. I ignored calls from Janice. I cancelled my nighttime meeting with Dario, knowing I'd need to prepare. By the time it was eleven o'clock and time to go, I'd worn a groove in my apartment carpet. Would Dark Iron even show up? I had nothing beyond Chuck's note, no way to confirm the meeting without tipping the mage off that something was amiss. All I could do was go and hope that surprise was on my side.

I brought the soul trap. As much as it creeped me out to have the thing in my pocket, I knew it would guarantee that Dark Iron would speak with me, even if I wasn't the mage he expected. He needed it back. I had a feeling it was the only thing keeping that Argentina mage from cursing him to a fiery death.

The address Chuck had given me was north of where I lived in Fells Point. I passed Patterson Park where we'd LARPed this past weekend, parking near the CVS on Fayette so I could cover the rest on foot. From there, I walked for blocks, with my sword on my back. It wasn't the only weapon I was carrying but it was the most obvious. And it was the one I'd rely upon the most if this turned bloody.

I *knew* it was going to turn bloody.

The building was a two-story brick, on a street lined with identical homes. I was glad I walked since the street was so narrow that with even with cars parked half-on the sidewalk there would have been barely enough room to squeak by. Feeling very exposed on the empty street, I checked the numbers and ducked down a narrow space between two buildings. In the walkway was an entrance that led to what would have been called a garden apartment—fancy word for basement.

Ten minutes 'til midnight. I was early, but I was sure Dark Iron was even earlier. It was his style, and I was counting on him being here, waiting for Chuck. Slowly I eased open the unlocked door, counting to three until I stepped a foot over the threshold.

"*Haxa luz.*" A ball of light appeared before me and I sent it forward to better see the room. It was a cheap, low-rent apartment, a twelve-by-twelve room with a door that I assumed led to a bathroom, an open doorway to a shadowed kitchenette, and a back bedroom. Tiny, without a lot of room to hide. It should have been encouraging, but I was far from confident.

I drew my sword with one hand, touching my finger to the third charm on my bracelet. Heat surged through me and the room lit up, every magical trap and ward highlighted in white.

I'd expected to see some sort of magical protection in the

room. I wasn't disappointed. One spot lit up right in front of my feet past the threshold, and another midway through the room. The windows had some kind of charms on them as well.

And a figure in the corner, previously invisible, glowed. He saw me, and now I saw him. I dropped the charm, jabbed my finger on a needle I'd hidden in my pocket, and palmed my butter knife. "I've got something you want."

The figure shifted, becoming fully visible. Dark Iron stepped forward to the dusty metal table. "And what am I expected to do to get it back, hmm? Confess my sins?"

"Why kill Raven?" I asked him. "She was loyal to Haul Du for over a decade, loyal to you. She wouldn't have said anything about the soul trap or the Dupont Circle mages. There was no reason for you to kill her."

He leaned against the table. "Me? All the evidence points toward Fiore Noir. Your friend Raven was just one more in a long line of their victims. Sad, really."

"Even *I* could tell Fiore Noir didn't conduct that ritual. Don't bullshit me, Mitchell."

Dark Iron winced as I used his real name. "Raven was a good mage, but she knew too much, and I couldn't trust her. The last few days she was busy filling your ears with confidential information—things Haul Du mages vow to keep within the group. Her loyalties were elsewhere. She knew the price she'd pay."

"The *price* was being thrown out of Haul Du," I snarled. "Not being stripped naked, bolted to an office floor, and sliced up with a knife. Nothing she knew about the Dupont Circle murders, Bliss, or the stolen soul trap was worth killing her over. It was all conjecture, what she'd heard from others. It's not like she could bear witness on any of that."

He shrugged. "No, but it was a matter of time until she found something and took it to the Conclave. The timing was right, with all the Fiore Noir mages being accused of murder."

"Was it worth it? You've lost Haul Du all because of a stolen soul trap. Why would you even need such a thing? You're a Goetic mage."

Dark Iron scowled at me, his hands steady by his side. "There are magics that can't be worked through demons, or charms, or hexes. Some spells need death magic, and some spells need soul magic. You're an idiot if you don't recognize that."

I glared back. "I'm an idiot because I think there's nothing magic can bring that is worth murdering someone? That's worth stealing their soul, taking away any chance at eternity?"

The scowl turned into a smirk. "Yes. Because there are times when the blood of a few must be spilled for the greater good. Go on with your naïve Templar hopefulness. Go on thinking you're saving the world when you're just making it worse."

"Well it's all for nothing. You've lost your magical group, you've lost the soul trap, you're about to lose your freedom, and if I'm reading the situation with that mage in Argentina right, you might just lose your life."

"I think not."

Magic sparked in the air. I had less than a second to act. He was too far for me to reach with my sword, so I ran my fingers along the butter knife as I threw it at him. It wasn't a sharp weapon, so instead of stabbing into him like a dart, it bounced off his chest and onto the floor.

"*Combustio.*"

Nothing happened. Dark Iron blinked in surprised and looked down at the knife on the ground. I'd blown all the spells from it breaking into Eleanor's garage hideout last night, and hadn't had time to do more than one simple spell, one every Templar knows how to use—a null spell. Activated with the blood from my poor, needle-jabbed finger.

The mage kicked the knife away, but the room was small enough that he'd need to actually leave to escape its radius. And leave he couldn't—at least not without going through me.

I pulled the soul trap from my pocket. "You confess to Raven's murder, turn over evidence to the police, and I'll give you this. Maybe it will save your life."

Dark Iron backed up and put a hand in the pocket of his jacket, his eyes on the soul trap. I edged closer, sword at the ready. Not that I expected him to do anything. As long as the null spell on the knife held, none of his magic would work.

"No."

And with that word he shot me. There was a bang, flash right through his jacket pocket, the smell of burning fabric and pain like a hot knife across my arm. I might not have faced actual combat before but I'd spent years training and instinct took over. I jumped on top of the table and swung, my vision blurring with the pain that came with the motion. The mage jumped backward, the blade slicing a narrow, diagonal line from shoulder to chest.

My arm burned like fire. A second shot rang out, but I didn't feel it. It all seemed to happen in slow motion—the jerk of the hand in his pocket, the swing of my sword as I tried to bury the blade in his shoulder. The gunshot went wide as he jerked backward. The momentum of my swing pulled the injured muscles in my arm and I nearly threw up.

Gunfire rang out, over and over. I jumped off the table, still swinging as I came at the mage. He stumbled backward, dancing away from my sword and shooting from the hip. My arm was in agony, my aim just as bad as his at this point.

We rounded the table, his pistol clicking empty. I darted to the side, kicking the table to make sure he didn't have a clear path to the door. And then I brought the sword tip to his chest.

"I yield." Dark Iron dropped to one knee, taking the empty gun from his pocket and sliding it across the floor before lifting his hands. "I yield."

Blood dripped from his shoulder and waist where I'd cut him. It didn't seem to bother him. In fact, he didn't even wince as he shifted his weight.

I hesitated. There was nothing the police could do. There'd be no evidence that he killed Raven, and nobody alive in Fiore Noir had seen his face. Magical divination wasn't admissible, and neither was the confession delivered at the point of a sword. Raven's death looked a lot like yet another Fiore Noir murder. All Dark Iron had to do was appear shocked and angry, and there would be enough doubt to set him free. He'd wiggle his way out of the legal system. He'd never serve a day in jail. But could I stand here and coldly drive my sword through his heart? As much as Raven's death ached, as much as I hated this bastard, I'd never been a killer.

Some Templar I was. Although, to be honest, Knights hadn't been warriors for centuries. We were rich academics, playing at arcane martial arts.

Dark Iron shifted to the other knee, the blood a red stripe down his shirt. "Arrest me. I'll come willingly. You know how useless that will be, though. I'll walk right out of that police station just as quick as I go in. Call the police or let me walk out of here now. Your choice."

He was right, but what was my alternative to calling Tremelay? Let him go and hope that mage in Argentina caught up with him? I couldn't execute a man who knelt in front of me, unarmed. As evil as he was, killing him wouldn't be like banishing a demon or sticking a lance through a sandwyrm.

Raven would have taken his head off for killing me. I'd promised her I'd have her back. I'd promised her I'd avenge her death.

Dark Iron stood and brushed the dust from his pants, giving me a stiff bow. "Until next time then, Templar."

He turned to leave, turned his back on me, and something snapped. I remembered Raven, her eyes and mouth fierce, her hands balled into fists with her skin sliced.

I couldn't let him just walk away.

The tip of my sword slid through his back like it was a sawdust practice dummy. His arms flew wide, time seemed to stand still.

I couldn't have placed my aim better if I'd tried. I'd impaled him right below the fifth rib. Blood flowed like a river out along the blade of my sword. His lungs made an odd sound, a cross between a whistle and a bubbling noise. I stared at his back, fascinated, noting how his shirt puckered into the wound, how his hands, empty of any weapon, flailed helplessly around.

I yanked my sword out, watching the blood out of the corner of my eye. So much blood. He crumpled to the ground, and as his head hit, it turned sideways—enough that I could see his expression. The surprised look on his face finally faded. In its place wasn't anger, or hatred, or fear, just a sort of emptiness.

I heard my sword clatter to the ground, felt the sticky blood on my hand and looked down, realizing with an odd detachment that it was a mixture of Dark Iron's and my own. The pain from my gunshot wound dulled to numbness.

I'd killed a man. I'd stabbed an unarmed man in the back.

It always seemed so easy in video games, in books, and in movies. How many times had I shouted at the television for the hero to just go ahead and put a bullet through the villain? But this was different. This was real and I'd just made the decision to end another's life. I'd taken my sword, with its spells, my *consecrated* sword, and put it through a man's back.

I slumped to the floor in a pool of blood and pulled my phone from my pocket, smearing the screen with red as I frantically tried to get the touch-screen to work. I would face justice for Dark Iron's killing. What I'd done…well, I'd face whatever consequences my actions caused. Jail didn't worry me, as much as the state of my soul did. The demon mark. My family. Oh God, my family. How would they take this? Templars weren't supposed to judge, and this took judgement to a conclusion, down a path we hadn't walked in centuries. We'd once paid the price for our bloodshed. I'd pay the price for this, too. Eventually.

But right now I was scared and there was only one person I could think of to call, only one person who could understand what I was going through, only one person who wouldn't condemn me or think me evil, or a bad person for what I'd done.

Dario picked up on the first ring, just as I knew he would.

"I'm in trouble," I told him, tears filling my eyes. "I need you."

There were a million things I expected Dario to say —things like how I should have let him handle this, or about the waste of perfectly good blood. I didn't expect him to sit down beside me on the sticky floor and remain silent.

It helped. Just having him beside me helped. After a while I began to notice that the wet coating my pants and arms was congealed and cold, that the pain in my arm was growing in intensity. I'd bandaged the wound as best as I could, counting myself lucky that Dark Iron had been such a poor shot.

Taking a deep breath, I unclasped my hands, flexing my fingers and taking shallow breaths.

"I've never killed anyone before." My statement was partially for Dario, partially for me. The words seemed abnormally loud, echoing in the room.

"It gets easier," the vampire replied. "I know you don't want to hear that, but it's true. Eventually it's the quick and easy solution to a lot of problems."

I didn't want it to be the quick and easy solution to a lot of problems. I thought about the necromancer last week, avenging the murder of his family and remembered the chain of death one murder had set off. "There will be repercussions. It seemed like the only solution, but…"

He sighed. "You weighed the risks of leaving him alive and made a decision. Most likely he would have killed you and killed more people that you love. Was Raven the first? I doubt it. I doubt a man can go from scholastic study of the occult to bolting a colleague to the floor and stabbing her to death without hundreds of black marks already on his soul."

I'd knew I'd made the right decision—the only decision I could. But that only made my choice slightly easier to live with. The bad in the world *wasn't* always nonhuman monsters. I'd been prepared to kill monsters in self-defense, or while in battle. I'd not been prepared to kill a human. I'd stabbed him in the back. I'd stabbed an unarmed man in the back.

I'm sure my ancestors had done the same. I thought back on the Crusades, of the shameful acts some of us committed in the name of God, claiming the loss of life was for the greater good. That was dangerously close to the justification the death mages and Dark Iron had used. I'm sure the Knights back then felt equally justified. I'm sure eventually killing was easier for *them* too, just as Dario had said.

I didn't want it to be easier. I'd come here knowing I wanted to kill Dark Iron. I could guarantee that I was going to face this choice again. I didn't *ever* want that choice to be easy. I wanted to agonize over it each time. If I made the choice to take a life, I wanted to always know the serious nature of that act.

I stood, wincing and gently touching my arm as I did. "Can you all assist with clean-up? It's probably best if the police think Dark Iron slipped away. He's not their main target in this anyway."

Although he should have been. The Stranger. The man

behind the curtain. The man who had killed at least five people. I'd have to make up some excuse for Tremelay about why we didn't need to keep pursuing him.

Dario stood beside me. "We'll need a lot of bleach. You humans are so messy about these things. Such a waste of good blood."

I rolled my eyes. And *there* was the blood joke I'd expected. "I hear evil mage blood isn't good for you. Your cholesterol would go through the roof. You should be thanking me."

A faint smile curled the corner of his mouth. "So, do you want this to just disappear, or do you want to send a message?"

"Message to who? I'm the only Templar in town, putting his head on a spike with a note stapled to his forehead is only going to land me in jail."

Dario shook his head. "Nothing so obvious. Body parts with broken magical items delivered to certain individuals could ensure no mage east of the Mississippi would ever think of messing with you."

Vampires. I don't even think drug cartels did such things. Or maybe they did.

"No, that would probably get every mage east of the Mississippi to band together and kill me. Mages are rather sensitive about being threatened. Bullying techniques don't work with them."

Dario pursed his lips and nodded. "Okay. Gone-gone it is. By sunrise, there won't be a trace that this happened. I'll send a doctor by your house in the morning to stitch you up, too. That one's not going to heal on its own."

The vampires had a doctor on retainer, one who made house calls. I guess I shouldn't be surprised. They wouldn't need to be stitched up, but I could imagine their Renfields did on occasion.

I stooped and picked up my bloodied sword, thinking that I had a lot of cleaning of my own to do. It was a bit too hot to drive around wrapped in the blanket from the trunk of my car to hide the fact that I was covered in blood, but that's what I'd have to do.

"Thanks," I told the vampire, feeling guilty about leaving him with all this. He nodded, his eyes warm and full of affection.

What kind of affection, I didn't know. That spark was still there between us, and as much as I wanted to tamp it down and keep our relationship businesslike, I wasn't sure how that was going to work out.

"Tomorrow night, one hour after sunset at Sesarios," he reminded me.

I blinked. This was over. Done. Why would he want to continue to meet me every evening when there was nothing left to report?

Oh.

"I'll be there."

I drove home, sweating and sticky in the musty trunk blanket, my sword rolled in the extra cloth by my feet. Watching carefully for passersby, I dashed up to my apartment, thankful it was dark and that my cheap landlord didn't bother with adequate outdoor lighting. Once in my apartment I washed all the red down the tub drain, knowing it would take much longer to wash the stain from my soul.

It was close to sunrise when I got the text from Dario indicating I could rest easy.

Rest easy. I picked up the little resin fox figurine that had somehow fallen off the shelf and had rolled next to the sofa.

"I killed a man," I whispered to the fox, its garnet eyes glittering back at me. "I think he deserved it. Raven would definitely think he deserved it, but it's hard to live with. I judged a man guilty and I took his life."

Rubbing my thumb over the carved lines that represented fur I sighed. "And Balsur…any demon who wants my soul bad enough to have one of his minions impersonate an angel isn't going to be shrugged off easily. I need to get rid of this mark, to cut off his access to this side of the veil."

I walked over to my bookshelf and replaced the fox figurine, wishing the wise animal truly had answers for me. I'd made my choice. I'd chosen to kill Dark Iron. I'd chosen to stay in Baltimore, to act as the protector of the pilgrims in my city. Those choices came with a cost. It was a cost I was prepared to pay.

ACKNOWLEDGMENTS

A huge thanks to my copyeditors Kimberly Cannon and Jennifer Cosham whose eagle eyes catch all my typos and keep my comma problem in line, to Meredith Bond at Anessa Books for her formatting expertise, and to my brother, Frank, for lending me his Photoshop brilliance in cover and ad design.

Most of all, thanks to my children, who have suffered many nights of microwaved chicken nuggets and take-out pizza so that Mommy can follow her dream.

ABOUT THE AUTHOR

Debra lives in a little house in the woods of Maryland with her sons and two slobbery bloodhounds. On a good day, she jogs and horseback rides, hopefully managing to keep the horse between herself and the ground. Her only known super power is 'Identify Roadkill'.

Keep in touch!
debradunbar.com

A Demon Bound

Satan's Sword

Elven Blood

Devil's Paw

Imp Forsaken

Angel of Chaos

Kingdom of Lies

Exodus

Queen of the Damned

The Morning Star

Half-breed Series

Demons of Desire

Sins of the Flesh

Cornucopia

Unholy Pleasures

City of Lust

Imp World Novels

No Man's Land

Stolen Souls

Three Wishes

Northern Lights

Far From Center

Penance

* * *

<u>Northern Wolves</u>

Juneau to Kenai

Rogue

Winter Fae

Bad Seed

www.ingramcontent.com/pod-product-compliance
Lightning Source LLC
Chambersburg PA
CBHW032055180726
48284CB00004B/1345